"You a

Keanan's formal speech lapsed with his manners. The faint Irish inflection danced down her spine. "It is improper to address me thus, sir. Miss Bedegrayne, if you please." She added enough tartness to make him laugh. Grudgingly she had to admit it was a pleasant sound, even if it always seemed to be at her expense.

"I will wager, those impotent sycophants you call suitors probably repent their forward impulses when your voice loses that sweet quality." His indigo eyes entranced her. "You have made two mistakes with me, Wynne. One, I am no gentleman. Oh, I can play along when there is a need. However, bone deep, I will never change. And two, while there is nothing wrong with honey, I tend to crave tart things, like damsons."

"Damsons," she repeated stupidly.

"Uh-huh," he murmured, lowering his face closer to hers, upturned. "And you."

She felt his breath on her face. His lips were almost touching hers before she realized what he was about to do. Stirring herself from his trance, she held her ground and threatened, "Do not kiss me, Mr. Milroy. Not only do you risk losing your upper lip, because I will undoubtedly bite you, you will also lose my aunt's favor when I scream for assistance."

He jerked her closer, swallowing her breathy objection by kissing her. His lips, warm and firm, swung the ground upward, throwing her off balance. She clutched at him to steady herself, but he was already pulling back. He had lost the teasing light in his eyes. The emotion that gleamed there now was a dark, sultry promise.

"Oh, I dare, my damson." His breath was uneven. "I never refuse a challenge or an offer."

To my favorite storytellers:
Jessica, Cameron, and Cassandra

A GENTLEMAN AT HEART

Barbara Pierce

ZEBRA BOOKS
Kensington Publishing Corp.
http://www.kensingtonbooks.com

ZEBRA BOOKS are published by

Kensington Publishing Corp.
850 Third Avenue
New York, NY 10022

All Kensington titles, imprints, and distributed lines are
available at special quantity discounts for bulk purchases
for sales promotion, premiums, fund-raising, educational or
institutional use.

Special book excerpts or customized printings can also be
created to fit specific needs. For details, write or phone the
office of the Kensington Special Sales Manager:
Kensington Publishing Corp., 850 Third Avenue, New York,
NY 10022. Attn. Special Sales Department. Phone: 1-800-
221-2647.

First Printing: April 2002
10 9 8 7 6 5 4 3 2 1

Printed in the United States of America

One

London, 1809

Instincts.

A man who did not pay sharp attention to them was kicking the dust of his own grave. Keanan Milroy lifted his face to the sun. He inhaled deeply, noting the direction of the wind as it teased the left side of his face. His gaze sought out and locked on to the fighting ring in the distance.

Climate and fighting science flashed behind eyes of cool, intelligent indigo, calculating the best position to attack. The crowd of eager spectators parted for him as he confidently strode to the hastily constructed stage. Today he would be fighting on wood. Double ropes. Stakes. No one had taken the time to plane a rounded edge to them. The last tidbit of information shuffled through his mind and slid into place. The sky was clear, so rain would not make the boards slick. He eyed the rough edges of the four stakes. It would not make the fight any less deadly.

"Reckless Milroy!"

Keanan barely felt the hearty slaps on his back. He doubted any of these men who had come to watch him fight truly wished him luck. They were here to cheer two men into pounding each other bloody. No one cared who the victor was, as long as they had wagered on him. Keanan intended to be that man.

Nodding to his second, he ripped off his hat and tossed it high. A cheer went up when it landed in the center of the ring. This action notified his opponent and the spectators that he had arrived. It was also a token of defiance. Keanan preferred the latter, rather than believing he was clinging to years of tradition. After spending most of his eight and twenty years being defiant, he considered himself an expert.

Sam "Dutch" Olsson raised the rope and forced his bulky frame through the opening. He jumped off the four-foot stage and ambled his way toward Keanan. Dutch had been a decent fighter until he had shattered his right wrist in a fight three years earlier.

"You're looking fit," Dutch said, giving him an approving nod, "and mean enough to piss on the king himself."

"Is Weaver here?" Keanan asked, referring to the man he intended to knock out. If half the gate money were not enough of an incentive, then the stake of £300 would go a long way for easing a bruised face and scraped knuckles.

"Nah, but he'll show. The stake is too comely to resist."

"More appealing than a freshly bathed petticoat," Keanan agreed. He nodded in the direction of the barouche. Once inside, he would strip down to the waist and wait until he was called. "You know where to find me."

"On your knees and hands clasped?" Dutch laughed, when he heard Keanan swear. "Add me to your prayers," his friend shouted from behind.

"I'll chap my knees when they allow a braying ass like yourself through the holy gates."

Dutch snorted and waved him off.

Keanan glanced back, but his friend had already blended into the crowd. Knowing Dutch, he was probably off to increase his wager now that he had left his fighter restless and irritated.

He shook his head and headed for the barouche. Prayers. It was just like Dutch to say something so asinine to simply rile him. He was well aware that what faith Keanan had, had been snuffed out years ago, and its passing had not been gentle. When the smell of blue ruin and filth had made it falter, fear, beatings, and starvation had withered it into dust. The only thing he believed in was himself. His abilities were limited to his cunning and the power restrained beneath his flesh, muscle, and bone. Everything beyond was just fanciful twaddle.

Keanan hesitated at the door of the barouche. Turning, he scanned the growing crowd. Since prizefighting was illegal, there was always the risk of an unwelcome magistrate set on ruining their efforts. Keeping his gaze on the crowd, he reached up and tugged at the knotted silk fogle at his neck.

Every fighter wore colors. He slipped the black-and-red fogle from his neck and idly wrapped, then unwrapped it from around his left hand. A few hours from now, his victory would allow him to claim Weaver's colors.

No one had ever claimed Keanan's colors. He fought and kept everything he owned. The reminder of the times when he had been more vulnerable primed his driven nature. It all came down to finely honed instincts, and his instincts were warning him. This afternoon, he was about to face more than a jug-bitten bruiser.

"You Bedegraynes attract misfortune," Amara Claeg muttered, retying the ribbons of her bonnet for the third time. "And I must seriously ponder my own sanity, having agreed to accompany you on this outing."

Wynne Bedegrayne merely smiled. Her acquaintance with Miss Claeg over the past two years had enlightened her to the workings of her companion's mind. Amara viewed herself as a coward. Wynne supposed having a mother like the overprotective, strong-willed Lady Claeg would make anyone fade into the shadows to avoid notice.

Two years ago, Amara had proved she was stronger than

she believed when she had assisted Wynne's younger sister, Devona, in a wild scheme to rescue Amara's older brother, Doran, from Newgate. Naturally, the nervous young woman preferred viewing the entire ordeal as another example of a Bedegrayne bullying a helpless Claeg.

Wynne saw it differently. No coward would have paraded herself in front of the *ton* dressed in a ridiculous costume, pretending to be Devona. Nor would she have stood up to Wynne's older brother, Brock, and Devona's then-betrothed, the menacing Lord Tipton, when they threatened to ruin her unless she revealed Devona's whereabouts.

Wynne gave the parasol resting lightly on her shoulder a twirl. No, Amara was not a coward. Sadly, even her special outings with Wynne over the years had not dissuaded her from the notion. Still, Amara never refused her invitations. Her continued association with what her mother considered those *horrid* Bedegraynes never faltered, and what had once simply been the act of fulfilling a promise she had made to her older brother, had grown into friendship.

"I vow, I despise your arrogance."

Her companion's waspish tone snapped Wynne back to her present predicament. She took no offense at the comment. In fact, it heartened her. "Why, Miss Claeg, I pride myself on my arrogance," she said cheerfully, causing Amara's jaw audibly to click shut. Unable to conceal her good humor, she leaned closer, bent on further devilment. "It is said, and I am certain your dear mama would agree, that the Bedegraynes must have received an extra dosing when the angels were passing out all our fine qualities, such excellent bloodlines and even teeth." To prove her point, she displayed her fine white smile.

Amara made a helpless noise that sounded suspiciously like suppressed laughter. "Mama would have agreed to no such thing, Miss Bedegrayne." She took a deep breath and squared her shoulders. "If unearthly creatures have had a hand in creating a Bedegrayne, it is obviously the devil and his succubus," she quoted in a shrill voice that eerily reminded Wynne of Lady Claeg.

Looking away, she stared beyond the crowd to the canal in the distance. "Small wonder you are so surly. If I had to listen to that woman spew poison every day, I would scarcely find the will to climb down from my bed."

Apologetic, Amara gently touched her on the arm. "That sounded dreadful." A wet sheen darkened the blue depths of her eyes. "You were correct; I am sulky, and too callous for not recognizing the cruelty of her words. I do not deserve your friendship."

Wynne sighed. A fine pair they made. Snipping at each other like scrawny lapdogs when they should be thinking of the young life they had come to protect. "Amara, you can be rude, whiny, and quite more irritating than either of my sisters. However, I keep my promises, and more to the point, I have grown used to your blue sulks."

Amara's tormented expression softened. Her eyes narrowed as she pounced on the one word Wynne regretted having uttered. "Promise? What promise are you keeping?"

"The one I made to myself," she effortlessly lied, not certain whose fury she was avoiding—Brock's or Amara's. "The same one drawing us here."

"Oh, Wynne. Tell me we are not here for the sake of the Benevolent Sisterhood."

"Naturally, we are not here for the sisterhood. We are here for the people who need us." She ignored her friend's unladylike groan.

The Benevolent Sisterhood was Wynne's creation. Once it had been a clever, empty ruse to help a childhood friend. Years of hard work had breathed purpose into it. Not only did the small charity provide food and clothing to the unfortunate lost souls of the city, she also tried to save the few she could.

With the exception of her younger sister, Devona, and Amara, none of polite society knew of her work; she pre-

ferred the role of an anonymous angel. She was the fourth
child of Sir Thomas Bedegrayne, and the last unmarried
daughter. She could quite imagine her father's opinion of
her mingling with the lower classes and of the minor risks
she took.

Amara tried nudging their casual stroll away from the
disturbing crowd, which seemed to be made up of mostly
men. "Wynne, this has to end." She raised a gloved hand
to stave off an argument. "The *ton* hails you, the handsomest
of the Bedegraynes. A most virtuous lady. The rarest jewel
in the Bedegrayne crown."

She was also considered heartless, the coveted maiden
who offered a man nothing but a beautiful mask disguising
her heart of ice. It mattered little that the men who whispered
such remarks had been rejected by her father. She feared
their assessment was accurate. "I know what they call me."

"Then consider this. What will Sir Thomas do when he
learns of how you have been fooling him and the rest of the
family for years?"

The roar of his outrage would deafen her for a sennight.
"Compliment me on my resourcefulness?" she innocently
offered.

"Lock you in your room and marry you off to the next
male who comes up to scratch. I care not to contemplate
my fate when my family learns of my part."

Guilt bubbled, fighting its way to the surface. Amara's
parents were miserable, self-absorbed creatures. Punishing
Amara would be looked upon as family entertainment. "Perhaps we should enjoy our picnic along the canal another
day?"

Instead of appearing relieved by the suggestion, Amara
was furious. Pink blotches bloomed on her cheeks while she
struggled to speak. "Do you think I could leave you alone
in this place?"

"Sweet Amara, my face may give the impression there is
little else to address. However, I can assure you, I am not

alone. I arrived with two footmen and that young maid who replaced Pearl Brown. How I miss Pearl's competence," she sighed, feeling a twinge of envy, for her sister had snatched her favorite servant off to the Tipton household.

"What use are servants who are not about?"

"What use are servants who do not follow orders?" Wynne flippantly countered, then relented when she saw how upset her friend really was. "Gar and Inch are close by, looking after my interests."

"And what of the fool girl you refuse to discharge. Silly Milly?"

"Hush, the last time she heard you call her that terrible name, she was quite inconsolable for hours."

"Completely worthless, if you want my opinion. Always claiming she has a weak heart. Where is she? Safely tucked away in your carriage, pretending she is a fine lady?"

Whereas, Amara, the self-proclaimed coward, was standing beside her, prepared to protect her from the unrefined world. "I managed to coax her from the carriage. She is keeping an eye on our young charge."

Her friend said nothing. Their walk had taken them to the banks of the canal. Facing away from the crowd, the place looked peaceful. They were not the only ones who were enjoying the view. Several couples strolled past them, and a merrymaking group of six were preparing to picnic farther up the bank. The occasional masculine roar in the distance reminded them the tranquil patch of beauty was deceiving.

Amara was the first to break the silence. "Is it a child?"

"A girl. Barely twelve years old." Not bothering to conceal her disgust, her flashing green eyes hinted at the steel hidden within the lady. "Her mother contacted me through Devona's cook. The family is struggling. The husband is useless and a drunkard. Perhaps worse. He plans to auction the girl tonight."

Puzzled, she asked, "For what?" The dawning horror had

her reaching for Wynne. "Should we not summon the magistrate? This man could be dangerous."

"What man would stand in the way of a father's rights? For all I know, the magistrate will be participating in the bidding."

"Wynne!"

Outrage soured her stomach. "She is just a poor, unimportant girl. Do you think anyone will care if there is just one more prostitute peddling herself in the shadows?"

There was a reckless fury glittering in Wynne's gaze, the kind that warned Amara there was nothing she could say to deter her friend from her actions. "Why this place?" she asked, already resigned about her role in this rescue.

"I have need of this canal." Wynne gazed out at the water, her mind playing out the plan.

Another cheer had Amara glancing back at the crowd. Something important—and probably illegal—had drawn this crowd. The imbalance of so many males around them frightened her. "What about *them?*"

The parasol twirled on her shoulder while she contemplated the source of Amara's concern. "Have you ever witnessed a prizefight?" She laughed at her friend's gasp. "Do not fret. Their appearance was unexpected, but the confusion can be used to our advantage. Trust me, these men are too concerned about their wagers to bother with the fair sex this afternoon."

Keanan ended round twenty-two by burying his fist in Weaver's soft belly. The man had crumpled and was still dry-heaving over the ropes in his corner.

"I warrant he'll piss blood for days," his second and kneeman, Tom Grandy, observed, but not without some sympathy. Like Dutch, Tom had spent some time in the ring, but had gotten out at the urging of his young bride. Unable to walk away completely, Tom volunteered to second any fighter who asked him. Crouching down, he offered his knee for Keanan to rest. The fighters had a half-minute break before they were to come up to the mark.

Dutch, acting as bottleman, wiped a sponge over Keanan's face and chest. "Are you fighting, lad, or asking Weaver to dance?" He ignored Tom's low chuckle. "Weaver has gotten soft. You could have floored him twenty minutes ago."

Keanan did not bother disagreeing. A round lasted as long as both men kept on their feet. Weaver rarely went beyond two minutes before he was knocked down. "Such a high stake requires more than a few minutes of amusement. Besides, Weaver used to be one of the best. A man's final fight deserves to be a worthy battle." He was speaking for himself as well as his opponent.

"Sentimentality, Milroy?" Dutch sneered, probably recalling his last fight and its lackluster finish.

Keanan matched his second's expression by baring his teeth. "Just earning my keep." No one had ever accused him of possessing feelings, let alone allowing them to rule his life.

"Time!" the referee shouted. "Fighters to the center and set-to."

"Finish him," Dutch ordered.

Keanan's emotionless gaze flickered over his opponent. Weaver was in poor shape. The former champion of Paddington was winded and listing to his left as he came up on the mark. Blood sprayed from his nose with each exhale, making the wooden ring a hazard.

The two took up their positions, setting-to like half-starved dogs prepared to tear each other apart for the amusement of the spectators. The umpire declared the round open. The blood was rushing too loudly in his ears for Keanan to hear him. He saw the man's lips move, and moved in to attack.

There was no fancy science to his actions, no dancing

around his intentions. He stepped forward, prepared to accept what punishment the weakened Weaver could issue. His opponent swung wildly, the tired muscles in his arm causing him to lose control of the sweeping arc. Keanan dodged a cannonball-sized fist and purposely stepped on Weaver's foot. The man tripped, landing in an ignoble sprawl.

"Foul!" Weaver's seconds screamed over the roaring crowd.

The fighters ignored them all. Weaver jumped to his feet with more agility than Keanan would have credited him with and charged. His loss of control would be his undoing. Keanan tightened his fist. A clean strike using his larger knuckles would be less damaging to his hand. Weaver came in low, aiming on tackling him, but Keanan was quicker. His right fist connected at the man's temple. It was a flush hit. His opponent's eyes rolled back in his head. He collapsed without making a sound. Of course, little could be heard as the frenzied crowd chanted his name.

"Reckless . . . Reckless . . ."

It was a cognomen he could never truly claim. A mocking tribute he abhorred. Keanan lifted his arms in grim triumph. The adulation meant nothing. The money even less, since he was already a rich man. Weaver was not the only one retiring from the ring.

"Miss Bedegrayne, I know ye have a mind toward a schedule," Inch said, yelling over the din of the crowd. At six feet and two, the raw-faced young man had to bow down to be heard. "Reckless Milroy is giving Weaver a fine thrashing. Weaver is bleeding claret all over himself. His defeat will craze these drunken coves."

Gar came up from behind and joined them. Somewhere in his thirties, he had been a part of the Bedegrayne household for almost twenty years. Catching the footman's last words, he bleakly nodded. "The lad is right. Our distraction could prove dangerous. I suggest we get to it, miss, before a winner is declared."

Wynne and Amara had moved as close to the spectators as they dared. Over the cheering mob, she critically observed the fight. The pugilists did not seem evenly matched. The tall one with shaggy brown hair was about six inches taller, and several stone heavier than his opponent. The other appeared younger. What he lacked in weight, he made up for in build. She winced as the artistry of fine sculpted muscle proved lethal when he planted a blow into the giant's stomach. The injured man wheezed and grabbed his middle. Exuded by a gruesome pressure, blood sprayed from his nostrils.

"I shall be sick," Amara whispered, cupping her gloved hand over her mouth. Her face appeared as white as the lace at her throat.

Any other time, Wynne would have agreed. She could not decide which she found more appalling, the men subjecting themselves to such brutal abuse, or the men cheering them on. She thought they were all animals.

"Do not dare faint on me, Amara Claeg," she warned in a crisp tone, "or I shall have Gar lay you out on the ground where you drop. It would be a pity to ruin such a lovely frock."

Her friend had turned away from the fighters. Her breathing sounded ragged while she struggled to maintain her composure. Wynne placed a comforting arm around her.

Skirting the circumference of the mob, she said, "Easy and calm, Amara. We are simply two ladies enjoying our outing." Wynne turned, addressing Gar. "Watch after our Mr. Egger," she said, referring to the man who planned on selling his own daughter. "I pray we shall never meet."

"Look to our lady," Gar ordered the other footman. Tugging on his cap, he slipped into the crowd.

Amara stepped out of Wynne's embrace. "I am better, thank you."

"What lady would not have a case of nerves at the sight of blood spilled?" she asked, pleased the starch was back in her friend's back.

"Your eyes did not even flutter when that awful man punched the other one," Amara accused.

Keeping her attention on her surroundings, Wynne kept her voice light and pleasant. "Well, it is a matter of timing. I am planning a wondrous swoon once this is over. It will most likely top any fit you can muster."

The vision of Wynne swooning drew a reluctant smile from Amara. "You are just saying that to make me feel better. I vow I have never seen you upset, nor a hair out of place."

"Just living up to my reputation," she said simply. Noticing her maid, her grip tightened on her parasol. "There's Milly, and bless her, she has managed to keep hold of Jenny Egger."

"The girl looks terrified."

Small for her age, Jenny Egger was doubling her stride to match the pace of the harried maid. Her wide brown eyes searched each passing face while she fiercely clutched Milly's hand. The fear and desperation in the girl's expression broke both women's hearts.

Summoning a welcoming smile, Wynne resisted the urge to hug the girl, sensing the comforting gesture would not be accepted. "Come closer, Jenny and meet my good friend Miss Claeg." The girl offered Amara a shy greeting. Wynne switched the conversation to a more favorable topic, smoothing over any awkwardness. "Did you and Milly find a treat?"

"Ginger biscuits, miss. A brimming 'andful!" she declared, reacting as though a fist filled with sweets were as rare as a purse of gold.

"Lemon is my favorite," Wynne mused. "What do you say we share a plate once we have reached our destination?"

Delight flared in her gaunt face at the notion of an unexpected treat. Then, wariness immediately doused her excitement. Despite her youth, she was shrewd and knew that nothing worthwhile could be had without cost. "I'm fond of biscuits, miss."

"Then you shall have them, Jenny." Her attention returned to her maid. "Do you think you were followed?"

"I did my best, Miss Bedegrayne. I kept us moving through the crowds like you told me. If her da' was set on watching us, he would have missed the fight." A man stumbled into Milly, causing her to shriek. "Drunken bounder," she mumbled, grabbing Jenny.

"Gracious me!" the man exclaimed, his watery gaze disturbingly keen. "Four pretty birds roosting among a scratch pack." He tried to put an arm around Amara, but she stepped aside. He chuckled at her nervous movements. "Even a clever cur dog can pick out a ticklish scent." He lunged wildly, forcing the women to scatter in opposing directions. Laughing at his devilry, the man continued making his way through the crowd, more interested in seeking out his next drink than terrorizing well-bred ladies.

"Scoundrel!" Milly shouted after him.

Amara wrinkled her nose in distaste. "Did anyone understand a word he said? Tangle-footed ramblings."

Wynne place her hand on her abdomen. The fluttering she felt in her stomach had started to work its way up her spine. "Forget the man. Something is wrong. Different." Observing the area around them, she tugged Jenny closer. "Come along, ladies. I fear we must hasten our departure."

Milly followed after them, lagging behind several steps. "Wot o' the menfolk, miss? Why are we rushing 'bout?"

"Fighting's over," Jenny solemnly replied. The announcement silenced further arguments.

Wynne moved them along a path that kept them parallel with the canal basin. The chaos of the fight was behind them. Still, many of the men present worked in the area. Wharves surrounded the four-hundred-by-thirty-yards ba-

sin. There were also a hay-and-straw market, pens for live-
stock, and sheds for warehousing the goods that traveled
down the canal. These same men, high on spirits or the satisfaction of viewing a good, bloody fight, were making their
way back to their posts.

The bustling activity was one of the reasons the location
had been a perfect choice for Wynne. Her father, Sir
Thomas, owned numerous warehouses north of the basin.
Over the years, she had attended her father when he had
come to oversee his investment, so she was familiar with
the area.

Mr. Egger, fearing young Jenny might run away before
he sold her off, had been keeping her close. Since the man's
drinking habits prevented him from holding a post, it was
a simple matter to have a representative offer him honest
work at the wharf unloading cargo. The position secured
Jenny's whereabouts and provided an escape route via the
canal, using a packet boat.

Everything had gone along according to her plans, except
for the fight. Illegal activities such as prizefighting could
hardly advertise their intentions. The magistrates, unless
they had been bribed, tended to act most severely when they
discovered these events in their jurisdiction.

The unforeseen fight had lured Mr. Eggers from his post.
Upset that her plans were ruined, Wynne had considered
summoning the magistrate herself. Those two bruisers had
most undeniably deserved it. However, once she had calmed
down, she realized the fight added a useful ingredient to her
plan. It provided a splendid distraction. Mr. Egger had become too involved in watching the fight to bother with his
daughter. He had counted on her fear of him to keep her
obedient, but the man had never reckoned with Wynne Bedegrayne.

"Miss, how much farther? My heart is pounding me
ears!" Milly complained.

They were moving too fast to portray themselves as ladies

partaking in a leisurely stroll. It could not be helped. Before long, Mr. Egger would discover his daughter was missing. Calculating the money he would lose, it would be enough to rouse him into searching for her.

"Almost there. Once we cross the bridge." Wynne gestured toward the bridge they were approaching. "Only a bit more to the boat."

"You, there!" an enraged male voice bellowed.

TWO

"Me da'!" Jenny screamed. Her grip on Wynne's hand was fierce as any clamp. "If 'e takes me back, I'll be dead in the morn. I willna' survive his fists."

Wynne believed her. She quickened her pace. Mr. Egger was not alone. Two men followed in his wake. She could only pray Gar noticed their trouble and was close. Even so, one man, three women, and a child were no match for three strong laborers.

Hampered by their long skirts, the race for the bridge ended before it began. The three men surrounded the women, effectively cutting off their escape. The drunk's earlier crude comment about a pack of dogs chasing down and caging their prey flashed in Wynne's mind. Her heart hammering in her breast, she cursed herself for underestimating the man's greed.

"O, Jenny, me heart. Flying off without a kiss?" The man's smile lacked warmth, and the vulgar intent in his expression shocked Wynne into action.

She placed herself in front of Jenny, trusting that Amara would protect the girl from behind. Milly marked the third point of their misshapen triangle. Frightened by the men, the maid was already weeping.

"Stand aside, sir, or I shall summon the patrol," Wynne imperially informed them. She collapsed her parasol, prepared to use it as a weapon if necessary.

The men cast knowing looks to each other and snickered.

Mr. Egger opened his arms wide, palms forward, the disturbing gesture an invitation for the women to share in their jest. "Well, miss, this lonely stretch of soil seems law-barren. 'Ere we look to each other. Right, Jen?"

Jenny, frozen in place, clasped then unclasped her fingers. "Da', leave them be. They meant no 'arm." She whispered to Wynne, "More than 'is eye has touched gin. Leave. Now, afore 'e turns."

A part of her desired nothing more than to walk away from Mr. Egger and his odorous acquaintances. Guilt and regret weighed unevenly on her shoulders for placing everyone in danger. Silently she cried out for her footmen. Their presence might be enough to deter these men from the intent she could read on their frank visages.

She had to stall them. This was not the first time she had confronted unwanted advances. Lord Middlefell and his odious cronies rose unbidden in her mind. Absurdly, those men were considered gentlemen. However, when it came to undignified groping, there was no class distinction.

Slipping into the attitude of a lady speaking down to an inferior was a role to which she had been born. "Mr. Egger, you will be pleased to know I have offered your daughter a position in my household."

His stunned expression would have been laughable if their situation were not so dire. "Fer wot? Jen has no skills worthy o' a lady." His bloodshot eyes narrowed; suspicion was already seeping into his gin-soaked brain.

"To assist the kitchen staff," she snapped, showing her displeasure at being questioned. "We have detained you long enough, sir." The inaccuracy of her words tested her hold over her own alarm. It twisted and expanded within her like a feral creature demanding to be released. "My man is getting our carriage. Be assured we shall take good care of your Jenny." She tried to brush him aside. The dismissal had worked countless times with unwanted suitors. She gasped when the man dared put his hands on her.

"Remove your vile hands, sir," she tossed her head back, her haughty demeanor in place despite her rising panic.

Jenny rushed forward and tugged on her father's arm. "Da', she 'as a legion of menfolk that will kill ye for touching 'er. I'm begging ye. Don't hurt 'er 'cause she's willing to 'elp."

His putrid breath steamed through his nostrils. Seizing Wynne, her feet dangled uselessly several inches off the ground, he shook her, although his wrath was focused on his pleading daughter.

"Ye told her, ye mouthy whelp. Whatcha do, go crying your plight on every fine-pressed skirt tha' passed?"

Seeing her chance of escape hopelessly crushed, the girl was crying in earnest. "No, Da'!"

Wynne struggled, but the man's grip was unrelenting. "Milly, find Gar. Anyone," she ordered, when she saw the maid hesitate. It heartened her, knowing the frightened servant was reluctant to abandon her. "Run!"

Milly took two steps backward. Her slender form trembled.

"Damn me, Rand, don't let 'er get away!" Egger bellowed.

The man swung his arm around to grab Milly by the waist. She ducked low, missing his arm, then spun out of his reach. Half crawling the first few yards, she managed to get to her feet and run. Rand sprinted after her.

Amara took advantage of Egger's distraction. A swirl of outrage and stirred dust, she pounced on the man's other arm, breaking his hold on Wynne. Jenny, Amara, and Wynne all tumbled to the ground.

"Take her to the boat," Wynne said, pushing Jenny into Amara's arms. "Stay with her."

"But—" Amara began to argue, the words dying with her exertion. It took all her strength to pull Jenny away from Wynne. She screamed the moment Egger's accomplice hooked his arm around her neck and caught Jenny by her braid.

Wynne ran in the opposite direction, hoping to draw one of the men away from Jenny. Egger was too quick. His large hand grabbed at her bonnet. The secured ribbons caught her by the throat, hurling her backward into his embrace.

Laughing, his arm slithered under her breasts, clamping her to his solid frame. He cruelly tugged her bonnet again until he could untangle it from her hair. The bonnet discarded, he murmured his approval. "Take a look, mate." He easily shifted his weight to counter her struggles. "Mane like gold. I feel like a rich man, just touching it." He buried his face into her hair.

She growled and squirmed away from his touch. Wynne had wanted Egger's attention to shift away from Jenny. Now that it had, she understood the girl's frantic need for escape.

"Wot do ye think, luv?" He pressed a kiss to Wynne's cheek. "Jen's scrawny hide might buy me a night of gin and doxies. Selling ye will keep me living like a king!"

"By God, you are a dead man if you do not release my lady at once!" Gar said, gripping his side as if it pained him.

"This fancy trussed prig wants to fight for ye." His tongue licked her cheek. She choked; the threat of becoming ill was strong. "I'll 'ave her skirts waist-high, an' be poking her in the dust afore yer courage brings ye close. Off now, this is no' yer concern."

She did not know what had happened to her footman, but it was obvious he was in no condition to fight these two men. She flicked her tongue over her dry lips. "Gar," she rasped; a single tear rolled down her cheek. She knew he would willingly die for her. Reaching up, she raked her nails down Egger's face.

Muddled by the pain, he released her. Swearing, he checked the damage to his face. "Damn cat. I'll teach ye!"

Wynne was not waiting around for any lesson. On all fours, she scrambled out of the way of his blind lunge. Gar went into action. He charged Mr. Egger, knocking him flat on the ground. The men, locked in a vicious battle, rolled toward Wynne. Egger wildly flung his fist out. It clipped her across the cheek. She cried out, the momentum knocking her onto her right side.

Desperation erupted into a fight for their lives. Amara sunk her teeth into her captor's thick forearm. Hollering and twisting, the man tried to get free from his captive, but Amara was mad enough to draw blood. Her teeth buried deep, she refused to release him.

Her cheek throbbing, Wynne ran toward the trio. Jenny was kicking the screaming man in the calf. Untangling the girl's hair from his fingers was relatively simple. He was too concerned about freeing himself.

"Run, Jenny!" Wynne urged. The girl appeared confused. "The boat!" she yelped, narrowly missing the fighting men rolling on the ground. "Amara!"

Gazes clashed, and understanding flashed between them. Separating would make catching them more difficult. Unclenching her jaw, she broke her hold on the man's arm. Staggering back, she paused only a few seconds, and then started running in the opposite direction of the bridge. The man raced after her.

Egger brought his fist down, digging it into Gar's wounded side. Sweat and blood carved little channels down his grimy face. His gaze shot up and focused on his friend. "Not 'er! The other one."

Gar lay unmoving under Mr. Egger. Wynne did not know which one the man wanted to get his hands on, nor did she care. Whoever he caught would suffer greatly. She pivoted and ran after Jenny. That child would be free of her horrid father, even if it took her last breath to achieve it.

Jenny slowed once she reached the bridge. Not sparing a glimpse backward, Wynne yelled, "Run!" Perspiration stung her bruised face. She cursed the skirts she wore, wishing she had a pair of her brother's breeches.

"I won't go back," Jenny shrieked, climbing up on the low stone wall of the bridge. "I'd rather die!" She jumped off the bridge.

"No!" Pressing her hand against the stabbing pain in her chest, she quickened her pace. The water in the canal was not particularly deep. However, she had seen the loss of hope and desperation on Jenny's face. She would drown if Wynne did not reach her.

She reached the spot where Jenny had gone over, and peered down. Jenny was facedown in the water. Her arms were extended, her braid a limp rope coiled on her back. It was impossible to surmise whether she had been struck unconscious from the fall or was just willing herself to drown. The girl's skirts bloated with water were sinking her frail form. Wynne lifted her leg, preparing to follow Jenny into the water.

Something heavy collided into her, imprinting her tender flesh into the sharp stone. Winded from the impact, she watched helplessly as Jenny slipped deeper into the depths. Rough hands heaved her from her perch. Through pain and tears, she fought Egger.

"Let me go!" she begged, vowing only for Jenny's life could she lower herself to this man. "She is not dead. I can save her."

"Ye ruined it all!" Egger raged, not seeming to hear her plea. Wynne slipped his hold, but he snatched her ankle and dragged her from the wall.

She dug her hands into the dirt, trying to slow his progress, trying to claw her way back to the canal. She shook her head in mute denial. Jenny was already dead.

"I 'ave ye, ye feisty bitch. I'll sells ye to a score o' men before the night is finished. I'll gets me coin, then I'll strangle ye with my bare 'ands for killing me Jen."

Her hands plowed through the dirt; any efforts to slow this madman were ineffective. Her skirts had ridden high on

her thigh from his rough handling, and her futile kicking
had managed to scrape every inch of her exposed legs.

Despite the warm weather, a coldness threatened to steal
her thoughts, bury her deep so she could hide from the pain.
It was tempting to give in to the numbness. She bit back a
cry as she arched her back to avoid being gouged by a sharp
rock.

A rock.

Twisting so she was partially on her side, she reached
back, felt her fingers close over the rock. A sob of relief
escaped her trembling lips. She had a weapon. She doubted
Mr. Egger was used to his victims fighting back.

The abuse she was enduring must have sifted into his
consciousness, or more likely, he calculated the money he
was losing for damaged goods. Swearing under his breath,
he dropped her ankle and bent down to scoop her up like a
sack of grain. Wynne did not hesitate. She slammed the rock
against the side of his head. The force of the blow snapped
his head to the left. Reaching for his temple, he lost his
balance. He plopped down in the dirt, nearly sitting on her
feet. Wynne scooted backward. If he made a move in her
direction, she intended to crack his skull again with the rock.

"I'm bleeding!" Amazed, he held his hand before his eyes
to examine the amount of blood on his fingers.

Propping himself up with his left palm on the ground, he
seemed harmless. She rolled over to see if her shaky limbs
would permit her to stand. Jenny needed her.

He attacked the instant her attention shifted. His heavy
weight flattened her facedown in the dirt. Her precious rock
was inches out of reach. Impotent rage unfurled within her.
She turned her head, prepared to scream.

Abruptly, the weight pressing her down was lifted. She
crawled forward, grabbed her rock, and twisted to face her
aggressor. At the first grunt of masculine pain, her hand
came up, stilling her quivering lips. Her struggles had not
gone unnoticed. A large man loomed over Mr. Egger. His

fury was a living current that cascaded over her even from the distance. Clutching a fistful of Egger's shirt, he coiled it tight and hauled the man up.

"I bear no tolerance to bullies," the newcomer said; the low, rough tones were a growl. The warning carried the promise of violence.

Wynne made a small, vulnerable noise in her throat. Her liberator's attention instantly focused on her. Eyes, so dark from the distance that they appeared a soulless black, pinned her in place. Without blinking, he seemed to examine her from head to feet without shifting his gaze. The bruise on her cheek throbbed. She did not realize she had been holding her breath until need had her struggling for air.

"The bastard hurt you," he said, the coldness directed at the man in his firm grip. Fierce and powerful, he stood there, silently proclaiming himself judge and executioner. Already dismissing her, his attention switched to Mr. Egger. "This is your lucky day, my friend. A man with such fists should be lending them to the ring instead of brutalizing a beautiful young woman."

Mr. Egger struggled to shake himself loose, but the stranger was stronger. In defiance, he spat saliva and blood in the stranger's face. "No one's business, but me own," he muttered.

Her blond defender mopped the spittle from his face with the side of his free arm. "Now, I disagree. You see, I know a thing or two about using my fists, both in and out of the ring. I think a man like you can benefit from a little knowledge. Some say I'm a natural when it comes to the teaching."

"Billet eater!"

Those cold eyes narrowed, glittering in their intensity. "Lesson one: Flattery doesn't impress me." His fist struck fast into Mr. Egger's abdomen. The air wheezed out of the older man's lungs. He would have doubled over if the other man had not jerked him back up.

Wynne had witnessed all the violence she could tolerate. Inching away from the men, she kept her gaze on them for fear they might prevent her from leaving.

Jenny! She whirled, running straight into the arms of her footman.

"Gar!" She embraced him, never happier to see him. "Jenny," she choked, anguish closing off her throat. "She— the canal." Time could play tricks on a distressed intellect. Wynne was not certain if more time had elapsed than a drowning girl could spare. "The canal!" she repeated, pulling him toward the muddy banks.

A small crowd had gathered at the water's edge. Relief made her light-headed when she noticed Jenny sitting on the ground. She would have joined the girl in the dirt if Gar had not caught her arm.

"The girl is safe, Miss Bedegrayne." The footman's statement soothed her raw nerves. "Inch came back to see what was causing our delay, and saw her go in. I expect a bellyful of canal scum will give her a case of collywobbles; otherwise she's fine."

Milly hovered over Jenny. She sprung to her feet at Wynne's approach. "Oh, my poor miss," the maid sniffled, pity brimming in her eyes as she noted Wynne's disheveled hair and soiled frock. "I felt horrid leaving you in the hands of those awful men."

"You followed my orders and brought Gar to us," Wynne wearily murmured, feeling the need to reassure her maid. "You have my gratitude."

Milly's brows came together in puzzlement. "But—no, miss. I didn't find Gar. It was the other one." She nodded her head at something in the distance, a malicious glee brightening her expression. "I never knew a man who deserved a thrashing more than that Mr. Egger. And who better than the champion himself."

Wynne turned back, watching the men. Mr. Egger was no longer a threatening figure. The fighter had him secured on the ground with one knee while he tied the inert man's hands. Neither of them noticed her scrutiny.

"Miss Bedegrayne," Jenny called out.

She walked over and crouched down beside the girl. Not caring which one of them she was reassuring, Wynne hugged her.

"I'm so sorry, miss. I was crazed. I thought 'e would take me away and I couldn't bear—"

"Hush," she crooned. "If I had gotten away from your father, I probably would have joined you in the canal." She smiled, attempting to make light of the ordeal. Her gaze rested on Inch. "Thank you for saving her. I was too late."

The footman blushed under her tender regard. "No thanks needed, Miss Bedegrayne. I just wished I could have reached you as well."

She shook her head. "You chose the correct person to aid. All I need is a bath and I will be better for it."

Her servants glanced away, recognizing the lie, but were too respectful to disagree.

Wynne gently smoothed back a wet strand of hair from Jenny's face. "Are you well enough for the boat? Considering your father's present disposition, I think we should go forth with our plans."

"Considering all ye've done for me, if I said no, I wouldn't blame ye for dumping me back in the canal." Jenny stood; accepting a wool blanket, she wrapped it around her shoulders.

The feeling of control was a balm. It pushed away her various aches. There would be time later for musing over her mistakes and perhaps indulging in a few tears.

"Inch . . . Milly, both of you will accompany Jenny on her journey. I will send a carriage for your return home from Leicester." Gar had retrieved her discarded reticule. Sensing her request, he handed her the soft bag. She reached in and removed a small pouch. "Everything is arranged. The Headleys are expecting your arrival. They are good people.

I hope you will be happy there." She offered Jenny the pouch. "Inch has already purchased the boat tickets. This is for the unexpected. I regret we will not be able to share that plate of lemon biscuits." Her altercation with Mr. Egger proved that the unanticipated had a way of ruining one's meticulous plans.

Jenny impulsively embraced her. Concerned she had offended Wynne, she took a few nervous steps backward. "Ye are a kind woman, Miss Bedegrayne. I won't be forgetting ye in me prayers." She meekly followed behind Inch and Milly.

"Wynne!"

Amara ran toward her and Gar. She had arrived with reinforcements. Her brother-in-law's man, Speck, strode a few paces behind. Wynne concealed her groan behind a smile. All hope of concealing this afternoon's events from her family faded as she watched the grim-faced servant's approach.

"Do you think he is bribable?" she asked her footman, not taking her eyes off Speck.

"He's Lord Tipton's creature, Miss Bedegrayne. What do you think?"

She sighed. Since his marriage to Devona, her brother-in-law had taken up the task of keeping the impulsive Bedegrayne clan in line, and that included her father, Sir Thomas. Speck was the man's eyes and ears. She did not stand a chance of deceiving him.

"You missed all the excitement, Speck," she said, opting for a lighthearted, teasing tone.

The manservant, whom her sister referred to as "the gargoyle" snorted at her friendly greeting. He was short and thickset, with sharp brown eyes that assessed and noted every mark on her face and arms. "Where is he?"

At his fierce, ruthless expression, Wynne fortified herself, expecting she was about to witness another violent altercation. She looked left, seeking out the two men she preferred to forget. Her mouth parted in a surprised O. "They were there a moment ago. Two men. Mr. Egger and the fighter. Gar, did you see them leave?"

"No, miss."

Amara slipped her shawl from her shoulder and gently settled it over Wynne's shoulders. "We should summon a physician."

Speck's eyes gleamed. "What fighter?"

Amara glared. "Speck, the interrogation can wait. Can you not see that both Wynne and Gar are injured?"

Agitated, Wynne shrugged off Amara's coddling embrace. "Why are you all acting as though I should be seeking out my bed? I may be a little bruised; however, I can assure you all I am well."

The fact that she was snipping at them proved to all how unwell she truly was. She used both hands to smooth her hair from her face. "Forgive me. Perhaps I am more shaken than I would care to admit. But I am fine. Milly's fighter saw to it." If she closed her eyes, she could still see the burning rage in his eyes. He looked as if he would kill for her. She pushed away the disturbing thought.

Gar cleared his throat. "After Egger knocked the breath from me"—his face reddened at his failure to protect her— "Milroy took up for my lady."

Speck's sharp teeth came together, as if using them to sink into the footman's account. "I'll wager Egger didn't expect facing Reckless Milroy's fists. Unparalleled fighter, both in and out of the ring." He lifted his cap and scratched his head. "I can't believe that silly, fluttering piece of floss you call a maid chased the champion down?"

Defending her staff came automatically to her. To criticize them was to accuse her of faulty judgment in hiring them. "I have no cause to question Milly's story. I, for one, appreciate Mr. Milroy's well-timed arrival."

Wynne frowned, pondering whether a note conveying her gratitude might be misconstrued as an insult. The last thing she desired was to enrage a man who ensconced himself in violence. Something about him disturbed her on some level. All in all, she thought it best to stay away from Mr. Milroy.

Speck grunted, which could have meant anything. The events of this afternoon weighed heavily on her. Until she had word Jenny Egger was safely tucked away in Leicester, she doubted she would be able to relax. "Speck, what are you doing here?" Suspicion swirled and floated like smoke in her agile mind. "If your lord has ordered you to spy on me—"

"Not this time, Miss Bedegrayne. His ears are still ringing from your last scolding on the subject."

"Really." Tipton's audacity went far beyond the polite society they moved within, and well beyond her tolerance. "So Amara just came across you while you were strolling along the canal?"

"Yes—no."

Speck rolled up on his toes, then dropped flat on his feet. Not truly thinking the man was capable of normal emotions, she blinked at the sheepish grin she saw on his homely face.

"My lord didn't send me after you, miss," he assured her, casting a glance at the area around them. "Though by the look of things, Lord Tipton summed his assessment of you up right and tight." He hurried on before she could express her own opinion on that remark. "I have one vice." He paused. "Two." He counted on his fingers. "Three, but that's beyond the point. I came for the fight. I was on my way back to the house when I saw Miss Claeg racing down the road. If I had known Milroy would go against another challenger, I would have arrived sooner."

Bribing Speck was not an option. He was too loyal to Tipton, Wynne mused. A distraction, though, might gain her the time she needed to placate her family and gloss over the more harrowing details. The manservant himself had just volunteered his greatest weakness. She almost smiled. There would be no rushing her off to Tipton. No lecture. No bellowing Papa if she kept her head.

"Speaking of Mr. Milroy, I have a dilemma, Speck. The man literally saved our lives, only to run off without allowing us to offer our appreciation." She placed her hand to her brow for effect. "The champion deserves more than a polite note. I hate to impose upon you, but if you could find Mr. Milroy and thank him, it would ease my mind."

He tensed, considering the temptation she had just dangled in front of him. "What of you? His lordship would not like me leaving you."

No, he would not. She gave him an encouraging smile. "Amara and I have Gar to see us home. Please, Speck, I would not want Mr. Milroy to think me ungrateful."

The servant's hard look bordered on impertinence. Wynne concentrated all her energy on appearing calm and sincere. She considered herself quite an actress when the situation called for such talent. Unfortunately, most dealings with the *ton* demanded the polished skill. Speck's brow twitched, and she believed she had him.

He laughed in her face.

This was no polite chuckle, but rather a hearty, from-the-gut guffaw. "Oh, Miss Bedegrayne, you are quite a piece, aren't you? I always thought it was your sister who was the sly one." His laughter mellowed to a chuckle. "Her ladyship is all nerve and impulsiveness. But you—all sweet and pretty as a frosted cake. Most can't see past the fancy decoration to the cleverness beneath the surface."

Wynne started walking in the direction of their waiting carriage. "Very well. You win, Speck. Escort us home."

Amara caught up with her. "You should see a doctor. Tipton will be discreet."

He would also be persistent. He was the most arrogant, high-handed, overprotective male she knew who was not related to her by blood. She thanked God daily that such a man was not her husband.

"Gar should have his ribs checked. The mark on your cheek is already changing color," Speck observed.

"What if I promised to seek out Tipton while you meet the fighter?"

"Tempting, miss. Truly. It pains me to refuse. Then again, I cut my teeth on your sister's mischief." His brown eyes twinkled. "I've learned not to take a smiling Bedegrayne at just their word."

Three

Few gained entrance to the private study of Rayne Tolland Wyman, Viscount Tipton. The years being married to her sister, Devona, had gradually softened the *ton's* view of the enigmatic, handsome surgeon. Still, there were others who defiantly continued to call him *Le Cadavre Raffine*. The Refined Corpse.

At age fifteen, he had survived the horror of being accidentally buried alive. Resurrection men intent on collecting a new body to sell to a local surgeon had inadvertently saved him. His survival had been considered something unnatural, when so many had succumbed to the fever, including his older brother, Devlin. Shunned by his own family, he had left England to seek his fortune. Years later, he returned, a powerful adversary against those who challenged him.

It was his fearsome reputation that had intrigued her sister. She had required a man of his talents to save a childhood friend. Tipton had refused her.

Wynne smiled, imagining her sister's shock. It was rare for anyone to refuse the youngest Bedegrayne. Tipton, like many others, had underestimated her spirit and determination, not to mention the danger surrounding them.

She sometimes still awoke from nightmares, believing her sister was lost to them. Feeling chilled, she settled deeper into her brother-in-law's favorite green-and-gold upholstered rococo armchair.

She turned her head at the sound of the door opening.

Tipton's impressive form filled the opening. At two and thirty, he appeared to be a man in his prime. His build was lean, she thought, unconsciously comparing him to the fighter. Through eerily keen light-blue eyes, his gaze alighted on her, surveying and assessing the damage to her face, arms, and clothes.

"Good afternoon, Lord Tipton," she graciously addressed. "Where is my sister?" Realizing he was about to drop either his precious medical case or the small basin of water, Wynne rose from the chair to assist.

"Sit down, Wynne."

She merely raised a brow at the snarled command. "Tipton, you must be confusing me with my sister, or perhaps your own." She took the bowl from him and moved away to set it on a nearby table. "Much better. So where is Devona?"

He closed the door. "Doing the same thing you should be doing. Staying out of trouble." He hooked his arm through an ornate open-backed chair and dragged it next to her chair, watching her lean cautiously back. "Lucien has been giving her some sleepless nights, so I insisted that she take a nap."

Lucien Gordon Thomas Wyman was the newest addition to the family. At thirteen months, he was already favoring his formidable father physically and in temperament.

"Oh, the poor darling. Is he cutting more teeth?"

Some of the severity in his expression softened with the discussion of his beloved son. "Yes."

He bent down and reached deep into his medical case. Gripping a small bottle, he removed the stopper and poured a liberal amount of the dark-green oil into the basin. He swirled a small towel in the warm water and squeezed out the excess.

"Now, we could continue and talk about the trials of changing my son's napkins, but I would rather talk about you."

She tilted her face, allowing him to inspect the bruise on her cheek. "Why, Tipton, that is what all the gentlemen say to me," Wynne murmured huskily. She ruined her nonchalant pose when he pressed the cloth to her sore cheek. "Ow, that stings! Beast. What did you add to the water?"

"Wormwood. It should lessen the coloring."

"Any chance I will be able to fool Papa into thinking I just scrubbed my face too roughly this morning?"

Tipton smiled. "Never. Hold this while I look at the scratches on your arms and legs." He laughed at her expression. "I swear you can trust me. I am qualified."

"You are a surgeon," she corrected, feeling flustered. "And I can see to my own legs, thank you."

"Wynne, all my unchaste thoughts are directed toward my wife." He pulled up her feet into his lap. Gently but efficiently he removed her soiled shoes. When his hand touched her calf, she jerked her feet out of his lap.

"Oh, for heaven's sake!" She jumped up and walked so that the chair was positioned between them. "It is not that I do not trust you, Tipton. I do. But I would never allow one of my brothers to remove my stockings. If you insist on making me miserable, the least you can do is turn your back."

Amused, he complied. "This is the first time anyone has ever complained that my touch makes them miserable. I might have taken the comment to heart if I did not have a loving wife who generously feeds my self-love."

Wynne also turned her back and began working her skirt up to the garter. "Something tells me your self-love has never been in jeopardy." With a mild oath, she worked one torn stocking down her leg, then the other. She scrutinized her legs. "I will have a bruise on my ankle where Mr. Egger—" She let the words fade off. She did not intend to give Tipton any details if she could avoid it.

"Ah, yes, that would be the Mr. Egger who attacks unknown females for no reason." He sighed at her silence. "Come here and permit me to examine you."

Wynne dropped her skirt and returned to the chair. "Anything higher than my knee, and I plan on slapping you," she warned, placing her bare feet back in his lap.

In the late afternoon, no one walking along the bustling street of Upper Seymour paid more than cursory attention to the man sitting on the steps of one of the fashionable town houses. His head bowed, he leisurely peeled the skin from an apple, using a sharp knife. The sun, now eclipsed by clouds, had darkened the sky to an unfriendly gray. The threat of rain was not foremost in Keanan Milroy's mind. Severing a section of apple peel with the edge of the blade, he popped the sweet treat into his mouth. Frowning at the town house across the street and two doors to the right, he chewed thoughtfully.

He did not have much use for the fancy. Nor, he thought ruefully, did they have much use for him. Oh, there were the high-nosed lords who risked dirtying their fine coats by mingling and wagering with the lower classes. Keanan did not count them. They were a necessary evil to tolerate, like rats picking over the better parts of the garbage strewn onto the streets.

It was the magnificently trussed and perfumed ladies he had managed to avoid. At a distance, he had made several observations about these vain creatures. Dressed in ridiculously inappropriate confections that would be better served in a storefront window, they preened and posed in carriages and sedans, begging for the adoration of every male. Of course, these would-be sirens were equally horrified when a man decided to accept their silent invitation.

His friend Dutch once told him that it was the lady schooling that ruined them. No proper lady dared to enjoy a kiss, and she would certainly freeze at the notion of having a man between her legs for more reason than planting an heir in her belly.

Keanan pinched off another piece of peel and slipped it between his straight teeth. It was a shame these fancy ladies were nothing more than pretty shells for admiring. Otherwise, he deliberated darkly, his father, Wesley Fawks, Duke of Reckester, might never have sought out the beautiful Irish actress, Aideen Milroy. He claimed her body and heart, only to abandon her when his wife gave birth to his heir three months after Aideen gave him a bastard first son.

Anger, liquid and white-hot, coursed through him as it always did when he thought of the man who sired him. The hilt of the knife pressed deeply into his thigh. He softly muttered an oath. Relaxing slightly his grip, he continued peeling the apple. He was not particularly hungry. The action gave him an excuse not to rise and seek out his father. He was certain if he confronted him now, he would slit the man's throat.

Too irritated to carry on his pretense, Keanan swiped each side of the blade against his trousers and then sheathed it. A passing child caught his attention.

"You. Lad."

A boy, on the lesser side of ten, turned at the sound of his voice. Revealing the half-peeled apple between two fingers, he tossed it to him. The child caught the offering with both hands.

He sniffed the apple first, and then took a generous bite. "My thanks, gov!" he said, his mouth full of apple. With a jaunty wave, he pivoted and continued down the street.

The child already forgotten, Keanan stood. Stretching his arms above his head, he released the bowlike tension and absently scratched his stomach. His gaze lingered on the town house. He had followed the woman to this residence.

The corner of his mouth tugged into an unwilling grin. This was a first for him. He had never pursued a woman in his life. His fair features, along with a steadfast rule of keep-

ing to women who shared his interest, had removed the zeal
of the hunt from his liaisons. It also minimized the inevitable
tears and recriminations for broken promises of love.

Head down, he started walking. He did not understand
the whim that had brought him there. Nothing was going to
change. The woman was tucked away safely in her town
house, and he had no intention of doing anything about it.

Or did he?

He had not known what to expect when the dark-haired
maid practically collapsed into his arms, begging for his
assistance. Her lady was held captive by three brutes, she
had explained. How could he refuse?

The scene he had come upon had not been unexpected.
He had spent most of his life living in the poorest districts.
A man lifting his hand to his wife or shoving her about was
not uncommon. Or so it had seemed, until the small details
of the desperate drama revealed and portrayed a different
tale.

The man was already dragging her across the road as he
had approached. Keanan's attention had been immediately
drawn to the woman. Her long blond hair had come undone
in the struggle and trailed in the dirt like an artist's hair
pencil. Despite her vulnerable position, even from a distance, he could feel her determination to trounce her larger
adversary. Before he could call attention to his presence, the
woman, like a true fighter, had sized up her opponent and
attacked. If she had had a bit more weight to her, she might
have finished him off with that blow to the nob.

Keanan crossed the street. He retraced his steps, bringing
him closer to the town house. What was it about the woman
that drew him this day? Under all that grime, there was an
undeniable perfection to her face. Pleasurable bait, certainly,
but it was not enough for him to risk his neck for a beautiful
stranger. Perhaps it was her helplessness. He did not know
her reasons for being at the canal. However, her looks and
clothes revealed she had been completely out of her ambit.

Still, she was as game as any drunken moll in a bawdy house fighting for every penny due her. He never had seen such pluck in the refined. She intrigued him.

"Hey, ol' man," Keanan greeted a man sitting on his haunches, painting a decorative javelin-headed railing in front of one of the residences. "Who owns the house over there?"

The man cast a glance at the town house Keanan was pointing out. "That be Lord Tipton's dwelling."

An unanticipated shaft of pain splintered his chest. "He has a wife, I expect."

"A brave one too, for marrying a man most think is the devil's companion." Uninterested in Tipton's town house, his attention returned to his work.

Keanan stared at the house. So the woman was taken. The half-baked fantasy congealing in his mind faded at the disappointment. "Has the mark of the beast, you say?"

"No, the mark of a surgeon. Ye have to guard your dead loved ones around the likes of him."

Undisguised hope flashed in Keanan's eyes. If Dutch had witnessed the emotion, he would have most likely cuffed his foolish friend on the side of his head. "I think I was introduced to Lady Tipton once." He ignored the older man's snort of disbelief. Dressed in the manner he was, Keanan concurred silently that he did not appear to be the type of gentleman a lady would willingly associate with. "A pretty lass. Blond."

"Not her ladyship," the man disagreed. "I've done odd jobs for them. Lady Tipton's looks are agreeable enough, but she has a tangle of fiery curls tucked under her lace cap." He gave Keanan a speculative glance. "Must be someone else you met."

"Must be," he mused. Decidedly more cheerful, he walked away in the opposite direction from the town house. Whoever the blond woman was, she was not Tipton's wife.

He refused to dwell on the fierce satisfaction he felt about that revelation.

Perhaps she had suffered more at the hands of that scoundrel than he had guessed. Had she sought out a surgeon to set a broken bone? The thought made him want to seek out the man who had attacked her and use him as a sparring partner.

Lucky for Egger, he was safe from Keanan's lawless justice. After he had tied up Egger, he had hauled him off to place him in the hands of the nearest authority. By the time he had returned to the canal, his mystery lady and her entourage were gone. Very inconsiderate, considering the risks he had taken to rescue her. The woman owed him. Keanan intended to collect on her debt.

A sudden movement near the door caused Wynne to fling her injured foot from Tipton's lap to the floor.

"Good God, woman, are you trying to unman me? You are as dangerous as your sister," Tipton accused, glowering.

Before Wynne could apologize, the door swung open and Devona bounded through the doorway. "Tipton, I was thinking—" She paused, spying her sister sitting suspiciously close to her husband and high color suffusing her cheeks. "Wynne, no one told me you came calling."

Against her wishes, her color only heightened. She tucked her bare feet under her skirts. "Tipton said you were napping and should not be disturbed." Her gaze alighted upon her stockings thrown over the arm of her chair in the same instant Devona's did.

Slightly puzzled, her sister strolled to the side of the chair and lifted the embroidered white cotton by one finger.

" 'Tis not what you think," Wynne began, silently beseeching her brother-in-law with her eyes to straighten this awkward matter out with his wife.

"Really? And what should I be thinking, dear sister?"

"Enough, minx. Wynne is too muddled to recognize your brand of naughtiness."

Without invitation, he reached under Wynne's skirt and retrieved her injured leg. "As I was saying, nothing is broken, and the damage is minor. I will wrap the ankle for support to get you home, but I want you to soak it in cool saltwater before you retire. Do you want some laudanum for the discomfort?"

"You are considerate, but the ankle is hardly worth all this fuss. All I need is a cup of chamomile, and I shall be fine in a day or two," Wynne assured him. Shaking out the wet cloth she had balled up in her fist, she daintily touched it to her sore cheek.

Devona latched on to Wynne's wrist and pulled the cloth away. She audibly gasped. "Your face! Tipton, what is going on here?" She gently took the cloth from her sister's limp grasp and dabbed at the slight swelling.

Tipton's penetrating gaze centered on Wynne. "I despise stating the obvious, love. Your sister needed my medical expertise."

"Obviously," she muttered. "Well?" She glared at her sister.

Wynne mutinously sank deeper into the chair, feeling irritated and cornered. This was what she had wanted to avoid. She felt ill-disposed to explain the situation to either of them. "It was rather embarrassing. I was enjoying a picnic near the canal. You know the one, Devona. The one close to Papa's warehouses."

A concurring sound emanated from Devona.

She retrieved the cloth from her sister and applied it to her cheek. "Well, I twisted my ankle on some gravel and fell."

Empathy showed plainly on Devona's expressive face. She put her arm around her for comfort. "Oh, darling, how awful. What of the bruise on your cheek?"

"Yes, Wynne," Tipton mockingly urged, "what of the bruise?"

She did not bother glancing in her brother-in-law's direction. Clearly, the man did not believe a word she was uttering. "I landed ignobly on my face. I must have struck another rock. Speck came across us—"

"Speck? Speck was there?"

How much more should she admit, she wondered? "I thought at first Tipton set the gargoyle on me." She met his measured stare unblinkingly. "Nevertheless, the man explained he was there to see the fight."

Devona's brows came together. "What fight?"

She waved her hand haphazardly in the air. "Reckless Milroy and Waver somebody. I really did not pay the battle much heed."

"You attended a prizefight?"

"No. The prizefight intruded on my picnic," she countered. Wynne seized on the one subject guaranteed to distract her sister from her relentless questioning. "I should return home. You know how Papa worries. Do you think Lucien has awakened from his nap? I would love to see him before I depart."

Devona stared down at her sister, as if attempting to see beyond her words and demeanor. She shrugged, apparently satisfied. "I will see to Lucien myself. He would be heartbroken if he missed a visit from his aunt." She leaned down and kissed her lightly on her unblemished cheek. "I shall return shortly."

When the door closed behind Devona, Wynne risked a wary glance at Tipton. Intent on his task of wrapping her ankle, she was relieved she did not have to endure his stare.

"You handled her quite well. One would think you have been perfecting your technique for . . . oh, let us say, for years." He removed her foot from his lap. "You were correct. I was being a bit overprotective. Of course, how am I suppose to react when Speck comes charging in here, claiming you had been savaged by a madman?" He waited, giving her an opportunity to speak. She remained silent. Shaking his head, he picked up a pair of scissors, wiped them clean, and then placed them back into his medical case. "Can you bring it upon yourself to at least respect my medical opinion? If I were you, I'd avoid being pursued by overeager suitors for several days, and madmen for a sennight."

The scoundrel was baiting her. She refused to engage him in this matter. "Tipton—"

He overrode her words. "Truly, I am grateful. Whatever scheme you have hatched, you have managed to keep my wife out of it. That alone proves what a cunning baggage you have become." Crossing his arms over his chest, he leaned back in his chair and studied her. "Or mayhap it is simply in the blood."

"There is no need to be condescending, my lord." Wynne arose slowly; her inactivity had made her stiff. "Be a gentleman and turn around. I was not fibbing when I told Devona that I needed to return home."

Tipton pivoted the chair to face the fireplace. " 'Tis just the rest of your tale that deserves to be raked into the compost, eh?"

"Quite clever of you, twisting my words," she said, pulling up her stocking then tying the tapes above her knee. "What I meant was that Speck misunderstood the situation. Nothing was as dire as it seemed."

"Shall I summon Gar and prove you a liar, Wynne?"

She felt the rush of fear flood her senses. It quickly transformed to anger. "I cannot account for the reason why Devona has tolerated your high-handedness, Tipton." She smoothed her skirts back into place. "Finished."

Agile as any sleek beast, he got up from the chair and turned toward her. Although eccentric, Wynne had to admit her sister's husband was an excellent representation of a man in his prime. He was not handsome in the classical sense. Rather, his proud, chiseled features gave testament to the harsh life he had endured and triumphed over. A long mane of mixed honey and chestnut hues softened the severity most found in his features.

He surprised her by playfully pinching her chin. "It is a measure of trust."

She smiled. "So says the high-handed gentleman."

He did not match her lightness with a grin of his own. "Ah, but Devona anticipates my overbearing tendencies, and I have been onto her schemes from the very beginning. We count on each other to make certain neither one of us oversteps ourselves. This is where the trust lies. You shall see it is thus when you find yourself a husband."

Pondering that notion, she spied her bonnet on the table. Walking over, she retrieved it. It was hopelessly crushed. It would go perfectly with her mussed hair.

Wynne put on her bonnet. Staring into the mirror hanging over the chimneypiece, she tucked stray wisps of hair into place. "I may not be fated to marry, Tipton. I fear I am too picky." She also preferred her own council. Seeking a husband's approval would be tiresome, if not quite irritating.

Guessing her thoughts, her brother-in-law's light-blue eyes twinkled with amusement. "A husband is not so easily deterred from learning his wife's secrets as is her family," he warned.

She gave her misshapen bonnet one more tug before she faced Tipton. "Then I shall count myself fortunate I do not possess one."

Keanan entered the gaming hell, dressed more like a rake searching for trouble in the stews than a man who had been whelped in them. Gambling by means of a card game or the throw of the dice had never captivated him. Too much was left to chance.

He preferred to be in control of his own fate. Tonight he

sought the man who could bring him closer to the polite world he craved.

"Milroy!"

Keanan nodded his head, acknowledging the summons. He took his time finding his way to the gentleman's table. It would not do to appear too eager. Sighting the proprietress of the Silver Serpent, he switched directions to meet her halfway.

Somewhere in her forties, Blanche Chabbert had taken over running the small gaming house after the death of her husband ten years ago. In her capable hands, she had managed to triple the profits.

"Mr. Milroy, it is good of you to remember us." She genteelly offered her hand.

Bowing, he said, "Mrs. Chabbert. To my regret, my absence has deprived me of your enlightened companionship."

Being the focus of his devastating charm had her twittering, "Rogue!" Giving up all formal pretenses, she threw her arms around him. "Keanan Milroy, look at you. All dressed up like a first consequence gentleman. I almost didn't recognize you." She gave him a playful push.

He endured her good-natured teasing and motherly petting. He had been barely fifteen when Blanche's husband, Henry, had hauled him, kicking, into the small rooms they kept for themselves in the back of the gaming hell. He was bleeding from his mouth and nose when Henry had rescued him from a severe beating by a gang of boys, even though at the time, Keanan had been far from grateful. It had been four against one. Terrible odds for someone his size and age. Even so, he'd had two on the ground crying for the mothers who had abandoned them, before Henry had run them off.

"Blanche, my love, we've got a boy who fancies himself a fighter," Henry, a man who made his living encouraging others to play the odds, had crowed over his latest discovery. "Not much to look at. But what food doesn't add to that lanky frame, age will, lad. In your prime, those fists will be your fortune."

Henry's words resounded in Keanan's head. The old gambler had been right. He and Blanche had taken a half-wild boy into their home. They had provided food and a place to lay his head when he would accept it. He had too much pride and mistrust to remain, yet he always had returned. The bait Henry had dangled was too tempting. The sly old man had offered to train him for the ring. Eventually, he had even put up the first few stakes. It was a debt Keanan could never repay.

"What are you doing here, love?" Blanche asked, interrupting his thoughts. "You know I enjoy seeing you, but you've never been one to squander your coin playing cards."

Unlike your father.

He flinched, reacting as if she had spoken the insulting comparison. Retreating from her embrace, Keanan scanned through the smoky haze in the room, seeking one man in the crowd of shadowed faces. Recognition made his breath hitch. There in the corner sat Wesley Fawks, Duke of Reckester. His noble sire.

"How long has he been here?"

Blanche was not fooled by his dull, reasonable tone. "Now, Keanan, I want no trouble from you."

Seething, Keanan watched his father lay down his cards. Laughing, the man who refused to acknowledge him nudged the player to his left and reached forward to collect his winnings. The normalcy of the scene almost sent his unnoticed son into a murderous rage.

"He isn't worth it," Blanche hissed, her hand stroking the sleeve of his coat in an attempt to soothe him. "If you can't think of yourself, then think of me. I depend on his kind to patronize my establishment. To turn one out is like refusing them all." Her eyes begged him to understand. "They drink themselves senseless and lose half their fortunes before they sober. It is a revenge of sorts, is it not?"

Restrained frustration had him removing his hat and threading his fingers through his short, dark-blond hair. He clapped his hat back in place. "Not enough, madam. Not for me. Never for me."

Blanche flinched at his vehemence. She had always been too kind-hearted to comprehend such hatred. "I can't talk to you when you are in this state. Dressed as you are, I assume you came for a respectable purpose. Hold tight that anger, or you'll be allowing the foolish old sot to ruin your evening plans. A shame, for I thought better of you."

Attacking his sire did not suit his purposes. He was a gentleman now. There were subtle ways of gaining his revenge. "You're right, of course, love." He took up both her hands and kissed her knuckles. "Ply him with drink and weak cards. May he awaken in Queer Street come dawn."

Recognizing the storm had passed, she beamed affectionately at him. "There's my lad. You have enough Irish in you to summon a curse from hell and fire it straight into his black heart."

Keanan hugged her. He thought of the man waiting for him. If it pleased her believing Reckester was safe from his bastard son, then he would not shatter her illusions.

Four

Anticipation thrummed through Wynne as she and her papa sat in their coach. They were just another link in a long chain of coaches snaking down the street, the participants each awaiting their turn to be escorted down by liveried footmen. Twelve days had passed since her encounter with the unsavory Mr. Egger. A light dusting of face powder concealed the remaining trace of the bruise on her cheek.

"Bothersome, this pomp, when all a man craves is something to relieve the dryness in his throat," Sir Thomas Bedegrayne complained for the third time.

"Papa, Lord and Lady Lumley revel in providing the most spectacular event of the season. Even you manage to turn up for their yearly ball," she reminded him.

"I had my gels to marry off," his low voice boomed in the small confines. "How else were these young bucks going to get a good look at you?" The dim interior had him squinting at her. "Your sister Irene did her duty. She married her viscount almost thirteen years ago."

Wynne sensed a lecture brewing concerning her unmatched state. Their frequency had increased over the past two years. She longed to stick her head out the window and count how many carriages were ahead of them until her reprieve.

"And my sweet baby, Devona. She secured a fine husband in Tipton," he arrogantly declared, pretending he had a hand in their match.

"More likely was bullied into it," she countered. "Papa, I am attending the ball. Lady Lumley has most likely shaken the trees for London's most eligible, and we are about to witness a showing that will put Tatt's in the pale. Be content."

Sir Thomas's bushy brows came together. The gray wild hairs reminded her of a ghostly caterpillar. She pursed her lips.

Her father made an exasperated sound. "Crusty as an ace of spades at her husband's funeral. Stubborn, too. That pretty face of yours has given me more grief than a dear papa should bear."

"Really, Papa." It was an old lament. The coach lurched forward, then suddenly halted.

"A plain gel wouldn't quibble about her suitors. She'd be pleased to receive any man's card."

She switched tactics. "Not every man is suited to be your son-in-law."

The turnabout logic pleased the old devil. "Quite. Quite."

A harried footman flung open the coach door, granting Wynne her desired reprieve.

It was a maddening crush. Most of the *ton* seemed to have accepted Lord and Lady Lumley's invitation. Wynne and Sir Thomas helplessly rode the rising tide of delicate muslins and silk, pressing their way forward to the obligatory greetings of their host and hostess before making their way to the entertainments of the evening.

Identically dressed twin girls, wearing ribbons and conservatory roses in their hair, stood at the entrance of the ballroom passing out nosegays. Wynne accepted her flowers and was about to move on to the ballroom, when her father touched her on the arm.

"A man needs fortification to withstand such plumed pageantry." His shoulders hunched when he realized his presence had caught the attention of one very persistent widow. "God-awful matrons. Always bothering me, seeking to ruin my blissful unwedded state."

Interested, she sought out the recipient of her father's glowering. She recognized the god-awful matron in question as Lady Malion. After losing her husband five years ago, she had been not so subtly pursuing Wynne's father for the past eighteen months.

"Ah, yes. Matrons are always matchmaking. Not unlike persistent papas." Wynne affectionately reached for a handful of side whisker and tugged him closer. She kissed him on the cheek. "Go hide in the card room, Papa. Aunt Moll should be about, and will keep my ardent suitors at a respectable distance. Careful strategy will keep both our blissful unwedded states intact."

Sir Thomas showed all the signs of a father brewing an objection, but it sputtered out with the knowledge that he had been masterfully maneuvered. If he remained to oversee his daughter, he would have to endure Lady Malion's amorous attentions. "A frumpy, one-armed pea-goose for a daughter would be less trouble," he grumbled.

Laughter and candlelight competed for brilliance in her eyes. "I adore you, too, Papa."

"Do not underestimate your aunt. I am not the only Bedegrayne who would prefer seeing you spliced to some proper gallant." Satisfied he had the last word, he went off seeking safer entertainment.

Many in the crowded ballroom had witnessed the intimate byplay between father and daughter. The myriad of responses varied. Some envied the cherished relationship of father and child, while others thought that the senior Bedegrayne exceedingly indulged his daughters. The results were progeny who were too willful, too educated. Too finicky.

From across the room, Keanan discreetly watched the

woman. If he had not been told it was she, he would not have recognized the elegant, refined woman in the rose gown as the bedraggled, distressed waif he had rescued at the canal.

He had a name to place with that fair face: Miss Wynne Bedegrayne. Once he had Tipton's name, the rest had been relatively simple. Either due to the viscount's notoriety or to his own peculiar selection of intimates, Keanan quickly learned Miss Bedegrayne was neither wife, mistress, or hired help. She was Tipton's sister by marriage.

Beyond that revelation, he had gathered little more information about the lady. He considered his recent introduction to polite society fortunate. Although his presence at the ball was motivated by his ambitions, he saw no reason why he could not indulge in the evening's pleasures. Gaining an introduction to Miss Wynne Bedegrayne had suddenly become a priority.

"Ho, Milroy. My apologies for abandoning you, sir."

Keanan raised a hand to still the man's protest, though his attention still remained on Miss Bedegrayne. Her presence had subtly migrated the unattached males to her side of the ballroom. They hovered around her in a growing circle like drones supplicating their queen bee. *Simpering, flattering fools.* He scowled.

Misunderstanding the reason for Keanan's ill temper, the man suggested, "I realize a man of your caliber might find the Lumley function a bit tame."

Tearing his gaze away from the woman, he gave the young lord his complete attention. His new acquaintance, Caster Evett, had recently claimed the title Marquess of Lothbury upon the death of his father three months earlier. Lothbury had enthusiastically embraced his miserly father's demise by embarking on a hedonistic spree of horses, women, and gambling. The last vice had led him to cross paths with Keanan.

"I do not follow," he said, modulating his accent so it

was more fitting for his surroundings. He considered the talent a gift from his mother. "What caliber do you mean?"

The young marquess blinked. "Nothing offensive, I assure you. It's just sipping tepid lemonade and having young misses fluttering their lashes at you does not compare to the exciting atmosphere of the ring."

Either Lothbury was concerned about his new friend's reaction to the ball, or perhaps the man was already regretting his patronage. This would not do. He needed this entrance into society. "There is nothing like a good fight to fire a man's blood, Lothbury. But standing here admiring the exotic butterflies flap around the room can stir a man in a different way. Yea?" He gave him a conspiring wink.

Both men chuckled.

Keanan deliberately focused his interest on the woman. "Speaking of exotics . . ." he trailed off, waiting for his friend to catch up.

Lothbury scanned the opposite side of the room. Not surprisingly, he settled on the proper lady. His hazel eyes warmed with awareness. "Ah, yes, Miss Bedegrayne. Quite beautiful. And quite unattainable. More than one man has cast his lot for her hand, only to be refused by the aloof Aphrodite Urania."

"Goddess of the heavens," Keanan mused. Blanche had a fondness for Greek myths. "It suits her. I want an introduction."

"That can be arranged. You are new to our circle, and thus a curiosity. It is one of the reasons why I have been selective of the events you've attended. Our efforts should have the gentlemen clamoring to lift a toast to the *ton's* favorite pugilist, and the ladies yearning after your marvelous physique."

He had no quarrel with Lothbury if it contented the man to believe he was responsible for their presence this evening. His new friend possessed an affable manner that was amusing if not dangerously naive at times. The young marquess needed his friendship just as much as Keanan had use for his.

"I trust the execution of our endeavor to you, my lord."

Wynne's desire to dance had dwindled the moment she had seen her great-aunt's pale countenance. Her health had been poor after a rather nasty fall nine months earlier. The injury had made her a veritable recluse. Glancing back for the third time, Wynne was pleased to see her aunt sitting beside her old friend Mrs. Cryer, engrossed in a lively debate.

"Cease fussing, Wynne." The familiar voice had her whirling in delight. "Your aunt is in good hands, and enjoying herself. She would be upset learning you have refused two earls and a viscount on her behalf."

"Brook! Or rather, Lady A'Court." She embraced her friend and coconspirator from Miss Rann's School of the Ladies' Arts. "When did you return to England? The last I heard, you were extending your wedding tour of Italy another month."

"A business matter demanded Lyon's attention," Brook confessed. Her upswept blond tresses, a similar hue to Wynne's, lent a superficial impression that the two women were related. "It was idealistic of us to assume we could vanish from our responsibilities for long."

"Well, I for one am pleased to have you around. Papa is lamenting my unwedded state again, and I fear I shall be married before the year is out if he has his way."

Peripherally she spotted the Marquess of Lothbury making the rounds, renewing his acquaintance with various young ladies who had caught his eye. It did not astonish her that the new marquess would be searching for a bride.

"Perhaps, as a newly wedded lady, you could offer some advice in choosing the proper husband?" Wynne asked, surprised that Brook tensed at her question.

"Miss Bedegrayne," the Marquess of Lothbury called out, dividing her attention.

Brook squeezed her hand. "Lyon has arrived. I must leave you." She rushed off. Wynne observed her friend greet the sullen earl. Ten years Brook's senior, the silver in his dark locks made him seem more dashing than old.

"Miss Bedegrayne, this evening I have been spared chasing you about the room." The marquess's tone rebuked as well as expressed his pleasure.

Wynne curtsied. "My lord. I was renewing an old acquaintance. Are you familiar with Lord and Lady A'Court?"

"Not particularly," he said, dismissing the subject. "I, too, am making acquaintances, both old and new. Come, my dear Miss Bedegrayne." He offered his arm. "I have a new friend who desires an introduction."

Bemused, Wynne allowed the marquess to escort her across the room. Because he was a year younger than herself, she considered herself quite safe from his favor. A man in his position would clearly require a young woman not quite so on the shelf as she was at three and twenty.

"Sir, a moment, if you please."

It took all the polished skills of deportment she had learned at Miss Rann's school not to gape openly. Seeing *him* again brought back the mortification she felt about that awful day near the canal.

Unaware of Wynne's mounting horror and the fighter's comprehending scrutiny, the Marquess of Lothbury made his introductions.

"Mr. Milroy, a pleasure," she said; the words were false and he knew it.

Keanan credited her for handling what was an apparent shock. The tremor in her extended hand might have gone unnoticed if he had not been examining her reaction to him so attentively.

"Miss Bedegrayne." To prove to them both that he could be chivalrous, he accepted her hand and bowed. "Rumors of your beauty reach beyond this ballroom. When Lothbury revealed your presence, I insisted on an introduction."

The bland conversation seemed to steady her. The wariness had not left the cool, intriguing depths of her green eyes, but her bearing had lost that restless movement, signaling the need to bolt.

"You are most gracious, sir." She took a deep breath; a nonverbal decision flashed in her expressive eyes. Swift determination set her jaw. Her chin lifted a notch. "Pardon my boldness, but I must ask. You seem familiar to me, Mr. Milroy. Have we met?"

Her daring, aggressive approach was most unexpected. For a lady who had secrets and a reputation to protect, she risked much in challenging him so publicly. His admiration grew toward her, even though he could not resist poking at her composure.

"Miss Bedegrayne, I can assure you, I would not forget such a meeting." He intentionally held her gaze, wanting her to understand his warning.

Despite the orchestra playing just outside the doors in the gardens, and dozens of conversations continuing around them, he heard her small, startled gasp. She muffled the sound by nipping her lower lip with her teeth.

The action drew his gaze. The woman had incredible lips. They were neither thin nor too full. She had left them unpainted. However, their natural hue did not require artifice. Like morning dew on a raspberry, there was a sheen outlining her half-formed pout. A hunger rose within him that he had never thought possible. He fought against the demanding urge to claim her tempting mouth, wondering if she tasted as sweet as any summer berry.

"Miss Bedegrayne," Lothbury interjected, breaking her gaze away from Keanan's magnetic spell. "Mr. Milroy is relatively new to society. I doubt you would have encoun-

tered him unless you share an appreciation for pugilism."
He gave her a considering glance. "Perhaps one of your
brothers?"

She was more than willing to give the marquess her complete attention. "My lord, both of my brothers are out of the
country, and my father cares little for the sport. You are
correct," she conceded, looking at Keanan. "I can think of
no situation in which we would have met."

So she intended to deny the encounter. He saw no advantage to revealing her lie, so he smiled, letting her know he
had teeth and could use them at any time of his choosing.

The voice of a newcomer breached their little group.
"Miss Bedegrayne, why is it I must wend my way through
half the males in this room to secure your hand for a dance?
My dear, do you never tire of holding court?"

Keanan recognized the voice. He had enough reasons to
dislike the gentleman. Listening to him attempt to exert his
claim on Miss Bedegrayne enraged him on a very primal
level. He pivoted, placing himself in front of her.

"Milroy," Drake Fawks, Lord Nevin sneered. "The Lumleys' status has fallen greatly if they are inviting the likes
of you."

Lothbury stepped forward. "You insult me, Nevin. Mr.
Milroy is my guest."

Nevin was a blond giant compared to the marquess. His
eyes, an icy aquamarine in color, glittered threateningly.
"You insult Miss Bedegrayne, forcing her to address this
miscreant." He held a commanding hand out to her. "Come,
my lady. What you have endured goes beyond etiquette."

A frown wrinkled her brow as her gaze shifted between
the three men. "Lord Nevin, these men have been above
reproach, which is more than I can say for your behavior.
Attacking these men in front of me—"

"Do you know who he is? What he is?" Nevin demanded.
Miss Bedegrayne's eyes narrowed to calculating slits.

"More to the point, I know who you are, and what you are to me. And one of those being, *not my husband!*"

Realizing his error, Nevin took an entreating step toward her. "Miss Bedegrayne. Wynne."

Deliberately provoking him, Keanan blocked his progress. He welcomed the fury he saw in the other man's eyes. "Oh, I dare, sir. Can you state the same?" he taunted.

"Mr. Milroy," she crisply spoke, her tone sounding like a reprimand. "I believe, sir, you were about to claim me as a dance partner."

Damn the woman! Did she not understand how much he relished challenging this particular man? Or perhaps she did, and thus her impulsive interference. He could all but taste the scent of Nevin's blood, and she was fretting about the scandal.

Scandal.

Keanan gave Nevin his back. The slight shrug of his shoulder, blatantly expressing his lack of fear that he would be attacked from behind. He stared at Miss Bedegrayne. Her slender fingers so tightly gripped the blades of her closed fan that he expected it to snap under the strain. Her expression, filled with eloquent concern and embarrassment, pleaded for him to accept her refined retreat.

However, he was not one of them. From the corner of his eye, he could see them whispering to each other, waiting to see what he would do next. He refused to hide behind politeness. Most of all, a woman's skirts!

"My apologies, Miss Bedegrayne. I did not hear you correctly."

She audibly cleared her throat. Finally, noticing their audience, her gaze discreetly slanted to each side. "Our dance, Mr. Milroy. You promised me a dance."

"I regret the contradiction, my lady. I made no such offer."

Her cheeks blanched at the first few twitters of laughter, feeling the first sting of humiliation.

Lothbury coughed into his hand. "Uh, Milroy."

Nevin's fingers curled, appearing clawlike, but he did not carry out the lunge his eyes promised. "Bastard," he impotently muttered.

Miss Bedegrayne held his gaze. Whatever she sought, she found him lacking. She lowered her lashes, but not before Keanan noticed the moist gleam of tears. "Ah." She wet her lips, attempting to force the words out. "My mistake. Gentlemen, you must excuse me. I regret my presence has denied you all the pleasure of turning the Lumleys' ballroom into an exhibition at Fives Court. I bid you all a good evening." Holding her head up with all the grace of a queen, she strode through the crowd, painfully aware that she was the cause of their amusement.

It had not been Keanan's intention to humiliate her. Anger and pride prodded him to tread over her feelings. Frustration had him raking his fingers through his hair. To chase after her now would only heighten her embarrassment.

Nevin stepped closer. Their stature almost equal, he spoke in low tones so his words carried no farther than the recipient. "I should call you out for deliberately hurting her like that. However, duels are for gentlemen. We both know you do not qualify."

Brushing past Keanan, he rebuked Lothbury with a scathing stare. "My lord, I would choose my friends with greater care." Stiffly he pushed his way through the guests, following in Miss Bedegrayne's wake.

Glancing at Lothbury, it was apparent to Keanan he had fallen in the marquess's esteem. "I lost my head. I am the bastard Nevin accused me of being."

His friend made a disapproving noise. "I thought her quite brave, choosing you over the man intent on marrying her." He was watching the dancing couples in the center of the room, so he missed the denial that flickered in Keanan's eyes. "Only tomorrow's gossip will tell us if we have lost ground in civilizing you, my friend."

Keanan cared little for what people thought about him. What bothered him was the look on Miss Bedegrayne's face when she heard people laughing at her. He did not believe for one second that she was upset by his refusal to dance.

Searching the room, he hunted for a glimpse of her rose colored gown. A sensitive creature, she was probably seeking a quiet place to cry.

There.

His gaze locked on her. She stood near the doors leading to the garden. Keanan cocked his head, trying to see who was halting her graceful exit. Couples danced their steps in front of him, giving him teasing flashes of her.

The dance ended when his patience had all but vanished. He had been about to ignore his own sage counsel and charge after her. Seeing that it was Lord Nevin who had delayed her departure froze him in place. He unconsciously gritted his teeth, watching them together. Their retreat into the torchlit gardens had him taking a step forward. So Nevin had his eye on Miss Bedegrayne. An ambitious lady would welcome the interest of an earl and future duke, he darkly mused. Unfortunately for her, Nevin was a swine, and Keanan lacked the conscience to warn her off. Not when she could aid him in ruining the man.

Having tolerated her share of overbearing males this evening, Wynne had hoped Lord Nevin would heed her hint and leave her alone in the gardens. She sat on a small stone bench overlooking a large, shallow pool. The reflective flames from the freestanding torches provided a quiet, meditative setting.

"Wynne."

She nudged her slipper into the decorative loose gravel at her feet. "Are you just persistent, Lord Nevin, or simply hard of hearing?" she wondered aloud.

Gravel crunched as he came closer. She stood, wanting

to escape him and the rush of embarrassment she had felt in the ballroom.

He halted her with a touch. "Please." He guided her back onto the bench and then settled beside her. "You told me to wait, but I fear I do not have the patience. I need to explain a few things." Lord Nevin stared out at the pool, which had initially beckoned her to seek solace there.

"You are presumptuous, my lord, if you believe I owe you the consideration to listen to you—or care, for that matter."

Her words were a lie. For the past six months, a reluctant truce had formed between the womanizing rake and her. To her surprise, she had discovered a man who was intelligent, humorous, and so unlike the superficial persona she had automatically applied to anyone of his good looks and carefree character. While she loathed confessing the news to her papa, she had believed she was developing a *tendre* for the impossible man.

"Why were you talking to Milroy?"

It took her thoughts a moment to follow the question. "Lothbury insisted on introducing us," she explained. "I saw no harm."

"Did you not?" he asked, not really needing an answer. "Somehow, Milroy discovered my interest in you. He sought you out as a means to attack me."

"My lord, what fever fires these demented hallucinations? Mr. Milroy and I met by chance." She made a helpless gesture. "Lothbury tells me Milroy is a champion pugilist by profession. The man is clearly enjoying the fame and connections his victories have gained him."

She did not understand Lord Nevin's irrational dislike for the fighter. Even if he had been acting in a reasonable manner, she still would not reveal the truth of why Milroy desired an introduction.

"Lothbury is a maggot," Lord Nevin passionately proclaimed. "He drinks too much, gambles to excess, and he owes debts to unsavory gentlemen. His connection to society made him Milroy's perfect choice."

The corner of Wynne's mouth lifted into a slight smile. "Hmm. Drinking to excess, gambling, and womanizing. I would guess these sins would be familiar to you."

Instead of recognizing the irony, his grim expression became unreadable. "More than you know."

In the ensuing silence, she thought of her papa. He was not a man to cross when he was deep in a game. Perhaps her aunt was tired and would not mind giving her an escort home. Asking her meant she would have to walk back into the ballroom. Nevertheless, she was too sturdy to crumble at a few whispers. Wynne rose.

Lord Nevin clasped her hand within his. "Promise me . . . because of our friendship. Keep your distance from Milroy."

It was too much. Grimacing, she slipped her captured hand free and headed back to the ballroom. She had no intention of ever speaking to that pugilist again. Still, Nevin's command grated. She was not in the mood to humor the man.

He seized her arm before she had a chance to walk through the open doorway. He need not have bothered. What Wynne noticed twenty yards away had rooted her.

Lord Nevin's grip tightened to the point of pain. "Damn."

Mr. Milroy was seated beside her Aunt Moll. The two of them looked on as her aunt laughed at something the man murmured in her ear. She affectionately patted him on the cheek.

Wynne did not struggle free from Nevin's hold. She tilted her face upward; her cool green eyes held his. "Forget the warnings and the sworn oaths. That man is charming my aunt. Why is he a danger to my family? Who is he to you?"

The blond highlights in his long brown hair glistened in the candlelight as he leaned closer. A loose strand freed itself from his queue, swung forward, and brushed lightly against her temple. "Keanan Milroy seeks to destroy my family. He despises me and is ruthless enough to use any pawn. Do not be fooled by his charm."

Charm? The man had insulted her in front of everyone. Still, she believed Lord Nevin's assessment that Mr. Milroy was ruthless. Wynne had seen the rage on his face when he dragged Mr. Egger off her. She had witnessed the violence as he delivered retribution for the other man's crimes.

"How do you know all of this?"

Lord Nevin's attention returned to Mr. Milroy flirting with her aunt. His jaw hardened with an audible click. "He is my half-brother."

Five

Keanan's motives were murky, even to himself, as he followed the servant up the stairs to Mrs. Molly Bedegrayne's drawing room. The older woman had imperiously requested an introduction two days ago at the Lumleys' ball.

"Are you the gentleman who boorishly refused my niece a dance?" she had demanded, her sharp eyes examining him, noting every detail.

"Yes, ma'am."

He had expected her to order the footmen to expel him from the residence. To his amazement, she tossed her head back and laughed. Through her teary, humorous gaze, she reached forward and patted him on the cheek.

"Mr. Milroy, I warrant my niece has never been treated thus by any of her suitors. I credit she will recall your novel approach for years."

If she meant the lady would never forgive him, then he agreed.

Mrs. Bedegrayne proved to be unlike any member of the *ton* he had met. Sitting on a blue-and-gold gilded high-backed chair, she had enthralled the group, regaling them with tales of her youth. She considered everyone around her a dear new friend, and her refreshing enthusiasm captivated him. Later, it had been impossible to refuse her invitation to come calling.

"There you are, my dear boy." Mrs. Bedegrayne limped

forward to greet him. She wore an unembellished gray gown with crisp white Vandyke trim edging her sleeves and hem.

"Madam, are you well. I could call another time?"

"No, no. It is an old injury that aches me. No need to fuss." Taking him by both hands, she led him into the drawing room. "I am pleased you accepted my offer. When I last saw you, I wondered if you had agreed just to appease an old woman."

Settling onto the sofa she gestured toward, he removed his hat and placed it on his lap. "I must disagree, Mrs. Bedegrayne. A woman of your beauty is considered ageless."

Her fingers fluttered up and adjusted her lace cap, which in Keanan's unsophisticated opinion appeared fine. "Aunt Moll to you. I see your dear mama brought you up well."

The casual reference to Aideen Milroy still managed after all these years to drive jagged glass splinters into his gut. Years of practice and discipline had him wrapping the seething emotions within him tight and dragging them deep. A woman like Aunt Moll would never understand the duality of compassion and treachery that had made up his mother. "I lost my mother when I was thirteen."

The awkwardness of not knowing how to offer him comfort had her fidgeting. "Oh. Oh, my. Forgive my prying. I did not invite you here to summon old pain."

Shrewdly he studied her. "Why did you invite me here?"

"Aunt Moll," a female voice called out from downstairs. One of the servants must have intercepted the new arrival, for a muffled conversation took place outside the drawing room door.

Wynne Bedegrayne.

Young eyes met old. *The sly old matchmaker,* he thought, not bothering to hide his grin. "Your niece wasn't pleased to see me hovering around you at the Lumleys' ball; she will think less of me sitting here in your best room."

She sniffed into her handkerchief and then used it to wave off her concern. "Wynne was miffed at your outlandish behavior, and rightly so. However, I have gained more than silver hair and wrinkles over the years. I see things you young ones miss. You may be a slippery one, Mr. Milroy, but you are redeemable."

He could not prevent himself from asking, "What about Lord Nevin?"

Aunt Moll leaned forward. "I prefer you for my niece," she admitted, pleased that she had managed this discreet meeting.

Well, this should be entertaining, Keanan thought, adjusting his position slightly so he could see Miss Bedegrayne's reaction. It was rather perverse of him, but he enjoyed rattling the lady.

"Perhaps she is out?"

Almost to the top of the stairs, Wynne waited for her lagging friends, Amara and Brook. "Amara, the front door is unlocked. The servants are absent. Why would she beg me for a visit and then depart without a word?"

Brook delicately shrugged. "It has been some time since I have seen your aunt. Still, at her age, the mind becomes weak. She merely could have forgotten."

"I suppose," Wynne said, not convinced. She rubbed the tingling feeling in her neck away with her hand. Not waiting for her friends, she knocked at the drawing room door.

"Enter, dear," her aunt bade from within.

Some of the tension in her shoulders eased at the sound of her aunt's voice. Nothing was wrong. Her aunt was safe. She was not lying at the bottom of the stairs with a broken leg, as she had been found nine months past.

"Good afternoon, Aunt Moll." She pushed open the doors. "I have a surprise for you. Look who—" Her words took flight. Sitting in her aunt's drawing room, as if he had every right to be there, was *that man*.

Aunt Moll waved her handkerchief, beckoning her closer.

The teasing glimmer in her eyes revealed to Wynne that her shock had been expected. "As you can see, my dear, I, too, have a surprise."

She heard Amara's sharp intake of breath. Her friend had arrived late to the Lumleys' ball; even so, there had been a wealth of gossips eager to share the tale.

"Lady A'Court and Miss Claeg." Her aunt used the arm of her chair as a brace to stand. Espying Wynne's concern, she shook her head in denial. "Just a little stiff if I sit too long. Lord Tipton warned me this would happen. If I give up on this old limb, I will be forced to squander my last days bedridden."

Her aunt's movements became less stiff with each step. She embraced each woman before making her way back to her chair. Mr. Milroy reached out, gripping the older woman by the upper arm, and assisted her into her seat.

"Ladies, please join us." Aunt Moll touched her heart. "Dear me, a gathering like this requires refreshments. Wynne, ring for Aberly."

"Is he about? He did not answer our knock."

Her aunt frowned. "Probably sleeping in the pantry again," she murmured, not particularly upset by the notion. "Oh, I suppose the refreshments can wait. Wynne, come sit beside Mr. Milroy on the sofa."

She would rather have gone off to chastise Aberly for shirking his duties. Brook's and Amara's seat selections gave her no option but to comply with her aunt's wishes.

"Mr. Milroy." Wynne mumbled the greeting, refusing to look him directly in the eye. She sat.

"Miss Bedegrayne."

He shifted; one shoe brushed against her gown. The accidental graze only called attention to their proximity. His large, muscular build quite overwhelmed her.

"Ladies, formality demands an introduction. I am Keanan Milroy."

Oddly detached from the group, she listened as her aunt

made the proper introductions to her friends. She slanted a speculative glance in his direction. *What of your ties to the Reckester family, Mr. Milroy? Most would flaunt their connection to a duke.*

Noticing her regard, he nodded, sending a faint, smug smile in her direction. Conceited savage! He believed her enthralled by his masculine beauty. It irritated her beyond tolerance that she did, indeed, find him fascinating. She would have been grateful to blame her interest on his kindred resemblance to Lord Nevin. Unfortunately, except for hair color, the two men did not share blatant similarities. She doubted she would have recognized their blood ties on her own.

Wynne absently rubbed her lower lip with her finger. His name was Keanan. The word conjured images of hard, deadly edges in her fertile imagination. That description seemed to apply to the man as well. Mr. Milroy stood a few inches shorter than his half-brother.

Regardless, what he lacked in stature was generously compensated by battle-honed muscle, she decided, recalling the encounter at the canal. His linen shirt had been open that day, revealing the masculine contours of his chest. She had not seen such perfection except when appreciating marble statuary at one of the museums.

His face might be considered by some as severe as his body. It was lean and angular, a consequence of his harsh, disciplined life. Such features alone did not invite closer deliberation. What made him approachable were his eyes. She had mistaken them for a merciless black at a distance. In truth, his eyes were indigo, lined with lashes almost too pretty for a man. Their dark, unfathomable blue depths, instead of being cold, intrigued her, made her want to peer deeper to find the man cloaked beneath his pride and impudence.

She could not fault his attire. His cutaway-style blue dress coat matched the color of his eyes. The lighter blue waistcoat within was accented by an indistinct gold thread pattern. His buff-colored trousers appeared as clean and starch-pressed as the high cravat he wore.

While Brook spoke of her travels, Wynne continued her discreet observations of Mr. Milroy. He did not seem aware of her appraisal. Absorbed in the conversation, he politely encouraged her friend by asking various questions about her journey.

She told herself her curiosity was merely a protective measure. Besides Amara, this stranger knew details about her life that she had managed to conceal from her family. He *had* insisted on an introduction the other evening, regardless of his rude behavior once Lord Nevin had joined them. Muddling the situation further was his hostility toward his own family. His reasons were his own. What questions she had wanted to ask Lord Nevin had been forgotten at the sight of Mr. Milroy flirting with her aunt. If what the earl had said was true, then the man posed a threat to her family.

"And what is your opinion on the subject, Wynne?" Aunt Moll asked, pulling her from her private thoughts.

Frantically she tried to recall fragments of their conversation. Nothing. She silently pleaded to her friends for help. Brook returned her regard, expecting something insightful from her. She saw concern reflected in Amara's visage. Lowering her gaze, she stared at her hands. It was utterly mortifying to admit to herself that she had been caught gawking at Mr. Milroy. She would rather have Speck set a broken limb than confess it to the others.

Feeling pressured to speak, she mumbled, "I have yet to form an opinion, Aunt."

Her answer seemed to increase Amara's alarm. Brook was now staring at her strangely, and her aunt had yet to shut her mouth. Not caring if he was innocent, Wynne glared at the source of her inattention. Mr. Milroy had propped his left elbow against the arm of the sofa. The back of his hand was pressed against his quivering lips to prevent himself from laughing outright.

What a widgeon, she mentally scolded herself. "Perhaps I did not hear you correctly," she prompted, deciding she had reached the pinnacle of her embarrassment.

"We were discussing your brother, Brock, dear," Aunt Moll gently explained. "Lady A'Court had commented on the risks at sea. Even if your brother survives the diseases of the natives, he must face foul weather and pirates to return home to us. It made me most distressed, thinking about him in danger. I had wanted your opinion on the subject."

"Oh." Wynne rubbed the spot between her eyes. She had misjudged. This embarrassment seemed endless.

Her aunt inadvertently came to her rescue. "What is it, Wynne? A megrim?" She pointed at Mr. Milroy. "You, sir. Touch her cheek for fever. Perhaps the stomach illness that plagued you a sennight past has returned."

She slapped his hand away. "When I need a medical opinion, I shall summon a physician, Mr. Milroy." It relieved her that he did not endeavor to touch her again. "Aunt, I am well. Truly. All I need is some air." She stood, satisfied that her excuse made more sense than her feeble attempt at joining their conversation.

"A stroll in the garden might be the very thing to revive you, dear," Aunt Moll suggested. "Mr. Milroy, why do you not join my niece? I will not worry if she is in your care."

Her aunt could not have been more obvious. This was dreadful! Wynne concealed her misery at the notion of being alone with him. She considered herself quite clever; there had to be a polite manner of discouraging him.

"It is not fair to abandon Brook and Amara, Aunt."

"Nonsense, we are having a lovely chat," the older woman replied, obviously pleased she had maneuvered her willful niece into a romantic tryst. "Off with you two. Enjoy the garden. If you come across Aberly, tell him to send up some refreshments."

Before she could think of another excuse, Mr. Milroy had placed his large hand in the middle of her back and practically shoved her through the door.

They made their way downstairs in silence. Aberly was in the front hall, balanced on a chair. He was wiping the dust from the frames of the numerous paintings that cluttered the walls. She broke away from Mr. Milroy and relayed her aunt's instructions to the butler.

Returning to him, she wished he would go away. The embarrassment had faded, leaving her mind clearer. She had garnered a reputation for dissuading her suitors with a cool, uninterested glance or a witty refusal. The knack seemed to have deserted her. Naturally, she blamed him. He unsettled her.

"Mr. Milroy, you must not feel obliged to do my aunt's bidding," she began, satisfied by the indulgent quality in her voice. "She tends to be overprotective. I can assure you, I am quite fit. Please do not misconstrue your departure as a failing to keep a promise to my aunt."

The doors to the garden stood open. Confident he would agree, Wynne almost stumbled when he gripped her upper arm, assisting her down the three steps to the garden's stone path.

He paused. His hold forced her to halt also. Audibly taking a deep breath, her gaze was drawn to his chest. Being outdoors did not diminish his overwhelming size. She still felt slight and edgy standing next to him.

Realizing she was still staring at his chest, she moved on to his face. Something amused him, she could see. The light in his eyes did not erase the shadows she saw in those dark-blue depths. Rather, it skipped across the surface like a flat stone skipping across the water.

"You are used to getting your way around men, aren't you, Wynne?"

His formal speech lapsed with his manners. The faint Irish inflection danced down her spine. "It is improper to address me thus, sir. Miss Bedegrayne, if you please." She added enough tartness to make him laugh. Grudgingly she had to admit it was a pleasant sound, even though it always seemed to be at her expense.

"I will wager, those impotent sycophants you call suitors probably repent their forward impulses when your voice loses that sweet quality." His indigo eyes entranced her. "You have made two mistakes with me, Wynne. One, I am no gentleman. Oh, I can play along when there is a need. However, bone-deep, I will never change. And two, while there is nothing wrong with honey, I tend to crave tart things, like damsons."

"Damsons," she repeated stupidly.

"Uh-huh," he murmured, lowering his face closer to her upturned one. "And you."

She felt his breath on her face. His lips were almost touching hers before she realized what he was about to do. Stirring herself from his trance, she held her ground and threatened, "Do not kiss me, Mr. Milroy. Not only do you risk losing your upper lip, because I will undoubtedly bite you, you will also lose my aunt's favor when I scream for assistance."

He jerked her closer, swallowing her breathy objection by kissing her. His lips, warm and firm, swung the ground upward, throwing her off balance. She clutched at him to steady herself, but he was already pulling back. He had lost the teasing light in his eyes. The emotion that gleamed there now was a dark, sultry promise. Her innocence prevented her from understanding how dangerous the need she saw there could be.

"Oh, I dare, my damson." His breath was uneven. "I never refuse a challenge or an offer."

She could still feel him; her lips thrummed from the ferocity of his swift kiss. The sensible action would have been to turn around, returning to her aunt and friends. She looked up at the windows, relieved to see none of the servants watching them. The drawing room overlooked the street. There were no witnesses to the kiss. It was one more secret they shared.

His fingers were still wrapped around her arm. Suddenly aware of the heat, the calloused texture of each digit, Wynne shrugged him loose. He released her. She strolled farther down the path, accepting that she had grown rather lax lately when it came to sensible actions. Besides, she had yet to figure out what to do about Mr. Milroy.

"Why are you here, sir?" she queried. "And do not expect me to believe your favorite manner of enjoying an afternoon is visiting a widow whose niece you deliberately insulted several evenings earlier."

He caught up to her. Removing his hat, he roughed up his short, damp blond hair into disheveled spikes. "No."

"No, what?" she demanded, feeling flustered again. The devil could come fetch him and fly him back to the underworld. What manner of man was he who used mundane gestures to tempt and seduce? And what kind of woman was she to be enthralled?

She glared at him. Blaming his breach of etiquette for her upset, he settled his hat back on his head. Looping his arm around hers, he steered her to the right toward a hedge wall. No one from the house would be able to see them. She halted, refusing to move another step until he answered her.

"I am used to people answering my questions, Mr. Milroy." He tugged her arm, but she slipped free from his hold. "Again, sir, why are you here?"

"Aunt Moll considers me one of your suitors."

"A role you undoubtedly encouraged," she charged. "My aunt is a kind woman. Losing her husband when she was still a young woman has marked her. I am certain a clever man such as yourself would know the correct questions to ask, and then use that information to charm a vulnerable old woman who romanticizes unrequited love."

"Rather clever of me, wasn't it?" he admitted a little too cheerfully. He walked under an apple tree and reached above his head to grip a limb. White petals fell like snow when he shook the limb to test its strength. "Or it would be, had I thought of it." Contemplative, he stared at something beyond her shoulder. "Tell me, Wynne. Or shall I call you Winnie?"

"Only if you are not overly fond of your teeth," she sweetly replied.

Mr. Milroy smiled, ruefully touching his mouth. "Oh, I am. Do you know how rare it is for a fighter to keep his teeth?"

"Blind luck, Mr. Milroy?"

He shook his head. "Skill, my dear." He released the limb and stalked over to the bench where she sat. He did not sit. Rather, he propped his foot on the bench and leaned his arm on his bent knee. "Considering how we met, Wynne, I am surprised you are so willing to cast me as a villain."

He paused, giving her time to relive the incident. How could she not, when part of that nightmare was standing in front of her, demanding she remember?

"I may not know my way around the fancy, but I had imagined you would be grateful I hauled that bastard Egger off you."

"I was. I am." Agitated, she pulled and twisted the fingertips of her right glove. "Is that why you asked about me, insisted on an introduction? You wanted to see how grateful I was?" She touched her brow. The pain was getting worse as she contemplated the unthinkable. "My plan was sound. Egger should never have been aware of our presence. Yet word had reached him. Warned him. Were you part of it? Did you think to blackmail me, thinking I would pay for your silence?" She sprang off the bench, needing the space between them.

"Whoa." Mr. Milroy raised an arm, blocking her escape. He danced back a few steps, proving he was willing not to touch her as long as she remained. "Calm down. You have quite an imagination, sweet, and I can guess the name of the man who put the fear in those lovely green eyes. 'Cause it certainly wasn't me." He expelled a puff of frustration. "I was there, Wynne. The man who saved you? Remember?" He lowered his arms. She could run past him if she desired. "Damn Nevin straight to hell for filling your head with such dross!"

Vehemence and regret laced his heated response, prickling the tiny, invisible hairs on her arms. Whatever his part, his anger toward Lord Nevin was genuine. "Do not blame your brother for my accusation, Mr. Milroy. I am not a puppet who needs another to give intellect and voice to hollowed wood. My opinions are my own."

Ignoring her defense, he seized upon the two words that confirmed his suspicions. "He actually confessed our kinship to you? Nevin must have been pressed if he needed our loathed association to sway you. Ah, to have seen his face when he choked up the words," he sighed wistfully.

"He has a high opinion of you, too." She glanced in the direction of the house, briefly wondering why no one had sought them out. "Listen, sir, it is clear you and your brother—"

"Half-brother," he coldly corrected.

"Half-brother, then," she impatiently amended. "Your quarrel is your own affair. I am more concerned about your role at the canal."

"If Nevin—"

Her hand gesture silenced him. "Lord Nevin is not privy to the events of that day, nor do I see any reason to enlighten him. Contrary to your misguided belief, my thoughts and actions are my own." Her lemon yellow skirts printed with a scarlet Grecian border design gave a satisfying swish as she changed directions, leading him this time. "Now that we have settled your concerns, let us focus on the subject, Mr. Milroy."

"I dare not interfere with a lady who governs not only her words but her actions, too," he lightly mocked.

"Your presence that day." She charged forward, ignoring his sarcasm.

"Was by accident or invitation, depending on your view." He shrugged, not caring one way or the other. "Your maid begged my assistance. She was a frantic little thing. How could I refuse her?"

She had to be certain. "Until that day, you and Mr. Egger had not met?"

He winced. "Must you apply equal address to me and your attacker? I can understand not wanting an intimate connection to him, so why not please me by using my Christian name."

She wrinkled her nose. "I do not think so."

"A simple name, really. Keanan. Say it, Wynne," he cajoled. "Say it for the man who saved your virtue."

Wynne eyed him warily. "You would accept this informality as reward for your heroic actions?"

"That, and all you would willingly offer. Let me hear my name from your lips," he entreated.

Wynne felt as though she was crossing some undetectable barrier if she gave in to his request. Mr. Milroy had baited his challenge well. To deny her errant knight was comparable to thrusting a sword through his heart as a reward for trouncing her adversary. The breach of propriety would cost her nothing. She doubted she would see him again once Lothbury tired of showing off his favorite pugilist.

"Keanan, I owe you my life. I regretted not telling you that day, but you were gone by the time I had collected myself," she revealed, meaning every word.

His delight dazzled her, making him seem younger. The smile he bestowed for a ridiculously paltry boon shamed her. He asked little for the risk he took, if what he said was true.

Unexpectedly, Lord Nevin's warning resounded in her head:

"He despises me and is ruthless enough to use any pawn. Do not be fooled by his charm."

Charm. Once, she thought he did not possess the quality. This afternoon, he gushed to the point of swamping her very senses. It would be so easy to believe him.

However, Wynne was old enough to be considered quite on the shelf, despite her pleasing countenance. Her papa called it pickiness on her part. She believed she had learned a thing or two about a courting male. The first rule was to look beyond the obvious. If the man was handsome and satisfied a lady's requisites in a husband, then he probably mistreated animals or had an abundance of children from his various mistresses. The second rule: never believe a man's flattery. No gentleman she ever encountered wasted time with flowery speech unless he was after something from the intended lady.

The sound of female voices had her checking the house again. Aunt Moll had decided it was time to view the results of her matchmaking. Mr. Milroy lifted his head at the sound, understanding his time alone with her had ended.

"I want to see you again," he said, no playful cajoling lessening the command.

"Why?"

He snorted, using the edge of his shoe to kick at the gravel. "Why else? I have not stopped thinking about you from the moment I saw you on your back, fighting for your life. Even seeing you cleaned up, head high, appearing every inch a queen, has not deterred me."

Before she could ask him why being finely dressed for a ball should have discouraged him, he silenced her by touching her cheek. Sunlight dappled his face, causing the minuscule beads of sweat on his jaw to glisten like frozen snowflakes on a glass pane. Good grief! The man felled her sound rules in one blow.

Her aunt and friends were almost upon them.

"Promise to receive me, Wynne!"

Her slender brow lifted. "And if I refuse?"

He fingered the hair framing the left side of her face. A strand or two came free in the tender combing. Instead of shaking them off to catch the breeze, Keanan tucked them into his waistcoat pocket. He gave the approaching women a distracted wave.

"Would you refuse the man who rescued you from a villain? I am certain if I discussed this situation with Lothbury and his cronies, he would be shocked by your lack of appreciation."

Lord Nevin was correct. There was nothing this rogue would not do to gain his desires. "How dare you blackmail me, sir?"

His heavy-lidded gaze burned her lips, remembering. God save her, she could not prevent herself from remembering their kiss, too.

"We both know what happens when you challenge me, Wynne." Fathomless indigo eyes clashed with her passionate green. "For some reason," he murmured for her ears alone, "I predict neither one of us can do much to thwart it."

Six

Rae Fawks, Duchess of Reckester, joined her husband and son at the morning table, purposely positioning herself between them. Primly dressed in a cream-and-gray muslin check-weave morning dress, she nodded to the footman, signaling him to prepare her a plate.

"Good morning, Mother," her son, Drake, dutifully acknowledged her. She stared at his handsome profile as he returned to the morning paper. The years had crept up on him, changing her only child into a man. She should be dreaming of the grandchildren he would be giving her, not being forced to confront the past.

Her husband did not seem to notice her presence. His eyes bruised from lack of sleep, and most likely suffering from the previous evening's debauchery, he solemnly chewed the sausage he had speared on his fork. His lack of interest in her presence was nothing new.

In their almost nine and twenty years together, instead of the bond of love and respect that, as a new bride, she had once dreamed of, indifference shared their marriage bed. Not long after Drake's birth she realized there was no room for her. However, she was not the kind of woman who quietly accepted her discontent. It had taken strength, and a certain ingenuity, to maneuver a rake like Reckester into offering marriage. Rae always drew on that internal fortitude when dealing with her husband. These instances were the only moments when she felt visible.

The footman placed her plate in front of her and filled her cup with steaming coffee. She had no real interest in eating. The food and cutlery would merely give her hands something to do.

"You promised to make an appearance at the Graftons', Reckester," she softly admonished.

Something in her voice must have warned him. Her husband stirred from his slouched position, focusing his red-rimmed eyes on her. He blinked, already appearing bored. "I was involved, madam."

Drink, cards, or his latest mistress could have detained him. Her feelings had calloused over the years. Rae would not demand an excuse. The lies tended to sting more than the truth. Nevertheless, her grievances aside, she was prepared to make him address their current predicament. After all, the blame was entirely his alone.

"One hears gossip at these functions. I fear one of your many transgressions has surfaced, Duke."

"What?" He pointed his fork at her. "Are you bringing up the singer again? I told you, like most of the gentlemen who observed her performance, I paid her a visit to compliment her on her, uh, abilities. Nothing more to it, no matter what anyone says."

Singer. Actress. Barmaid. Prostitute. There had been so many, they had lost their names and were noted only by their professions. "Not your little canary, Reckester," Rae gritted out. "I speak of that little tart who bore you a bastard. Do you recall her, or are they all a blur when you are stewed?"

Reckester's expression became pensive. Once, she had considered his dark blue eyes soulful and poetic. She had been too entranced by his title and seduced by his charm to notice his feckless core. Checking her son, she saw he was not immune to their conversation. His gaze might have rested upon the newspaper, but his grip had turned his knuckles white.

"Aideen Milroy. Irish. A tolerable actress, but Christ, what a face," he recalled, sighing. "Haven't seen her in years."

Not looking up, Drake said, "Not surprising, father. The woman is dead."

"Dead?" He assimilated the news. He pressed his fingers into his eye sockets and then dragged them downward until he could prop up his head. "Ah, yes. Aideen. The years. Sometimes I forget."

"The women you bedded last week are already forgotten. A woman dead fifteen years would not concern you," Rae said, not liking the faraway look in his eyes. "What does concern this family is her bastard."

"Keanan? The boy is harmless." He dismissed the matter and resumed eating.

Refusing to be deterred, she met his gaze and leaned forward. "That boy is a man, Reckester. He can no longer be swept aside if he continues to embraced by the *ton.*"

Giving up the pretense of reading, Drake set his paper aside. Fingering the edge of his plate, he said, "Lothbury supports him. And others. Milroy's success in the ring, and his unsanctioned connection to our family, have opened many doors. The notoriety of the man and the whiff of an old scandal are too delicious for most hostesses to resist."

Of all the sins Reckester had committed, Rae considered his involvement with Aideen Milroy his worst, the most unforgivable. Perhaps it was selfish of her to blame the dead woman. In the end, it had been Rae who became his duchess.

Nevertheless, while she had weaved her dreams about the handsome man she had claimed as her own, Reckester had carelessly planted his seed in the actress. Furious, and determined that she would be the one to carry his heir, she had allowed him to seduce her.

It had been a near thing. Rae suspected Reckester had developed an affection for the actress, whereas he had only felt lust and duty when he had looked upon her, his wife.

Still, she held the advantage. Her father was an earl. Her husband might not care whom he bedded, but his title demanded more selectiveness in whom he married. Second, her dowry could not be overlooked. Reckester enjoyed the tables too much to pass up the annual income that marriage to her would bring. It was not the first time money had erased a youthful indiscretion.

So Aideen Milroy had succeeded in being the first to bear Reckester a son. Three months later, Rae had made certain the victory had been a bitter one.

Now after all these years, the son had managed the impossible and was welcomed in their sphere. To protect herself and her family, she was not above crushing another Milroy into dust.

"Lothbury is a child," she sneered. "The rest are sheep. The Reckester name used to wield some influence."

"Still does," her husband muttered.

"Then showing the young parvenu he does not belong in our little world should pose no problem." She cast a sly glimpse at Drake. He sat stiffly in his chair, his hands curled into fists. "Oh, one more little tidbit from the gossips. It seems Mrs. Molly Bedegrayne received Mr. Milroy at her residence yesterday afternoon. I believe her niece, Miss Wynne Bedegrayne, was also present."

She considered their cozy family chat a success when Drake pushed back from the table. Sending his chair flying across the room, he departed without a word.

Keanan entered the Dour Monkey, a small tavern on Little St. Martin's Street not far from Fives Court. Earlier, he had joined Lothbury to observe a sparring match between a pair of third-raters. The marquess, quite the enthusiast, had been looking forward to engaging John "Gentleman" Jackson in hopes of securing a subscription to his rooms at 13 Bond Street. To his friend's disappointment, Jackson had not made an appearance. Discovering that his gold snuffbox had been lifted ruined the day. Sympathetic, but not in the mood for listening to his friend lament his favorite trinket, Keanan decided to seek out friendlier company. He noticed Dutch sitting alone at a corner table.

"My, my, quite the dapper bruiser, Milroy. I hope it isn't catching," Dutch taunted. He gulped down his beer and banged his tankard, signaling the barmaid for more.

"I've learned being rich is not enough. Looking rich, smelling rich"—he bent low to sniff Dutch's hair and grimaced—"Christ, man, smelling human would make you palatable to the ladies. When's the last time you bathed?"

His friend accepted the jibe with his usually untroubled aplomb. "The ladies like me just fine. Don't ye, Mary?" He patted her backside.

"Meg, y'old sot." Slamming down two beers, she stomped off.

Both men laughed.

Keanan raised his tankard, clanking it against his friend's. "Aye, why change what works? Ladies just fall on their backs when you enter a room."

"Speaking of ladies,"—Dutch sagged forward and pinched the fabric of Keanan's coat—"trying to impress a fancy one?"

He sat back in his chair and sipped his beer. "Nah. I met Lothbury at the Court." Keanan shrugged. "He almost cried when he realized a pickpocket would be enjoying his personal mix of snuff this evening."

"Pure shame, that," he nodded, commiserating. Cupping his beer, he stared thoughtfully into it. "Is it worth it, Keanan? The clothes, new lodgings, the preening, high-nosed peacocks for friends."

"I am a champion, Dutch. Just enjoying my rewards," he said, a cocky grin in place. "What brains I've managed not to have beaten out of me have done me well. The purses

I've claimed have been respectable. Some money I invested; some I gambled. Both risks have made me very rich."

Bracing his beefy hands on the scarred wooden table, his friend regarded him solemnly, his black brows elevated. "So you're rich, Reckless Milroy. Let me lift my tankard to the champion. But tell me this. Does it really change those others' opinions?" He nodded in the direction of two young gentlemen unaware of the exchange across the room. "To the likes of them you will be an outsider. Worse, a bastard."

"Not just anyone's bastard," Keanan harshly reminded.

"Reckester refuses to recognize you, man. The fighting mob cannot seem to forget. Enjoy the amusements your gold brings you. You deserve them. Just don't fool yourself into thinking you can be one of them. It will give the high and mighty the pleasure of proving you're not!"

Frustration and denial pumped through him. Just because Dutch was correct did not make accepting it any smoother. "See here. It's—"

Raised voices distracted him. The chairs and tables being shoved aside made the argument falter. He recognized the man charging toward him.

Nevin. Something had fired the blood of his half-sibling. He suspected he knew the reason—or rather, the lady who inspired this confrontation. He propped his leg on an empty chair, waiting him out.

Nevin was not alone. Another man, not as tall but certainly built to handle himself, matched his half-brother's stride. His dusky skin, heightened by exertion or the heat of their private argument, was damp from perspiration. Whatever the man was saying did not impress his companion. Shouldering past him, Nevin approached Keanan and Dutch.

"Is it not the way of younger brothers, Dutch?" he said conversationally, taking perverse satisfaction in his brother's growl. "They always shadow their older brothers, aping them." Restrained muscles coiled, he took a deceptively casual taste of his beer.

"You are not my brother." Each carefully enunciated word bespoke his admirable control.

The dark-headed stranger stepped forward, attempting to intercede again. "You prove nothing by challenging him," he argued, his slight accent indicated his Spanish origins. "Mr. Milroy's skill in the ring is unmatched. Let us go. Once your ardor for violence has waned, you will see I am correct."

"Listen to your friend, Nevin," Keanan advised. "Jackson may pronounce your sparring skills adequate, but dancing around the ring wearing muffles on your hands to protect your pretty looks isn't the same as facing a seasoned bare-knuckled fighter." He swiveled his chair, giving him his back. "Go home, little brother. I'd enjoy breaking your bloody noble claret-jug too much." He swallowed the rest of his beer and lifted his tankard, signaling for another.

"Arrogant, conniving bastard!" Nevin roared, lunging at Keanan before the insult was out of his mouth.

Keanan purposely allowed himself to be propelled forward into the wall. Bracing his hands against the flat surface, he sharply kicked backward with his right foot, the blow striking Nevin's midriff. A sputter of violently expelled air was the only sound he issued as he fell rearward onto a recently vacated table. Tense silence followed the magnificent collision.

Keanan stood over his stunned, furious brother. "Obviously, getting knocked on your arse is a new experience for you." He offered his hand, the other one curled into a fist just in case Nevin required another reminder of who was the elder, meaner sibling.

"Go to hell!" He knocked the extended hand away and climbed to his feet. His companion murmured in Spanish. No one could convince Nevin to give up this suicidal confrontation. The man lifted his hands in a fatalistic gesture. Wishing them luck, he moved to another table.

The proprietor appeared, endeavoring to soothe the disgruntled patrons. Chairs and tables were righted around them. A nervous barmaid served them beer, compliments of the Dour Monkey. No damage had been done to the tavern, and the proprietor had not wanted to further offend his affluent customers.

Accepting a beer, a cynical smile creased Keanan's stern expression. "Nevin, I am curious. We have lived in the same town for most of our lives, and you have managed to ignore my existence. What prompted you to find me? A sudden desire to claim your beloved brother?"

A disapproving noise came from Dutch's throat. "Keanan, beating your half-brother won't be as satisfying as you imagine."

"I disagree. Besides, how can you be so certain I'd not relish pounding this pup senseless?"

"You could try," Nevin sneered, daring him.

Dutch rubbed the ache out of his damaged wrist. "If you were using your noggins, you'd both realize each is thirsting to appease your honor. Considering your brash approaches, each will fail."

Keanan glared at him. "Remind me to thank you later for your boundless confidence, Dutch."

"You misunderstood," his friend objected. "I'm not questioning your skill or ambition. Just your target."

Standing added to Nevin's condescending air. "You are nothing but a crippled drunk pontificating on a subject that is not your concern. Who do you think you are to boldly speak of my business?"

Keanan chuckled. "Ignore him, Dutch. You know how important blood ties are to the Reckester family." He clamped Nevin's wrist before the thought to attack had formed in his brain. Hauled closer in an unrelenting hold, the only thing the man could do without disgracing himself

again was to be seated. "Dutch, you might want to say your
farewells to fair Meg before we depart."

Accepting the opportunity to escape, Dutch put on his
hat and stood up. "Aye, a fine idea, that." He bent down
and whispered, "Have a care with the pup, Milroy. I have a
fondness for this tavern. They won't be letting us back if
you bust up the place." Nodding, he went off to flirt with
the barmaid.

"Here we are, the pair of us, sharing a table and lifting
a tankard of beer." Keanan shook his head, amused his
crushing grip was the only thing keeping his companion
from taking a swing at him. "Who would have guessed we
could be civil after so many years of ill will?"

Nevin twisted, fighting the hold unmanning him. It took
only seconds to understand that he risked breaking his wrist.
"I would not piss in your direction, even if the wind was in
my favor. Now why would I care to be civil?"

"Because I'm stronger, pup." Keanan deliberately used
the provoking nickname. "You were the one who sought me
out. Why don't you have your say, then leave."

"Fine." Brilliant aquamarine eyes intently met his. Resistance vibrated through their contact. "Release my wrist
first."

"A truce, then. The next swing you take will be your last.
Your Spaniard friend will cart you out of here."

"Agreed."

Keanan freed him. His expression dispassionate, he
watched Nevin massage the abused limb. "Your reasons?"

His brother did not pretend to misunderstand. "Your presence in my life. Of late, no matter where I go, it is your
name I hear discussed, your face I see across the room."

"I break no laws attending gatherings I've been invited
to, or coming into clubs as a benefactor's guest," he said
matter-of-factly. "My presence may inflame your sensibilities; however, in truth, there is little you or your precious
family can do about it."

"Cling to that belief if it brings you comfort, Milroy." Nevin rose. "Oh, I offer you a warning. Miss Bedegrayne is off limits. Confront me if you must. The lady is an innocent in this affair."

He found Nevin's warning profoundly irritating. The man did not know him, yet considered him monstrous enough to prey on young innocents. Regrettably, it was true. He was ruthless. Using Miss Bedegrayne as an instrument of revenge against the Reckesters was not above him.

Uneasy, Keanan shifted his shoulder. Essentially, his existence had been a constant battle. Whether it was for a dry place to lay his head, or a meager scrap of food that guaranteed his survival for one more day, he quickly learned that mercy, decency, and honesty were qualities owned by those who could afford them. Until recently, they had been beyond his reach. Now, he had the means but lacked the heart. He was too scarred, too hardened ever to reclaim them.

"You would accept my word, Nevin?"

"Never," he avowed. "Still, you have met Miss Bedegrayne. She is an honorable, guileless creature who could never understand the pettiness of a baseborn gutter orphan."

Keanan closed his eyes, thinking of the disheveled woman struggling in the dirt to fight off a brute thrice her weight. He thought of the woman he had tasted in the garden. Twice Nevin's guileless sainted angel had needed him. Each need was distinct, yet he was positive she would deny both of them. The idea of her duplicity made him smile. He knew more about Miss Bedegrayne than his half-brother did. The lady sauntered between her world and his. He was too intrigued not to figure out the reason.

"My grievance lies with the Reckesters."

Nevin's jaw grew taut, his nod, a clipped assent. "I consider myself warned. We are in agreement then?"

Could he leave Miss Bedegrayne alone? Just thinking of her filled Keanan with a sudden desire to find her. He had speculated often whether their second kiss would taste as remarkable as the first. Would her slender form melt against him, craving the blinding heat that two bodies entwined begot? It was impossible denying his fascination for the lady. Not for a rival—certainly not for his enemy.

"I confess I cannot imagine an hour when you and I would ever come to an agreement."

Wynne added another entry to her logbook, beaming approvingly at Mr. Jubbs. The solicitor had become the Benevolent Sisterhood's newest patron. Borrowing a silver container from his desk, she sprinkled the pounce liberally over the ink. Tilting the book, she blew the loose powder off the page.

"Mr. Jubbs, on behalf of our charity, allow me to thank you for your generous purchase of barley and oats. We will oversee the distribution to the local workhouses," she promised, mentally calculating how many men she needed to move the heavy sacks of grain.

She extended her hand; the man eagerly rushed forward, clasping it. "Miss Bedegrayne, how could I refuse a request that was so charmingly delivered?"

She gently reclaimed her hand. "I fear I would be out of a job if the city were littered with generous, worldly gentleman such as you, Mr. Jubbs. Good day."

Milly stood at the door, fidgeting. Seeing her mistress, she straightened. "Miss Bedegrayne, did you get your corn?"

She ushered her maid through the door. When she had entered the solicitor's office, the sun had been shining. Now, it looked like rain. "Yes, Milly. More than I hoped. If our good fortune continues, I might risk asking Papa to lend us space in one of his warehouses."

"He's likely to give you the lash. And you won't be the only one frying in the grease."

"Fustian! Papa is quite supportive of my philanthropy.

As Papa tells it, the Bedegrayne family has endured being under the hatches a time or two."

"Being forced to wear last year's fashions is not the same thing as starving, miss."

"Why, you impertinent little goose!" Wynne gave her maid a playful nudge as they strolled down the street. "I see the influence of Jenny Egger is at work." Feeling too pleased with herself, she said, "Tell me again, Milly. How did Jenny look when she saw her new home? Sending her off to the country was the correct decision. It was all worth the danger, was it not?"

"Aye, miss. You should have seen her thin face when the city was out of sight." Milly reflected, wanting to describe it accurately. "Like the sun, I think, creeping up on a spring dawn. The nerves and the stiffness seem to fade with each passing mile." Her smile faded. "Her da' still haunts her dreams. She woke each night, a scream crowding in her throat. Inch and I took turns keeping watch, hoping it would ease her mind."

The maid fell back a few paces, making room for two very determined ladies and their entourage. Catching up, she noticed Wynne's distress. "There are only so many battles you can fight for the girl. I reckon, a fierce dragoness and you hold equal when it comes to protecting the young ones."

"Miss Bedegrayne!"

Several yards ahead, an approaching gentleman raised his hand. Baffled by his identity, she took note of his gray eyes and straight black hair framing a pleasant, well-fed visage.

"Good afternoon, sir. It appears we shall have rain, does it not?"

"And spoil your lovely bonnet? The heavens would not dare!" he effortlessly replied, a little too smoothly for Wynne's tastes.

"Fie, sir, I am not so fragile as not to withstand a spring rainstorm. Indeed, I think the air would be better for it."

The man did not return her engaging smile. Cocking his head, he shrewdly concluded, "Have so many months passed that you do not recall an old friend, Miss Bedegrayne?"

Something in his gaze shook the clues to his identity around in her head like puzzle pieces in a glass bowl. His smile settled them in place. The man was Brook's husband. Since their last meeting, he had gained weight. It flattered him. "Lord A'Court. Forgive me. I have a tendency toward woolgathering."

"Trying to decide which slippers and gloves match which frock, I warrant."

Insufferable, patronizing prig, she thought. How had she ever forgotten him? Oh, there had been a time or two over the years when she had engaged him in conversation. However, once Brook had expressed her tender feelings about the earl, she had discouraged his attentions. "And how is your lady, my lord? You must convey my aunt's gratitude for Lady A'Court's visit."

"I shall." A pedestrian careened into the earl, earning a scowl. "May I be blunt, Miss Bedegrayne?" He continued without gaining her permission. "A wife shares her concerns with her husband. She mentioned another visitor attending your aunt. A Mr. Milroy, I believe?"

"That is correct." It surprised her Brook would have mentioned Mr. Milroy. To avoid gossip, she had specifically asked her friends not to discuss her aunt's attempts at matchmaking. Still, what did she know of the dealings between wife and husband? Perhaps a loving vow dissolved all others.

"My wife considers you a close friend. Because of that friendship, and the fact your brothers are out of the country, I feel it is my duty to speak out against your association with Mr. Milroy. I know my wife agrees. A man of his reputation might seem dazzling to an inexperienced lady."

"I am hardly a dewy-eyed maiden, sir. Your concern is unnecessary." Her reticule swung dangerously as she held up a hand, demanding his silence. "My brothers may be absent, but my father, Sir Thomas, can adequately flush out and dissuade an ambitious fortune hunter."

"I have offended you."

"Not at all, my lord. I am honored, even grateful for your counsel. The next time I see your wife, I shall compliment her on her excellent choice in a husband." She extended her hand, dismissing him.

From his expression, she could see he was questioning whether or not he was being slighted. Warily he bowed. "Your servant, Miss Bedegrayne." He walked away, lifting his hand against the sky to shield him from the beginning splatters of rain.

Very odd. "Who requires a husband when obviously one can gain a friend's on loan?" she asked aloud.

Milly snorted. "Your servant, miss?" she mocked. "He does not seem the bowing, scraping sort, don't you think?"

"That assessment would apply to most of my disrespectful staff," Wynne dryly retorted.

Any hope of getting home before the rain was a lost cause. It struck the ground with a resounding force that left their surroundings a steamy blur. Walking in tandem, her footman held an umbrella over her head while they hurried into the house.

"Mae," Wynne greeted the housekeeper. She stepped into the hall, shaking at her damp skirts. "What a sight it is out there! I thought the horses might be washed away."

Milly moved past her. "I'll be seeing about a warm bath, miss."

"You will do no such thing, silly girl," the housekeeper admonished. "I will not have you dripping all over my clean floors. Go on up and change out of your wet things, and then see to Miss Bedegrayne's. I'll tell the kitchen we need water sent up."

"Thank you, Mae. Is my father home?"

"No, miss. He mentioned something about going to one of his clubs. Shall I send up a tray? Or will you be going out this evening?"

Wynne removed her wet bonnet and handed it to Milly before dismissing her. Papa preferred his clubs to eating at home. The habit had become ingrained years ago, after the loss of his wife. Even his children's growing out of the nursery had not dissuaded the firm ritual. No matter, she concluded. The notion of sitting in front of the hearth immersed in a good book held its own appeal this chilly evening.

The housekeeper clapped her hand over her mouth. "Oh, miss, I almost forgot. A missive was delivered while you were out." She collected the letter from the silver salver used to hold visitors' calling cards. "The boy delivering it was told to await your reply, but I sent him on his way, seeing you were not expected back for hours."

Wynne touched the garnet seal. A bold, ornate "KM" had been pressed into the melted wax. Breaking the seal, she read:

> *Miss Bedegrayne:*
> *I've just been warned off by one of your most ardent knights. I think we should meet to discuss our special alliance. Meet me at the Park Lane entrance to Hyde Park tomorrow at 3. Don't bother sending regrets. I'll come and collect them if you fail me.*
>
>   *K*

Wynne crushed the letter in her hand. It was simple to deduce her knight. No man disliked Mr. Milroy more than Lord Nevin. If their meeting had not come to blows, she suspected they would be fighting a duel in her name soon if she did not take steps to prevent it.

Lifting her head up, she noticed she was alone. Milly had gone upstairs to change, and Mae had departed for the kitchen. Shivering, she hugged herself and headed for the library. One of the boys could carry her reply to Mr. Milroy. In all likelihood, he was already feeling provoked. She did not doubt there would be trouble if she did not heed his command.

Seven

Keanan dug the toe of his boot into the small chink he had discovered in the Bedegraynes' garden wall, and used the additional height to hoist his leg over the top. It was built for adornment, and getting over it did not require any grand skill.

Crazed, he decided after questioning his motives again for the thousandth time. What else did you call a man skulking around a lady's garden in the dark? The dense fog only seemed to add to the menace of the act.

The need to see her, to talk to her again, had been pressing him hard toward this action since Nevin had tried to warn him away from the lady. Declaring himself, as if *he* had the right to protect her. Arrogant pup! He had not looked so haughty sitting on his noble arse.

Still chafing from Nevin's belligerence, he had sent her a bullying summons. It did not surprise him that she had ignored it. She even had her staff shoo the messenger away. His observations of Miss Bedegrayne proved her to be a feisty, courageous creature who would poke her chin up at the three Furies if provoked. Keanan found spirit in a woman quite admirable. He also thought she was addled. A man was in a bad way when those combustible qualities began to appeal to him.

Stumbling over a small bush, he muttered a curse. He might as well be paddling through white soup. If he was not careful, the Bedegraynes would discover his body come morning, his head bashed in by a stone bench.

A light flared within the house, then floated across the room. Grateful for the muted light, he moved closer, wincing at the noise of the gravel grinding under his boots. Approaching the ceiling-to-floor French windows from the side, he almost yelped at the unexpected appearance of a woman's face peering through the glass. He moved deeper into the shadows just as she opened the panel.

Wynne stared out into the fog. Her state of undress revealed she had remained at home this evening. The gown she wore was white. It was slit down the front, and small, tasseled tie cords gave him stimulating glimpses of a lilac underdress. She wore her straight, waist-length blond hair in a simple plait down her back to keep it in place. Keanan held his breath, afraid the slightest noise would draw her attention to him. Whatever she saw in the darkness was not within the garden. The blankness in her stare hinted at otherworldly thoughts. Tilting her head, she listened. The droning of insects, punctuated occasionally by the barking of several dogs, echoed around them. Without warning, she retreated back to the safety of her lighted room.

Positioning himself so he remained concealed, Keanan watched her light the oil lamp near the chair closest to the hearth. Retrieving the lilac-and-white-striped cashmere shawl she had tossed earlier over the back of the chair, Wynne sat down and spread it over her legs. She picked up the book near the lamp and began reading.

Observing her enjoying her solitude, a rare contentment washed over him. She idly twisted an errant strand of hair around her finger as she lost herself in her book. A woman like Wynne Bedegrayne represented all that he craved: wealth, breeding, beauty, intelligence, and mettle.

Plotting the ways he could claim such a woman, he was jarred from his musings by a loud clatter. The fog was too dense to identify its source, but it came from behind and to the right, close to the very wall he had mounted. Before he could move, Wynne came charging out of the house, a sword firm in her grasp.

He had forgotten to add *addled,* to his list. Her courage was terrifying. Afraid she would hurt herself, Keanan caught up to her in five strides. One arm curled around her waist, and the other clamped around her mouth. She stiffened at his touch.

"Delivering you from harm is becoming a habit," he murmured in her ear.

Relieved she knew her intruder, Wynne sagged against his chest. The teasing quality she detected in his low whisper ignited her fury. Taking advantage of his loosening hold over her mouth, she set her teeth into the soft flesh between his thumb and first finger.

"Ow, you vicious hoyden!" Keanan cursed, releasing her. "Don't you know who I am?"

She whirled to confront him, her father's sword poised to run him through if he lunged for her again. "I will show you vicious." She struck his arm, using the flat of the blade. "That is for scaring me witless, you half-Irish lout!"

"Wynne!"

She swung the blade, intending to strike him again. Instincts blazing, Keanan blocked the blade with his hand. She froze at his pained hiss.

"You've drawn blood, woman." He sucked on the wound. "Damn. Have you avenged your honor, or am I going to lose fingers taking that sword from you?"

Wynne had not meant to cut him. She had just wanted to hurt him a little. He snatched the sword from her limp grasp, muttering on about crazy females.

"How bad is it?"

"Bad enough," he fumed, all male outrage that he had been done in by a female. "What if I had been a milken after your silver, you fool? Did you think to chase him away with a little sword?"

"It stopped you, did it not?" she mocked, then realized her error. He was furious and wounded; provoking him only proved she was addled. "Come inside," she entreated. "I will tend your hand."

"Later." He gave her an encouraging shove toward the open window. "Go inside. I want to check around first."

Wynne departed without arguing and shut the window. She understood he would not be satisfied until he discovered the source of the noise. With her mind turning over the reasons for his presence this evening, she collected the supplies she would need to clean and bandage his wound. When she returned, he was standing by the fire, studying the spine of her abandoned book.

"Did you find anyone out there?"

"No. It could have been an animal or someone passing by." He held up her book. "What are you reading?"

Unsure of his mood, she cautiously advanced. "Miss Porter's *Thaddeus of Warsaw*. Have you read the tale?"

Scowling, he dropped the book on the table. "No." Not liking the sympathy in her gaze, he tensed when she brushed by, setting the bowl of water and the bandaging material on the floor beside him. Defensively he added, "I know my letters. Blanche saw to that. I can pick out words, but not enough to make a book pleasurable, as it obviously is for you."

"Blanche. Is that your mother?"

"No. A friend." He cupped his good hand under the injured one to prevent the blood from dripping on her floor. "Her husband staked me when I first started fighting."

"Oh." Kneeling beside him, she touched him on the leg, gently bullying him into the chair. With the length of his arms resting on his legs, she pried open his injured hand. The blade had cut across all four fingers, although it did not look particularly deep. "Good. I feared we would have to call Tipton to stitch you up."

Mr. Milroy's bowed head was so close, his breath stirred

the hair at the crown of her head. "Tipton. He be your sister's husband."

His knowledge of her family surprised her. She could not imagine Lord Nevin sharing confidences. "Yes. He is an excellent surgeon. I have often assisted him when he visits the prisons and workhouses."

"Such places are not for women," he said, his anger at her swiftly changing to anger on her behalf. "Your menfolk need a lesson in taking care of you."

Dipping his hand into the bowl of tepid water, she rinsed the blood from his wounds. "Mr. Milroy, I suspect you think you know a thing or two about me or my family; however, you are mistaken."

She lifted his hand from the water and was pleased the bleeding had almost stopped. Pushing a cloth into his hand, she had him dry it while she opened a small jar of ointment. "The smell is quite unpleasant," she confessed, wrinkling her nose as the scent filled the room. "Tipton highly recommends it for sealing small wounds."

When she finished wrapping his hand, Keanan flexed his fingers, testing their strength. "It's sore. Dutch would grieve if you have done lasting damage to my fist."

"I assume this Dutch is another friend?" She gathered up her bowl and supplies. Walking to the door, she deposited them in the hall for one of the servants to collect.

Espying her shawl on the floor, he picked it up and laid it on the arm of his chair. His fingers stroked it, savoring the softness. "Aye, and a good one. He's a fighter, too. Met him when I was still green and worked my fists more in anger than fight cunning." He shook his head, laughing at the memory. "Our first mill, I took a facer. Broke my nose." He fondly rubbed the spot. "Christ, I was mad! Blood running down my chest like a river, I floored him in ten minutes. We have been friends ever since." He tapped his nose. "And no one has ever gotten close to busting me on the plant again."

Wynne steadied her hands by reaching for one of her father's decanters. Keanan spoke of blood and violence with a fondness she found incomprehensible. Still, she liked him. Sitting before the fire, dressed in black breeches and coat, a pressed cravat at his throat, he looked like any other gentleman she had encountered. However, the differences between them stretched out like an impassable crevasse.

She returned to his side, a glass in her hand. "Papa's best tonic," she answered the unspoken question his lifted brow indicated. "Cognac. Smuggled, I assume, though Papa would perish if I dared speak my suspicions aloud." He took the glass from her. Her gaze fell on the soft bandage, reminding her of what she had done.

"Do not fret, Wynne. The cuts will heal." His grin warmed her as if she had been the one drinking the French brandy. "Only a half-Irish lout would be so stupid as to grab a sword by its blade."

She had no quarrel with his opinion. Wynne stared down at her sleeves. She had pushed them up when tending to his hand. Working the sleeves back into place kept her fingers busy while she contemplated the best manner in addressing her concerns. "Mr. Milroy—"

"Keanan," he corrected. "I've spilt blood for you. At the very least I should hear my name upon your lips."

She met his smile with a vague half smile. "Keanan, why are you here?"

His gaze sharpened with interest. "Isn't it clear? When you ignored my letter . . . had my messenger thrown out on the streets by your servants, did you not believe I would inquire as to the reason?" Firelight reflected in his dark blue eyes, but it was a cold light. His beautiful, strong features emphasized by shadows and light made her feel as if she were dealing with a night creature from the pit rather than a mere man. Man or fiend, she was wary of both. Holding his emotionless gaze, she carefully sat in the opposite chair.

"Mr. Milroy, I was out for most of the day. My housekeeper sent your boy on his way because she did not know when I would return. She gave me your rude summons the moment I returned."

"Was I rude? You must forgive me. A man of my stamp has so much to learn," he mockingly confessed.

She shifted in the chair. Tension curled her hands into fists. "Well, I am willing to make allowances," she murmured, adding a cutting edge to her tone. "When one works so hard at being a bastard, it is difficult giving up an inspiring performance."

Silent as a snake, his arm struck. Latching on to her arm, he dragged them both out of their chairs. Standing on the tips of her toes, real terror settled into her chest, making it difficult to breathe.

"You little fraud."

The accusation befuddled her. "W-what?"

The tautness of his grip lessened, permitting her heels to touch the floor. Their forced closeness made her heart pound so fiercely, she assumed he could hear it.

"You," he murmured, bringing her gaze up to his face. "I have heard the talk about you. Men sit around dreaming of your beauty, wishing it were they who had the right to touch you, kiss you."

His lips hovered over hers. Intuitively, her head tilted up, offering. Her chest tightened in anticipation, fear and desire an unyielding, disturbing tangle.

Keanan's stare focused on her mouth, yet he did not take it. "They all ask aloud, Why has no one claimed Wynne Bedegrayne? Men have cut their hearts out over you, offered up fortunes, and you have rejected them all. Why?"

He shook her, compelling her to meet his gaze when all she wanted to do was look anywhere else. She knew what they said about her. Some thought she was too selective. Others wondered if it was a matter of pride, since she no doubt had been humiliated by her younger sister's precipitate marriage. No one, not even her precious family, realized the awful truth.

For two seasons, a particular intimate group consisting of Lord Middlefell, Mr. Dugaud, Mr. Therry, and Mr. Esthill had been taking private delight in tormenting her. For these spoiled, jaded gentlemen of the *ton,* her virtue had become an amusing wager.

At first, disbelief had kept her silent, and then later, shame. They were cunning, else her father and Tipton would have spent their dawns in abandoned dew-drenched fields. There was no proof of their delinquency, so publicly accusing them would gain her nothing. She never spoke of her vile encounters with them. For her, the game had simply gone on so long, she could no longer tell the difference between sincere affection and polite guile, leaving her wary of all men.

"You have your answer." She sucked in her lower lip and lightly bit down before releasing it. "I have heard all the slurs, sir. They say the man who lies with me will wake in a bed of frost." Tears rose close to the surface again. "I am surprised you risk touching me. Should not ice burn?" Her twisting attempts to flee were futile. Vulnerable and upset, she kicked him.

"Hold still, you untamed—" Keanan scooped her up into his arms to keep her from hurting herself.

"Put me down!"

"Aye, your highness. That I'll do." He plopped down in the chair, holding her tight. She opened her mouth to scream, but he muffled her efforts by kissing her. Pulling back, his indigo eyes were heated by more than the reflective glow of fire. "I do not mind an enthusiastic squeal from a wench," he said, laughing at her futile lunge for his face with her nails. "If you scream, your people will find you enjoying the pleasures of sitting on a man's lap. What will your respectable father say to this business?"

"You are the spawn of the devil," she hissed.

"On that we agree, my damson."

Her forehead butted up against the hardened, contoured muscle of his chest. "I was insane for sending that letter, agreeing to meet you at the park. I had hoped to prevent you and Lord Nevin from engaging in a duel. Instead I have only encouraged your boldness."

Surprised, he pulled back to see her face. "You agreed to walk out with me tomorrow?"

"I told you I was out. I sent a footman over to your residence with my reply. Did you not receive it?"

"No." He pressed his nose to her hair and inhaled. "I had matters to attend to."

"Well," she huffed, not mollified by his gentling manner. Sitting on his lap like a wanton made her all too aware of his virility. "I would consider it a favor if you would burn my reply. You and Lord Nevin may shoot holes the size of a goose egg into each other. I am absolving myself from feeling sorry for either one of you."

He chuckled, nuzzling her temple with his beard-roughened chin. "You asked if I burned when I touch you? Aye, I do, but not in the way you think. I called you a fraud. And that you are, hiding behind your rules, pretending you can manipulate your feelings, like plucking strings on a marionette." He stroked the back of her head. Grasping a section of her braid at the base of her skull, Keanan pulled her head back until he could see her face. "Your eyes cannot quite hide it, you know."

"Hide what?"

He stared, as if peering into the very heart of her. "So volatile, that flame burning within you. It cannot be doused by water, stifled, or tempered by neglect." His fingers probed and caressed her stiff neck muscles, seducing her to relax. "Such a flame needs a man's tending."

Despite her resolve, her body was softening in his arms. Wherever his fingers roamed, her flesh warmed, her muscles eased. Unintentionally her back arched, stretching for something her mind had not begun to fathom. Keanan understood. Lashes lowered, lips already parted in anticipation, he pressed his mouth to hers.

Being untouched, she expected gentleness, the sweet worship joining lips in a sublime union of heart and body. Conversely, Keanan was a man of experience, and not especially interested in her heart.

His ardent kiss became a fuse trailing to a cache of unexplored sensation. The explosion was meteoric. Wynne's senses fractured like soaring pieces of twisted, searing shrapnel. The world dimmed except for him, his mouth on hers, his hands on her body. Her lips moved under his, wanting to contribute. Her hands vainly threaded his short hair, seeking an anchor, but the wild storm he had created besieged her.

Soon touching her with his lips did not seem to satisfy him. Using his tongue he breached her, halting the forming plea to cease. She could not catch her breath. Misunderstanding, he used his teeth to nip and cajole her compliance. Tiny shivers rebounded up and down her limbs. A lethargy she would have attributed to illness stole her strength. Keanan's mastery of the kiss marveled as much as it alarmed her. She felt enthralled within his embrace, a sway she had never intended to give any man.

Sensing her increasing withdrawal, he pulled back and stared down at her. His pupils were dilated saucers of midnight. The slight catch in his breath revealed he was equally moved by their kiss.

"Lovely Wynne," he mused, stroking her lower lip with his thumb. "I'll wager you have not kissed Nevin in such a manner."

Regret was the cool breeze settling in after passion's tropical storm. The kiss meant nothing more to him than a means to outdo his brother. Realizing her appalling position, she climbed out of his lap.

"I have no intention of appeasing your curiosity."

Unperturbed by her departure or her mulish attitude, Keanan reached down and retrieved his abandoned brandy. "Want to know how I know?"

"No." She swallowed a gasp. The man had managed to untie four of the knotted cords holding her dress together. Offering her back, she retied each cord.

He chuckled, she guessed, at her belated modesty. "I'll tell you anyway. If you had melted in Nevin's arms like you do mine, he would have wedded and bedded you years ago. No man can resist the alluring fire of a responsive woman."

He moved closer. Sensing he might try to kiss her again, she stepped out of reach. "You should go. My father is expected soon."

"Liar," he said, sneaking a quick peck on her cheek before she could retreat. "Earlier, I came across Sir Thomas. He was ensconced at his club, happily surrounded by his cronies, and by all accounts winning. Knowing your father better than I, you also comprehend it shall be hours before he rouses himself up from the table."

She blushed, irritated he had seen through her ruse. "There is the small concern of the servants discovering your presence."

Giving up his game of pursuit, Keanan rested his hand lightly against the chimneypiece. Flanking the fire, two half-nude fireplace atlantes painted a weathered copper, shouldered their burden of marble.

"Ah, Wynne," he murmured, shifting his glass so the amber liquid caught the firelight. "No one will know of my visit. You are good at keeping secrets." Striding to her, he pressed the glass into her hands. "Drink this. It will help you recover from the horror of having endured the pawing of a man you consider beneath you." He shrugged her aside and returned to the open French window.

Outrage gleaming in her eyes, she whirled, prepared to charge after him. The urge to pick up her father's sword tempted her. "How dare you, sir! Twisting this incident so the shadow of blame falls plainly on my face when you are at fault."

A fighter could be nothing else but a fighter. Face-to-face, he matched her anger. "I figured I would get the blame come morning," he said, clearly entertained. "Poor Miss Bedegrayne, mauled by the arrogant, uncouth bastard, Keanan Milroy." He made a small sympathetic noise.

"I commend your choice of words. I would not even improve upon the order," she sweetly assured him. Wynne strolled over and collected her father's sword. She needed every advantage when dealing with Mr. Milroy.

"Still wanting a poke at me, Wynne?" he taunted.

"Just wanting to make certain I have your complete attention." She would have laughed at his uneasy glance at the sword if she were not so incensed. "I have every right to be vexed at the man who kisses me senseless, then vilifies me for liking it." He leaped out of her way when she suddenly pivoted, the point of the sword slicing inches from his thigh.

"W-wha—you liked my kisses?"

Pacing until she came to a wall, she spun around and returned to his side. "Why would I not? You face is pleasing, your breath is not sour, and you can be agreeable when you choose," she rattled off, preferring to forget the emotions she felt. "It was quite pleasant."

For some reason, the compliment offended him. "Pleasant," he repeated through clenched teeth.

She gracefully lifted her hand, halting his motion toward her. "Naturally, I speak for myself. You seem surprised. Did you think me a fickle creature who would eagerly accept your kisses, only to deny enjoying them?" Of course he had. The twit! "Get out." She shoved him backward.

"Hold on." He complied, else risking contact with the leveled sword. "If you are not nettled about the kiss, then why not prove it. Kiss me again, lovely Wynne."

Jabbing the sword at his gut, she had him cursing and

stumbling backward out the door. "I feel pressed to offer some advice, Mr. Milroy. The next time you kiss a woman, restrain yourself from gloating. No lady wants to hear that the sole reason she was in your arms was to provide a method for besting your brother. It is humiliating." She closed the panels and secured the latch. Ignoring him, she returned the sword to its place on the wall.

He pounded on the frame, causing glass and wood to clatter in a perilous manner. Refusing to act like a coward, Wynne went to the window. She did not unlock it.

His seething stare was intimidating, but she refused to concede. Without warning, his anger crumbled. Laughing, he bumped his forehead against a glass.

"So you like my kisses, Wynne Bedegrayne?"

She hesitated, then shrugged. "Yes."

"And you think I'm an arrogant arse."

"Very impressive, Mr. Milroy. You deduced all that and did not even require my palm."

"Aye," he nodded, relieved. "Still able to cut mere mortals with the edge of your tongue. I would have been disappointed if my kisses befuddled the skill out of you."

Befuddled! His conceit roiled in her stomach like ground glass. Incensed, she glanced back at the sword on the wall. Reading her thoughts, he tapped on the glass, drawing her attention back to him.

"Now that we have settled our business, I will be off. Keep the windows locked. Something was in your garden. I will not be around to chase it away if it comes back." The corner of his mouth lifted in an indulgent grin. "Don't forget. Tomorrow. Hyde Park at three."

"I will not be there."

"You will not be able to resist. You may be cross with me, Wynne, but you have a fondness for Nevin." He frowned, displeased at the notion. "Keeping me entertained will save Nevin's hide one more day." Kissing his hand, he touched the glass. "Dream of me." The fog swallowed his departure.

Tugging the curtains closed, she returned to her chair and book. Taking up the book, she realized she had lost all interest in reading. Wynne gazed at the fire, contemplating Keanan's not-so-subtle warning that he and Lord Nevin would one day resolve their grievances by bloodshed. Lamentably, she had become part of their battle. It was due either to providence or the machinations of a devious man. She believed in both, yet could not fathom which one guided her.

His kisses must have befuddled her, after all.

Eight

No one had ever accused Devona of idleness, or patience. Still, all her aborted starts in the direction of her father and son must have appeared to the observer as some type of nervous affliction. She concealed her cringe when her father lifted her young son high above his head and then pretended to drop him. Being a new mother, she could not help but contemplate the horrors of the innocent game gone awry. Lucien giggled, not understanding that he was supposed to be terrified. She appealed silently to her husband, Rayne, to take charge of the situation.

"Thomas, your grandson just gorged himself on some of Cook's pudding. You will likely sample it yourself if you continue tickling him in that manner." Her husband winked at her.

"Take charge of your son, gel," Sir Thomas demanded, dangling the wriggling child outward for her to collect. "You should have more sense than to turn him loose on his unsuspecting grandsire."

Devona took Lucien from him and nuzzled his cheek. "Yes, Papa." She peered over her son's wispy blond locks at her husband; appreciation and love shined in her eyes. What she never tired of was seeing those same emotions reflected back.

Her marriage to Tipton was enduring, in spite of the dire predictions from various members of the *ton*. He was not an approachable man, she ruefully admitted to herself.

Rayne bore too many scars from his past to grant trust indiscriminately. Devona knew she not only had his love, but also his trust. They had been hers almost from the beginning. Time and healing had allowed him to open his small circle to include the Bedegraynes. The one thing no one could fault Tipton about was his devotion to his family.

"I thought Wynne would come with you. She has not visited us in a sennight." It bothered Devona that her sister seemed reluctant of late to discuss her confidences. In some ways, she had become quite secretive.

"She promised to call on Amara Claeg," her father said, shaking his head. "Don't know why she troubles herself. Lady Claeg will always blame us for her son's death. The Claeg gel might be as gentle as a tame pony; nonetheless, befriending her is like inviting a vengeful adder to rest upon your breast."

No one had endured more confrontations with the hostile Lady Claeg than Devona. Of all the Bedegraynes, she had been the most despised because of Doran Claeg's unrequited love for her. In the end, his love had caused his death. Amara was the only Claeg who understood Devona was not to blame. She had maintained their friendship, despite her mother's demand that she sever all connections to the Bedegraynes.

A slammed door in the distance had everyone glancing at the open doorway. The feminine murmur and the rhythmic click of four paws heralded the presence of Tipton's sister and her dog.

Sir Thomas perked at the noise. The motherless sixteen-year-old had earned a place in the old man's heart. Nothing fired him more than cheek and determination. Madeleina Wyman was fashioned with both. Her lively temperament sorely tested her brother's patience. The pair often did not agree, which led to many loud discussions, a few tears, and the occasional crash. Their confrontations had always made Devona homesick for her brothers and sisters.

Madeleina rushed into the drawing room. Her Maltese, Flora, was at her heels. The dog's long white hair appeared to have been recently combed. It swept the floor about her as though she was adorned in a flowing robe. Crisp pink ribbons secured the hair above her eyes, revealing dark, alert canine eyes.

The dog had been a gift from their friend Dr. Sir Wallace Brogden before he and her brother had departed for India. He had hoped a grieving girl could find comfort in a pet. Brogden's instincts had been accurate, although his choice still puzzled her. Madeleina loved the outdoors. She spent hours digging and creating her gardens. It had been her sanctuary long before Rayne and Devona had come into her life. Why he had chosen a creature that seemed more ladylike in appearance and mannerisms than Rayne's sister could only be viewed as a facet of their friend's dark humor. Nevertheless, Flora and Madeleina had become instant friends.

Resting her cheek against Lucien's, Devona gave her sister-in-law a welcoming smile. "Good afternoon, Maddy. Flora looks freshly bathed. Was she digging in your flowers again?"

Madeleina grimaced. Her cream-and-green sprig gown looked fresh, though a small dirt smudge on her jaw confirmed the small battle between dog and mistress. "I swear she thinks I am hiding her bones." She kissed Devona on the cheek and tickled Lucien on the chin as she passed. "Brother," she acknowledged. Brightening at the rising man, she exclaimed, "Papa Thomas! No one told me you were visiting."

Sir Thomas embraced her. Flora, upset she was not being included, whined and circled around them. "What are you doing here?" He directed his glare at Rayne. "Maddy, gel, you should be in one of those fancy ladies' schools. Devona, what was that prissy school I sent you gels to?"

"Miss Rann's School of the Ladies' Arts. She still runs the school, you know. Never have I encountered a woman so obsessed with the proper folding of napery. Wynne and I both agreed no lady's education is complete without her lecture on the twelve steps of sitting." She grinned at the girl's groan.

Baffled, her father frowned. "Twelve steps? What steps are there to sitting on your arse?" He reddened at Madeleina's mirth for his slip.

Light-blue eyes, so much like her brother's, twinkled. "The woman is cracked."

"Madeleina," Rayne reprimanded.

She moved closer to Devona, her sun-streaked light-brown hair swinging jauntily, matching her proud stride. Her hands parted in invitation to Lucien. He squirmed in his mother's arms, eager to climb into his young aunt's embrace. Devona handed over her son. Madeleina cooed, murmuring nonsense until the little boy shrieked his glee. Like her brother, Madeleina was learning to widen her tiny circle of love and trust.

"There was an incident at the school," Devona explained to her father.

"Several, by my account," Rayne countered.

Madeleina swayed; the motion exposed her agitation as much as it soothed Lucien. "One mistake and I am branded for my villainy forever."

Her husband's eyes transformed into an intriguing pewter hue whenever he was angry. That color was focused on his sister. "A small creature was killed because of your waggery."

"Who knew Miss Rann feared birds? All I wanted to do was liven up her staid instruction. She was the one who felled it with a book."

Devona recognized a fight brewing between them. "Rayne, she has a point. Releasing the bird into the room was harmless. No one could have predicted the tragic outcome."

Irritation flickered in his expression at her interference.

"Supporting her side will only encourage her outlandish behavior. You do recall the reason why we sent her to the school?"

"I have to agree with the gels, Tipton. No reason to fuss over a little bird," Sir Thomas interjected.

Madeleina's rocking picked up speed as Rayne glowered at all of them. "There is the small matter of the fire."

Devona's father's bushy brow lifted. "Fire?"

Hurt and defiance smoldered in Madeleina's eyes. "If you are so certain I set that fire to that girl's bed, then how can you sleep at night? I might set your house ablaze." Her arm tightened around Lucien.

Having placed herself between fighting siblings more times than she could count, Devona positioned herself so neither could see the other. Flora, assuming her swinging skirts was a new game, tried nipping at her hem. "Maddy, your brother does not believe you are responsible for the fire, so desist in goading him. Is this not so, Rayne?"

"She is merely an innocent bystander in a series of regrettable incidents," he dully agreed.

Provoking beast, Devona silently thought. The infuriating man obviously did not understand how to handle the sensitive nature of a budding young woman. She would be certain to set him straight later in private. "Papa, the school was closed due to an outbreak of typhus."

Concern for Madeleina had Sir Thomas scowling. "Bloody putrid fever!"

"Once word reached us that a few of the girls had taken to their beds due to a fever, Rayne insisted on examining the girls. He confirmed the local doctor's suspicions and then promptly removed Maddy from the school. He did not even bother packing up her clothes."

Refusing to confirm the tale, Rayne stared at his clasped hands while Maddy and Lucien danced over to study one of the paintings hanging on the wall.

Cloaked within grief, wariness, and pride, neither of the

Wyman siblings seemed capable of admitting their affection
for the other. Still, a callous man would not rush to the side
of his sister if he thought her in danger. Nor would a young
woman have been distressed at leaving her brother's house
to go to school if she did not find comfort in being a part
of his family. Devona had faith they would someday settle
their differences.

"Maddy, do not wiggle Lucien so," she warned. "Pearl
fed him pudding."

"Oh, he seems fit to me." Maddy lifted him up high. She
brought him close to rub noses. "Are you not, my sweet
little man?"

Lucien grinned. He then proceeded to vomit all over the
front of her gown. Shrieking, she jumped back, yet her hold
on Lucien never faltered. Flora barked at her mistress's upset. Horrified, Maddy handed the boy back to his mother.
Regurgitated pudding dripped off her chin. Without a word,
Rayne tossed her his handkerchief. Devona applauded his
control. His only sign of amusement was a muffled snort.
Sir Thomas laughed outright, probably relieved he had not
been his grandson's target.

Maddy mopped her chin. "Oh, vile," she wailed.

Gar stood by the door of the carriage, preparing to help
Wynne and Amara down. If he wondered why they were not
driving into Hyde Park instead of abandoning the carriage
at the Park Lane entrance, he kept his questions to himself.

Amara looked splendid in her walking dress made of fine
cambric. A twilled blue silk mantle rested on her shoulders.
Her dark-brown hair had been swept up and concealed
within a matching headdress. Slender strands of hair had
been selected with care and curled. The wind blew them
across her face, tickling her nose. Distracted, she brushed
the irritant away.

Wynne's choice of gown had been influenced by her

thoughts on Keanan's reaction. She wore a white sarcenet underdress, with a green crepe robe over it, hoping it heightened the green in her eyes. Her blond hair was tucked beneath a cap of green crepe and intricate lace. White kid shoes and gloves completed the image she wanted to project. She was a confident, privileged lady. The woman who had clutched Keanan Milroy, begging for his kisses, had been an aberration. She had no intention of repeating the experience.

"No offense, Wynne. Our last outing did not end well. You can understand my trepidation concerning our joining Mr. Milroy," Amara said, interrupting her thoughts.

"He saved my life."

"Then blackmailed you. It is not like you to fudge the finer points."

Wynne looked back, reassured to see Gar following them at a discreet distance. "He was rather annoyed with Lord Nevin when he issued the summons. A later meeting allowed him to explain his intentions."

Amara halted, recognition flashing across her expressive features. "A clandestine meeting? I thought you had more sense. This is something Devona might do—"

"It is not as sordid as you imagined. Since you think I have lost my good sense, I do not see the need to continue the subject," she said. A shard of guilt splintered her indignation because part of her knew that Amara was speaking the truth.

They continued walking in silence. Almost to the entrance of the park, the crowd thickened. Everyone seemed excited about the fair.

"You have feelings for him," Amara whispered. Awe resonated in her voice. "Wynne, loving a man beneath you can only lead to regret. I recall reading a treatise a few years back on the very subject."

Love. She flinched at the thought. How could she love the man? They were barely acquainted. Devona had once said that her affection for Tipton had struck her heart like a lightning stroke. Wynne believed her. Her sister always rushed headlong into life. Falling in love would be no different. Her reckless sister had found happiness, but Wynne considered it luck. Too many Bedegraynes trusted their fate to impulse. She had sworn to be more sensible.

"Cease being a snob, Amara. Mr. Milroy, despite his profession, has behaved like a gentleman." She decided not to mention his kisses.

"Gentlemen have vied for your attention before only to be rejected. Mayhap you feel beholden to him for his bravery. Reward him. You have the right. Just do not encourage him."

"Miss Bedegrayne, your friend offers sage counsel," Keanan said, approaching them from behind. "Forgive my tardiness. Lord Lothbury insisted he join us on our adventure."

Wynne and Keanan took turns making formal introductions, all pretending their meeting was accidental.

"Miss Claeg," Lothbury murmured, bowing over her hand. "Now that you have shed your mourning garb, I hope to see you about town more. I insist on claiming your first dance."

The marquess's words flustered Amara speechless. She tended to be awkward around gentlemen, an affliction Wynne had not been able to alleviate. Accepting his proffered arm, the pair walked several steps ahead.

"You rogue," she accused. "How did you guess?"

Keanan leaned closer, boldly brushing a brief kiss to her cheek. He did not pretend not to understand her charge. "Ah, Wynne. Last night you thought with your heart. Today, I suspected you would armor yourself with logic. Bringing a companion to protect yourself from my lecherous intentions was wise"—he fingered the lace on her cap—"but entirely futile."

"Amara is my friend. Gar"—she glanced over her shoulder and smiled at her footman—"will tear off your arms if you misbehave."

His gaze followed her to the footman. Each man soberly sized up the other. Nodding to the servant, he returned his attention to Wynne. "A well-built guard you have, my sweet. If you insist on calling a fight, I am willing to oblige. A good fair always demands a prize ring."

"Beast," she said, not really angry. She expected Mr. Milroy to act like the gentleman that she had sworn to Amara he was.

Enjoying the atmosphere of the fair, it was easy to forget she had been maneuvered into attending. Music filled the air. Couples broke into impromptu dancing all around them. In the distance she could see some of the quality sitting on quilts, observing the festivities from a distance while servants served them meals on fine porcelain. She had partaken in those picnics in the past. Now she looked forward to mingling with the masses. They would not starve, she decided, observing an old woman sitting on a stool, flipping fritters. It was one of a thousand smells, mingling with sunshine, the animals, and people, begging to be explored.

"Well, Miss Bedegrayne, what would you like to see first?" Keanan asked. "The stage was built for a play, it seems. We can make our way over to watch a hero triumphing over a villain. There is a wild animal show. I will hold your hand and protect you from the ferocious beasts. Or perhaps you are hungry? I thought I heard your innards growl a second ago."

"It was impolite of you to notice."

"I disagree. A gentleman always sees to his lady." He cupped his hands and yelled to his friend. "Lothbury!"

Still flushed, Amara and the marquess joined them. "With a mob like this, it would be easy for folks to get lost." He winked and nudged Keanan.

"Miss Bedegrayne and I have decided to eat before we explore the fair. Will you join us?"

Amara's lips parted as if to speak, but Lothbury was already making their excuses. "I promised Miss Claeg we would find a place close to the stage for observing the play. Do not let us detain you. We can meet up later for the fireworks." He was already leading her away before anyone could argue. Helpless, Amara silently appealed to her friend.

"I cannot leave my friend in his clutches. She will never forgive me," Wynne said, moving to go after them.

Keanan stilled her by grabbing her arm. "Lothbury may be a bit too impressed with himself, but he is harmless. He will keep Miss Claeg safe." He shrugged. "The man is a marquess. That alone should still her mama's tongue if the gossip reaches her ears."

It was not Lady Claeg she feared. The ambitious woman would be thrilled learning her daughter had caught the attention of a marquess. It was her brother, Brock, who was likely to throttle her if anything came of this budding friendship.

"Gar, look after Miss Claeg. She intends watching the play with his lordship."

The footman's eyes narrowed on Keanan's. "She's not the only one who needs a keeper, miss."

"I will look after your mistress, Gar. She will come to no harm under my care." He extended his hand, willing to seal the vow with a handshake.

Gar accepted it, and for a few seconds the men tested the strength of their oaths. Grimacing, the footman released his grip. "I am not the only man coming after you if I hear different." Nodding to Wynne, he threaded into the crowd in search of Amara.

"Come on." He took her hand. "Let me feed you. Maybe then you will swallow down that frown."

Feeding Miss Bedegrayne did indeed improve her disposition. She was smiling at him when he lifted her up and set her on the merry-go-round.

"I feel foolish," she said, nervously clutching the ropes strung up to the center pole.

"Rot. Everyone likes to see a pretty maid rosy-cheeked and giggling." He paid the man for her seat and waved farewell.

Two men spun the giant wheel. Keanan watched Wynne tighten her hold on the ropes on the first turn. Her skirts flared with the increasing speed. She tilted her head back and laughed. While watching her pleasure, desire washed through his blood like strong spirits.

He wanted her.

If she were any other woman, he would not have hesitated. He was a healthy man, fired by the natural urges a man feels when an attractive woman has caught his eye. Wynne Bedegrayne possessed a singular allure that could twist a man into knots. He had sensed it the moment he saw her. Claiming her would be a mistake, and the price dual-edged. Unfortunately, the risk was as tempting as the lady.

Once the ride was over, he ran forward and grabbed her off the wheel. Still laughing, she held on to his arms as if he was the only means of keeping her on her feet.

"Wonderful!"

"Aye, my favorite part, too," he said, his right hand splayed across her lower back, pulling her closer. "If I keep you dizzy and weak with laughter, you will never want to leave my arms."

Shock widened her eyes. "I fell for a ruse? You fiend!" On wobbly legs, she tried to step back. "How many women have you put on a merry-go-round just to take advantage of their dizziness?"

He liked how she bristled. Then again, he preferred her in his arms more. "Counting you?"

Her reply came out like a hiss. "Yes!"

Taking up her hand again, he kissed her palm. "One."

"Oh."

The misty, romantic expression on her face nibbled at his

conscience. To diminish the importance of his admission, he said, "The fairs I attended were to prove myself in the ring. Afterward, I was tired, sweating and my knuckles bleeding from cutting them on some bugger's jagged teeth; I was poor company for any woman." Sighting the tent he had been searching for, Keanan hailed the man standing by the entrance.

Suspicious, Wynne asked, "What are you about, sir?"

"Nothing worthy of that frown, I swear. Silhouettes. A simple memento of the fair."

"Enter, my lord and lady," the man entreated, eyeing the expensive cut of their clothes. "By Jove, what beauty." He took Wynne's hand and led her to the only chair in the tent. Several oil lamps lit the area, casting multiple shadows on the canvas walls. "For once, I curse my meager tools. I only wish I had marble to immortalize you, my lady."

Figuring he was paying for the showmanship as much as for the skill, Keanan handed a guinea to the man's assistant.

The silhouettist prattled on, praising his subject's beauty while he made minute adjustments to Wynne's position until he was satisfied with the sharp profile shadow on the white sheet behind her. Instead of tracing the shadow as Keanan had expected, the man picked up his scissors and black paper. His gaze fixed on her silhouette, he began cutting at an amazing speed. Two minutes later, he held his copy up to the shadow.

"Excellent, no?"

"Pure artistry, sir," Wynne marveled.

Keanan pulled out a few more coins. "I would like a copy made, and both of them framed. Is this possible?"

"Yes, my lord. I have a shop in the Strand where it can be framed. If I was you, I would fill each room with her image, so no matter where I wandered, her image would be there to comfort me."

It was an admirable pitch. Keanan shook his head. "I only require two. Send them to this address." He handed over his card. Wynne slipped her arm through his, distracting him. "Why fill my rooms with paper effigies when I have the real woman to gaze upon?"

Wynne was taking pleasure in her afternoon with Keanan. Alone with her, his mood was light and indulgent. After the silhouettist, they had walked from stall to stall, examining the various wares. Every temptation was offered. There were bolts of fabrics, lace, ribbons, slippers, and fans to impress a young lady. Keanan had insisted on buying her a fan and a pair of slippers she had admired. Biscuits, sausage, venison, fruit, and a half-dozen other choices beckoned to be tasted. In the background, a mock battle was being waged on the Serpentine River. A rope dancer juggled balls over their heads. Four theatrical, very drunk men called out slurs, goading the others into a sword fight. At least, she had assumed they were part of the entertainment.

They found Amara and Lothbury at the wild animal spectacle. Wynne joined the couple while a gentleman who recognized Keanan delayed him.

"I had dark thoughts of murder when his lordship dragged me off," Amara confessed, her voice softened so the men could not hear their conversation.

"Forgive me, I did not expect the men would confront us with a strategy worthy of the late heroic Nelson. I sent Gar after you, to insure Lothbury behaved."

Amara's cheeks flushed, darkening the work of the sun. "There is no need for apologies. Lord Lothbury was most kind. Witty, too. I cannot recall a day when I have laughed so."

Wynne returned her friend's smile. Too much tragedy had shadowed Amara's young life. Silently she thought Brock would be thinking murder as well if this day led to Lothbury's offering for Amara's hand.

"Miss Claeg, Miss Bedegrayne, I would be honored to

fetch you both something to drink," Lothbury suggested. "The dust is thick from both man and beast stomping about."

Both ladies consented, and Lothbury disappeared into the crowd. Wynne tried to see beyond the shoulder-to-shoulder mob, seeking out Keanan. She thought she saw a glimpse of his sleeve, yet she could not be certain.

Trumpets blared, signaling the commencement of the wild animal exhibition. Two huge black bears lumbered into the dirt arena the crowd had circled around. A man cracked his whip at the feet of each bear. Growling, the animals stood to full height. Revealing their mouths full of deadly teeth, they slashed their large paws into the air. The crowd roared its approval.

"Do you think it is safe to stand so close?" Wynne questioned.

"I think they are trained to act fierce in front of the audience," Amara replied over the din. "The ropes around their necks ensure they remain out of reach."

One of the men took up the lead rope of the bear on the right and ran alongside him as they circled the ring. Everyone shrieked and tried to step back when the bear passed by them.

Unease grew in Wynne. Any animals she had observed had been within cages. This excited, unpredictable crowd could trample a person. She and Amara collided when the people around them pressed closer. Large globes were tossed to the bears. One of the bears missed, but it did not diminish the cheers. Trumpets blared again, heralding the king of all cats. Entering between the poised bears, a lion stalked into the area.

"I think we should leave."

Amara leaned her ear closer but did not look away from the arena. A second lion paired with the first. "We have to wait for Lord Lothbury and Mr. Milroy. Besides, I doubt we would be able to move more than a few steps."

Wynne wanted to turn around to search for Keanan. There simply was no room to move her shoulders. Looking to the right, she noticed Gar had been separated from them. He was too far to hear her shout, so she waved her hand, gaining his attention. The footman acknowledged her summons. Even so, it would take time for him to work his way to them.

Her attention returned to the animals. The bears had been returned to their cages. Some of the tension in her chest should have eased. It had not. The two badly scarred lions were dirty and most likely half-starved, she decided, noting their visible ribs. They had to be in order for them to fight on command.

The lion on the right crouched low, then lunged for the other's throat. Using its muscular limbs, the other lion arched and batted at its opponent's head. The vicious battle for dominance had begun. With much growling and thundering, another lunge toppled the animals backward. Rolling in the dirt, they were a confusing tangle of claws and teeth.

An abrupt blow from behind thrust Wynne several yards into the arena. Clumsy from the shock, she fell forward, landing on her stomach. She froze. Time slowed, so that seconds seemed like an eternity. The sounds and shouts around her faded into the background. All she saw were the lions. Biting and slashing into each other's hides, they rolled mere yards from her position. Coughing on dust, she inched backwards, fearing that if she stood she might alert them to her presence.

Jerking her gaze up, she saw that from across the ring, people were shouting and pointing. She could not tell whether they were encouraging her to move or commanding her to halt. In the end, the decision was made for her. Masculine hands shot under her arms and dragged her out of the arena. One of the lions, spotting the movement, snapped its massive jaws in her direction.

His face white and rigid, Keanan pulled Wynne to her feet. She whispered his name, and the world tilted as he lifted her into his arms. She could barely breathe, yet she could not make herself let go. Shouting orders, he impatiently followed Gar and Amara as they forced an opening away from the lions.

Out in the open, Lothbury rushed to them, their drinks balanced precariously in his arms. "What happened? Did she faint?"

Amara took one of the drinks and pressed it to Wynne's lips. "She lost her footing and fell into the arena," she explained to the marquess, causing him to swear. Forcing her to sip more of the warm cider, she asked, "Do you hurt anywhere?"

Wynne shook her head. Still panting, she leaned back into Keanan's supportive embrace. The solid strength and warmth of him steadied her. "I cannot seem to stop shaking." Her hysterical giggle had everyone glancing warily at Keanan.

"Gar, see to the carriage," he ordered. "I will see to your mistress."

Her footman hesitated. It did not surprise her. He was loyal to the Bedegrayne family. After this incident, he probably did not trust her care to anyone.

She blinked when Gar crouched down beside her and took her hand. "Miss Bedegrayne, the blame is mine. When you waved, I knew you were in trouble. If I had done my job and stayed close, you would not have fallen like you did."

"Oh, Gar. No one blames you. The crowd was boisterous and unpredictable. We were all being jostled like trunks in a high-speed mail coach." She patted his hand. "See to the carriage. We will meet you at the entrance."

Wynne glanced up at Keanan's face after Gar departed. His attention was still fixed on the back of the footman. There was more color in his face, but tension made the muscles in his neck prominent.

"He truly is not to blame, you know. The crowd—"

Keanan took out his handkerchief and tenderly wiped the grime from her face. "I am the one responsible. I should not have left your side."

Lothbury cleared his throat, gaining their attention. "I plead my guilt as well. I could have waited until Milroy returned to you ladies."

"I doubt any of you men could have helped," Amara said with a slight hitch in her voice. "I stood beside her and—I am so sorry, Wynne."

Wynne got up. Ignoring Keanan's protest, she hugged her friend. "How fortunate I am to have so many who care. I repeat, none of you are to blame."

"Taking on the responsibility yourself, Wynne?"

She took offense at his mocking tone. Still, it confirmed his nerves were mending. "No," she replied crossly. "It means, Mr. Milroy, someone else shoved me!"

Nine

Someone had tried to kill her.

Keanan sat across from Wynne and Miss Claeg, consumed by his grim thoughts. Still wanting to believe it had been a freakish mishap, he had commanded her to repeat the tale numerous times. Her account remained the same. Someone had put his hands on her back and pushed her into the path of those lions.

With Miss Claeg's assistance, she had brushed most of the dust off her gown. Calm again, no one would ever know she had almost died.

"You did not have to ride with us, Keanan. I told you, I am fine." She held up her filthy gloves. "These are ruined, of course. A small sacrifice, really. I would have taken off a layer of flesh without them."

Her carefree demeanor, instead of soothing him, ignited his temper. "To Hades with your fine gloves! Is that all you care about? A coldhearted lout tried murdering you in front of a thousand witnesses. Am I the only one present who is feeling a chilly ache in my bones?"

Keanan had judged Miss Claeg a docile woman. In his limited experience with her, he had seen her flustered, delighted, and concerned for her friend. He had believed the two women were an odd pairing of extreme temperaments. Realizing the fragile-looking woman was livid enough to consider rapping him on the head with her reticule upped her in his estimations.

"Mr. Milroy." Miss Claeg's frigid tone dripped icicles of condescension. "We are quite aware of the events. Badgering her to tears might make you feel superior but will do little to address the issue."

He removed his hat and scratched at his disheveled hair in frustration. "I do not want to make you cry, Wynne." He glowered at Miss Claeg. Speaking in her presence made him feel awkward. Smashing his hat back on his head, he complained, "Do you know how I felt when I pressed through the mob and saw you inches away from two brawling beasts? Such a fright I endured, I expect during my morning ablution I'll be counting new silver on my head."

Wynne's lips trembled. Considering her strange mood, he could not tell if she was holding back her amusement or her terror. Part of him hoped she was laughing at him. He could not bear to see her cry. Having Miss Claeg in the carriage, he was not in any position to soothe her.

"I may be at fault," she whispered, her hands kneading the fabric of her skirt as if it were stiff bread dough.

Had he thought her calm? Something had shattered her painstaking facade. Brown lashes dammed her tears, making her eyes green, tumultuous pools.

"Jenny," she said, her gaze seeking out her friend.

Miss Claeg shook her head, denying the suggestion. "You cannot be certain."

"I blundered the affair. He struck me, the type of man who would demand revenge if given the chance."

They were treating him like he was a bloody invisible servant. His eloquent curse brought their wary attention in his direction. "Speak to me." He enunciated each word. "Who is Jenny? Why would a man want revenge on you, Wynne? What trouble are you facing?"

The tears had retreated. A pained, resolved expression pinched her face. "Mr. Egger."

"Because I pounded him once or twice for touching you?" There was no reason to tell her that Egger had difficulty walking when he had finished with him. A sensitive lady like Wynne shunned violence. Keanan sensed she had trouble accepting his former profession. She needed no reminders that, like Egger, he should be avoided as well. "He wouldn't dare cross me."

She stared patiently at him, giving him time to figure out the possibilities. Temper thickened his accent. "Don't you think it's time you tell me why you were tangling with Egger?"

Miss Claeg shifted, preparing to argue, but Wynne silenced her with a quick shake of her head. "My actions involved him, Amara. He deserves knowing what he stepped between."

"Can you trust him?"

"Yes."

She held his gaze, unwavering as her faith in him. Such trust curdled his insides. The desire to tell her that he was not worthy rose like bile, burning the back of his throat.

"I took his daughter from him. Jenny. Thirteen-years-old, and he had it all planned to sell her virginity to the highest bidder."

The notion was appalling but not all that uncommon. His interests never roamed to the young, desperate girls earning their wages by selling the only asset they owned. However, there were countless others who were not so discriminating.

"Who is this girl to you?"

He saw confusion. Anger flushed her cheeks. Her chin rose an inch. "Why does there have to be a connection? What her father planned for her was depraved and cruel. It would shame me, and my family, if I had simply closed my eyes and ignored a plea for my aid!"

Passion radiated through her as she spoke of a needy girl. The world was filled with them. Too many. Keanan and his mother had spent too many years miserable and hungry not to be able to understand. He also knew firsthand of the quality's callous treatment of strife that did not concern them.

Leaning back in his seat, he contemplated her reaction. A part of the tale was missing. He was certain of it.

"How did Jenny Egger know you would help?"

Wynne glanced away. Her continued silence confirmed that she was not prepared to trust him with all her secrets. The carriage slowed and then stopped. "I believe, Amara, this is where you dismount from our adventure."

Wynne had tried to dissuade him from climbing into her carriage. Having Gar throw him out, after Keanan had saved her life yet again, seemed mean-spirited, even though the act would have simplified her life.

Telling him about Egger should have satisfied him. She had not anticipated that one answer would cause other questions to surface.

Looking out the window, she noticed they were home. She recognized the voice of one of the footmen as he called a greeting out to Gar. "Our coachman will take you wherever you want. Again, you have my gratitude."

Keanan reached for her arm, forcing her to remain. "Do not be too reckless with your thanks, Wynne. You haven't shaken me loose. I want to meet your father."

Wordless dismay moved her lips. He was too sharp not to notice.

"Poor Wynne. What will you do?" he asked, all mock sympathy. "You think you are above judging me when walking anonymously about a fair. Yet the thought of giving my name to your father has you wringing your hands."

"I never wring my hands, Mr. Milroy," she said, liking the frost in her tone. "Please, join me. Meet my father. At least one of us will gain pleasure from the encounter."

The door opened. Wynne halted her departure. "You think you have me all figured out, do you not? You accused me of judging you. Yet I am the one who feels like I am doing penance for some nameless sin."

His eyes, like the man, were enigmatic. "Shall I put a name to your sin?"

She left him, not deeming his question worthy of a reply. Or perhaps she feared it. Gar helped her descend from the carriage. His gaze flickered to the man behind her. "Mr. Milroy will remain for refreshments. It is the least I can do for my brave hero."

Keanan Milroy was not the only one who could use mockery to his advantage.

"Lord Nevin, you understand I would never have breached a client's privacy if these were not dire circumstances," the nervous man said, his fingers tapping against the worn black portfolio he clutched.

Mr. Walter Tibal had been his father's man of affairs for twenty years. Somewhere in his fifties, his flesh had never seemed to fit his scarecrow frame. He was clever with figures, and his resourcefulness had always kept the Reckesters out of dun territory. Now, it appeared his father's excesses had become more than a drain on the family fortune.

Drake stared down at the activity on the street below. He preferred it to the defeated expression on his companion's face. "How bad?"

Barely stifling a weary sigh, Mr. Tibal opened his portfolio and retrieved several documents. Pushing his sliding spectacles back into position, he silently reread the information he'd gathered. "His Grace's gambling debts have exceeded the figure you and I had agreed upon were tolerable losses."

Nothing remarkable about that news, Drake thought, rubbing the stiffness creeping into his neck. "Do you have a figure?"

"At best estimate, sixty thousand pounds."

Half a year's rents, gone, on the turn of a card or a slow horse. Drake closed his eyes, cursing his father's weakness

for gaming hells. Both his mother and father looked to
him—no, demanded—that he seed the next generation by
marrying a respectable woman to breed his heir and to keep
the coffers brimming to counter his father's losses.

He thought he had found his bride. Wynne Bedegrayne's
lineage befitted the Reckester requirement for respectability,
while her beauty enticed his fevered fantasies. Sir Thomas,
unlike his own sire, was a shrewd man who did not succumb
to excesses, thus ensuring bountiful dowries for all his
daughters. Marrying Wynne Bedegrayne would have ful-
filled his personal and his family's financial needs.

Nevertheless, Sir Thomas would never part with his precious daughter for a mere title. Regrettably, it was the sole
asset he possessed that could not be wagered away on some
dark gaming table.

Mr. Tibal cleared his throat. He placed the papers he
clutched on the desk. "Several of His Grace's, um, associ-
ates, have approached me about the promissory notes."

For a moment, the fantasy of telling those vultures to pay
for an arrest warrant drifted like smoke in his mind. Sitting
in a debtor's prison might prevent his father from squander-
ing the remainder of his son's inheritance. The idea tempted
him, but, in the end, duty forced him to be practical. "What
can we sell?"

"Well, there is no need to start selling off the household
goods. You are not quite that destitute. I recommend you
sell off your shipping interests. Granted, there will be a loss,
since the West Indies venture has yet to come to fruition,
but we all do what we must in these difficult days," Mr.
Tibal said. His logic, as usual, could not be faulted.

Grinding a fist into his palm, Drake bitterly accepted that
his fourth attempt to resurrect his family's wealth had failed.
For every business transaction he negotiated, his father
poked more holes, bleeding the profits dry or forcing him
to sell off prematurely.

"Sell them. Sell them all," he told the man, praying his

sire remained out of sight until he had control of his rage. He did not trust himself not to lay his hands on him and throttle him for his weaknesses.

The door closed behind him. Alone, he contemplated his shrinking legacy. So far, he had managed to keep their financial woes from being common gossip. His reputation was already tarnished. Most thought him a rake, a replica of his scoundrel father. Granted, he had not lived a monk's existence, but his actions were hardly comparable to Reckester's. Perhaps he still had time to woo Miss Bedegrayne and her imperious father.

Word had reached Sir Thomas Bedegrayne's keen ears before they had crossed the threshold. If the housekeeper was curious about Keanan's presence, she kept it to herself. All business, she took Wynne's bonnet and soiled gloves then shooed them down the hall toward the conservatory.

"Papa's latest hobby," Wynne explained, while they walked through a hall lined with diversely themed paintings. "Tipton's sister, Madeleina, is a botanical enthusiast, although her passion leans more to landscape architecture. Her knowledge of plants and design theories are most impressive, considering her age."

"How old?"

"Sixteen." She opened the door to the left.

They had returned to the library. Keanan gazed fondly at the chair near the hearth, recalling the feel of Wynne in his arms. He almost suspected her of having ulterior motives, until she continued across the room and pushed open the set of heavy, dark-stained doors along the right wall. Giving the chair a wistful glance, he followed her down the steps into the conservatory.

"Papa."

Sir Thomas Bedegrayne turned away from his work at the sound of his daughter's voice. He was an impressive man, both in height and brawn. Over six feet, he wore a sailcloth apron tied around his lean waist. His sleeves had been pushed up, revealing sun-weathered, hairy forearms. This was no pampered gray-haired aristocrat who idled away his life in dark clubs. Whatever the man's business, he did not build that muscle potting posies.

Wynne hurried into her father's waiting arms and embraced him. Sensing his attention was focused on her guest, she looked back at Keanan. "Papa, I have someone I would like you to meet. This gentleman is Mr. Keanan Milroy. Mr. Milroy, my father, Sir Thomas Bedegrayne."

Sir Thomas still kept his arm around his daughter, his stance obviously protective. The flint in his blue-green eyes was scarcely welcoming. "Mr. Milroy, your name seems familiar. Where would I have heard of you?"

"Mr. Milroy is a pugilist by profession, Papa."

"A man is in a coil when the womenfolk feel compelled to speak in his stead."

"I hide behind no woman's skirts, sir."

The older man's eyes narrowed. Apparently satisfied with what he saw, he nodded. "Good, good." He gave his daughter an affectionate squeeze before releasing her. "You look tired, gel. Why do you not go rest while I chat with your Mr. Milroy?"

"Ah—" Embarrassed and helpless to stop her father from treating him like a brazen suitor, she silently questioned Keanan about his feelings regarding her dismissal.

It was not Sir Thomas's actions that disturbed him. He expected nothing less from a father intent on protecting his daughter from an unknown male. What did bother him was the growing ease with which he and Wynne communicated with each other. A small gesture or a glance, and he knew what she wanted, how she felt. It bred an intimacy he had never shared with another person.

"Miss Bedegrayne." Reverting back to formal address out of respect for her father, Keanan accepted her hand and bowed. "The pleasure of your company will feather my dreams this eve."

Accepting that neither man wanted her presence, her departing glance warned him that she was placing the consequences of this meeting on his head. She was putting thoughts in his head again, he realized, scowling at her back.

"Do you know anything about horticulture, Mr. Milroy?" Sir Thomas picked up a trowel and added dirt to the pot in front of him.

"No, sir."

"Neither did I. Little Maddy Wyman tells me anyone can poke cuttings into soil. A soul needs patience and caring to make them take hold."

"I thought it took water, sun, and fertilizer. Loads of fertilizer."

The baronet's bushy brow lifted at the remark. Chuckling, he stabbed the trowel into the mound of dirt. "Truthfully, I can't tell the difference between an exotic hydrangea and a weed. Don't particularly care. With my sons off traveling and my gels up and marrying, I think Maddy feels I need tending like one of her gardens."

"Wynne isn't married," he silkily reminded, not liking the idea that this wily old devil was plotting to marry her off.

Removing his apron, Sir Thomas waved him over to the wrought-iron table and cushioned, padded chairs. "Aye, my Wynne has led the lads a merry chase. Too picky, is my opinion. Blessed with my fair lady's face and my damnable stubbornness. A maddening combination, I must say."

"You have my sympathies, sir."

Sitting down, Keanan casually rested his hand on the inexpensive checkered gingham tablecloth. He assumed that the family on pleasant mornings used the table for breakfast. The house he recently purchased was lacking a conservatory. Glancing about at the flowing baskets of ferns and wild strawberries, he could envision the benefits of the earthy ambiance.

"Quite a prize, my Wynne. Clever, talented—have you heard her play the harp? No? Gentle on the ears, she is. Sings, too, although my Irene is the best out of the three."

Keanan made an ambiguous sound, wondering why the older man was apprising him of Wynne's virtues. He owned adequate senses. A man would have to be half mad not to want her. Intuition told him that her sire had expectations far above a duke's bastard son. So he settled back, guessing the old man would eventually appease his curiosity.

His wait was brief.

A large hand slammed down on the table, vibrating the metal surface beneath. He remained seated. His body tensed and he prepared to move if the man attacked. Keanan prayed he could talk the man out of fighting. He doubted Wynne would speak to him again if she learned that he and her father had milled in the conservatory.

Perhaps Sir Thomas had perceived Keanan's impatience, or he had tired of the game he played because he had not gained the reaction he had expected. Either way, his intent was direct and serious.

"Do you know what else my gel is, Mr. Milroy?" His fathomless blue-green gaze was as hard as his grip. "Honest. She does not lie to her papa. At least, not until she met up with you."

He almost smiled. Wynne was hiding more secrets than her association with him. Provoking Sir Thomas by pointing out that fact would not serve his purposes as well as having the lady indebted to him. Instead, he said, "It is no secret I met your daughter at the Lumleys' ball."

"And insulted her. Aye, the tale reached my ol' ears, even without my gel's assistance. She has pride in spades. Why would she be slinking off to meet you when she told me she was visiting Miss Amara Claeg?"

Being reminded of his inferior status was almost as irritating as Sir Thomas believing he could match him in a fight. The corner of his mouth lifted in a sneer. "Mayhap my disinterest presented a challenge to your spoiled daughter." The disbelief on the man's face was comical. "Or the awkward meeting at the Lumleys' was a mistake, and we decided to amend our bad impressions. Then again . . ." he said, his chair toppling over at his rapid ascent. Red-faced, his companion appeared weary of Keanan's mocking theories. "Wynne told the truth. She and Miss Claeg were together when I encountered them at the fair."

Sir Thomas was too astute to have missed Keanan's slip. Using her Christian name bared the growing intimacy he had tried to conceal.

"Mr. Milroy," he said, righting the knocked-over chair. He patted it, encouraging Keanan to rejoin him. "I think you have been baiting the Reckesters, and any other person you have deemed an obstacle between you and what you want, for so long that you do not know any other way of dealing with people. Like me." He sat in the opposing chair and clasped his hands on the table. "Deal straight, lad. Why did you come here, besides vaunting your interest in my gel?"

He had bullied Wynne into introducing him to her father. Her reluctance, while justified, had angered him. Holding her in his arms the other night, her mouth moving experimentally over his, had felt too wonderful. That kind of perfection gave an unsuitable man ideas. He should have realized that even an outraged father would not be able to prevent him from staying away from Wynne.

"Two reasons, sir. I've come face to face with that stubbornness you spoke of, and worried she would not tell you what happened this afternoon."

"Then why not you be the one to tell me?"

Keanan tersely explained the incident at the wild animal exhibition. The intensity with which the older man listened sent echoing waves of unease through his own system.

When he finished, Sir Thomas had visibly aged. There was no doubt the notion of losing his daughter had shaken him. Rubbing his side-whiskers, he broodingly lifted one brow. "You said two reasons, Mr. Milroy. What could be worse than almost losing my Wynne?"

Fairness prodded Keanan to forewarn him. In the end, it would not make any difference. "Losing her to me."

Ten

Her chaperone was a dragon. Well, she was at least dressed as one. If anyone could manage to look dashing in brilliant green scales, with a droopy red-felt tongue hanging off her chin, it was her impulsive Aunt Moll.

Convinced her niece was settling too comfortably on the shelf of spinsterhood, she decreed drastic measures were needed. Ignoring Sir Thomas's reluctance to have his daughter go off without him, her aunt had browbeat Wynne into a costume. Before she had thought of a reasonable excuse not to leave the house, they were on their way to a masquerade at the Pantheon on Oxford Street.

Aunt Moll had refused to listen to her protests. Wynne had retaliated by slipping into the acerbity she was accused of perpetuating. Maybe she was brooding. She had grounds, even if she loathed sharing the source with her aunt.

Ten days had passed since she had left Keanan and her father in the conservatory. He had departed an hour later, not bothering to summon her to say farewell.

Her father had been less evasive. Charging up to her sitting room, he had found her curled up in a chair near a window, working on her needlepoint. Uncertain of his temper, she stiffened when he pulled her into a powerful embrace.

The emotion-choked murmur against her shoulder proved Keanan had done what he had sought out to do. He had guaranteed that her father enjoyed an accurate accounting of the incident at the fair. She had tried relieving her father's concern, but Keanan's forthrightness and her nonchalance were at odds. Her father had preferred a stranger's tale to hers.

It should have hurt. She had tried to turn Keanan's confession into a betrayal. Hours later, she had come to admit there was a relief in having her father know. The escalating omissions to him and the rest of her family weighed heavily on her.

"So if I am sulking, then so be it," she whispered to her reflection in the full-length looking glass. Like many of the ladies, they had visited the ladies' cloakroom to add the finishing touches to their costumes.

"Do not tarry, girl. Put on your mask," her aunt chided behind her; the bulging eyes of the dragon leered over Wynne's shoulder in the reflection.

Holding the mask up to her face, she held still while a maid tied the ribbons. Wynne tilted her head, surveying the results. Aunt Moll had made her queen of the butterflies. Her winged mask, created from translucent white crepe and wire, was a fanciful creation of paste jewels and gold swirls. Quite beautiful, it effectively concealed the top half of her face.

The gown alone could have been worn in any ballroom. It was fashioned from white mull, with gold floral embroidery adorning the boldly wide V neckline, the melon sleeves, and the hem of the skirt. Several petticoats underneath provided a graceful sway to the skirt with every movement. An extra length of gossamer fabric was attached to the back of the bodice, giving her the effect of wings.

"Delightful," Aunt Moll sighed, leading her out of the room. The quarter train of her bright-green gown trailed behind her like a dragon's tail.

The scene before them would have credited any artist hoping to capture the color and joy of life on his canvas. The large, high-ceilinged room was filled to capacity. Music and the din of conversation merged into a disjointed comity. The musicians, unaware of their competition, played in the back on a raised stage festooned with red curtains. Below them, a menagerie of beasts and mythological characters mingled with traditionally attired patrons wearing cheap masks purchased at the door, fulfilling the costume requirement of the evening. The Gothic vaulted galleries on either side were overflowing with young lads plotting mischief, and tired onlookers.

"Not quite the ambience it had seventeen years ago, before the fire of seventeen ninety-two," her aunt admitted. "I recall the nights in my youth, when my dear Mr. Bedegrayne would bring me here for masquerade. Ah, those glorious nights! They called the Pantheon 'the winter Ranelagh.' Mr. Walpole declared it 'the most beautiful edifice in England.' And it was. I have memories of walking through the majestic rotunda, my hand tucked in the crook of Mr. Bedegrayne's arm."

"You loved him."

Aunt Moll blinked, clearing the old images of the Pantheon from her wizened face. "Did. And do. True love cannot be packed away like brittle fragments of a forgotten nosegay." She nodded approvingly to the approaching couple. "Devona, my dear, and Tipton. How fortunate we all chose this evening to attend the masquerade."

Tipton's grim amusement glittered through the shadowed eyeholes of his mask bearing an exaggerated hooked nose. "I recognize a royal summons when I hear it."

Devona dug her elbow into his side, but her oversized coat padded the impact. "Ignore him, Aunt. I was delighted by your invitation." She embraced her aunt and then her sister. "Wynne, you never uttered a word you were attending."

She and Tipton traded commiserating glances. "That is the problem with a royal summons. No warning." Wynne grimaced at her sister's masculine togs that had been fashionable a hundred years ago. "Who are you purported to be?"

Devona's grin was pure imp. "Monsieur Claude Du Vall."

"The French highwayman? Was this—" she began, letting her question fade when she remembered the last time her sister had employed the costume. Two years ago, Devona had talked Amara into assuming her identity while Wynne assisted her sister in an escape attempt at Newgate. With Amara disguised as the flamboyant Frenchman, Brock and Tipton should never have guessed they were observing the wrong female. Naturally, like many of her sister's schemes, it had been an absolute debacle.

"You are correct, Wynne," Tipton said, accurately judging her thoughts. "A sensible woman would avoid reminding her husband of her reckless past."

"Killjoy," Devona taunted, unconcerned. "Confess. The costume was clever. Amara must have fooled you for a time."

Tipton stroked one of the white plumes fanning out from her mask. "Never. The moment I noticed Miss Claeg, I knew she was not you."

Devona seemed ridiculously pleased by her husband's certainty. She rewarded him by giving him a quick kiss on the cheek.

"Miss Bedegrayne?"

Wynne turned, recognizing Lord Nevin's voice. His formal attire and the simple black mask suggested his presence at the Pantheon had been impulsive.

"Pardon me for interrupting." He bowed to Wynne and then bowed respectfully to her aunt. "Would you grant me the honor of this dance?"

"I—" Flustered, she silently beseeched her family for assistance. A month ago, she would have genially consented to his request. She considered him a friend. Nevertheless, his undeclared kinship to Keanan disturbed her. Circumstances placed her between these two men. In her heart, she understood that of the three, she risked the most.

"No fretting, my dear. I am capable of finding my own seat," her aunt assured her, taking away her excuse. "Tipton, you should dance with your French beau before she dreams up trouble for us all."

Wynne's sister gave her a parting hug. Whispering in her ear, she said, "The gossip about town is, a certain lady has Nevin finally coming up to scratch, sister." Devona kissed her cheek. Tears welled in her eyes as she allowed Tipton to lead her away.

She whirled, almost colliding with Lord Nevin. He touched her only as long as it took to steady her. For once, she was glad she was wearing a mask. She prayed it concealed her distress. The midsummer moon was shining down on them all if her sister truly believed such tittle-tattle pleased her.

Awaiting her reply, Lord Nevin offered his right hand as if it never occurred to him that she might reject him. Why would he? Both of them were performers in an unwritten play that couples for generations had abided by to conclusion. No sane, respectable woman questioned the consequences!

"You honor me, my lord," she said, curtsying. With her left hand on his right, they strolled the perimeter of the ballroom.

"Have the amusements of town displeased you, Miss Bedegrayne?"

Surprised, she slanted a discreet glance in his direction. "No more than usual, my lord."

"Then the company, perhaps?" he persisted. "Of late, you have been conspicuously absent."

So he had been seeking her out. His attentiveness added weight to her already sinking heart. "My father lays claim to the displeasure of which you speak. I daresay I shall be the continued recipient for more days than I care to count."

They took their positions at the beginning of the line for the country dance. Two lines were formed: one side, the men, and the opposing side, the ladies. The separation effectively ended Lord Nevin's questions. Meeting his gaze from across the opening between them, she could tell he intended to pursue the subject.

The music commenced, forcing Wynne to concentrate on the sprightly figures of the dance. Lord Nevin and the woman next to her moved forward and exchanged places. There was no opportunity for him to speak, for she and the second gentleman in the line copied their actions. The next dance figure was a *moulinet.* Each couple took turns crossing right hand to right hand in a half circle, then switched hands and circled in the opposite direction back to their original positions. Since they were the lead couple, Wynne and Lord Nevin moved to the center again. Clasping hands, they lollopped down the middle.

She smiled, enjoying the innocent abandon of the dance. Noting her pleasure, he returned the smile. They ended their merry jaunt with *brisé,* or circling around and then moving back to their positions at the end of the line.

The end of their turn was punctuated by numerous howls from rambunctious gentlemen in other sets. Considered too much the custom of barbaric nations, clapping, hissing, or yelling of any kind during the dance was generally disapproved. The masquerade provided an anonymity that made these formal rules readily dismissed.

Feeling someone's gaze upon her, Wynne glanced across at Lord Nevin. He watched the couples ahead performing their steps. Looking from side to side, she could find no one seeking her attention. She scanned the galleries above. She suspected that her aunt had chosen to retire there so she could watch the activities below. A suspicious person would conclude that her mischievous aunt was matchmaking again. Lord Nevin's presence this evening revealed as much.

A masked figure to her right drew and held her gaze. Definitely male. Like her dance partner, he was attired in a dark-colored coat and breeches. The expression molded into the mask was one of humor. It did not match the tightly compressed lips of the man who wore it. His hands gripped the railing as he stared down at her. Wynne shivered. There was no doubt in her mind that she was the one he had focused his attention on.

Keanan? She could not be certain. The man was careful, just staying out of the candlelight. If it was him, she could understand his animosity. Sir Thomas was not one to dally in choosing his words. She had heard enough of them lately on the subject of Keanan Milroy.

The dance ended just as they took the position as the second couple in the lines. Curtsying to his bow, she placed her hand in his and they began their promenade around the ballroom.

"Would you care for something to drink?" Lord Nevin asked, breaking the silence.

"Yes," she replied, gazing up at the shadowed figure above. His eyes burned her with their intensity. "Ah, no. No, thank you, my lord." If it was Keanan, then separating from Lord Nevin seemed prudent.

"I fear I have bored you, Miss Bedegrayne. Forgive me."

"You do that very well."

"Pardon?"

She gestured with her unfettered hand. "Come, now, Lord Nevin. Our acquaintance stands on years. I have observed your many facets. You even tried courting my sister."

"And was it not you who pointed out to me that Devona and I did not suit?" Lord Nevin squeezed her hand, signaling her to halt. As he stared down at her, the candlelight deepened the bluish hue to his eyes.

"Yes."

There had been a time when her motives for interfering between her sister and Nevin were not as clear. Jealousy

directed at her beloved sister had been unpalatable, all the
more so since Devona had never once voiced an interest in
the handsome rake.

"No offense, my lord. It was a bad match, and I think
you know it. In truth, once Tipton entered her life, there was
no other for her." She began walking, and he had no other
choice but to keep pace.

"Noble reasons, Miss Bedegrayne. Shall you confess
your indecorous ones as well?"

"Such as?"

"Jealousy, madam. You were not bothered by the notion
that I fancied a Bedegrayne, just simply that I was attentive
to the wrong one."

Speechless, she stared at him, horrified that her passing
infatuation had been so obvious. She highly doubted that
she was the only lady in the *ton* who had contemplated winning his affection. Looking up, she noticed her aunt waving
her handkerchief at her. Her relief expressed itself in a gasp.

"My aunt—"

Cutting her off, Lord Nevin continued, "I wanted you to
know. I have for a time noticed the error of my direction,
and have long sought to correct it." He grasped both of her
hands. "Miss Bedegrayne. Wynne. Please tell me I am not
too late."

"I—" Anguish tore at her. She did not have the heart to
hurt him. "I must rejoin my aunt. She signals me from the
gallery."

He looked up and saw she spoke the truth. She sensed
he wanted to pursue their discussion but feared pressing her
would force the rejection.

"I will escort you," he said, his tone clipped.

"There is no need. The stairs are here, and she is only a
few yards from the top. Please, we will talk another time."
Pulling away, she blindly headed for the stairs.

"Indeed we shall, Miss Bedegrayne," he muttered, frowning at her hasty retreat.

* * *

Moving quietly through the merrymaking throng, his stride matched theirs. He felt invisible, his mood inverse to the revelry. Blending into the shadows, he observed them. They were too absorbed in their conversation to note an audience. Her nervousness showed just as before, when she noticed him in the gallery. He had wanted her to see him, although he doubted she recognized him. The mask and the poor lighting protected him. He sensed her fear. It had diminished the anger he had felt earlier, upon her arrival. Her presence this evening had shocked him. Achingly beautiful in white, she had not protested Nevin's attentions. The revelation was a bitter tonic. He scowled as the earl tried to detain her from leaving. She broke away and disappeared out of sight. He guessed she was heading for the stairs. Ten days ago, he had chastised her for her wickedness. This evening proved the lady needed another reprimand.

A maelstrom of emotion constricted her chest while she followed the current of people ascending the stairs. Perhaps she had misunderstood Lord Nevin. The thought brought her little comfort. Wynne had all but run away from a man intent on declaring himself.

Why? She blamed Keanan Milroy. His dark indigo eyes called out to her soul. Whenever she was around him, she had to fight down the craving to stroke the noble contours of his face burnished brown by the sun. Just thinking about his damnable kisses still made her lips tingle. Once, she viewed him as an aberration to her small world. Of late, she worried that her feelings for the man were not a shallow flame. What a fix! She was falling in love with the most improper man.

Gloved masculine hands reached for her, halting her climb. A warm, solid chest muffled her high shriek. Her nose practically pressed into his coat; she inhaled his scent. The recognition was immediate. It represented danger as much as it offered a refuge.

"Keanan!" Noticing her heart's tempo increased whenever she was in his proximity, she pushed away. A single painted eye glared down at her. She gaped at him. If he was a cyclops, then who the devil was the man in the humorous mask?

Eleven

"Do you make a habit of grabbing every maiden you pass?" Wynne used the tart question to conceal her awkward surprise. She had been so certain he was the man watching her from the gallery. Seeing him here, especially after his confrontation with her father, amazed her. She should have had more faith that it would take more than a justifiably incensed father to discourage Keanan Milroy. She relaxed against him as people on the stairs pushed them together in passing. Calming, her faculties returned. Peeking over her shoulder, she was grateful Lord Nevin had not followed.

"He isn't there," he said. The concise words proved he had known her whereabouts and the company she kept all along. "I wonder. Who did you think to protect: me or him?"

"Both," she admitted, her stubbornness showing. "He is my friend—"

"Friend?" he scoffed. "Nevin wants you in his bed. Did he not make his intentions clear when he detained you below, or is he still plying your delicate ears with syrupy words of adoration?"

His nasty tone did not inspire her to ease his curiosity. Besides, she doubted the truth would improve his present temperament. "You observed us?"

"I entertained your aunt while Nevin courted you." The accusation was clear in his eyes.

"Aunt Moll! I forgot. She must be worried. I have to go

to her." Wynne took a step away from him before he reached for her wrist and pulled her back.

"Your aunt is well. If you leave me now, you will have ruined all her crafty plans to bring us together."

The man had a manner of rattling her composure. Her teeth clicked audibly when she closed her mouth. "This evening. She meant for you and me—" She finished the thought with a joining gesture. "I believed—" Wonderful! Completing a sentence was becoming a feat!

For some reason, Keanan did not have any trouble understanding her. "Lord Nevin was not invited by your aunt, although you cuddled up nicely to him."

"I did not—" She was doing it again. "I only danced with the man. My sister mentioned—Devona!"

Acknowledgment glittered in his dark gaze. "Your sister tried her hand at matchmaking, did she?"

"Apparently so." Wynne frowned thoughtfully, repeating her sister's earlier words in her mind. "She said that Lord Nevin was asking after me. She is so deliriously happy in her marriage bed, I guess she decided I needed a hard prod toward my own."

"Taking the tumble, Wynne?"

His derision shattered her contemplative demeanor. "When it becomes your business, I will let you know." She forced her way into the flow of human traffic, preventing him from halting her escape.

It took only minutes to reach her aunt. She was not alone. A male companion attired as a court jester sat beside her. "Aunt Moll."

"Wynne, my dear." She regally held out a hand. "Did you run off our Mr. Milroy? Pity—I had thought better of him."

"No need to alter your opinion, Mrs. Bedegrayne," Keanan said behind her. "Your niece wanted to check after you before we wandered off."

"Aunt Moll, if you please," her aunt chided. "You are

amongst friends." She patted Wynne's hand, drawing her attention. "You are acquainted with my dear friend, Mr. Keel. He is the proprietor of Keel and Bottles, a perfumery off Bond Street."

"Yes, indeed. I have visited your establishment often, Mr. Keel. It is a pleasure to see you again."

Friendly, albeit nervous in their presence, the man vigorously nodded to both Wynne and Keanan. "Lovely nieces, Molly. Each one I meet, I swear is prettier than the last. Mr. Milroy, I witnessed your last fight. A pattern card of science and skill, sir. Most impressive."

Using Keanan's reply to his flattery as an opening to discuss the match, the men moved a few steps away to relive the finer points of the match.

"Should I apologize for the ruse?" her aunt asked.

"Only to my father, if he should learn of your role. You know he has forbidden me from seeing Mr. Milroy." Her gaze flickered to Keanan while she sat down in an abandoned chair. He was too lost in his conversation with Mr. Keel to notice they were discussing him.

Aunt Moll grimaced. "That was his anger and fear for you at the fair raging. When it recedes, he will reconsider."

"We share the same opinion, Aunt. Tonight's outing proved his threat about locking me in my room for the entire season was toothless. However, I fear his dislike for your young champion will never improve. I would not be amazed if Mr. Milroy had a hand in forging this low estimation."

Her aunt sighed. "Two pride-puffed males. It was inevitable the two would clash over the care of you."

Wynne wrinkled her nose. "You make it sound as if a declaration has been made. I can assure you, Mr. Milroy has not issued any offer worth repeating to a gentle audience."

The comment had her aunt laughing until tears gleamed on her lashes. She used her handkerchief to dab at the corners of her eyes. "The last time I saw so many sparks, lightning struck that beautiful old oak I loved." Her frail hand trembled slightly as she lifted it to Wynne's cheek. "I see how you look at each other. Both of you think each is clever at this dance, but I view it all through old eyes. There was a time I sought out my beloved, Mr. Bedegrayne." She stopped; her throat visibly tightened at the glimpse of old memories. "I was told by my friends and family that marrying a second son was not an advantageous match. He could not offer me wealth or title, nor was he the handsomer of the two sons."

She touched her aunt's hand on her cheek. "I am partial about my papa; however, there must have been something about my uncle's character that caused you to favor him?"

"On our first meeting, he called me a gabbler," she fondly recalled.

"Were you not insulted?"

"Naturally. I threw my shoes at him. One hit him right between the eyes." She pointed to the spot on her own expressive face.

"I will wager he wanted to throttle you."

"He did. And he tried. Do you know what else he did?" At the shake of her niece's head, she continued, "He brought me lace handkerchiefs, because he thought the delicate lace would look pretty in my hands. He read poetry to me. There was always an odd catch to his voice when he did that I found endearing. He bought me a dozen pairs of slippers to replace the ones I threw at him, and later he gifted me with a special pair each wedding anniversary to remind me of our first meeting."

Love. Loss and time had made it bittersweet, but the memory of it still put a misty longing in her aunt's eyes. "Did he ever apologize for insulting you?"

"Never. He still accused me of being a gabbler." She shrugged. "I am. Mr. Bedegrayne observed my refined qualities and my faults. The wonderful man adored both." The dreamy, reminiscent expression sharpened as her thoughts shifted to her present concerns. "Your Mr. Milroy sees only his faults, and it blinds him to the fair qualities most take for granted. It will take an intelligent woman possessing courage and patience to breach an unwilling heart. However, I think the eternal love of such a man balances the risks."

"Miss Bedegrayne, are you satisfied your aunt is well cared for?"

Heads close in confidence, the women pulled back, each wondering how much of their discourse had been overheard. "Ah . . ."

Mr. Keel bounded forward. "No need worrying about Molly. I will look after her." The affection he had for her aunt showed on his face and in his protective stance behind her chair.

Feeling Keanan's gaze on her, pressing her to speak, she relented to her inescapable fate. "Thank you, Mr. Keel. It pleases me my aunt has such a good friend." She held her hand out to the only man capable of breaking her heart, and accepted the risk. "I am ready, Mr. Milroy."

Keanan and Wynne had departed with Aunt Moll's blessing. He was indebted to her. For some reason, the old woman had sided against her family to champion him. Her faith awed him as much as it terrified him. He had tried to tell her it was misplaced, but she would not hear of it. The instant she had learned of the confrontation with Sir Thomas, she had sent for him, the seeds of a plan to bring the young couple together already sprouting in her nimble brain.

Her fond memories of a masquerade, and the necessity of a costume, had led her to conclude that the Pantheon was the ideal setting for an assignation. He had agreed until Nevin had appeared, claiming Wynne for a dance. Watching her smile at the insolent pup, it had taken all his will not to leap down from the gallery and tear them away from each other. They had appeared too well suited for his comfort.

"Do you wish to dance?" He inwardly winced at the growl in his voice. Issued more like a threat, it would have caused any decent lady to shy away from such attention. Not Wynne. She seemed to tolerate his moodiness just fine.

She gave the crowded ballroom a disinterested glance and then moved away. "Not particularly. I get quite warm dancing in this costume."

The diaphanous fabric that draped across her back floated teasingly at her every movement. Cobwebs could offer more warmth. "Do you believe I will provoke a fight with your noble suitor, Wynne? Even I can restrain myself from my baser instincts. I realize you consider me a savage—"

"Stop, please," she begged, her gloved fingers reaching out to still his lips. She retreated, making him feel bereft at the loss of her touch. "If you behave like a savage, it is only because you wish to act so."

He allowed her to set their pace and direction. She seemed content to move toward the front of the building, away from the revelry and crowds.

"Lord Nevin claims to have feelings for me, Mr. Milroy," she admitted, sending his emotions into a frenzied roil of rage, fear, and denial. "I have not encouraged him. Nor do I wish him punished because you cannot bear seeing him humanized by his lighter passions."

Could she not see? He had little practice with the fair sex except for the occasional hour in the dark, sweating and grunting on a lumpy mattress to relieve his lust. It had not prepared him for handling a prickly female who seemed more wary than romantically interested in him. "It isn't his civilized veneer or the lack that makes me want to plant my fist into his pretty face. He thinks he has a right to claim you. Deserves you. I could kill him for the fancy!" Great. Those were exactly the kind of words a man used to woo his lady.

She blinked at the vehemence of his vow, but she did not step away from him. "No one can control another's thoughts,

Keanan." A hint of a mysteriously feminine smile had his insides clenching. "Even you."

"I have no desire to control Nevin. I just want to thwart any intentions he has for you."

They strolled through the opened entrance. Rain poured like sheets of water over the four-pillared outcropping of the Pantheon's Grecian facade. The cool evening air felt inviting, compared to remaining inside where the air was heated by the exertions of the dancers and the smoky candlelit chandeliers.

"Are you chilled?"

"No."

Not believing her, he let his fingers graze hers and gently tugged her to him. Her back to his chest, he wrapped his arms around her as he leaned against the wall. Silently accepting the warmth he had to offer, she listened and watched the rain.

Masked, their public display of affection did not seem so improper, as if their costumes protected them from censure. Of course, they were not the only couple seeking a dark place to share a few desperate minutes of intimacy. On the opposite side of the entrance, there was another couple ardently entwined. Soft murmurs and laughter from the woman drifted over to them.

"I pondered whether or not you would heed your father's command not to associate with me," he said, pitching his voice low.

Wynne turned in his arms so she could see his face. "Do not judge my presence as any concession. I simply was not privy to my aunt's grand scheme."

"And if you had been?"

He watched her nibble her top lip, and then her lower, while she mulled over his question. "I would still be here."

The generous admission felt like a balm to his senses. Confronting her father when his motives that day were at best murky had been foolhardy. He had departed, with the old Bedegrayne charging after him and swearing he would rather marry her off to a Turkish pasha than waste his precious daughter on an infamous fellow. What had he expected? A loving, patriarchal embrace welcoming him to the family? If he had, taunting a very capable gray-haired giant that he was stealing his daughter away from him was not the manner in which to go about it.

"Why did you do it?" Wynne asked, unerringly picking up his thoughts. Two coaches rattled past them on the street.

"He needed to know what happened at the fair. You never planned to tell him, did you?"

"One truth unravels several lies."

She separated from him at the appearance of two departing couples. One of the men took notice of her and leered, but his lady rapped him on the ear, bringing his attention back to his party.

"If you are so eager for truth, why do you not exercise the words yourself? What really provoked you to enrage my father?"

Keanan objected, "I did not—"

"You did. My father may be brusque by nature. Nevertheless, his temper is moderate. An hour in your presence had him muttering curses, punctuated by ardent exclamations for a sennight."

"I am not overly fond of him, either."

"I am so pleased you find this amusing." She waved his hand away when he tried touching her arm. "My father has never forbade me from anyone before. I was willing to risk—" She felt her throat closing up, preventing her from finishing. "Forget I said anything."

"Do not leave me," he entreated, meaning every word. Their meeting was not transpiring the way he had imagined. Keanan blamed himself. It was difficult explaining his feelings to anyone, and he had recently discovered that speaking them to Wynne challenged him beyond his comfort. At the sound of more approaching people, he moved to the side, shielding her from their scrutiny. "I want to show you something. Will you come with me?"

Wynne placed her hand over his on her arm. For once, she seemed uncertain. "I cannot leave my aunt."

"Aunt Moll is in the tender care of Mr. Keel and is pleased by her circumstance. Her hints for us to leave were not all that subtle." Keanan silenced her by rubbing her lower lip with the pad of his thumb. "I told her I would see you home. No one will miss us. To the casual observer, Theocritus's Cyclops has finally conquered the heart of his beautiful Galatea."

"Is that how you see me?" Wynne could not resist asking later once Keanan had secured them a hackney. She recalled the mythological poem of the gay, mocking sea nymph who tormented the ugly Cyclops. "Do you feel I tease and arouse hope in your heart, only to reject you?"

The interior of the coach was dark except for the muted light coming through the windows from the exterior lanterns. She sensed more than saw his agitated movements. "I spoke of the costumes—our anonymity to the public. There was no reference to your poor treatment of me." His voice confirmed his rising irritation.

If he had hoped his gruff manner would quell her, he had underestimated the complicated mix of nerves and stubbornness. "I doubt my aunt considered this costume a representation of Galatea. I rather preferred thinking I was queen of the butterflies instead of some callous creature." Good grief, now she was prattling.

He exhaled noisily. Muttering an oath, he said, "Be the bloody queen of anything that pleases you." He blew out another breath. "Forget I opened my mouth."

Watching him rip off his mask and toss it to the floor, an insight struck her. Too caught up in her own confusing feelings about Keanan, she had never considered that he

might have a few of his own. In her understanding, humor
surfaced. "What are we fighting about?"

His lips twitched. "Damned little, in my opinion." As
they laughed together, he reached for her. "Come here."

"Any closer and I will be sitting on your lap," she protested, amusement still lacing her voice.

"I'll let you know when it becomes a problem."

In a less friendly section of town, the torrent of heaven's
black tears beat down relentlessly on another coach. The
cool air and uncomfortable dampness heightened Lord
Nevin's savage mood. He had never shied from the notion
that Wynne Bedegrayne would be a demanding wife. Indeed,
he relished the benefits of channeling such passions to the
marriage bed. Feeling defeated, he slammed his foot into
the floorboards of the coach. First, he had endured Wynne's
indifference to his clumsy attempts at charming her. Later,
when he trusted his temper again, her crazy old aunt could
not seem to recall the whereabouts of her niece. Resistance
had trumped every calculated maneuver this evening. He
felt half mad from frustration.

Reaching his third stop, the coachman opened the door,
an umbrella readied in his hand. Not bothering to keep pace,
Drake trudged through boggy mud and entered the Silver
Serpent. A sneer diminished his handsome features as his
gaze swept the room. There was no relief in his expression
at the sight of the approaching proprietress.

"Where is Reckester?" Drake demanded. Any inclination
toward graciousness had left him hours past.

Not offended by his brisk manner, Blanche Chabbert's
shrewd gaze assessed him. "His Grace does not like to be
bothered. Who are you?"

"His son," he said, the words spoken as though his birthright was a curse.

"Ah, yes. You have the look of him. His eyes, I think. Like the other."

Not appreciating the comparison to Reckester, or to his bastard, he disregarded her startled protest and pushed past her.

Hands on her hips, she shouted, "And his rude manners, too."

She remained in his wake, which was fine with him as long as she did not interfere. Not seeing his father in the main room, he moved down the hall. Three doors lined each wall, leading to rooms used for private games. He opened the first door. The naked man and woman within did not hear him close the door. Obviously, the Silver Serpent had expanded on its private pleasures, he thought, moving on to the next door. Empty. Drake discovered Reckester in the third room. He considered it a small mercy that his father was engrossed in a card game rather than sampling some whore's wares.

"Well, well . . . it is young Reckmore. Come join us, man," one of his father's cronies beckoned.

Drake gnashed his teeth at the ridiculous cognomen. Some wit years ago had dubbed his half-brother Reckless, a nasty reminder of the family he lacked. Amused and drunk one evening, his father announced at one of his clubs that if his bastard was Reckless, then his heir must be Reckmore. The name had stuck, especially, after Milroy's exploits in the ring had brought him fame and recognition. Drake had managed to quell its use among his peers; however, his father's intimates still enjoyed needling him. He briefly wondered if Milroy equally despised his name.

"Come to play?" Reckester asked. His sloppy appearance gave one the impression he had resided in his chair for days. His coat misplaced, he wore his soiled shirt unbuttoned and the sleeves rolled up to the elbows. His shoulder-length light-brown hair hung loosely and looked to have been combed countless times with his fingers. Those red-rimmed eyes flickered upward, meeting his son's dispassionate gaze. "Thought you were off doing your mama's bidding."

The other men at the table snickered. Rebuffing them, Drake leaned forward, resting his left palm on the table, successfully blocking his father's view of the ongoing game. "An unnecessary bidding, if you did more with your time than piss the rents against the wall."

"Tibal came weeping to you about the accounts. Weak-kneed peach!" he roared.

Keeping his voice pitched low to avoid becoming next morning's gossip, he murmured, "Who do you think cleans up your affairs, Father? Those creditors do not simply disappear because your word is respected in town."

His attempts to stand were inhibited by poor balance brought about by an indecent amount of port. "Disrespectful," he slurred. He pounded his chest. "I take care of my own. I don't need you meddling. You and Tibal whispering behind my back, by God!"

"You are gambling more than our wealth when you tangle with those shady moneylenders. The last one hinted to Tibal that he was willing to snap the bones in each of your fingers to gain your cooperation."

His father's expression paled but was still mutinous. "Just bluffing. No one would dare touch me."

The blind arrogance of his boast shattered something inside Drake. Suddenly, his hands were on him. His fingers seized fistfuls of his father's ruined shirt and hauled him out of his chair. Reckester's glazed eyes were wide with shock and a gratifying dose of fear. "Keep out of this!" Drake warned his father's friends when one of them moved to intercede. "Look at you. Drunk, foolish, you foul the air."

Reckester worked his mouth. "Listen—"

"Keep your excuses. I have heard them all." He stared down at his father while he dangled in his grip. Disgust and pity had eroded his filial love. "Where is your dignity? You are like a disease. Your decadence and self-pity consumes our family, leaving nothing but putrid waste."

"Let go. Let go!" his father bellowed, an enraged, wounded animal. The accusations garnered Reckester the strength to push Drake away. Released, he fell sideways back into his chair, his arm shoving his cards into the air like one-winged butterflies. "I am your father. I am entitled to your respect and obedience, sir. What gives you the right to judge me?"

Using his palms, Drake pressed at the pain in his temples. He was losing the woman he wanted to marry; his birthright probably amounted to IOU's at various gaming hells; and tonight with his father's assistance, he was chiseling at the foundation of his reputation.

"My name gives me sanction. I leave you to your decay, Father. The quicker your demise, the sooner the title and estates are mine." He turned his back on him.

"You're not my only son," Reckester, gaining courage, staggered to his feet and shouted. "Hellfire, you aren't even the eldest. Have a care, young Nevin. A properly placed signature could have the *ton* calling you the bastard!"

Twelve

Keanan had left their destination a surprise. Wynne had withdrawn from him. Uncertain about her silence, he allowed the sounds of rain pounding against the roof of the coach, and the rumble of the wheels to substitute for conversation.

Even in darkness, her beauty called to him. Her winged mask still remained in place. Whether she kept it on to distance herself from her decision to accompany him, or to prolong the night's enchantment, he could not guess. The paste stones winked with her subtle movements. The intriguing glitter beckoned him closer, making him want to see if her eyes were equally inviting.

Her hand brushed his arm, halting his silent inquiry. The slowing coach prompted his midnight siren to speak.

"Where are we?"

The coachman opened the door, giving her a glimpse of the house shrouded in murkiness. Keanan had yet to hire a permanent staff to keep lanterns ablaze for their master's return.

"The property is mine," Keanan replied, descending the coach. Accepting the coachman's umbrella, he hesitated only when she made no attempt to move. "Regrets, Wynne?" He held out a waiting hand, his outer demeanor passive as he watched her lips part, challenged. He had long learned how to conceal his feelings from the world. In truth, he feared a candid revelation would have her fleeing into the night, leaving him alone in his cold, empty house.

Sucking in her lower lip in contemplation, she gazed past him to his dwelling. What inner conflict she fought ended with a decisive nod. She accepted his outstretched hand. Together they hurried to the door, acting as if speed would leave them untouched by the rain.

Taking out a key, he unlocked the massive walnut door and ushered her into the ink-black maw of the entrance hall. Keanan handed the umbrella back to the drenched coachman, and their sole light faded into the distance.

"Remain where you are. I'll light some candles," he assured Wynne. He moved confidently to a table and withdrew the items he needed.

"Where is your man?" she asked, her speech rapid and breathy, the result of her increasing nervousness.

Working on the promised light, he grinned in the darkness. Despite her fears, she always held her ground with him. Keanan could not think of a single female as brave. Or foolish. Her trust staggered him. It made him want to prove to her that it was not misplaced.

"Ah, blessed light." He took the single candle and lit the pewter branch of four. Once finished, he pushed the candle into the empty socket, and picked up the candelabra. "I have yet to hire servants," he explained, bathing her in the warm circle of his light. "The house stood abandoned for years. It needs cleaning and various repairs to make it livable. So far, I reside alone. You are my first guest."

Wynne trailed after him. He led her down the hall and to the left. Walking through a room and out another door, he suspected their meager light provided a respectable glimpse of the house. His. Pride filled his chest. He had never owned anything as grand as this old house. Its rotting floorboards, cracked plaster, and uninvited vermin could not diminish his prize. His new wealth had enabled him to replace the boards, recoat the plaster walls, and sweep the vermin out along with years of dust. Already, commissioned artisans labored adding elaborate detailing to the cornice, frieze, and architrave, restoring the old house to its former elegance.

"How do you live? Someone should be here at all hours, to look after things, and deter the clever thief. And what of your clothes? You need a man to see after you. How do you eat?"

Amused by her flurry of questions, he chuckled, "I manage, Wynne. I've had years of seeing to myself. A proper staff will only spoil me."

He wondered about the man she saw when she gazed at him. Did he truly look like a gentleman, a man entirely useless without an army of servants hovering around him, seeing to his every whim? He had worked to conjure such an image for her, but now he saw the flaws in such a fellow. Too caught up in his role, he had not allowed her to meet the man beneath.

"I did not mean—I was prying," she apologized, walking away from him to the large unadorned windows, her embarrassment acute and uncomfortable.

Keanan instantly regretted his mocking comments. The stiffness in her posture, and the prideful tilt of her head showed him that she had retreated, hiding behind politeness. An evening at the masquerade had seemed fated, because he longed for the unmasking.

"I will see to a fire," he muttered, kneeling down in front of the iron grate.

Drawing the edges of her cloak together, she said, "I am not cold."

Using a candle to ignite the small coal, he shrugged, dismissing her admission. "A fire provides light, besides warmth." He took up the bellows and fanned the small flame. "You might as well remove your cloak. It is so sodden with rain, it is more likely stealing heat than providing it." Using the tongs he added more coal.

"Your house is barren, Keanan."

He bristled at the observation. Hunched in front of the grate, he stared at the fire, remaining silent.

The rustle of fabric revealed she had heeded his advice and removed her cloak. "No servants tending you. No furniture for reposing. You are a man of contradictory natures. I cannot help but ponder them."

He jabbed the poker into the fire until he was contented with the results. "It is not my intention to be mysterious, Wynne. You are witnessing a man at the beginning of a new life. I simply have nothing of my old life I wish to meld with my new."

Frowning at his hands, he realized his gloves were soiled with coal dust. He peeled them off and tossed them into the shadows. He glanced up at her. She had placed herself a few steps behind him, clutching her cloak in front like a shield. Her bejeweled mask glinted in the fire, capturing his attention. Rising, he stretched his cramped muscles with the elegance and grace of a sleek malkin. Impulsively, his hand shot out in midstretch and ripped her mask off, the wire and mesh crushing easily in his grip. He tossed the ruined mask into the fire.

More offended than fearful, her green eyes reflected the flames. "Why the devil did you do that?"

"No masks allowed, Wynne," he declared, taking her cloak from her. "Not here."

His announcement caused her to become skittish again. *Interesting,* he mused. She moved out of the circle of warmth and light, returning to the window again.

"The weather is clearing." She opened the window. Tendrils of rain-purged fresh air mixed with warmed air from his fire.

Keanan shook her cloak out. It fanned out, inner lining outward in front of the fire. "Not really creative, Wynne. You will have to be more clever if you plan on avoiding my clutches."

Seemingly distracted by whatever she saw through the

window, she pushed back the stray hairs tickling her cheek. "Whoever said I was plotting an escape?"

He froze half crouched, like a predator sighting his prey. His nostrils flared slightly with each breath, the scent of her brought to him by the evening's breeze. The elemental strike of desire knifed through him. Keanan tried to master the lust her casual admission incited.

The woman was still a mystery to him. Her actions and words tonight painted her as a forthright siren, although he knew her to be an innocent. A light breeze caught the gossamer fabric of her costume, causing it to billow behind her. She appeared ethereal dressed in white. A yearning rose from deep within him. He wondered if she understood that any sign of willingness on her part would free the bonds of his self-control.

Keanan did not notice that he had taken steps toward her until the floating ends of her make-believe wings lightly caressed his face. She whirled around, her expression showing her surprise at his stealth. He lifted his hands slowly, palms forward, trying to gentle her. He wanted to reassure her that she was safe with him. However, they both knew it was a lie.

"Come back to the fire," he urged, when comforting phrases eluded him. She followed him back to the fire and settled on her cloak. "Despite your poor impression of my home, I do possess some luxuries. Are you hungry?" The negative shake of her head pressed him to ask, "Perhaps something to drink, then?" He hunkered down next to her, his larger frame taking up most of the space on the cloak.

That alluring, mysteriously feminine smile of hers was back in place. "Who would have guessed that I make you nervous?" She laughed then, her delight confusing him all the more, even as he snarled a denial. "Why did you bring me here?"

She boxed him neatly with the unexpected question. His innards prickled just beneath the middle of his ribs. Perhaps she was not the only one who possessed a fine case of nerves. Rubbing the spot, he stared into the fire.

"I have ambition. Always did. I needed to show you there was more to me than brawn and violence." Feeling her perceptive stare on him, he pushed on, shrugging off his discomfort. "This house is the beginning of the refined life I have planned for myself."

"These plans you have made . . . are you a slave to them? I put forth, what happens if the unexpected occurs?"

The unexpected. That summed up Wynne Bedegrayne storming into his life. Unbeknownst to her, she had jumbled his carefully crafted plans, leaving him bemused and hungry to fill needs he had never thought he felt. If he were a good man, hell, even a kind man, he would bundle her up in her cloak and stuff her in a carriage for home.

Bewitched, he decided. Hopelessly lost in those green eyes. Her innocence shined like a beacon, warming his soul for the first time in his life. How could he turn her away? Why would he want to?

Perhaps sensing his inner chaos, her gloved hand reached out and cupped his cheek. Keanan leaned into her impulsive gesture, accepting her comfort. She was here because she wanted to be. Greed bubbled inside him. Already wanting more, he leaped forward to the morrow, when she would cast him off. Self-preservation forced him to bury the automatic denial. He had spent his life surviving on meager scraps. He could be content on anything this lady willingly offered him.

"You are going to kiss me, are you not?" she asked too politely, almost concealing the passion that swam just beneath the surface.

Keanan took her hand. Bowing over it, he set to the task of removing the offending gloves denying him access to the flesh beneath. The next time she touched him, he wanted to feel her warmth and the silk of her flesh gliding over him.

"Aye, Wynne. I'll be kissing you. And more, much more, if
you let me."

His gentleness always surprised her. It seemed contrary
to a man of his size. Large fingers, as nimble as those of
any seamstress, peeled and worked her gloves off. Tracing
the shape of her fingers with his nails, he intertwined their
fingers. Wynne felt shivery from his contact.

"There is a strength in you that makes me forget how
small you really are," he marveled, comparing the size of
her hand to his.

She tugged her hand out of his, feeling the need to put
some distance between them. The action was instinctive,
something she had always done to protect herself from males
who had come too close. "Not that small," she argued.

Keanan's white teeth flashed at her fractious tone. "Aye,
just small enough." He leaned forward and kissed her.
"Christ, what a pout you have, woman. All I want to do is
devour you." He scooted closer. Framing her face with his
hands, he murmured, "I should be slapped for the fantasies
I've woven on your behalf. Your father is likely to hang me
if I act on them."

Since he had her head locked in his grasp, all she could
do was peek from side to side. "I do not see my father
lurking about."

He rewarded her sauciness by pressing a hard kiss to her
lips. "You tempt me. More than any—" Keanan drew a deep
breath, starving for air. His lips rested on her forehead for
a few seconds before he released her, pulled back. "Where
is your good judgment? You should scuttle my nob for laying
my hands on you."

For all his teasing, Keanan Milroy was not a jaded rake
seeking his latest seduction. He desired her. Wynne saw
proof in the way his hands trembled when he reached for
her. She heard the catch in his voice, as though the ardor

building within caused him pain. In spite of her innocence, she was not oblivious to the rigid swell pressing an intriguing outline in his breeches.

Even the air around them smelled different. Human musk and suppressed passion charged the air. Combined with her feelings for Keanan, it created a powerful aphrodisiac. It empowered her just as much as it swept away her lingering resistance. Perhaps he was feeling it, too. He just had more strength to delay the inevitable.

She bridged the several feet he tried putting between them by placing her hands on his broad shoulders. His muscled frame should have been impossible to manipulate. Nevertheless, he moved against her with gliding ease when she pulled him closer. Angling her face upward, she whispered, "I regret if this shocks you, but I have a few fantasies myself. If it pleases you, perhaps we can compare our interpretations of being devoured by the other."

His pupils dilated until there were only rims of indigo. Groaning, whatever oath he uttered was obliterated when his mouth clamped down on hers. The stunning ferocity caused her to gasp, but that, too, was swallowed up in his capitulation. Her eager innocence was never more apparent, for it paled in comparison to his experienced male onslaught. This revelation tempered her desire. Her slowing response did little to dampen Keanan's enthusiasm.

A tidal flood of emotion flowed from him. There was no tenderness, no reverence in the fingers that dug into her upper arms. This was need. As promised, he devoured her mouth. Firm, demanding lips gave way to teeth. He nipped her lower lip and then used the tip of his tongue, easing his branding.

"Open for me. Let me in," he entreated, nipping the length of her jaw.

She shivered, feeling her nipples tighten in response to his guttural plea. Wynne closed her eyes, uncertain of what he wanted from her. Was he asking for her trust, her heart?

She feared the choice had been taken out of her hands weeks earlier when he dragged that dreadful Mr. Egger from her.

Clutching his waist to steady herself, she shifted her mouth out of his reach, forcing him to pay attention to the words she had never given another man. "I love you."

His grip became almost unbearable. Noting her discomfort, he loosened his hold and rubbed the injured flesh. Keanan hauled her into his lap, hugging her closely to his chest, preventing her from seeing his face. Her confession had stunned him. Wynne could not fault his response. Saying the words aloud was making her feel light-headed. She had just bared her heart, leaving herself vulnerable for rejection. Doubt constricted her lungs until she could not breathe. His continued silence forced her to consider that she might have misunderstood his plea.

"Shall I take back my heart, Keanan?" she whispered, knowing such action was impossible.

Maintaining his hold on her as if fearing she might flee, he transferred her in his arms so he could see her face. "No," he said solemnly. His hand stroked the hair near her left ear and then moved on, exploring her intricate coiffure. Whenever his fingers brushed against one of the bronze combs securing her hair, he plucked it out. The weight of her hair, free from its confines, tumbled down her back. He smoothed her tresses with his fingers; his curiosity and admiration were evident.

"Why do you bind up such beauty?" Her hair sifted through his fingers. The length fell almost to her waist. Vanity had kept her from cutting it, even though she admired the shorter locks many of the ladies of the *ton* possessed. Watching Keanan rub his face in a fistful of her hair and marvel at its texture, she did not regret her decision.

"It is not proper, nor is it practical walking about with it unbound." She gave him an exasperated look when she sensed he was about to argue. "Not even for you."

He kissed her playfully, using his tongue to tickle her

upper lip. She granted him a smile for his efforts. "I don't think I could bear having other men see you thus." He kissed her again. The tenderness of it melted her heart. Keanan had leashed his hunger, attempting to prove to her that he was worthy of her gift. "Only for me, when we are alone like this, will you free your hair from combs and jewels?"

"If you like."

Elated, he slipped his right hand underneath her mane and cupped the back of her head, drawing her mouth to his. He suckled her lower lip. Draping one arm over his shoulder, she wiggled closer. He moaned at her movements. Needing to deepen their kiss, his tongue boldly pushed into her mouth. Before she could question the action, his tongue swirled against hers, enticing her to return his torment. Pleasure frothed through her. Hesitantly, she copied his movements. A low growl rumbled in his chest at her tentative probing of his mouth. Crushing her to him, his arm became an unyielding truss.

"Not enough," he mumbled. "Closer."

She kissed the small indentation of his chin. "Yes."

Wynne clung to him as his fingers worked the glass buttons down the center back of her gown. He was a quarter of the way down before impatience overruled caution. Muttering an apology, he tore open the back, sending a shower of tiny glass buttons clattering around them.

She expelled a nervous choke of laughter at the destruction of her gown. "Beast. How ever will I travel home now that you have ruined my gown?"

Keanan's feral grin did little to relieve her concerns. "Perhaps I have no intention of sending you home." Seizing the melon sleeves, he pulled the gown to her waist. "I could keep you naked at my side, drugged by my kisses. Aye, the idea has merit." He turned her in his lap so he could give his complete attention to the laces of her corset. "Infernal trappings."

Awareness tingled just beneath the surface of her skin.

Her body had never felt so animated, as if she could divorce her mind and body into separate entities. Liberated now from the corset, blood rushed into her constricted torso. Studying Keanan's grim determination, she knew he would not be content until his hands had uncovered every barrier. Still respectably covered from the waist down, she crossed her arms over her breasts, covering what the sheer chemise revealed. "There is an imbalance that needs remedying." She looked pointedly at his coat.

Keanan shrugged out of it. A few buttons undone, and his waistcoat was discarded. "I would rather be undressing you," he complained affably.

Wynne could not help responding to the wicked gleam in his eyes. The man's very nature tempted her in ways she had never contemplated. His expression all but begged her to join him in his mischievous love play. Deciding her protective stance was denying her what she truly wanted, she reached out to untie his cravat. She had never undressed a man before, and her first effort felt clumsy.

Keanan's fascination with her own body did not help her concentration. His finger idly traced one areola through her chemise, and then the other. Each breast swelled and tautened from his rapt attention.

Wynne unwound the long cloth from his neck and was pleased to see only three buttons on his shirt. The slight tremor in her fingers forced her to focus on her own task.

"Permit me, sweet lady."

She jumped at his voice, immediately withdrawing. He tugged the ends of his shirt trapped in his breeches and pulled the garment over his head.

He was beautiful. Years of labor and fighting had sculpted his muscles to masculine perfection. Her fingers touched his defined collarbone and trailed over the hard slope of his shoulder. Intrigued by the triangle of brown hair on his flat abdomen, she petted him and was delighted when he shuddered. Moving her hand lower to the buttoned flap on his breeches, his hand gripped her wrist.

"Not yet. I'll last longer if they remain in place until the last."

Bewildered, she frowned. "What are you prolonging?"

He groaned, placing a kiss at her temple. "Such an innocent." He untied the strings to her petticoats at her waist. "You deserve pleasuring, Wynne. Only my best. I need my wits to make that happen." He pulled her chemise out of her petticoats and was prepared to draw it over her head when she stopped him.

"So?"

He snorted in disbelief. "So, my sweet damson, how can I see to my task when your hands are stroking me like I was made from the finest pelt, and your greedy, hungry eyes are begging me to fill you!" To quiet her questions, he distracted her by removing her chemise and tossing it away.

"Stand up," he commanded hoarsely, helping her to her feet in case she tarried.

Unfettered, her gown and petticoats slid over the flare of her hips to puddle at her feet. She was nude except for her knee-high white silk stockings and her slippers. Staring at her abandoned gown, she fought the urge to drop down and retrieve it.

Her gaze flashed over Keanan's face at the unexpected low, soughing rumble deep in his throat. His teeth were clenched, the muscles in his neck corded in restraint. He had fallen on his knees; his hands were fisted on his thighs. The only part of him he allowed freedom was his gaze. With an intensity that would have frightened her in any other situation, he examined every part of her, committing her to memory. Striking his fist on his thigh, he swore and looked away. Suddenly ashamed, she plunged down to retrieve her clothing.

"No!"

His tortured demand startled her, causing tears to drench

her lashes. He wrenched her hands away from the fabric and hauled her to him by maintaining a steely grip on both her hands.

"Release me."

Mute with regret, he shook his head. Certain of his strength, his left hand slid to her lower back. Tilting her chin up to his waiting lips, he sank deeply into the kiss. It ended with a claiming sweep of his tongue, leaving her with the taste of him.

"Stay." His voice was as stark as his expression. "I thought—" He lowered his head and kissed her breast. A jolt of awareness burst within her. "I am not noble, Wynne. I thought I could offer you pleasure then turn you loose, hiding my baser needs from you. You deserve a proper aristocratic lover, a man who can—"

He looked up when her hands caged the sides of his head. "I choose you. I have bared my body and heart to you, something I have never done for any man." It was strange. When Keanan faltered, she found strength giving them both courage. "Men do not believe women are capable of true desire. They are fools. I feel, Keanan." She clasped a hand over her heart. "I need. All I want to do is press you to me, wishing I—" Defenseless, she closed her eyes, realizing how inadequate her words sounded.

A feather-light kiss on her eyelids opened them. She saw the joy in his eyes before it formed on his lips. The shadows were not completely gone from his eyes, but her admission had assuaged the guilt for taking something from her that he had decided he did not deserve.

Her arms curled around his neck. Keanan scooped her up and reverently lowered her to the floor. Meeting her steady gaze, he unbuttoned his breeches. He sat down to remove his shoes and stockings. Instead of stripping off his breeches as she had expected, he knelt at her side. Fingers grazing her thigh, he untied each garter and slid her stockings down, discarding them with her slippers.

Stretching out beside her, he placed his hand on her quivering stomach. The heat of his hand radiated down to the bone. He rolled toward her, his mouth claiming hers. A rush of excitement swamped her, reminding her of their first kisses before the noble nature he denied possessing dulled his ardor. She returned the kiss he had initiated, arching her body against him. The hand on her stomach shifted lower. She had not been aware of its progress until his fingers glided between the feminine folds of her sex. His calloused fingers, slick with her desire, rubbed the small nub protected within. Wynne moaned, her hips rising higher to meet his touch. Anticipating her demand, his finger sank within her, breaching the depths that would make him her lover.

"Keanan." His name was a whisper compared to the raging passion taking control of her body.

His head lifted. Their gazes met. His was triumphant while hers was glazed and needy. Latching on to her breast, he suckled, splintering her with pleasure. As he quickened the movements of his fingers, a pulse flared to life within her. Clasping his head, she bucked under his ministrations, knowing she would die if he did not . . .

There.

The energy building inside her winked to a pinpoint, then exploded into a million shards of starlight. She convulsed, a silent cry hissing through her clenched teeth. As she became conscious of her surroundings again, she focused on Keanan's face. He acted as if she had slapped him when unwanted tears filled her eyes.

"Did I hurt you?"

"No, no." Her head moved side to side, causing the tears to leak down her temples into her hair. "What did you do? I have never felt . . . it—it was extraordinary!"

"Really," he said, some of his former male arrogance leaching into the word. "Extraordinary, eh?"

"Arrogant swine." She gave him a shove, finally recalling he had yet to remove his breeches. Her hand captured the impressive bulge, making him groan. "What of you? Do you want—?"

"Aye, I want, and I burn." He said it as if it were a curse. "I will stop. Leave you be, if that is your wish."

So he found the strength to be noble after all.

Wynne caught the edge of his breeches and tried pushing them down. Her position was all wrong to assist him. Keanan sat up on his knees and peeled the skintight breeches down and kicked them away.

Rising up on her elbows, she parted her lips in surprise. Gracious! She had seen sculptures of the nude male form; however, she never believed a living man could surpass the cool marble perfection of an artist's imagination. And there was simply more of him, she marveled, her gaze fixed on the portion of his anatomy he had just uncovered.

What had always seemed so understated in art jutted aggressively out from a nest of wiry dark hair. Sitting up, she reached out and petted him. The length of him was surprisingly smooth and hot. She glanced up at Keanan. He stood rigid, his eyes firmly shut as if enduring a great torment. The flesh in her hand bobbed, pressing against her hand, insisting that she continue her stroking.

Curiosity soon gave way to growing concern. He was too big. She had two married sisters who had explained the happenings between a man and woman. If what she had gleaned were true, he could not possibly fit.

"I should not have given you time to think, I see," he said, guiding her back into a prone position with the length of his body. "Your face has lost its rosy glow, Wynne."

The hot length of his manhood pushed persistently into her inner thigh. The lingering effects of his earlier pleasuring faded with her increasing fear of the pain she would endure.

Keanan kissed her forehead. "Pain is the last thing I would have you feel," he said, accurately reading her thoughts. Moving lower, he kissed her nose, and then her mouth.

Gradually, she relaxed. His relentless tender assault on her mouth rekindled the waning flame of passion. Soon she was initiating the engaging tongue play he had used to seduce her. Using his fingers, he traced inflaming circles over her breasts and abdomen. Just beneath the surface, her stomach muscles clenched when his hand moved lower, her body already anticipating the astonishing release only he could awaken.

Testing her readiness, he groaned when proof of her desire coated his fingers. Shifting, he nudged a space for himself between her legs. Hooking her hands into his, he locked them over her head, holding them with his weight. His eyes, intense and nearly black, enthralled her. "No more waiting. I cannot stand being apart from you."

A roll of his narrow hips, and the rigid length of him unerringly found its dewy mark. Sweat beaded on his forehead and shoulders, and his eyes held hers as the pressure built, his body demanding access to hers. Keanan rocked his hips; the bulbous head of his manhood, slathered with her wetness, sank deeper.

Wynne sucked in her breath. He was barely inside her and she already was feeling stretched beyond her body's capabilities. She wiggled her hips as Keanan had done, hoping to ease the discomfort.

"Christ!" he muttered, releasing one of her hands to cup her buttocks. He pulled out, only to plunge completely into her, forcing her hips to meet his decisive thrust. They both cried out at the joining.

Keanan gave her no time to contemplate the stinging fullness of his penetration. His head pressed into her shoulder; he moved in and out of her like a man possessed. A gush of liquid anointed his rigid length, quickening his thrusts. Warmth expanded in her pelvis. The initial ache of their joining lessened, and new sensations seem to flow from him into her. She lifted her hips, attempting to meet his demanding thrusts. Keanan raised his head.

"Wynne."

Her name burst out of him, the feelings behind his meaning were too much to analyze. The kiss he pressed to her mouth was tense and desperate. Turning his head to the side, he drove himself as deep as she could take him and froze. For endless seconds, he did not even breathe. The hot pulse of his seed flooded her womb before he raggedly inhaled. Still joined, Keanan collapsed, giving her his full weight.

Wynne rather liked the feel of him on top of her. He felt solid. Safe. She sighed, noting the subtle changes to her body. Sated, his softening manhood nestled inside her. She clenched her inner muscles, trying to hold him in place. Her eyes widened when the softened flesh twitched.

Keanan laughed, almost dislodging himself completely. Propping himself up on his arms, he looked down at her. His eyelids drooped lazily, making him appear too satisfied with his present situation. She smiled, realizing she was responsible for his present arrogance.

"You have bewitched me, Wynne. And my cock. I confess we're both restless whenever you are about."

Thrusting gently, he tested the strength of her enchantment. She wrapped her arms around him, tugging him closer. Their physical rapture only heightened her love for him. If this was truly magic, she prayed it would last a lifetime.

Thirteen

Where was she?

Keanan stalked down Bond Street, ignoring the exclusive shops and their impressive inventories meant to entice the fashionable. His gaze skimmed over each approaching female, immediately dismissing them from his mind when they turned out not to be the lady he planned to encounter accidentally.

A fortnight had passed since Keanan had brought Wynne to his house. Aunt Moll's matchmaking had given them both a chance to explore their mutual attraction. Never had he dared contemplate that the lady would freely offer what he secretly coveted: affection as well as her luscious body.

Weeks later, he was still reeling from the aftermath. She had professed that she loved him, but he had tried not to allow the words to creep into his heart. Women had whispered those words to him before, more aware of their power than he, when he was younger and craved such devotion.

Perhaps, speaking them aloud had given Wynne an excuse to throw away her virginity on a man who could never be her equal. A lady, a real lady, would need a justification to bolster her courage when she faced her proper aristocratic husband on their wedding night. He did not blame her. Like all things in his life, Keanan knew Wynne's presence was transitory. If she did not end their affair, then her family would.

"Milroy!"

Dutch ambled toward him; his size and less-than-fashionable attire earned him a few rude stares from the people he pushed past.

"Where have you been hiding? For weeks there hasn't been a glimpse of you at the Court, nor any of your old haunts. Blanche Chabbert has asked after you. She said you have been avoiding the Silver Serpent." They stepped into the opening of a deserted alley, out of the way of the pedestrian traffic.

Keanan leaned against a brick wall, stifling the guilt he felt at abandoning an old friend. With each step he took toward the new life he had planned out, the further removed he seemed to be from his boxing past. "I have been working on my house," he said rather defensively, hoping Dutch would take the hint and quit pushing at him.

Dutch's grayish-blue eyes narrowed. Smelling weakness, he ruthlessly pressed onward. "You've been dallying with that fancy mort your brother pants after, haven't you?" His despairing groan echoed between the brick walls. He jammed his hand through his unruly patch of salted black hair. "Tell me, any prigging done was limited to your nocturnal whimsies?"

"I do not consider it any business of yours," he coolly replied.

The older man seemed oblivious to the dangerous edge he traversed. "Oh, you brainless merry-begotten fool!" he roared. "This is no well-ridden quim you can plow and then walk away, a few coins less for your trouble."

Blind anger rose, blotting out his civilized veneer. He charged, seizing the edges of his friend's brown waistcoat. Despite the fact that Dutch outweighed him by several stone, he managed to lift him off his feet and slam him into the opposing brick wall. "It isn't like that. Speak one filthy word in her name again and I'll break your good wrist." He shoved him again, reinforcing his point before releasing his hold.

Using the wall for support, Dutch rubbed his chest. "You might as well cut your own heart out and toss it in the Thames, Milroy, if you think the *lady* will be choosing you over your brother. No matter her heart, duty trumps love for their kind."

Keanan wiped the sweat from his forehead, using the sleeve of his coat. He did not need the older man's opinions on love when he had his own demons whispering in his ear. Hell, he had enough brains to understand that love was the idyllic dream idiots and romantics strove to capture. If his time with Wynne was an illusion, then all he wanted was a little more time to enjoy it.

"I didn't seek her out for love, Dutch," he spat, not certain which one of them he was reminding.

The bitterness in his voice took the residual anger out of his friend. He checked the street; they were invisible to the passing fashionable.

"Well." Dutch blew out the word. Crossing his arms, his contemplative expression focused on Keanan. "My sympathies to the lady, then. Ruining her will certainly make her unpalatable to your brother, and any other decent fellow who might consider her for a wife."

"She isn't ruined. Her family's wealth will keep her out of the streets," he growled, recalling how his mother had not been so fortunate.

"Still," Dutch drawled, preparing to twist the verbal blade he had already buried in Keanan's gut. "I hope you treated her with the courtesy you would have any tart, and spared her your mettle. No matter her wealth, breeding her lover's bastard will bury her."

Shamed, he turned away. He recalled the exquisite moment of climax. Instead of pulling out of her, instinct and obsession had overruled his common sense. Driving his cock deep enough to kiss her womb, his hot, spurting seed pumped into her body, not just once, but thrice. He had claimed her over and over, trying to sate himself. Only her increasing tenderness had halted him that night. The hunger even now remained. It was a living thing, growing more bestial the longer he was denied her.

Keanan scrubbed his face. Christ! A child. He had not thought, damn him. All he had focused on was her willing body, and her love. Love. Bloody hell. Self-preservation shut off the possibility. He backed away mentally from it, feeling stark terror. Their one night together had not been fruitful. He had lain with other women. No woman had ever claimed he had planted a babe in their belly. He clung to that revelation as if it was a talisman.

His silence was an answer in itself. Swearing, Dutch spat on the ground and walked away in disgust.

"How fortuitous, Wynne, I came upon you this afternoon," Brook said after they were seated within Ferry Hill, a small, natty public house intent on luring the patronage of rich when they had tired of shopping. "Walking about unescorted"—she made a disapproving sound—"I marvel at your boldness. My lord would have sent me off to the country if he had caught me at the deed."

Wynne silently agreed, recalling her last conversation with Lord A'Court. He was a man who prided himself on his sense of propriety. A lady under his hand would be forced to bend to his will, or be broken. Regrettably, she had encountered scores of such men.

"Scarcely boldness, Brook. Both my maid and footman are attending me." She could never reveal to her friend the true daring of her outing.

Somewhere, Keanan walked the nearby streets searching for her. To both of their frustration, conducting a discreet affair in town was more challenging than either had imagined. Maneuvering accidental meetings without alerting her family or stirring gossip required strategic skills neither of them could claim. Now she understood Tipton's haste to wed her sister. These constant interruptions and foiled plans were wearing on Keanan's temper. Even so, what could she have done? Once Brook had sighted her from her carriage, Wynne could not think of an excuse to break off their encounter.

"Still," her friend continued, "considering Nevin is close to making an offer, it would be prudent to restrain your natural enthusiasm for life and adhere to the demure womanly qualities a gentleman expects in his lady wife."

"What tripe!" Wynne gaped, surprised at the preaching nonsense she had just heard. Their friendship spanned many years. Brook's lesser standing might have forced her to heed closely society's dictates, and yet she had never before condemned others who were not as perfect.

"I would refuse any man who insisted I behave as a paragon. It sounds like a cold life, both in and out of the marriage bed."

The mention of marriage intimacies was too much for her friend. A cherry stain washed over her entire face. Putting her hand over her mouth, she broke several of her precious rules, by sobbing into her palm. Copious tears overflowed her eyes and then coursed down her cheeks. Never had Wynne felt so heartless. Rising and moving over to her distressed friend's side, she sat beside her, attempting to shield her from the curious.

"I meant no offense, Brook," she murmured, pitching her voice low and soothing. "Our father has raised us to speak forthrightly, and sometimes I forget to temper my opinions."

Brook vigorously shook her head, taking the handkerchief Wynne pressed into her hand up to her eyes. She dabbed at her tears. "You are not to blame. That is not why I—" She shuddered, finally gaining control over her upset. "I find myself weeping at the strangest circumstances. I am told it is due to the babe."

"A babe!" Delighted by the news, Wynne squeezed her friend's hands. "How wonderful for you! Lord A'Court must be thrilled."

"We have been wed too long for him to expect anything less."

She frowned slightly at the moody comment, but dismissed it like the tears as part of the nature of her delicate condition. Her sisters had suffered similar bouts of melancholy. Sympathetic, Wynne hugged Brook, unprepared for her visible flinch and painful cry.

"You are hurt." Ignoring Brook's protestations, she pushed up her sleeve. Ugly bruising mottled the flesh she exposed. "What happened?"

"D-do not tell Lyon," she begged, shoving the sleeve back into place. "It was an accident. J-just an accident."

"You fell?"

Wobbly, nodding her head, she explained, "One of the maids left a pile of linen on the stairs—"

"Brook!" Wynne did not need all the harrowing details to imagine the tragic possibilities.

"I am quite unhurt. The babe is unharmed." Clutching her reticule in an unyielding grip, she leaned forward, her eyes beseeching. "I beg you. Do not tell Lyon. If he should learn . . ." her voice trailed off, keeping her concerns to herself.

Wynne doubted such bruising could be concealed from a husband, she thought, recalling the intimacy she had shared with Keanan. Not an inch of her had escaped his attention. Lord A'Court would certainly tend after his wife. Since she did not want to upset Brook further, her thoughts remained unspoken. "I have no desire to stand between you and your husband." Her friend sagged against the back of the chair at the promise. "I do insist on seeing you home. You should be in bed, not jostled about in a carriage."

The pathetic gratefulness she saw in Brook's gaze made her feel terrible.

"You are so right. It is so kind of you to look after me. I consider you my closest, most treasured friend, Wynne."

While awaiting the A'Court carriage, she instructed her

footman, Inch and her maid, Milly, to follow behind them in the family carriage. The wind and passing traffic billowed their skirts. Both ladies fussed, smoothing their skirts back into place.

When she glanced up, Wynne noticed Keanan standing across the street. He did not greet her. With his back propped against a storefront brick wall, she sensed his gaze was focused on her. She longed to rush over and explain why she was abandoning him. However, publicly acknowledging him brought its own troubles, and Brook needed her now.

Two opposing phaetons crossed on the street between them, breaking their stare. Before it had passed, Keanan was already adjusting his hat and walking away. Brook's carriage halted in front of them, blocking his departure.

Wynne ascended after her friend, her mind already repeating the silent exchange with Keanan. Not able to resist, she glanced back, only to be disappointed he was gone. Nibbling at the glove seam of her first finger, she settled into the cushioned seat. From her limited experience, loving this arrogant, complicated man made her vacillate from euphoria to despair. She wondered if she would ever find her balance. Sighing, she tried to focus on calming her friend. It looked as if Brook was not the only one battling melancholy.

Sipping his favorite brandy, Sir Thomas Bedegrayne enjoyed the nightly routine. Since the death of his beloved Anna, he had sought solace in his clubs. There, he could find a hot meal waiting for him, companionship if he welcomed it, and opportunities to occupy his mind.

The demands of his family had dwindled as his children had grown. His heir, Brock, had given in to his restlessness and sailed off to India. Irene had married Sutton years ago and was happily making grandbabies for him. Nyle, his and Anna's changeling, had vanished from England years ago. He always felt the weight of his years when he recalled that his parting words to his second son were spoken in anger. He thoughtfully sipped his brandy and grieved.

Shrugging off the ill humor, his thoughts drifted to his youngest daughter, Devona. With more pluck than a weary papa could bear, she was thankfully Tipton's concern. He chuckled to himself, the memories of Devona's past mischief flickering through his mind. His gel would prevent Tipton from becoming too staid in his newly acquired respectability.

No, he no longer fretted over his youngest daughter. Rather, the one daughter he had considered the most sensible and the least trouble concerned him. He blamed himself. Anna's death had shaken him. Adrift in his private grief, it had taken him years to notice how Wynne had quietly assumed her mother's position in the household. Despite her youth, she had eased her siblings' hurts, shared their confidences, and created order in their household. Or at least she had tried to keep his grieving, motherless brood together until their father had figured out how he was going to survive without his beloved wife.

Now it was Wynne who needed him, whether or not she desired his interference. He had sensed trouble the day Milroy walked into his house and insolently told him he was taking his gel. His grip tightened on the glass of brandy. Randy buck! By God, he would face him at dawn if he touched his gentle, beautiful daughter.

Arrogant, intelligent, stubborn, and dismissive to the fashionable sway, this blue-eyed rake possessed many of the qualities he wished in a man for his Wynne, and yet he was marked by the taint of scandal. No amount of wealth and fame would wash away the lad's disgrace. Thomas had been curious enough to do some digging into Milroy's past, and the results had been fascinating. Nevertheless, trouble was following his gel, and if he were a wagering man, he would bet every coin he owned that this fighter was responsible.

"Bedegrayne. My apologies for being late."

One bushy brow lifted as he invited his companion to join him. "I'm a forgiving man, Reckester, when I need to be," he cryptically remarked, wondering again how far his sweet gel had fallen into the deep play of the Reckester warfare.

Reckester slumped into the chair, wishing he were less sober. Returning home and confessing failure to his wife forced him to ply caution when confronting this man.

He had never considered Bedegrayne part of his elite circle of friends. The man's blunt manner of speaking, not to mention his delivery, had always been wearing on his ears. Then there were the man's eyes. Like his speech, the blue-green stare he pinned his victims with was cold as a winter sea. He was one of the few people who intimidated him, although a few glasses of whatever spirits were at hand would ease the discomfort.

"Your note stated an urgent purpose to our meeting."

Perhaps directness had its own advantage. The quicker said, the sooner he could have the drink he craved. "I thought it was time we chatted, since my son has finally settled on your Wynne. My wife believes his interest is returned. Between the two of us, I think we can come to terms and post the banns. I am certain you recall the anticipation of the marriage bed?" The only lust ruling him these days was his portion of the Bedegrayne wealth.

"Which son?"

His mouth was already working before the meaning of the succinct question had sunk into his brain. Old sins had surfaced faster than expected, and yet, they were manageable. "I have one true son."

"And two who court my Wynne, Reckester." Bedegrayne leaned closer, his unblinking gaze locked on his own. "What kind of game are your lads playing?"

"None," he blurted out, stunned at the sudden turn of the

conversation. "Drake is the only blood I claim, the one I offer to your daughter."

"Milroy has your stamp. Do you deny him?"

Reckester slouched deeper into his seat, idly tapping a tattoo on the table with his fingers. He had never had any grievance against his bastard son. Rae's fury at his existence had prevented him from ever claiming him. Even so, he could not help but feel pride at the young man's success. Despite his wife's threats, he had been tolerant of his son's presence in town, as long as he did not interfere with his sire's interests. Unfortunately, Milroy had just crossed purposes with him.

"Milroy is a regrettable complication from my reckless youth," he brusquely admitted. "I doubt a man in your position would consider marrying off your daughter to my backdoor son whose mother was nothing more than an Irish whore."

He took Bedegrayne's silence as concurrence.

Reckester grimly smiled, sensing he had gained the upper hand again. "Milroy isn't a concern. If you caught him sniffing after your daughter, I would be surprised if you had not already run him off."

"I did."

His smile grew broader, more sincere in approval. "Good. Good. So all we have to do is work out the details for bringing our offspring together."

"Not quite," Bedegrayne drawled, his eyes taking on the glint of a ruthless pirate who would rather kill than share his hoard of gold. "There are too many bastards in your line, Reckester. I'm still picking them out as I go along."

Lothbury tapped him on the shoulder. Murmuring his apologies to the gentlemen who had engaged him in a spirited debate about which training enhanced a pugilist's skills, Keanan followed his friend into an outer hall.

"Is she here?"

The marquess sighed. His expression eloquently bespoke his reluctance. "Yes. While I have not sighted the lady myself, I was told her arrival was announced over an hour ago. Milroy, is this wise? Surely there are other ladies who draw your attention?"

Casting a look in all directions to make certain their conversation was private, he said, "No amount of discretion on your part has concealed your interest in the fair Miss Bedegrayne. That particular lady is under the protection of several fractious albeit absent brothers, a quarrelsome father, and a rather nasty brother-in-law. And let us not forget the enemies you will gain if you are the one to melt the ice maiden's reluctance. Agh—" Lothbury choked.

The strong hold Keanan had on the man's cravat forced him to take a leap forward or be strangled. He immediately released him, and to anyone passing by, it appeared he had rescued his friend from a dangerous tumble.

"I, too, can be rather fractious, quarrelsome, and utterly nasty if I hear any further speculation about my association with Miss Bedegrayne, or any comment besmirching her character," he vowed, keeping the violence that had flared barely restrained. "Am I clear?"

More embarrassed than hurt Lothbury coughed. Trying blindly to fix his wrinkled cravat, he muttered, "You are crazed. If it is not the woman, then it is bad blood. Either way, I envision a ruinous end for you, my friend." Cursing in French, his hands fell away in disgusted surrender. "These bloody knots are spoiled once you touch them."

"Hold still," Keanan commanded. In lieu of an apology, he put order to his friend's fancy knot.

Perhaps he was a bit crazed. He could not explain away his growing urgency to be near Wynne. His temper soured with every day he was denied her. By day, he plotted ways to see her, and at night she tormented him in his dreams. He awoke each dawn sweat-drenched and longing for her.

Never had his feelings for a woman brought him to such extremes of ecstasy and despair. It left him feeling hollow and in pain. He feared the power she held over him. Still, walking away from her seemed impossible.

"I think I improved it," Keanan joked, earning him a chuckle from his friend.

Lothbury sobered, saying, "Forget your dalliance with Miss Bedegrayne. We could slip off to my clubs, or one of the taverns near the docks if you feel like using your hands for more than lifting a tankard."

Keanan shook his head. His body already thrummed with the excitement of seeing her again. By wit or by scandal, he intended to steal her away.

"We received a letter from Brock this week," Wynne said to Amara.

The air was intolerable, despite all the doors and windows that had been flung open to offer some respite to the guests. The women rejected the notion of dancing and had instead found solace in the drawing room with a few other ladies. A slight draft wafted from the open doors that led to the unlit garden, so they had chosen seating close to the elusive coolness.

Wearing pale-blue silk this evening, she complimented Amara's choice of embroidered amber crepe. They sat in companionable silence, listening to the chatter around them. Soothing, joyful music echoed in the distance, reminding them of what awaited should they decided to join the others.

She was contemplating how to reintroduce the topic of her brother again, when Amara solved her dilemma. "I suppose your brother will move on to another exotic locale once he tires of India." Her lips compressed into a thin, disapproving line.

"I do not believe so."

The need to defend and explain surged through Wynne.

She stifled it behind a tight smile. Brock's decision to leave England had caused discord within the family. Papa thought it was restlessness; Devona, the desire for adventure; and Irene assumed her wastrel brother was shirking his responsibilities. Only Wynne had understood fully the demons driving her brother, though he had extracted her promise to remain silent on the matter before he had departed.

"I suspect he has missed England and longs to come home."

Amara's eyes flashed with unexpected anger. Her fanning reflected her agitation. "Sir Thomas is too tolerant. Your brother will only return, wasting his life in drink and the gaming hells."

And why do you care so much? Her promise stopped her from speaking the words aloud. Wynne was not clear on the depth of her friend's feelings for her brother, or the relationship between them. Nor was it her business. Whatever their differences, she hoped they had a chance to resolve them.

"Ladies," Lord A'Court greeted them. Brook was at his side, tucked protectively in his embrace. The pale pink satin she wore emphasized the high color in her cheeks. Murmuring a greeting, she appeared demure and fragile. Considering her delicate condition, Wynne was surprised Brook was feeling up to an evening out. Regardless, just as Wynne had hoped, the earl was looking after his wife.

"Miss Bedegrayne, please accept my gratitude for your compassion toward my wife the other day."

She hesitated, wondering what Brook had told him. Yesterday she had pleaded not to speak of her accident. Her expression revealed nothing as she met her friend's anxious gaze. "There is no need for gratitude between friends, my lord."

"Nonsense. Accompanying my wife home when she complained of dizziness was very generous." Taking her hand up without permission, he brushed a light kiss across her knuckles. Gray eyes flecked with blue glittered appreciatively in the candlelight. "Your servant, Miss Bede-grayne." He nodded to Amara. "Miss Claeg. We must beg your pardon, ladies. We have not yet spoken to our host. Come, my dear."

Lord A'Court tenderly cuddled his wife to his side. His devotion to his lady was apparent and enviable. Glancing at Amara, Wynne noticed her expression was wistful, too.

Brook looked back before they had crossed the threshold. She held Wynne's gaze, and then they were gone.

"What was that all about?"

She shrugged, assuming Amara was referring to the earl's excessive gallantry. "The man obviously adores his wife. He was just grateful."

"Hmm." Her friend did not seem convinced. She expelled an embellished sigh. "You are truly wicked, Miss Bede-grayne. Enamoring married gentlemen with your saintly deeds."

"A vain execution if you ask me. What use do I have for a married man if I cannot claim his title or his purse?"

Amara, indulging in a little wickedness, leaned closer and whispered what she could claim. Both ladies sagged into each other, giggling.

They were still laughing when the Marquess of Lothbury approached them. He formally greeted them, his eyes silently persuading them to share their jest. Nothing short of torture would ever gain a confession.

"Miss Claeg, would you grant me a dance?"

Amara looked askance at Wynne, who nodded her encouragement. "I would be honored, my lord."

With their departure, Wynne rose, moving outside to enjoy the cooler air. Rough hands seized her, dragging her deeper into the darkness. A hand clamped over her mouth, cutting off her scream.

"Stop kicking. It's me," Keanan whispered in her ear. He spun her into an embrace.

Too outraged, she punched him in the shoulder. "You daft donkey! I was so frightened I almost fainted."

"Not you, my sweet damson," he protested, chuckling when she bit his hand. "Your pluck bests most men." He tugged her deeper into the night.

Her fury receding, she whispered, "I cannot just wander off. My friend—"

"Miss Claeg is too enchanted by Lothbury's charm and attentiveness. I doubt she will give you a thought for at least two hours."

The cold calculatedness of the plan slowed her progress. "I will not have Amara hurt because of your . . . ah, eagerness for privacy."

Even in the darkness she sensed his grin. "No fretting, Wynne. Lothbury genuinely enjoys the lady's company. Allow them their flirtation while you enjoy my . . . ah, eagerness."

Choking on laughter, her hand clasped in his, they ran away from the house. "You must have the eyes of a cat."

"I confess, I feel like a beast when I am around you." He steadied her. "There are several steps. Have a care." He guided her up three stone steps.

"I overheard our hostess, Mrs. Hazell, discussing a new addition to her gardens. What is this? A temple?"

"The Temple of Virtue," he intoned, his low voice rebounding off the walls of the circular marble-columned structure.

"Be serious."

He nudged her through the arched doorway using the thrust of his hips. "I tend to get serious where you're involved. Want to be my sacrifice?"

"I have been kidnapped by a madman," she laughingly complained, wincing at her echo. "Someone is going to discover us, you know. We should go back to the house."

She heard the rustle of clothing. The back of her knees came up against a stone bench when she took a step backward. "Keenan? 'Tis unsettling being here. I feel like I am floundering in a pool of ink."

"There is nothing to fear."

His hands unerringly found her waist and hauled her up against him. The solid contact of his chest, hip, and legs molded to hers was reassuring. "Woman, I have missed you."

She felt his fingers trail up the bodice of her gown, over the swell of her breast, and ever so lightly along the length of her neck. Capturing her chin, he lifted her mouth to his. Their kiss was one of remembrance. It was an affirmation. She used her tongue, teasing him, and was pleased by his frustrated growl. His hand slid down, cupping her breast. He literally vibrated with restraint when his thumb caressed her sensitive cresting flesh not bound by corset.

"I have waited too long for this," he rasped, claiming another kiss.

Despite the darkness, vibrant colors filled her vision. Lethargy stole her strength as the colors seemed to swirl downward and pool into her loins. Wynne pressed closer, recalling the last time she had felt this way.

"No," she moaned, kissing his jaw. "Not here. We risk too much." He had removed his coat. Unable to resist, she unfastened several buttons on his shirt and slipped her hand inside. His chest muscles quivered at the contact.

"It is just us, Wynne." He took her hands and brought them to the buttons at his waist. "The ball does not exist here." Together, they unfastened his breeches. "No rules. Just the blessed night, weaving its magic over lovers." They swayed hip to hip, lost in a hypnotic dance.

Her body craved what he was offering. Every nerve in her body begged for the release only his touch could provide. Still, she tried to resist. "My gown," she said weakly.

Understanding her concern, he said, "There are different ways for pleasuring, and not all require the removal of all our clothing. Even if the notion is difficult to resist."

"Keanan."

"I'm a crazed man, Wynne." Bumping against the bench, he straddled it and pulled her within reach. "The days . . ." Gliding masculine hands moved under the yards of skirt and petticoat, seeking her legs. "Seeing you, but never being able to touch."

She could hear his displeasure, the days of loneliness and denial of his need. Fabric streamed over his arms as his fingers sought the heart of her. The air felt cooling against her steaming flesh. When he found her, she gasped, still unprepared for the rush of desire she felt.

"I am not alone in this," he murmured, nuzzling his face into her abdomen. Like a hidden spring, her body responded, moistening his demanding fingers with the nectar he hungered after. "So perfect. I cannot wait. Don't make me wait."

Her skirts fell back into place when he jerked away from her. Bereft of his stroking, she counted his rapid breaths as he struggled with his breeches.

"Come to me."

She stilled, too unskilled to understand his request. With a muffled sound of impatience, he clawed at her skirts, yanking her forward. Burying his hands under her skirts again, he effortlessly lifted her by the hips. Suddenly weightless in the blackness, she clung to him, trusting he would provide safe purchase. Keanan wrapped her legs around him, settling her in his lap. Proof of his need and readiness pressed against her soft, dewy curls.

There was something heady about this wickedness, the risk of being caught. She should want to push him away and run back toward the house before someone questioned her absence. It was Keanan, being enfolded in his embrace that coaxed her to forget the rules and the person she was raised to be. In his arms, she found acceptance and the joy of discovery. There also was a kind of power in their joining. Her lover was as vulnerable as she, trapped by the intricate threads of awareness, intimacy, and love. If he could have seen her face, he would have seen this knowledge burning in her eyes, sensing that it mirrored his own.

Keanan's thoughts were focused on one carnal purpose: possession. Lifting her higher, he positioned her and guided the head of his cock to her welcoming feminine portal. She melted, her flesh yielding to his penetration. Half buried in her gown, his arms tightened around her waist. His arousal flexed inside her, demanding the slick impetus that would catapult them beyond their world, allowing them to forget their differences.

"Move on me," he begged, kissing her exposed breasts.

"L-like this?"

She rocked against his pelvis, and the constrictive pressure of her sheath almost wrung out his release.

"Uh," he gulped. "More like this." Holding her slender hips in his hands, he demonstrated the motion destined to drive them both insane.

She repeated the action, almost killing him. "Better?"

"Aye," he said; sparks of light exploded beneath his closed eyelids. "I'm fond of repetitive exercise. Best for getting the move right."

Wynne moved, adding a roll to her hip when she came back down on him. If he could have spoken, he would have complimented her inventiveness. His creative goddess rubbed her corseted torso up and down him making his fingers itch to tear off the offending barriers. Keanan wanted her naked, their limbs tangled while he suckled her breasts. He wanted to mark her body with his mouth and his scent. What remaining sanity he possessed forced him to accept the restrictions to their lovemaking. With her womanly fragrance teasing his nostrils, he was too hungry for regrets.

He kept his hands on her, but it was Wynne who set their pace. Her lithe body hammered down on his, increasing their building tension. In the blackness, she was the center of his existence. She claimed all his senses, and he ached to give her more. Crushing his mouth to hers, his tongue plundered her. She did not submit to his unspoken command. Instead, she met him as an equal, her tongue and body mated with his until he was certain a man could die from such intense pleasuring.

Lost in passion, all her concerns were forgotten. She cried out when she climaxed; the beautiful sound of her fulfillment echoed in the cylindrical chamber. Her fingers dug into his shoulders as she arched against him, the inner muscles of her sheath convulsing.

His body answered her siren's call. Any previous thoughts of pulling out of her were buried under millennia of primitive instinct. Thrusting upward, he cupped her buttocks in his splayed hands, forcing her to take him deeper. He bit her shoulder, smothering his strangled cry as his hot seed jetted into her womb.

Gasping for air, he rested his forehead on her shoulder. Now that the pleasuring had cleared his thoughts, ugly rationality resurfaced. He found it as annoying as the sweat trickling down his spine. "I lost my head again. It's a wicked travesty to my good sense, love. We're taking on more risks than we need to."

Even while he chastised his carelessness, his cock thickened and hardened within her. She laughed when he cursed. He plunged deeper, her silkiness proving her own insatiable appetite.

"You did claim to be a servant of repetitive exercise," she reminded him.

"And you, my damson, are my lady. I desire only to serve you."

Fourteen

Stripped down to a pair of rusty brown trousers, Keanan listened to the sound of hammers and the idle chatter of the workers emanating from within his house. From his vantage point in the back gardens as he exercised with a set of dumbbells, he stared at the house, his chest swelling with pride. There was more work to be done, certainly. Nevertheless, the house had been improved upon since he had brought Wynne to see it.

The drawing room where she had given him her innocence had been the first room he had seen completed. Learning she was partial to the color green, he had discarded the upholsterers' suggestion for bold yellow in that room and insisted the firm incorporate a soft, inviting green, which reminded him of her eyes. A man of simple refinements, he had found himself agreeing to elaborate drapery to cover the floor-to-ceiling windows, an Axminster carpet, its design a replica of antique sources, and furniture chosen to please the feminine eye rather than to accommodate the masculine frame.

Despite his reservations, the results were surprisingly agreeable. In his mind he could conjure an image of Wynne sitting by the fire, lost in the entertainment of a book. Lamentably, he had yet to think of a respectable excuse to lure the lady back to admire her influence.

Sweat dotted his chest and brow in the morning air as he raised the set of dumbbells over his head and leveled them to his chest. His fighting days might be finished, but his mind and body still demanded the training discipline.

"You've lost flesh in your arms, Milroy."

He nodded a greeting to Dutch. "Ballocks," he countered, repeating the motion with unflagging, straight thrusts.

"Impressive. You've kept up your form. Are you still running?"

"Fifteen miles at dawn."

His friend crossed his arms and leaned up against the trunk of a crabapple. "Training for a fight?"

"I told you, I'm finished with that life." He dropped the weights. Reaching for a towel, he mopped the moisture from his face and chest. He shrugged when Dutch's brows lifted. "You expect me to get fat and lazy in my retirement?"

"Not you, though it seems a shame to waste that physique on impressing the ladies." He ignored Keanan's disagreeing grunt. "You've a keen mind and a talent for business. There are plenty of fellows who'd pay well for your expertise."

Reaching for his shirt, he shook his head. "Let Jackson keep his reign over the amateurs. I haven't the tolerance for men who claim enthusiasm for the sport and yet would cry over a little spilt claret on their fine linen."

"I think you underestimate the young bloods."

"And you overrate my interest." He pulled his shirt over his head. "I had nothing when Chabbert found me except a strong instinct to survive. Fighting put food in my empty gut and gave me a dry place to sleep. For most men, that would have been enough. Good fortune and experience have granted me a chance to exceed my destiny."

"Bah, fancy plumage to disguise a spiteful word. Revenge. Or are you so caught up in your playacting and sporting the blunt that you've forgotten your less noble purpose."

No, he hadn't. It hovered between him and Wynne, sometimes blinding him like the sun. "Hungry? I've hired some staff. I've a cook now."

Choosing a tactful retreat, Dutch pushed off the tree trunk

and followed him up to the house. "Done up proper, with a sideboard of delicacies in the breakfast room?"

"Aye, and a footman to pour your coffee. And a butler to toss you out if you offend me."

Rubbing his hands together in anticipation to their meal, Dutch said, "Fair enough."

The new butler met them at the door. Wigget was in his late forties. A pugilist in his youth, he claimed to have defeated Sam Martin, the Bath Butcher, in the spring of 1787, only to lose his right eye in a drunken tavern brawl three weeks later. Age had softened his fighter's build and silvered his hair, but there was something in his direct, single-eyed gaze that warned the observer he was a man who still faced the world with his fists raised. Keanan had hired the man immediately.

"Mr. Milroy, a gentleman is inquiring after you. He awaits your invitation."

He did not need to pick the card up from the salver to recognize the distinct initials. "He must be more desperate than I had anticipated to be calling on his bastard," Keanan bitterly mused.

"Will you refuse him?"

Proving to himself that the card meant nothing to him, he picked it up while he contemplated Dutch's question. Several amusing daydreams played out in his mind, all involving his sire leaving, his command rejected. He crumpled the card and dropped it onto the salver.

"Wigget, bid His Grace to join me in the drawing room." Forestalling his friend's objection, he said, "Enjoy your meal without me. I would not deny my father his tender reconciliation."

Keanan chose the japanned high-back beechwood armchair for their confrontation. His fingers curled over the bold scrolled armrests, finding comfort in their rigidity. The day had come. The lecherous old rake considered it time to acknowledge his firstborn. He thought back to the thirteen-year-old boy who would have traded his soul for Reckester's favorable notice but had the door slammed in his face, all ties denied. Now, the duke was willing to deal with him. Alas, it was his misfortune; he would discover the boy had been much more amenable than the man.

Wigget entered the drawing room. The duke trailed impatiently in his wake. "Sir, His Grace, the Duke of Reckester."

Nerves he did not know he possessed churned just beneath the surface when eyes too disturbingly familiar met his. The look struck him like a punch. Masking the reaction, he said to his butler, "That will be all." He did not stand, nor did Reckester step closer to offer his hand. In the background, Wigget closed the door.

Each took a moment assessing the other. Deciding the advantage was his, Keanan inclined his head, gesturing to a nearby chair. Instead of coming closer, his sire picked the large jade tub chair opposite him. Majestic lions grinned at him from the regal mounts at the armrests.

"You honor me, Your Grace. Considering the hour and our uncomfortable connection, I never expected your card."

The older man flinched, the lines above his brow becoming more prominent at the realization that someone he considered beneath him would dare chastise him for his breach of etiquette. Shaking his head, he shifted in his seat. "That is Reckester blood pumping through your veins. I don't know why I assumed you would be any less mulish than your brother."

"Half-brother," Keanan coldly corrected. "I have never blurred the distinction. I wonder, why are you?"

"Such bitterness," Reckester lamented, removing his gloves. Grasping the pair in one hand, he playfully slapped them against his leg. "My handling of you has been, at best, deplorable. I blame myself, my wild youth. If I had been stronger, I might have been able to save your mother from her tragic end."

The anger itching just beneath his skin exploded into blazing fury at the mention of his mother. Like an unquenchable fire, it consumed his civility. All his muscles tensed, poised to spring and attack.

"What outcome did you expect, Your Grace? You abandoned her. Unprotected, penniless, and stripped of her respectability because she had borne your bastard, she was tossed into the streets. Your actions denied her any respectable means of support."

His calm, merciless delivery battered his sire as efficiently as if he had used his fists. What suspiciously could have been interpreted as guilt, flickered in the older man's gaze before he masked it. Keanan longed to unfurl his hands from the scrolled armrests and mold them around Reckester's neck, choking him until that indignant expression of his had changed to terror. It was almost worth facing the hangman's noose. Keeping his hands where they lay, he patiently awaited the man's sputtering outrage. Despite his loathed cognomen, he rarely realized his aspirations in that manner.

"O-of course, she twisted the tale, poisoning my son so she had her final revenge," the duke bellowed, his body quaking. "Aideen Milroy was a tempting, ambitious, inconsequential actress before I lifted her skirts. The skills she acquired from my tutelage only increased her worth."

Distantly, Keanan recognized the baiting of a desperate man. He fought back the urge to strike him down, to break him as his sire had once physically and spiritually destroyed his mother. If he put his hands on him now, he would kill him.

Reckester did not deserve swift punishment. The ghost of Aideen's rigid, beaten body lay prone, dividing them. Even now, her dull opened eyes haunted him. Fixed in shock, the animated spark of her soul had been forever extinguished by the heavy hand of a drunken benefactor wielding a cane. Keanan had dealt with her murderer years ago. It had taken patience and cunning to get close to the man who through his carelessness had executed his poor mother, sending her worn shell to reconcile with the vitality Reckester had destroyed.

"On the subject of my mother, there is only one detail you and I will ever agree upon, and that is, you are solely responsible for my mother's fate."

The silky menace threading through his calm facade must have finally alerted Reckester to the risks of challenging an angry son's memories of his mother. If it had given him an advantage, Keanan would have explained to his sire that his plan of attack was weak and futile. Time had not glossed over the flaws of his mother. Even so, he had loved her as much as she had allowed. It just had never been enough. The duke cleared his throat and glanced away from his son's unwavering, fuming stare.

"I have not sought you out to speak of your mother."

"Indeed," he agreed too pleasantly. "She was not worthy of your regard."

"Damn you, must you continue to bait me? When you have lived as long, will you be able to proclaim yourself guiltless of misdeeds?"

"No more than any other man."

The image of Wynne in his arms surfaced in his mind, distracting him. Her guileless face glowing with affection for him stirred the remorseful specter that had lately bedeviled him. Mercy. It was a feeling only she had been able to draw out of him, one he had never been able to afford. Not now, never for this man.

"Speak quickly, Reckester. My meal awaits, and reminding me of our connection disagrees with my digestion."

The duke stiffened in muted affront. "You have no notion of what I've come to offer you, Milroy. I wager a part of you has longed for this moment for a lifetime. It merits a few minutes of your attention."

"Come to welcome me into the family, Your Grace? The last time I knocked on your door, I had it slammed in my face."

"Forget the past!" the older man roared. His gaze flickered to the door. "I cannot alter history, but I can amend it. There are details"—he lowered his voice—"crucial ones, which can make a nobleman, a bastard. And a bastard—"

"A nobleman," Keanan whispered, almost afraid to speak the words aloud. He closed his eyes, hiding the pain and hope he felt. "You are telling me that you married my mother?"

"An impulsive action. I lov—" he swallowed the word, when Keanan's eyes snapped open, daring him to finish the lie. "I lusted after her. Aideen was the most beautiful woman I had ever encountered. There was only one way I could claim her, and I was reckless enough to believe I could have her and satisfy the demands of my birthright."

"She never mentioned this marriage."

Reckester shifted closer, but he remained seated. "My family acted quickly when they learned of my blunder. You see, because of my father, I was already betrothed. Rae," he said, scrubbing his face. "I had dallied with her, and she was already with child. Bribes were paid. All records of my marriage to Aideen were supposedly destroyed." Silence prodded him to continue, "You did not know my father. He would never have accepted a lowborn Irish actress as my duchess. I owed my family. My marriage to Rae glutted the Reckester fortune, restoring it."

Keanan thought of the poverty he and his mother had endured. He nodded, absorbing the confession. "All it took was the ruination of a woman whose only sin was to have loved you."

"Aideen prospered from the bargain. She was recompensed with enough gold to buy her silence. All I had to do was disavow the union and her child."

The pieces of the past whirled in his mind like colorful tops. They collided with his memories, only adding to the chaos instead of giving him answers. "So she was offered her congé, like a discarded mistress instead of your true wife."

"She was recompensed," he insisted, still denying any part of the blame.

"Was she?" Keanan echoed. The old man's presence, his unexpected declaration, and his own turbulent feelings had blinded him. He had always trusted his instincts, but he had allowed old dreams to cloud a harsher reality. His father had never wanted him. If he was extending his hand, then there was a benefit to be gained.

His mouth took on a cynical slant. "Forgive me, Your Grace. You're either too befuddled by drink for me to credit this tale, or you lie. Neither explanation amuses me. Good day." He rose to summon his servant.

Reckester followed on his heels, grabbing his arm before he could reach the door. Keanan shook off his touch. "Why are you being so bloody stubborn? You cannot tell me you have not secretly yearned for this your entire life. I've watched you over the years, quietly maneuvering your way into polite society, never hiding your hatred of all who disclaimed kinship to you. I'm handing you your birthright, Milroy. All you have to do is take it."

He stared at his sire's hand. It was large, white, and probably as smooth as any lady's—the hand of a gentleman. How many times as a child had he dreamed of that hand tousling his hair or tanning his arse when he needed it? "You have proof?"

A guarded expression replaced his anxious plea. "I might."

Keanan pinched the bridge of his nose. Laughing, he shook his head. "Very clever, indeed. Approach and strike your enemy before he strikes at you. I almost believed you, except for one fact."

"You think I jest?"

The muscles in his face tightened until they felt like carved stone. Still, he forced the cavalier smile he did not feel. "You have a son, an heir. What you are suggesting would humiliate him. He would be tossed into an unsavory world, while it elevated a man who, up until this morning, you would not have deemed worthy to scrape the dung off your boots. Believe you, Your Grace? Such callous measures would undoubtedly christen you the truest bastard of us all."

"If you are answering the door, Speck, I assume my family has not summoned a runner to search for me?" Wynne said, rushing past Tipton's butler.

"Not yet, Miss Bedegrayne," the servant replied. His sharp gaze noted her high color and harried appearance. "Living for adventure these days?"

Untying her bonnet, her gaze locked with his. Speck, like his cunning employer, did not reveal much outwardly. She could not tell if he was teasing her or slyly hinting that he knew where she had been this afternoon. "Oh, I doubt you would find my adventures entertaining."

He accepted her bonnet and pelisse. "Ma'ap we swap tales someday soon."

Startled by his parting comment, she glanced back, but the manservant was walking away.

"Wynne!" Madeleina rushed to embrace her. Her Maltese, Flora, chased after her skirts, yapping a greeting. "An hour more, and your papa would have bellowed for a runner." She fluttered her lashes prettily, rolling her eyes upward. Although she was quite a bit younger, Wynne's tardiness had balanced the scales, making them equals. Her sister-in-law was always prepared to commiserate about the elders.

"Papa tends to dramatize."

"He is not the only one."

Clasping her hand, they strolled in the direction of the distant voices. "Why the frown, Maddy? Tipton becoming overbearing?"

Sir Thomas was not the only family member who had talent for the stage. Madeleina had perfected her sulking skills, much to her brother's annoyance. The skirmishes between the Wyman siblings had become legendary within the family. Wynne assumed they were catching up for all the years they were apart.

"I want to tour and study in Italy," the young girl said defiantly, her frown deteriorating into a pout. "You would think I asked for lessons to become a courtesan!"

"Oh, pet," she sympathized, understanding her desire to seek ambitions beyond wedding a respectable gentleman.

"Rallying an opposition will not likely change my position, Maddy," Tipton said in a brotherly, smug fashion that instinctively made Wynne want to give him a sisterly kick in the instep. He must have deduced her intent, because he added, "Wayward sisters need supervision. I have no desire to chase this hoyden all over Italy."

"Do not be a bore, Tipton. Living with my sister should have relieved you of all that starch." Ignoring Madeleina's smirk, Wynne kissed him on the cheek, taking the sting out of the observation.

"Maddy is not the only one who concerns me," he countered softly.

Dinner was a splendid, intimate affair. Tipton, denied his own family for so many years, often indulged his new family. There must have been at least sixteen dishes presented throughout the two main and dessert courses. Wynne touched her stomach and groaned, regretting the Shrewsbury cake smothered with hot raspberry jam and ice cream she had just eaten. It was tempting to have one of the maids loosen her corset.

Devona had chosen the music room to wait for the men while they drank their port and discussed business. Maddy sat at the pianoforte. Her brow wrinkled as she struggled her way through a simple musical composition. It took effort not to wince visibly when she muddled a chord.

"I think Maddy is improving," Devona said, trying to be encouraging. "Do you not agree, Wynne?"

"Her perseverance is commendable. Does Tipton listen to her play?"

Maddy snorted, increasing her tempo in an attempt to end her ordeal. "Ah, the sole pleasure in this wretched hour is when dear brother is bullied into hearing me play."

Wynne's sister shrugged, not contesting the comment. "Why do you think he and Papa are tarrying over their port?"

"Tipton," Sir Thomas said, alerting them to their presence. "Did your wife just call us cowards?" He joined Wynne on the sofa.

Tipton chose a seat close to his wife. "Merely pointing out the inescapable fact our Maddy will never entice an admirer with her musical abilities."

"Who says I want a husband?" Maddy sneered, the ensuing musical notes confirming her discord. "I already have a harrying brother."

"Nonsense, my gel," Sir Thomas said, shooting a notable look at his unmarried daughter. "You will have a multitude of suitors. Wynne, speak to the child."

"I will, Papa, as soon as I think of something to recommend about gentlemen."

Wynne met her sister's gaze. Her brow lifted as she thought of all the inappropriate proposals she had received over the years. Devona silently acknowledged the dilemma with the tilt of her chin. Both laughed, recalling shared tales. Countless years of confidences had allowed them to converse without words.

Sir Thomas scowled at his youngest daughter, wounded by her disrespect. "Tipton, I trust you to rein in your wife. I am an old man, and one impertinent daughter is all I can bear."

Wynne sighed, "Oh, Papa. Pray let us not bring up old arguments. It will only distress you." *And me.* She had hoped her father would be too distracted this evening to corner her.

"Old arguments? You are three and twenty and unmarried, my gel. What do you have to say for yourself?"

"Sadly, Tipton does not have a brother or handsome cousin."

Sir Thomas pounded the armrest of the sofa. "You were once such a biddable, intelligent gel. Why are you being so picky?" he demanded.

Tipton idly coiled one of his wife's curls around his finger. "I'd understood there have been a generous number of suitors courting her affection."

"Bounders, most of them."

Devona leaned into her husband's caress. "What of Lord Nevin?" she asked, earning a piercing glare from Wynne.

Her father dismissively waved off the suggestion. "The man could be shaped into a respectable husband. Decent to look at, titled, moneyed as far as I can tell. 'Tis Reckester who sours the deal. He came visiting, you know?"

Startled by the revelation, Wynne asked, "Lord Nevin has spoken to you, and you did not think to mention this? What did he want?"

"Sit back down and calm yourself. You look too pale for my liking," Sir Thomas commanded. "It wasn't Nevin. Reckester came to see me, prepared to sit down and settle the matter you and Nevin keep dancing around."

The room felt too stifling for Wynne. Her annoyance soared with each mistake Maddy made at the pianoforte.

"There is no understanding between Lord Nevin and my-self," she muttered through clenched teeth.

"But—"

Something in her expression quelled Devona from voic-ing her protest. The meal she had eaten churned in her stom-ach, making her nauseous. If she did not do something, her family intended to wed her to Lord Nevin. He was a decent man; however, he was not for her.

"What of this Milroy?" Tipton interjected. "There are rumors abounding that he is pursuing Wynne?"

He stared at her when he asked the question. There was no doubt in her mind that he was indeed aware of Keanan's interest.

Devona grew pensive. "Rayne, was not this Mr. Milroy the gentleman Aunt Moll introduced us to at the masquer-ade?"

The mention of his name mottled her father's face into a distressing purple hue. "Keanan Milroy," he raged. "Odd, neither you or your aunt spoke of the encounter. He did not dare approach you?"

He had done more than approach her that evening. If accidentally meeting Keanan at a public ball enraged him, then he would certainly murder him for taking her inno-cence. Wynne considered lying. She might have even been convincing if her aunt had resisted introducing Keanan to her sister and brother-in-law.

Bracing for the worst, she argued, "Aunt Moll considers Mr. Milroy a respectable acquaintance. There is nothing re-proachful about his behavior toward me."

"Deplorable, arrogant blackguard! I warned him to keep his distance. By God, I shall have the jackanapes pressed into service. Come, Tipton, you should be able to name a man or two who could cudgel him on the pate and haul him to the docks?"

Horrified by the turn of the conversation, Wynne rose to her feet. "No one is handing Mr. Milroy over to a press-gang. Tipton, I will never speak to you again if you assist him in this lunacy." Tears threatened, blurring her vision. She was prepared to dash off and warn Keanan this moment if she could not gain her father's promise to leave him alone.

Her sister stood and placed a comforting arm around her. "No one is going to truss up your Mr. Milroy and send him out to sea. Papa, assure Wynne that you were merely teasing."

"Tears?" Sir Thomas gaped while Wynne struggled not to cry. "No man sprouted from Reckester's careless seed is worthy of your compassion. Milroy is rough-edged, violent, a man who covets his brother's position."

She flinched at the truth of his words, even though her heart denied them. "You pass judgment on a man you do not know."

"He has a taste for pretty toys, my gel. That does not mean they are safe in his care, or that he will treasure them. Heed your papa, and strike him from your heart."

"You have already warned him off, I assume?" Tipton asked, attracting her father's attention away from her.

"Aye, I have. Walked boldly into my house and told me he intended to have Wynne. I told him he'd never gain my blessing on such a match."

Oh, wonderful, she thought. Where her father had failed, Tipton in ruthless thoroughness might find a more permanent way of discouraging Keanan. "You speak as if he is the enemy, Papa. Do I need remind you that he rescued me when I was pushed in front of those lions? He approached you to explain the incident because he feared I would not. If he said anything offensive, then you must have provoked him."

"Where have I failed, when my own child defends a scoundrel to her father?"

Devona's hand tightened on her arm. "What lions? You were hurt and did not tell us?"

Wynne immediately regretted her inadequate defense, realizing she had distressed her sister. "A small accident at a
fair," she assured her, regretting the pain she saw in her
sister's eyes. Both of them were recalling a time when they
shared all their confidences. "There was no reason to worry
you. Mr. Milroy protected me. I was unharmed."

Sir Thomas clung to his prejudice. "If he had not lured
you to the fair, your life would not have been risked. This
Milroy has mistaken my clemency for weakness. I shall meet
him at dawn if he seeks you out again."

Maddy's playing sounded as if she was paying more attention to their argument than to her sheet music. The man-
gled chords created a slicing pain in Wynne's temples that
she swore cut right through her skull. She dug her fingers
into her right temple, yelling, "Maddy, is it your intention
to drive us all mad with your cursed playing. I cannot bear
another minute of that awful clatter."

Stunned by the waspish tone directed at her, Maddy
curled her fingers into fists and jammed them into her lap.
Everyone was staring at Wynne in varying degrees of
amazement. She had never spoken a harsh word to the girl.
Guilt easily turned to anger toward the man she held responsible for her wretched conduct.

"I will not tolerate any dawn appointments on my behalf.
If either of you take any steps toward hurting Keanan, I will
simply tell everyone that I am his mistress. Imagine the
scandal, Papa. I doubt even you can bluster your way
through it."

"Now see here!" Sir Thomas's roar escalated over the
pandemonium that her threat caused. To her, the overheated
room filled with the irritating buzz of indistinguishable
voices, and the blur of colors heightened her nausea.

Wynne escaped the room. Moving blindly, her flight took
her down the hall to the stairs. Ascending to the next landing, she pushed open the first bedroom door and collapsed
at the open commode.

She was retching into the chamber pot when her sister came up behind her. Moments later a wet cloth was pressed against her forehead. The spasms in her stomach slowly relented. Boneless and weak, she turned away from the commode and slid to the floor. Her hand captured the falling cloth and pressed it to her mouth. Devona sat down next to her.

"I made a real hash of things," she said, folding the cloth and pressing it to her eyes. "Papa is probably summoning his carriage so he can put a ball through Keanan's heart."

"Tipton is managing Papa," Devona reassured her, pushing the stray tendrils of hair away from her damp face. "You are not in love with Lord Nevin?"

She sniffed. "No. Once I thought—no."

"Why did you not tell me you were in love with Mr. Milroy?"

As she calmed, her body trembled, the outcome from her earlier distress. "I did not set out to love him. At first, I did not even like the man. Later, it just seemed prudent not to speak of him, especially after Papa ordered me to avoid his company."

"Does he return your feelings?"

Misery pumped through her heart, leaving her exhausted. "He cares." To think otherwise would leave her with unrecoverable wounds. She replied to her sister's unspoken protest. "You do not understand. Keanan comes from bleak circumstances. He is not like us. Revealing too much of the heart is considered a sign of weakness in his mind. I do not know if he will ever be able to confess his feelings." Instead, he allowed his body to speak for him. In his arms, she felt cherished and protected. It was enough, she thought. It had to be enough.

She glanced away from the disbelief and sympathy she noted in her sister's expression, despising the notion that she deserved both.

"Will he offer marriage, Wynne? Will he add respectability and protection to his undeclared love by giving you his name, a home, a family of your own?"

"I have no answer for you," she replied starkly. "Not one either one of us will believe."

Fifteen

Keanan did not know whether it was the sound of the brimstone match striking steel, or the pungent odor of sulfur that first awoke him. Keeping up the pretense of sleep, he studied the intruder through narrowed slits. He was garbed in black and did not seem to be in any hurry while he lit the lamp on the table.

"Good, you are awake," the stranger said, though Keanan had not shifted from his curled position. "If I had put my hands on you, I feared in my present mood, I would not have been gentle."

Hating his vulnerable predicament, he sat up, and pulled the top blanket from the bed.

"Your modesty is quite charming, Mr. Milroy, and completely unnecessary. Considering my profession, I doubt your physique is any different than others I have observed."

Keanan gritted his teeth, bracing himself against that mocking, amused tone. His face more shadow than flesh, the man sat down in a chair, resting his cane across his lap. Furious, Keanan kept his distance, wondering if the cane concealed a more worrisome weapon, such as a long, deadly edged sword. Still, it did not keep him from growling, "Toss over my trousers."

The man chuckled. "I prefer holding the advantage."

"Aw, fuck," he swore, his manner of speech disintegrating into its rough origins. "You aren't one of those bleeding sodomites. I was fourteen when one of your sort tried to put his soft hands on me. I still managed to break his fat nose and several bones in his hand on our parting." The memory had him hoping his unwanted guest would come for him. He relished the chance at mussing up his face.

"Allow me, belatedly, to congratulate you on your triumph." The stranger scooped the discarded trousers on the floor with his wicked-looking cane and flicked them into waiting hands. "I took a few pokes, but my interest in you is not predatory." He laughed, unmoved by Keanan's succinct, mouthy opinion on what he thought his visitor was. "Damn, I like you. I can see why Bedegrayne despised you on sight."

His bowed head bobbed up. Pulling his trousers over his hips, Keanan fastened the top button. "What do you have to do with the Bedegraynes?"

"I'm family."

"No more games. I want to see your face."

The man obliged by leaning to the side and sliding the lamp closer. His gaze never faltered from Keanan's.

The bold streak of blond sprouting near his right temple was better than any calling card. "Lord Tipton. A bit late for a respectable visit, is it not?" His sarcasm made the viscount smile, but it was far from engaging. The tiny hairs prickled on the back of his neck. He eased into the chair on the other side of the small table.

"No one has ever accused me of being respectable. The same could be said about you."

"Ah, the crux of our problem." Keanan nodded, grudgingly respecting the man's forthrightness. "The old man sent you here to warn me off?"

"No, this visit was my idea. Actually, Sir Thomas was all for setting a press-gang after you."

If Tipton anticipated shocking him with the revelation, he would be disappointed. Keanan refused to give him a satisfying reaction. "He could try," he said, struggling to keep his voice level.

"Oh, Sir Thomas would dare anything when his family is at risk," he said, warming to the topic. "Not to worry, though. Wynne quite effectively neutralized his plans. If you have to look over your shoulder, it will not be on her papa's account."

He did not like the notion of Wynne stepping between him and her father. "I don't need a woman fighting in my stead."

"Well, you might as well get used to it. The Bedegrayne women can never be mistaken for fragile, timid creatures." Tipton paused, giving him a chance to ask the question that probably was burning in his gut. "Not even curious how she charmed her way around him?" When Keanan did not reply, the viscount shrugged, saying, "She threatened to reveal to all and sundry that she is your mistress."

A strange matching of awe and horror replaced his calm pretense. Keanan sprung up from the chair and began pacing. "The devil fetch her and all intractable females! I told her not to interfere in business that did not concern her." He glowered at his companion. "A firm hand to her backside is what that woman needs."

His tirade seemed to ease the tension in Tipton's posture. Settling back in his chair, he shifted that ominous-looking cane from his lap to a vertical stance near the chair. "I doubt Sir Thomas would disagree."

Keanan felt the blood drain from his head. "Has he touched her?"

"Well, well, is this not telling?" The viscount mused, "You want her beaten, yet are prepared to kill the man who tries. Shall I offer you my skilled opinion on your incurable condition?"

Keanan scrubbed the grit from his eyes. "I don't need your skills or your opinion."

"Fair enough. What do you want from Wynne?"

His lungs constricted, and he could not seem to breathe. Maybe he did require a surgeon, after all. Unconsciously he

patted his chest. "I do not want her suffering on my behalf."
What feelings he had for her were private, and Tipton would
not be privy to them. "Are we finished?"

That cold pewter gaze scrutinized him. A lesser man
would have been tempted to fidget. "I have what I came
for." The viscount stood without the assistance of his cane.
"I wonder how long it will take you to do the same?"

Feeling goaded, Keanan could not resist gibing, "For a
warning, I expected more from a man like you."

Before he could take his next breath, the point of a
twelve-inch blade was pressed into the shallow impression
of his throat. The stealth and swiftness of the move revealed
the lethalness of his nocturnal caller.

Tipton's amused expression belied the seriousness of the
moment. "If I were issuing a warning, my friend, you would
not have to question my, ah, execution." He withdrew the
blade and sheathed it. With a mocking bow, he let himself
out of the room.

Appreciating the reprieve, he felt his knees buckle, and
Keanan collapsed heavily into the chair. He would never
again misjudge the ingenuity of a skilled anatomist wielding
honed steel.

Reclining on her bed, an arm draped over her eyes to
block the brightening of the approaching dawn, Rae listened
to the coach on the streets below heralding her husband's
arrival.

She rolled to her side. If she had bothered to look out
the window, she would have witnessed her husband's ignoble
sprawl when he departed the coach. What his drunkenness
stole from his agility, it compensated him by bestowing
numbness, both of mind and body. Rae resented his respite
when all she could do was lie in her bed and worry. His
persistent pounding below meant the coachman had been
able to pull him to his feet and prop him at the door. The

scene below had been played out countless times over the years. It no longer amused her to watch.

The pounding stopped abruptly. One of the blurry-eyed servants had opened the door. Sitting up, Rae came to a decision. If she had no peace, then neither should he. Rising, she picked up her discarded woolen shawl from the chair and wrapped it around her shoulders.

Approaching the stairs, she could hear him talking to someone, even though their conversation was muffled. Her hand skimmed the railing, steadying her silent descent since she had not bothered lighting a candle. She focused on the welcoming light below.

She saw him as the last twenty steps of the staircase curled inward. What she had mistaken for dialogue were, in truth, incoherent murmurs of lust. One of the maids was doubled over the Italian rococo marble-surfaced console table in the hall, a wedding gift from her mother. Her skirts were shoved over her head, concealing her identity. Rae paused on the stairs, preferring to stare at the servant's white-knuckled fingers digging into the gilded scrolling of leaves and flowers than watch her husband's savage thrusts.

She managed a cool, brittle smile when she said, "A bit early in the day to be debauching the servants, is it not, Reckester?"

The maid screamed. Twisting onto her back, she struggled out of her master's embrace. "Oh, madam!" she wailed, horrified she was going to be sacked. The table, not made for its current abuse, rocked precariously.

"Damn you, hold still!" Reckester roared, managing to grab one of her kicking legs. The table tipped over, dumping the maid. Caught unawares, her husband collapsed on top, his breeches twisted around his knees.

Rae strolled past the embarrassing tangle. "Since you tend to be brief in these matters, husband, I will expect you in the library in a few minutes." She halted. Glancing back

at the sobbing maid, she said, "My dear, you are dismissed.
I will leave your references to my husband."

Entering the library, she was not as unmoved as she had
appeared. Picking up one of the porcelain doves from the
library table, Rae hurled it at the wall. It shattered quite
nicely. A second one joined its unfortunate companion.

Reckester charged through the door, the threat of retribution gleaming in his dark gaze. He had fastened his breeches,
but his pulled-out, rumbled shirt reminded her of his perfidy.
She seized another bird and threw it at his head. He ducked.
She missed him by inches. Translucent shards pelted him
like hailstones.

"Damnation, woman, don't plead a broken heart. In all
these years, you have never complained. I am not convinced
you even own one."

"You are welcome to your ugly sluts," she raged. Wisps
of gray hair had slipped from her immaculate braid. "But
keep them out of my house. I deserve that much."

Shaking off the shattered porcelain, Reckester brushed
past her to the brandy. "How was I to know you'd be prowling about at this hour?"

Rae clenched her teeth at his pathetic reasoning. He had
probably rutted with every female servant in the household.
"I hope she gave you the tetters," she purred with vicious
relish.

"Ah, finally a suitable incentive for seeking out your bed,
my duchess."

Strangling on her suppressed fury, she charged him. The
impact knocked the glass of brandy out of his hand. He
crossed his arms over his face, warding off her clawing
blows. She loved him. She hated him. The duality of her
feelings made her pray for his death, if only to end her
torment.

"Enough, you rabid bitch!" He shoved her away.

She fell against the library table. A table globe crashed
to the floor. "You disgust me," she spat. "You are quick to

bully a woman, and yet you cannot stand up to your own bastard. What did he do? Embrace you or have his servants throw you into the street?"

"Silence!"

"I know about your losses. Mr. Tibal was quite concerned and regretted selling our shipping interests. Who do you think bought up those shares? Shall I tell you or would you rather turn it into a game?"

Defensive, he grumbled, "Those shares will be ours again."

"Those shares belong to Keanan Milroy, and nothing short of death will force him to sell them back to us. Polite society enjoys gossip. Your endeavors and failings always provide them with new fodder. Do you know what else your bastard has stolen from us?"

"I can manage Milroy."

"Obviously, you cannot. Where you failed with Sir Thomas Bedegrayne, Mr. Milroy succeeded with the daughter." Smug that her barb had found its mark, she straightened, feeling more in control.

Reckester scowled, probably recalling his disastrous meeting with the baronet. "Bedegrayne will not hand his daughter over to Milroy."

"Marriage is inconsequential to a man like him. I cannot think of a more gratifying revenge than seducing the lady our son wanted for his bride."

"There are other ripe maidens and dowries," he said, dismissing the severity of their loss.

A slight stinging sensation drew her regard to her hands. She had not noticed that her fingers, fiercely rolled into fists, were causing her nails to cut crescent-shaped wounds into her palms. "Milroy is ruining everything. You promised to see to him."

The slyness in his expression did not comfort her. "You place too much importance on him. Families greater than ours have weathered the scandalous machinations of a by-blow." He yawned and stretched his limbs.

She watched him stagger wearily toward the door, probably off to his bed. The blind fool considered the matter of Keanan Milroy settled. Rae disagreed. The man was a risk to her family.

Men always underestimated women. It took a unique fortitude to nurture life within one's body and endure the searing pain of birth. There was no limit to the measures they would go to protect their own.

"Miss Bedegrayne, your absence has been noteworthy," Lord Nevin said, formally bowing over her extended hand. He did not sit but seemed reluctant to move from her side.

Aunt Moll, who sat at one of the tables in the room, looked up from her cards. Wynne inclined her head in the earl's direction, marking her approval.

"I have been unwell, my lord," she said, not wanting to explain her seclusion and the complicated battle of distrust between her and her father.

"Nothing serious, I pray."

"Not really. My father is overprotective."

She owed this afternoon's outing to her aunt. Once again, she and her calm persuasion had broken through her father's stubbornness. She had pointed out that her niece's abrupt absence from the town's amusements would stir as much talk as her association with Keanan Milroy. Her father had relented, but his disappointment scraped at her conscience.

"I assume you will depart for the country soon?" Lord Nevin asked, his aquamarine eyes filled with concern and a pain she refused to acknowledge.

She smiled at her aunt, silently assuring her that she was fine. "The season is almost over. I shall retire, and bear the shame of not securing a husband."

His jaw tightened at her light mockery of her unwedded

state. "Wynne, you could have married years ago. You could claim a husband this season if you chose. Instead you—" He resisted finishing the sentence.

"You may speak plainly, my lord."

For a few seconds, she watched the internal struggle he waged. Facing her polite lightness, his restraint burst its dam of civility.

"He will never grant you what you crave. A man of his stamp cannot love. If he defied convention and offered marriage, you would be just another possession to him. You are too passionate to accept such a cold contract."

There was no point in pretending she did not recognize the man who had stood between them. "For a man of logic, you lose all reason when you speak of your brother."

"Half," he said, the word slicing like a blade.

"Blood is blood, my lord." Wynne stood and shook out her skirts. She longed for a walk outdoors to clear her head. "You and Keanan obsess on your differences. Mayhap it is time to appreciate your commonalities."

"You will not listen. I feel responsible for the damage he will inflict."

"Let us walk in the gardens. I find the room a bit stifling," she said, loud enough to appease the curious. She waved to her aunt and mouthed her destination.

They walked in silence while she decided whether she should confess what her friend already suspected. Wynne did not want to hurt him. Her caring for the earl had been capricious. It had eventually transformed to brotherly affection once she had met Keanan. She suspected that was the confession he was prepared to argue about, so she chose a truth he would never be able to refute. "I love him, Drake."

He staggered visibly at her words. Her own heart ached, seeing the grief she was responsible for inflicting. "He will never be worthy of you."

"Your half-brother would agree, I suppose. Alas, I cannot direct the course of my heart."

Masculine laughter floated to them on the light, sweet breeze of honeysuckle and jasmine before they could cross the room. She froze at the mention of Keanan's name.

"I won a thousand pounds on Milroy. Though one cannot help but admire his punishing fists, I care little for the man," a man drawled.

"He has my respect," another man said. "I did not think there was a man about town who could attract Bedegrayne's fussy princess, let alone tup her."

"Aye," several men concurred, chuckling.

Lord Nevin stood a step forward. His visage was murderous. "I will challenge every one of those bastards," he vowed, keeping his voice low.

Wynne clutched the arm of his coat. "No, please." She was trembling. A part of her had never doubted that one day someone would discover her affair with Keanan. It was the men's cruelty and savage satisfaction in her ruination that struck at her heart. "I cannot have you issue challenges on what is essentially the truth."

He covered the hand that held him back with his own. It was a gesture meant to comfort. "God, Wynne." As he closed his eyes against the pain she had caused him, Wynne felt his condemnation as if it were a lash.

"Lothbury, you are his friend," one of the unidentified men interjected. "Why do you not lure him to the club? To honor him we will hold a supper and present the five hundred pounds."

"What you propose is too bold. Sir Thomas Bedegrayne will insist on meeting us all at dawn if he learns of our plans," Lothbury argued.

"His daughter is a whore," was the merciless reply. "Defending her will only make him a laughingstock."

"Enough," she whispered, feeling betrayed and as sullied as her reputation. "I can bear no more." She pulled on Lord Nevin's arm, trying to lead him away from the men. He resisted for a moment, then took a good look at her. Whatever he saw in her expression allowed her to drag him out of the room.

Worried about his silence, Wynne begged, "Promise me you will not challenge them."

Denied vengeance, his temper flared at her. "Do you think they plan to keep this scandalous tale to themselves? It is merely rumor now, which is bad enough. If Milroy accepts this reward, you will be ruined, and beyond all respectable alliances."

She stumbled. Only his hold on her arm kept her from completely disgracing herself. "I realize your opinion of Keanan is not lofty, but he would never betray me."

"You wagered your honor and your father's name to crawl into bed with him. I am glad one of us is so certain."

His sarcastic words hurt. "Curse you and your hypocrisy." She wrenched her arm from his grasp. "What bothers you is not the notion that I gave myself to a man, but rather that the man was not you!" Wynne marched away, ignoring his plea to halt.

Drake ground his fist into his hand. He wanted to race after Wynne and beg her forgiveness, right after he shook her for falling in love with the wrong man. The desire to turn around and challenge every one of those swaggering rogues for betting on her virtue pushed at him, too. He did neither. There was one man responsible, and he looked forward to seeing his half-brother pay for his misdeeds.

Rae watched Miss Bedegrayne enter the room. The young lady nodded to her aunt but did not join her eccentric relative. Instead, she found a seat near the window that gave her a decent view of the ladies' archery contest.

Years of being Reckester's duchess had given her control over her emotions. She could laugh and speak gaily even if she felt crippled and bleeding within. Blocking out the chatter around her, she noted Miss Bedegrayne's pale coloring

and the distracted brightness in her gaze. Granted, the young
lady had the rudimentary talent to fool the casual observer,
but Rae recognized a kindred wounded soul.

It appeared the seeds of rumor she had discreetly planted
had already borne fruit. The efficiency of innuendo whispered in polite society's cultured ear always surprised her.
It was rewarding to be on hand, witnessing Miss Bedegrayne's disgrace. If the situation had been different, Rae
might have regretted such a harsh punishment. In truth, she
thought the young lady quite intelligent, and she would have
been a charming countess for her Drake.

Her opinion had altered at the first hint of a *tendre* for
Mr. Milroy. Whether the dear lady had been foolish enough
to offer more than her sympathy to her enemy was not an
issue. Implication was as lethal as action in their world.

The duchess smiled at the stone stillness in the young
lady's carriage, and only felt admiration. Miss Bedegrayne
would need such courage for the rest of her life. She was
the key to getting to Mr. Milroy, and Rae was callous
enough to stake the lady's reputation out as bait to lure
him into her trap.

Sixteen

The attack came from behind. The black roan stallion that had been delivered from Tattersall's an hour earlier kicked its hind legs into the empty air as Keanan was tackled to the ground. He rolled away from the nervous animal, taking his tenacious attacker with him. The dirt rose and clung to them like smoke, blurring his vision and clogging his lungs.

An unscrupulous fighter when the situation demanded, he twisted his body forward. His attacker landed a nasty punch to Keanan's right kidney. Grunting, he responded by ramming his elbow into the man's throat.

The man fell back, clutching his throat. Keanan leaped to his feet, prepared to kick him into the street. The blow never landed. His attacker was too busy sucking in air to defend himself.

"Hell, Nevin. Spit out one reason why I shouldn't drag your blueblood arse within range of my stallion's hooves and let him finish the task."

"Y-you—" Lord Nevin choked.

"Save your breath," he retorted. "I've heard all your remarkable opinions about my character." Taking pity on him, Keanan knelt down and untied his cravat. He took a moment and examined the bruising that was already forming at his throat. "Nothing is crushed. It looks like your fancy knot padded the blow. By rights, a direct hit like that should have killed you."

"You," his half-brother croaked, the disbelief evident in his ruined voice, "trying to kill me?"

"Any man who attacks from the back is either a coward or intends to do some killing himself." He showed his teeth. "Neither is much of a loss to this world."

Nevin's mottled coloring deepened at the insult. "For a few, my death would matter."

"No doubt." Keanan stood and wiped his hands off on his trousers. Approaching the agitated stallion, he crooned soothing nonsense while he stroked its neck. The horse shook its head and tried to step on his foot. Shifting his position, he chuckled. Eventually, Keanan felt the animal's muscles relax under his touch. "If you had hurt this fine beast, I might have been tempted to deal with the complications."

Recovering from his injury, Lord Nevin got to his feet and came closer. Unconsciously, his expert gaze checked over the stallion. "You have chosen well."

Keanan nodded, uncomfortable with the praise, and slightly appalled that he wanted it. Gruffly, he said, "Now that you are feeling agreeable, would you kindly explain your unusual greeting?"

"Wynne."

He stooped down and retrieved the currycomb. "I have no time for your warnings, Nevin. What is between me and the lady is our own."

His movements were as efficient as they were gentle. For one season in his best-forgotten childhood, he had worked in the stables. He would have to hire some grooms to care for the horses he purchased. Still, he found pleasure when once it had been hard, unrewarding work.

"How can you stand there smiling after what you have done?"

The frustrated rage in his half-brother's cracking voice had him pausing. "You are going to have to speak plainly. Not all of us present have had the benefits of a tutor."

"You seduced her. Do not bother denying it. Wynne admitted as much after we overheard several gentlemen, including your friend Lothbury, discuss how they planned to celebrate the ruination of a beautiful, generous lady while you gain the five-hundred-pound purse."

Keanan tried not to dwell on the image of Wynne sharing tearful confidences with Nevin. He forced himself to concentrate on the heart of the accusation. "You think I seduced her and then went about town bragging to all who would listen that she was my mistress?"

Even knowing they were not evenly matched, his temper prodded Nevin into grabbing Keanan by the shirt and shoving him. "You were in town long enough to study your enemy. You knew I was in love with Wynne. Seducing her away from me was too tempting for a scoundrel like you. Why would you care if a young woman becomes a casualty in your private war?"

He could not deny it. In the beginning, Wynne had been the key to Nevin's vulnerability. Her connection to the family had encouraged him to pursue her. What he had not expected was that soon he would crave her as much as he desired revenge on the Reckesters. Seduce her? How could he steal what was so generously given? Keanan recalled Reckester's visit and his improbable offer of legitimacy. He suddenly felt cold with the dawning horror that someone had figured out that Wynne had become his vulnerability as well.

"Will you accept the purse?"

The question jarred him from his thoughts. "This money. It was for some sort of bet?" He snarled at Nevin's derisive expression, "What bet?"

"Rebuffed suitors can be cruel, especially when a younger sister marries before the elder. First, there was talk that there must be something wrong with her, if her face and her father's wealth could not secure her a match. Her family squelched the rumors, but they could not prevent them from making the wager. Five hundred pounds to the man who could seduce her."

"Bedegrayne would never permit such an insult. Nor Tipton."

"True. As I said, they have been discreet. It is part of the game."

Eyes narrowing, Keanan took a menacing step toward him. "What about you? Are you part of it?"

Nevin shook his head. "I found out by chance."

"And you did nothing to end it?"

Defensive, he argued, "Would it have been any kinder for everyone to know? I did what I thought best. I went to Wynne and warned her. She agreed that no one should know of their wager."

Wynne kept her secrets, and for what price? Every man who approached her, she greeted with distrust. The existence of that terrible wager on her innocence had kept her from finding a man to love, from marriage and a family. Her one failing had been trusting him, and now these vultures were preparing for a celebratory feast.

They stood nose to nose. Furious that he had been an unwitting pawn, he attacked. "You stand here crowing about your noble motives. You are just as guilty of manipulating our fair Wynne. Telling her and keeping her family out of it served you well. You wanted her."

"More than you, it appears. I am willing to marry her."

Keanan ignored the taunt. "I would guess she was reluctant. A sensible reaction, considering our sire. Abruptly, she was thrust into the awkward position of not being able to trust any man but her loyal friend." He seized Nevin by the coat. "You cunning son of a bitch."

"Cunning, indeed," Wynne said with heartrending sadness. "Gentlemen, there is no need to best each other. I feel liberal enough to offer you both credit on your magnificent performances."

"Wynne, how long have you been listening?" Keanan tensed, wanting to go to her, but she was poised to flee.

"Long enough, not to trust either of you." Her attempt at laughter was a dismal parody. "And here I rushed over to stop you from killing each other."

"You have no part in this," Nevin said.

"Hatred consumes. What feelings you have for me, gentlemen, if you are even capable of them, certainly are in the pale."

Not caring whether he spooked her, Keanan released his half-brother and ran after her, hauling her into his arms. "I did not know of this wager."

Her green eyes glittered, not with tears but cold with fury. "Perhaps not. You had other uses for me, and I was ripe for seduction. How could you resist?"

"You know it was more!" he said, shaking her for refusing to look beyond her pain.

"Cannot speak the words, Mr. Milroy? Despite all your nefarious deeds, you simply refused to lie about your heart. Nobility, after all."

Too stunned to move, he stood as she gently shrugged out of his grip and walked away from him. Desperate, he reached for her again.

"No! Keep that pity for yourself."

Impotent, he released her. He had never felt so alone.

Lord Nevin walked up behind him. "Letting her go?" he asked, somber. "I was right about you."

The subtle baiting was not enough to penetrate the numbness he felt. He had ruined her. It did not matter whether it had been intentional. She was too wary of him and his anger at the Reckesters to trust him. Her lack of faith ached more than any injury he had ever received in the ring. "She is too angry to listen. And I have better things to do than crawl for your pleasure."

* * *

Reckester entered the Silver Serpent, searching for the lady who could satisfy at least two of his needs. Perhaps three, if she was willing.

"Your Grace." Mrs. Chabbert curtsied, giving him ample view of her generous bosom. "It has been days since we last saw you. I hope you have not found a new establishment for your amusements?"

"Nay, I have been to the Midlands," he said, affectionately patting her hip. "Could you find me something for this headache? I am too sober to bear it." He had kept away from spirits because he needed to think clearly while he made his plans.

"A pint pot of beer will revive you, Your Grace," the woman said, setting the drink in front of him. "And another for your ails." She gave him a flirtatious wink.

Reckester swallowed down the contents of the first. The bitter taste provided its own comfort. Pushing the empty pot aside, his fingers circled the second. "Have you seen Milroy?"

The casual question had Mrs. Chabbert gaping. For all his years of frequenting her establishment, he had never acknowledged her friendship with his son. "Uh, no, sir. Sometimes it's weeks afore I see him."

He nodded, glancing at the second pint of beer. His tongue constricted in anticipation. No, he needed a clear head. The papers he had stashed within his coat were too valuable, and he tended to get mouthy when he had too many. "Put the word out that I am looking for him." After one regretful last look at the beer, he stood.

"You could stay while I send a boy for him?"

"Too tempting, I fear."

Reckester shouldered his way out the door into the night. There were a few other places he could check before he returned home. The hackney coach he hired had moved on without him despite the promise of extra blunt if he remained. He had never feared the night. Hell, he had passed out in worse sections of town. Still, seeing it through wary, sober eyes made him feel vulnerable and nervous. He clutched the edges of his rumpled coat and strolled down the street, refusing to allow his gaze to meet anyone he passed. Nor did he glance back at the curious dragging noise he heard from behind. The blow to his head lit up his vision like a flash of lightning. Pain was a whiny scream in his ears. The second blow blinded him. He coughed, tasting grit and blood, not realizing he was facedown in the dirt. The third blow deprived him of life.

Keanan swore when he sighted the Reckester crest on the approaching coach. The door opened. The identity of his unwelcome visitor had him sneering, "If I wanted an un-licked cub for a companion, you would have received an engraved invitation."

"Milroy," Lord Nevin said, unperturbed by the insult or the unfriendly greeting, "I stopped being a lad at two and ten when our benevolent father took me to the stews and bought me an education no book or grand tour could ever provide. Climb up, and spare yourself the hunt for a hack-ney."

Snarling his gratitude, Keanan climbed into the coach. His half-brother had also chosen to dress in black for this evening's festivities. "Have I mentioned your exalted peers have the morals of plague-ridden dock rats?"

"Once or twice." Nevin signaled the coachman to com-mence. "Tell me, what rung are you hanging from if you are crawling your way up to join the rats?"

Morose, Keanan decided he was somewhere between their droppings and carrion. "Tried to see her, you know." He pressed his fingers into his closed lids, attempting to stem the increasing pressure. "Christ, what a tangle. Me standing there, screaming her name like a madman. Servants blocking the door, keeping me out just as much as they were preventing her incensed father from taking aim and putting a ball through my eye. Everyone shouting threats and pleas. Aunt Moll stood at the window watching the folly, looking both sad and disappointed that I turned out to be the cur all had warned her I was."

Making a defeated gesture, he dwelled on the fact that Wynne had not roused herself to the window to gloat over his inability to get past the barriers she had thrown in his way. "Tipton is probably waiting somewhere in the shadows with his fancy lethal cane prepared to slit my throat if Bedegrayne fails at murdering me himself."

"Normally, learning that another family was crying for your blood would have overjoyed me," Nevin admitted, emotion darkening his blue eyes. "Not this time. Not for this price."

"The damage can be fixed," Keanan insisted, his anger flaring to life again. He would bargain, beg, or kill to heal that wounded look he had seen in Wynne's expression. "I am willing to call a truce concerning us if needed."

His half-brother stared thoughtfully out the window. "Considering your feelings, you must truly love her to offer this sacrifice." The sounds of the street filled his silence. "If I agree, this does not mean I like you."

"Nor I you, Nevin."

The bargain was struck.

"We thought we might find you here," Devona said, standing on the steps leading down into the conservatory. Tipton, attired for an evening out, was steadfast and supportive at her side. Wynne fiercely envied the closeness they took for granted.

"Since Papa has ceased yelling, I assumed you both had grown weary of his present tirade and departed." She sat, hands clasped, at the small table they sometimes used in the morning.

Her sister sat next to her, covering Wynne's cold hands within her warm ones. "I cannot bear this discord betwixt you and Papa. He refuses to speak a word directly to you, and you did not eat one bite of your supper."

"He is entitled to his anger. I have shamed him and our family with my selfishness. Mere deprivation of a meal is better than I deserve." She caught Devona's beseeching glance to her husband.

Coming out from the shadows, Tipton chose the chair on the opposite side. His fingers lightly brushed her jaw. "You have skipped more than one meal, Wynne. You have lost weight and are too pale for my liking." Always the surgeon, he pressed his fingers to the pulse at her wrist and frowned, not pleased at its hurried rhythm. "I thought you a fighter, dear sister. I never envisioned you a martyr."

Her chin came up at his mocking challenge. "I am not seeking pity, Tipton. Nor do I run from my responsibilities," she said, already regretting her stab at his past. "Forgive me; that was inexcusable."

"Apologizing for speaking the truth. Now you disappoint me," he teased, unruffled by her comment. "I prefer seeing you chin up and prepared to take a poke at me instead of curled up nursing your hurts alone."

"I was not quite candid about my association with Mr. Milroy. My deception has come to haunt me, and all of you will be drawn into a scandal if the rumors persist."

Tipton smiled one of his rare gentle smiles that were generally reserved for his wife. "I have lived more than half my life shrouded in superstition and scandal. Then Devona entered my life. She and her schemes did little to quell the gossips." He picked up his wife's hand and leaned over to kiss her fingertips.

"You had each other. I am not in a position to make assumptions about Mr. Milroy." Her hand slipped from her sister's grasp and rested on her abdomen. Though it was still invisible to the cruel, shallow world they lived in, Wynne did not need a physician to confirm her delicate condition. She longed to share her suspicions with Devona, but in fairness, she had to confront Keanan with the news before she told her family. She doubted either side would be pleased by the news.

"Why did you not tell us about this sordid wager?" Devona demanded. "Papa or Tipton would have dealt with those men."

"For that very reason, sister. I would not risk the men I love for what seemed like a childish game in the beginning. I thought they would tire, become bored. My acceptance to Mr. Milroy's advances seemed to fuel their wickedness."

"Do you believe Milroy participated in their group?"

Wynne sensed the thread of menace in Tipton's tone. She shook her head, still prepared to defend her lover. "He was a novelty to some due to his connections and money, but I suspect he was not accepted by all. No, he was too focused on his hatred for the Reckesters to bother with silly club wagers."

"Not too focused," her sister said, not unkindly.

Wynne, struggling not to cry, ignored the concerned look the couple exchanged. "No, you are quite right, and it is the root of my fears. Was I simply a means to bedevil Lord Nevin, or just an amusing windfall?"

"Confirming either casts your Mr. Milroy into a most criminal guise."

She despised doubting him, but the exchange she had overheard between Lord Nevin and Keanan did not ease the ache she felt. "Whether or not he is *my* Mr. Milroy has yet to be proved."

"Maybe Papa has the right notion. Tipton, how difficult is it to summon a press-gang?" Devona wondered aloud.

For the first time in hours, Wynne smiled. Her sister was always a little ferocious when it came to protecting the people she loved. No matter what happened, she had the love of her family.

* * *

Heads lifted, and murmurs stirred in their wake as Nevin and Keanan entered the club together.

"Milroy, you might have convinced Lothbury and his cronies to keep their triumph to themselves. However, our amicable entrance will be the talk of the evening."

Tense, and not feeling particularly friendly, he gritted his teeth and cordially nodded as they passed several tables of gentlemen playing hazard. "Altering their focus was our primary intention. I trust you can tolerate the strain of my company."

"Just, Milroy," was Nevin's dry reply.

The Marquess of Lothbury met them at the entrance of the private room. His anxious gaze traveled onward, preferring to linger on Lord Nevin. If he was curious about Nevin's presence, the man decided it was safer to hold his questions. Once, Keanan had regretted exploiting the young lord and his enthusiasm for pugilism to gain him entrance to the elite of society. Now he understood that he had also been well used.

"You have the makings of a tolerable footman, Lothbury," Keanan drawled, pleased to see him recoil. Irritation suffused his pale features. "What is your opinion, Nevin?"

His half-brother pretended to consider the question. "His livery is too somber. Yellow appears to be his color."

The marquess was too intimidated by them to challenge the insult. Needing to stand as their equal, he appealed, "Milroy, we are not enemies. I honored your request, convinced them that you would accept their congratulations in the same secrecy in which the wager was forged."

"Why allow the shredding of a decent woman's reputation to diminish your pleasure?"

Lothbury glanced warily at Nevin, obviously not pleased by his presence or his opinion. "Perhaps we should keep this amongst friends."

"A regretful impossibility," Keanan interjected. "I have learned to survive my disappointments, and so shall you. Nevin stays."

"Not exactly a cordial recommendation," his half-brother grumbled from behind as they followed the marquess into the room.

Eyes narrowed, Keanan curled his upper lip in disgust. "If you had not been more interested in pressing your own advantage, then you would have dealt with these purported gentlemen or alerted her family."

Undisguised sorrow furrowed Nevin's brow. "I had reasons, none of which I care to share with you at this time. Still, I would have changed my selfish course if it prevented Wynne from learning their depravity."

If his half-brother could bend his stiff neck, then so could he. "We both can offer reparation when we finish this."

Lothbury was speaking quietly to one of the four gentlemen seated at the table. Somewhere in his forties, the man wore his thinning brown hair in a style that had to be the result of a crimping iron. His narrow lips curled in artificial delight at the sight of Keanan.

"Gentlemen, arise and hail our victor."

All heads turned in their direction. His host was the only one daring enough to approach them. "I am Digaud, the leader of our exclusive society. You, Mr. Milroy, are a man whose reputation precedes you. Allow me to introduce the intimates of the Malefaction Society. The gentleman to your left is Lord Middlefell; the man next to him wearing the fascinating embroidered berry waistcoat is Mr. Therry." The older gentleman added with a sneer, "A merchant." He gestured to the man to the right. "Mr. Esthill, the future Lord Otten, and you are acquainted with our newest member, Lord Lothbury."

Keanan stared down each man in turn, memorizing their faces. "I assume Lord Nevin does not need an introduction."

Digaud bowed. "No need at all. My lord, you are welcome, though I confess I am enthralled by your unlikely alliance."

There was a negligent shift in his posture. "Then I shall not puncture the diversion with candor," Nevin said carelessly.

The tiny muscles around Digaud's eyes hardened. "Rivalry rarely holds my interest, unless blood is spilled in the affair. Our motto is *de mal en pis.*"

"From bad to worse," Nevin translated for Keanan.

"In which a wager can be placed," Mr. Therry added. The feral gleam in his eyes seemed out of character with his portly figure and his soft face.

Lord Middlefell, a raffish fellow not much older than Keanan, already had a notorious reputation for gambling. Where Reckester had failed in his wastrel's life, this man had thrived. "Then there is the prospect of tweaking the madam."

Brows lifted, Keanan appeared intrigued. "You cheat?"

"A minor manipulation of fate, if possible," Digaud explained. "Some wagers never see fruition if we do not prod some of our participants."

"The bets most worthy of note involve the least likely players," Mr. Esthill said, rolling a guinea between two fingers.

"Like Miss Bedegrayne," Lord Nevin tightly suggested, struggling to rein in his anger.

"Precisely." Digaud nodded approvingly, as if the earl were a clever pupil. "A most difficult wager. I had lost hope of collecting on it."

Keanan vibrated with restrained excitement at the admission. He had disliked the pompous dilettante on sight, and relished an excuse to mess up his immaculate attire. "You were the one who suggested the bet?"

Mr. Therry cleared his throat. "I believe I was the one two years past who presented Miss Bedegrayne as a possible challenge."

"Not so, sir," Mr. Esthill argued. "You only observed that the lady would be ripe for a husband after Tipton eloped with the youngest daughter. It was something of a scandal at the time, although old Bedegrayne did his best hushing it."

Lord Middlefell sipped his brandy. "A delightfully virtuous female, brimming over in just the right portions. To be the serpent that corrupted paradise . . ." he shuddered, lust glazing his eyes.

"Obviously, your serpent fell short of its mark," Mr. Esthill jeered.

"My, uh, serpent remains untried in that particular paradise, I confess. Who knew beauty possessed sharp teeth? I still possess a small scar on my wrist from our tête-à-tête."

Keanan had not realized he had taken a step forward until Nevin grabbed his arm and brought him back by digging his fingers into his arm.

For two years, Wynne had endured their covert machinations in silence, foolishly believing she was protecting her family. He could well imagine Middlefell ambushing her during some country house party, thinking she would bear the rape of her body as bravely as she faced an attack of her wits.

Keanan wanted to go to her and pull her close and soothe her, just as much as he wanted to shake her for the chances she had taken. Her stubbornness had escalated a cruel wager, evolving it into a dangerous game of pride and lust. At the fair, someone had calmly shoved her into the path of a lion. He glanced at Lothbury, recalling that he had provided the man with the opportunity to manipulate the fates. Was it one or all of them who wished the lady harm?

Lothbury edged away from Keanan's fixed glare on the pretense of pouring himself a drink. Crystal clinked against crystal while he flickered uneasy glances in their direction.

Digaud spoke to Lord Nevin. "I had a side wager with Esthill that you were our man after she rebuked Middlefell.

There seemed to be a genuine liking in your regard that promised you success where so many others had failed."

Can you believe this? his half-brother's outraged appearance seemed to query. "That's me," Nevin growled, stalking over to the marquess and seizing his drink. "Always genuine." He downed the contents of the glass in one swallow.

"You," Mr. Therry wagged his finger at Keanan. "I took you for flash-gentry when I laid eyes on you."

Keanan kneaded the knuckles in his right hand, his face lit in grim amusement. "I am no thief, fancy or otherwise. How can a man steal his birthright?"

Everyone chuckled except Nevin.

Mr. Therry's flushed jowls wobbled when he laughed, crushing the folds of his cravat. His eyes were glassy from drink and lack of sleep. "Unparalleled in the prize ring you are, sir. Without a doubt, my gilt's on you. A drawing room is another kind of ring. It has sticky rules of its own, and you fooled the lot of them. A real man of parts, I say."

"Must come from my mother," Keanan said, so casually that only someone who knew him would recognize the lazy menace it cloaked. Nevin tensed, muscles readied, proving that what he lacked in jaw he had to spare in wits. "Christ knows my sire would rather piss on fools than act like one."

Therry laughed so hard, his face turned an alarming red. Shaking his head, Middlefell thumped him on his broad back. Keanan wished them all to fiery hell. From the corner of his eye, he noticed Digaud signaling Lothbury with a look. The marquess bent down and retrieved a wooden chest from the lower shelf of the cart. The seams of his coat strained at the shoulders from the weight as he walked to the table. He placed it in front of their host.

Digaud removed an iron key from a hidden pocket and opened the lid. Contained within were hundreds of gold guineas and silver shillings. Five hundred pounds gleamed and beckoned greedy fingers to sift and fondle. All he had to do was ruin a young lady to possess it.

"If my contacts are correct, this is merely a paltry sum to you. Consider this a token of gratitude, Mr. Milroy, for outmatching a lady we had concluded was beyond the flesh. May you enjoy the transitory pleasure it brings you." He lifted his glass in a toast.

Mr. Esthill raise his as well. "To the serpent who plundered paradise!"

"The serpent!" Middlefell echoed.

The notion that the lewd toast aptly described his actions left a burning, acrid taste in his throat. Was he any better than these miscreants in hurting Wynne? Oh, he might have been blind to the act—needed to be, so that he could have her and seek retribution from the Reckesters. Unfortunately, these gentlemen could not make such a claim and would suffer doubly for their sins.

"All this for a whim," Keanan murmured to himself, measuring the sides of the chest with his hands. "You have had your fun. I fill my pockets with gold and silver." Looking up, his indigo eyes searched each expression, hoping to see more than greed, lust, or merriment. "What of Miss Bedegrayne? Where does she profit from the game?"

Lord Middlefell sniggered, "You tell us, Milroy. You were the one who dragged her out into the night and down to the temple. Did she scream when you pushed her to the floor and shoved your prick into her?"

A chilling breeze wafted his back at the question. Keanan did not recall seeing Middlefell that evening. Perdition! No one should know about the temple. He had been so careful that no one witnessed their departure, and they had been quiet in their lovemaking. His shoulder still bore the passion mark of her teeth when the need to cry out her pleasure had been too much to endure.

Lothbury.

Keanan's searing stare halted the marquess from taking a self-preserving step backward. Realizing his peril, he did not even blink. The man had supposedly been off distracting Miss Claeg that evening. He could have abandoned the lady in someone else's care. That accomplished, there had been nothing preventing him from following after them and spying.

The few steps to confront his traitorous friend were a blur. The thick muscles of his arm uncoiled like a whip, while his fist delivered a hammering blow into his jaw. Thrown backward, Lothbury crashed into the cart, receiving another hit to the head on his descent. Keanan pulled him up by his crotch and squeezed. Hard.

"Jack raw-head!" one of the men behind him exploded at the animallike cry from the marquess.

Not satisfied by the man's response, he clamped down on his wretched balls and twisted. Dispassionately, he watched Lothbury's sweaty face go white. Blood and spittle bubbled between his teeth as air was expelled.

"Hurting?" he asked, his voice soft with the silky promise of violence. "I have just begun, you frigging member mug. Who's going to stop me from twisting your tackle completely off and feeding it to your horse? I warned you once how nasty I could be when crossed."

"U-gulb." The indiscernible sound came from deep in Lothbury's throat. Eyes rolling upward, his spine arched and tensed.

Keanan released him and stepped out of range. The marquess fell on all fours and vomited.

"Slightly excessive for idle talk," Digaud said, instinctively covering his genitals when Keanan swung his gaze in his direction.

"Depends on the topic," he admitted. "Nevin can tell you, some talk gets me awfully disturbed."

His words cued his slackjawed sibling into speaking. "I could not leave my bed for a sennight the last time," he exaggerated, shooting him a look that was both awe and horror. Nevin positioned himself behind Mr. Esthill and the door, effectively blocking their escape. "In fairness, since

Lothbury here is too busy casting up his accounts, perhaps you should explain his blunder."

"Miss Wynne Bedegrayne."

A nervous titter erupted from Mr. Therry. "Milroy, we all assumed your presence this evening confirmed our suspicions that the lady was just a stratagem to thwart—" He used his eyes to designate the unspoken foe.

Keanan frowned. "Gentlemen, you are too concerned with my business. It ends this night."

Mr. Esthill pushed the chest at him. "We have no quarrel with you, sir. Take the money and leave."

"Not so simple." He inverted the chest. Coins thundered across the table and cascaded to the floor. Keanan heaved the chest at the nearest wall, denting the plaster. It landed inches from Lothbury's head, but the man was too consumed in his misery to flinch.

"You offend me." His arm swiped the table, sending a spray of coins into the flabbergasted faces of Lord Middlefell and Mr. Therry. "Your vile wagers sicken me. I should shove each coin down your throats until you choke on them for hurting her."

Lord Middlefell was not intimidated. "Gallant sentiments from Reckester's bastard and an Irish whore. Am I the only one who finds this amusing?"

Digaud made a concurring noise. "An angle we had not considered, Middlefell." His effeminate narrow features scrunched in delight at ferreting out a vulnerable niche. "Mr. Milroy, do you honestly believe this act of chivalry will sway Sir Thomas Bedegrayne into handing over his daughter to you? Even with her ruined, you are still beneath her."

It was a direct hit to his guilty heart, but Keanan was loath to let any of them witness it. "Another wager, Digaud? Even you cannot be that maggoty."

Affronted, the man puffed up, not used to anyone bullying him. His smile oozed insincerity. "Oh, I can do more than sit here and place wagers, Mr. Milroy. By the time I finish regaling society with my interesting speculations about Miss Bedegrayne, all will be able to procure and enjoy her for shillings."

"Bedegrayne would never stand for such slander," Nevin argued, angry their presence had upped the stakes of the wager.

Digaud laughed. "That is the wonderful thing about innuendo, sir. It slips through the cracks of righteousness."

"Having an old house, I know a thing or two about cracks, and I do not mind dirtying my hands to fix them."

He lunged for Digaud before the man had the sense to run. Grabbing him by the back of his neck, Keanan rapped the man's face on the table and then sent him gliding across the surface. Coins scattered in his wake as his feet followed his head in a graceless dive toward the floor.

"I'll kill you myself," Middlefell raged, leaping from his chair.

Keanan jumped backward, missing the lord's swing. His fist found its target even as he stuck his foot out for the escaping Mr. Therry. Both men went down, each searching for his wind.

A flash of metal drew Nevin's gaze from the fight. Spotting the blade curled around an eager hand, he kicked the back of Mr. Esthill's chair, forcing him to collide with the table. The man lost his grip, and the knife skidded out of reach. Before he could stand, Nevin clasped the edge of the table and brought it up, catching Mr. Esthill under the chin. Dazed by the blow, he slumped back into his chair. Nevin tipped it with his foot, sending it crashing.

Keanan stepped over the unconscious Mr. Esthill. "Impressive. You have my appreciation."

His half-brother shrugged. "Equaling the odds, though I think you could have taken them all on without my help."

"It is valued, anyway."

He bent down and turned Digaud over on his back. Tugging him up by his cravat into a sitting position, Keanan slapped his cheeks. Puzzlement, then fear tightened the man's visage when his lids flickered and his gaze fastened on his attacker.

"Good. I see I have gained your attention." He knelt down over Digaud, trusting Nevin to watch his back. "You have issued some threats, and now I take a turn. Forget Miss Bedegrayne. Any correspondence of this fictitious wager will be immediately destroyed. If anyone tries to discuss the lady in question, you will summarily dismiss them. I think you can manage that."

Lord Middlefell, still panting for breath, braced his weight against the table. "Digaud, ignore him. What will he do, challenge us all?"

Recognizing a more formidable opponent, Keanan released Digaud. "Aye, if that's what it takes to keep you from rattling your bone box. Weapons are not the exclusive property of gentlemen. I will bury you all in dawn appointments until reason or the devil buys your silence."

"Mr. Milroy is not the only one present who will issue a challenge," Lord Nevin's warning rang out. "I offer myself as your second. Will you accept, sir?"

After all these years of despising the man, growing respect was thick as todge in his throat. "I do. My thanks again."

"If Mr. Milroy fails, I shall persist in his name."

He would be damned if he actually started liking the man. Standing, Keanan glanced down at his knuckles. He had scraped them on Lothbury's teeth. Blood welled in the cuts, and the sting was becoming a nuisance. "Speaking out against the lady will also bring the wrath of her family down on your heads. Until now, the lady's silence and your sly discretion have kept them from pounding on your doors. Open war will give Tipton a chance to peel the flesh from your lead-punctured corpses."

"Enough," Digaud begged. Sitting up on his own, a knot

the size of a lime was forming on his forehead. "I have no knowledge of any wager on Miss Bedegrayne."

"Nor I," Lothbury concurred, appearing too sickly to stand. "Our grievance ends this evening."

Not on your life, Keanan thought, but kept the words to himself. The marquess owed him an explanation for betraying him and Wynne, and he would not be content until he got it.

Mr. Therry, retrieving an unbroken decanter from the floor, nodded. Popping the stopper, he drank deeply.

Lord Nevin prodded Mr. Esthill with his toe. Cradling his side, and a few broken ribs, he gave his agreement in a painful hiss.

"Middlefell?" Keanan demanded. The man's gaze held venom and retribution. They were feelings he understood well. "I am willing if you are."

"This no longer involves the virtuous Miss Bedegrayne," was his flat, defiant statement.

Keanan had made some enemies this evening. Nodding, he started toward the door. "Agreed." The hand he had extended for a handshake curled into a fist seconds before he punched him in the nose. Bones cracked, and blood burst from Middlefell's nostrils like from a squeezed tomato. "Nor does this."

Clutching his ruined nose, Middlefell screamed, offering no rejoinder.

Shaking the sting from his bruised hand, Keanan opened the door with his uninjured one. He could hear Nevin breathing heavily behind him, the excitement finally catching hold of him. Outside the room, their private discussion had drawn a crowd. Earlier, Digaud had ordered the footmen not to permit anyone entry, and despite the distressing sounds coming from within, the servants had honored the command.

Gentlemen moved past them to get a look at the wounded. Off on the right, he noticed Tipton blocking Sir Thomas Bedegrayne from the room. The two men seemed embroiled in a heated discussion until the older man noticed them. His silver, bushy brows lifted, giving Nevin an inquiring look. He murmured a comment in the viscount's ear.

Keanan braced himself. He fully expected Bedegrayne to assault him, creating a scandal he would be hard-pressed to dismiss in front of such a legion of witnesses.

Tipton pivoted toward them at their approach. Their presence did not appear to surprise him. "Leave any scraps for the family?" The man's expression was unreadable, but Keanan swore there was approval warming his tone.

"Why complain about a nonexistent wager?"

Tipton's light-blue eyes gleamed wickedly. "A nonexistent wager." He mulled over the notion. "I regret I have never seen you in the prize ring, Mr. Milroy. I admire finesse."

He glanced down at his bloodied knuckles, which were already beginning to swell. Keanan cocked his head back at the room. "Those men prey on the vulnerable. They just underestimated how formidable a fighter from the streets is when he's riled and nasty."

Sir Thomas Bedegrayne looked like a man who loathed bestowing gratitude on a man he had disliked on sight. Not that it mattered. In Keanan's present mood, he was tempted to shove that appreciation back down the baronet's throat, along with a few teeth.

Something in Keanan's eyes must have revealed his violent thoughts. Instead of backing away, Bedegrayne seemed ready to meet any challenge. "This isn't finished between us, Mr. Milroy," Bedegrayne warned.

No gratitude. Fine. He preferred it that way. "Whoever said it was, old man?"

Seventeen

It was three in the morning when Drake returned home. He and Milroy had parted ways once they had exited the club. Standing with him against the Malefaction Society had been a decision based on emotion. Wynne's misery at their hands clawed at his gut. His half-brother was correct. Drake's silence about the wager had pulled her into the unscrupulous game. He would have made a pact with Old Nick to assuage his guilt.

Oddly, he could not regret standing with a man he had been expected to hate since his birth. Exuding strength and confidence, Keanan Milroy was an astounding foe. The manner in which he vanquished his enemies proved he had shown some restraint when handling his unwanted sibling, a fact for which Drake was eternally indebted.

This night's adventure also enlightened him to a difficult truth: Milroy loved Wynne Bedegrayne. While the man had not said the words, he had purposely taunted five gentlemen into focusing their hatred on him. Drake could not think of a more quixotic sacrifice, nor a deadlier one.

Opening the door, he froze at the activity within. Candles lit the hall and numerous rooms. He could hear voices in the distance and wondered if his father had stirred the house up again in one of his drunken rages. Somewhere above, his mother would be brazening out the hostile beast. A part of him was tempted to back out the door and find other accommodations. Duty had him putting a reluctant foot on the first step.

A maid appeared from above. Her droopy eyelids widened upon recognition. "My lord!" Whirling around, she disappeared, crying out, "Ma'am! He's here!"

Indistinct agitated feminine voices heightened at the news. Drake did not realize he was bounding the steps two by two until his mother met him at the top. She wore a long, unadorned white nightgown. Her long black hair that had silvered around her face hung loosely down her shoulders; her nightcap had been forgotten. He was used to seeing her immaculate, her feelings locked behind a mask of cool tolerance.

Two steps and he was gripping her arms. He shook her, wanting the horror and sorrow in her tearful gaze to vanish. "Tell me!"

"Reckester is dead."

Denial was a snarl on his lips as he pushed her away and strode toward his father's door.

"I summoned a physician when they brought him home," his mother said, imploring him to understand that she had done all she could. "His color was terrible, and the wound—" Shuddering, she froze at the threshold, refusing to enter.

An elderly man he did not recognize stood over his father, wiping his hands. Another man, younger, perhaps in his forties, leaned against the wall with his arms crossed over his chest. His blue uniform and red waistcoat identified him as part of the horse patrol.

"My lord, I am Dr. Moore. You are the son, I take it?" the older man asked, the weariness of the hour roughing his voice.

His throat swelled with emotion at the fresh slash of scarlet defacing the pillow under his father's head. "Does he live?"

"He had already expired when—" He gestured to the other man. "This gentleman found him."

"Peters, milord," the man said, unwinding from his casual pose. "I spotted two nimmers bending over him not far from the Silver Serpent. They scattered at my shout, nipping His Grace's coat and boots in their flight."

"Did he . . ." He swallowed and tried again. "Was he able to tell you what happened?"

"No, milord. He looked no better than he does now. Some patrons of the hell heard my shout and came running. One or two of them identified him so I was able to bring him home."

"There was little anyone could do," the physician said, tipping Reckester's head to the side, exposing blood-matted hair and a hideous indentation where the back of his head should have been.

Drake looked away, gasping for air devoid of the stench of death. His mother was sobbing just beyond the doorway. He brought his clenched fist to his brow, striving for mastery over his sour stomach.

Clearing his throat to fill the awkward, grief-stricken silence, the officer said, "Bashed in the head for his clothes and purse, is my guess. Since you have no need of me, I'm off to report to my conductor."

"I want you to find the villain who did this. Hire as many men as you need."

The officer's proper reply droned in his ears and then he departed. Sweat trickled down his back as he stared at his father. The physician had adjusted his head, concealing the violence. It offered him little comfort. The ghastly image would be burned in his brain forever. All he had to do was close his eyes to see it.

Drake approached the bed. His hand touched his father's arm. The lack of life he felt beneath his fingertips had him retreating. If his father had found peace, his visage did not reveal it. The final moments of pain had been eternally frozen. There was dirt and bruising on one translucent cheek.

He spun away, seeking the cleansing air of the open window. Someone had murdered his father. Had it been an unfortunate robbery, or had his father crossed the wrong foe? Creditors both honest and corrupt were still hounding their man of affairs. A cuckolded husband, perhaps? Or a bastard son determined to have his vengeance? The possibilities bombarded his skull until they became merciless daggers. He startled at the hand on his shoulder.

The elderly man's gaze was sympathetic. "There is nothing you can do for him now." He cocked his head toward the sound of crying. "Help me get her to bed. She needs some laudanum, and from your expression, I would say, so do you."

Until that moment, he had forgotten about his mother. Once he believed there had been no love between his parents. Hearing her watery weeping, he decided that he had an incomplete understanding of the sentiment. Burying his grief, he followed the physician out the door.

Keanan arrived at the Bedegraynes' front door at precisely eleven o'clock. He felt optimistic when the butler had not shut the door in his face and had requested that he wait in the drawing room. Seeing Sir Thomas Bedegrayne at the threshold smote his hopes into dust.

"Do you intend to keep her from me?"

The older man closed the door. "Do you think it is possible?" There was no anger in the question, just curiosity.

"No," he bluntly replied. "We had words when we last parted. I need to see her. I want her to know she does not have to be afraid anymore."

"Are you telling me I cannot protect my own, Mr. Milroy?"

The old man would be challenging him to a fight before he left this house. "A man can only protect what he can see."

Sir Thomas's brows rose. "And you think you see my gel better than her papa?"

"Begging your pardon, sir, but a wily lady such as your daughter requires a man's full attentiveness."

Nodding, her father said, "I cannot disagree with your logic." He opened the door. "You, there," he called out to a passing footman, "fetch Miss Bedegrayne. She has a caller." He stared at Keanan. "What I have not reasoned out is if you are the man to do it." He left Keanan mulling over how a man went about convincing him.

Wynne headed for the drawing room, uncertain who would call upon her so early in the day. The only one she knew who cared so little for rules was Keanan Milroy. The mysterious caller had spoken first to her papa, and she doubted her father would have consented to their meeting, least of all allowed him in the house.

As she opened the door, her lips parted at the sight of him. He was dressed more for a brisk canter through Hyde Park than for calling. Suddenly uncertain, she peered behind her, wondering if Papa was off, intent on breaking out his prized flintlock brass-barreled blunderbuss pistols.

"I did not use trickery to see you, Wynne. He knows I am here." Keanan removed his hat and scrubbed at his short hair in the brisk, agitated manner that she had always found endearing.

"And he was agreeable?"

"Bedegrayne feels indebted for the moment. I am not counting on this lapse being everlasting." Any humor he felt was strictly on the surface. His fingers crushed the brim of his hat, while his stare glutted on every movement she made. "I need to touch you," he helplessly admitted. "Will you let me hold you?"

He was already crossing the distance and gathering her

to his chest. Burrowing his nose into her hair, he inhaled deeply, drawing in her essence.

She rested her cheek against his chest, finding strength in the contact. "Papa told me what you did," she murmured, thinking her statement had as many omissions as her father's tale. All she knew was that Keanan and Lord Nevin had confronted Middlefell and his cronies and ended their game.

He drew back far enough for the meeting of their lips. This kiss was meant to soothe. It was not filled with the drugging passion she knew was capable between them.

"You should have told me." Recalling how he had learned of her private distress, he pressed his fingers into the flesh of her upper arms. "I could have ended their game weeks ago. It is your damnable pride, woman. You would rather shoulder a burden that would bow a man instead of asking for help."

Her green eyes frosty, she walked out of his embrace. She preferred the anger instead of the vulnerability with which he had greeted her. Wynne had already given him so much of herself. If he took another piece of her soul, she feared the hollowed remains would shatter.

"Why should I have confided in a man who played his own games?" she demanded, pleased by the raw frustration in his answering scowl.

"I had my reasons," he growled. "Hell, Wynne, maybe you can tangle your family up by twisting the guilt, but I fight dirty, too. This is not about Reckester."

"Oh, I disagree. If Lord Nevin had contemplated his immortality with another agreeable lady, you would have hunted her, not me."

Her quiet certainty had him floundering, "Ridiculous. I might have approached this fictional woman. Perhaps—"

"Seduced her?"

He muttered under his breath a perfectly obscene oath. "If you want truth, Wynne, I cannot say how far I would have pursued her. Is that what you want to hear?"

"I seek not your confession. Nor do I judge you," she said tightly, her tone implying that she did.

"Your heart is as green as your eyes for all this fluttering outrage." He paced away from her, his hand rubbing the steady throb in his neck. "I was not chasing after another woman. It was you I wanted. You I pursued."

The puzzled exasperation she heard in his confession ruffled her pride. "I have no quarrel with your actions, Keanan. It is your, ah, *raison d'être* that has given me some restless nights."

His eyes fired to a cold black. "You could not resist, could you? Throwing French words at me like a man would throw his fist when a man's back was turned. No one more than I is aware of the chasm between us. I never pretended to be an educated man, leastways, not from the kind of tutoring your precious brothers can claim. Fight me if you like, my damson, but even you cannot deny this truth. It was my mouth suckling your breast, my flesh surging deep, averring you as mine. Greedy for the pleasure only I can give, not once were you thinking of our differences, or my lack."

She refused to be ashamed of their lovemaking. It was the words he refused to speak that made her want to sink to the floor and weep. "You boorish braggart! I am aware of what was offered and what was taken. I also am quite aware of what you rejected."

He stood there, his gaze steady on hers. Curiously detached, Wynne watched his fingers curl as if he was imagining her within his grasp. He exuded such passion with a glance. It saddened her that whatever he felt simmered within, never boiling over into the words she yearned for as much as his touch.

"Coward," she spat, reveling in seeing his cheeks whiten, the insult stabbing through skin and muscle to the bone. "Why did you come here?"

"Why, indeed? You ungrateful hellcat!" he exploded.

"You have been shadowed by trouble since we first met. I have ended it."

Her fingers trailed along the delicate surface of one of her mother's favorite vases. "Perhaps, for me. What about you? These men are not used to being thwarted."

His expression became guarded. "Well, neither am I. It's something you and those scoundrels should pay heed to."

He had put himself at risk. They could have already issued challenges, and he would never admit it. "You are not responsible for me, Keanan Milroy."

"Nor you for me," he said, matching her banked frustration. "It's no business of yours."

And more's the pity, she thought, because he spoke the truth. "It is a clever talent you have, disseevering your body and affection. I cannot pinch off my feelings so ruthlessly. So I have to choose."

Wary now, he bared his teeth, "Ultimatums, Wynne?"

She lifted a reckless shoulder, defying the bowing strain in her spine. "If you like. My role in your campaign against your father is over, since I have no intention of marrying Lord Nevin." Sensing his protest, she cut him off with a look. "You have risked your life protecting my reputation. My being your mistress negates your noble deed."

Horrified, he tried to approach her but halted at her retreat. "You are not my mistress!" he thundered.

"Oh." She staggered against the pain. "Well, less than."

"No! You are twisting my meaning, damn you!"

She placed her hand on her stomach, already mourning him. "You have never allowed me into your life. Not really." She turned to face him. "Oh, I know of your hate, your ambitions. What of love, Keanan? There must be people in your life you care about?"

Her calm query seemed to agitate him. "One or two— does it matter?"

Against her wishes, tears filled her eyes. "Indeed, sir.

Why have I never met these people that claim a place in your miserly heart?"

"They have no place in your world, Wynne. Neither do I."

"Oh, please. Have the courtesy of admitting the prejudices are your own. I have never thought less of you for your poor upbringing. What shatters my heart is that wanting me shames you." She turned away and wiped frantically at her falling tears.

Appalled, he grabbed her arm, preventing her from retreating. "Ashamed? What idiocy! My breath freezes in my chest, just looking at you."

"Do you think you are the first man to tell me that I am beautiful?" she cried. "Scores of men have spouted forgettable lines of flattery, hoping to gain my heart. I felt nothing, except regret that I could not return their sentiment. You were the only man who ever made me truly feel. I offered you everything . . . risked all, in hopes . . ." Her voice failed, consumed by anger and grief.

"What did you hope, Wynne?" he relentlessly pressed.

She shook her head. "No more. I cannot give you more without destroying myself. Leave me something after you have moved on."

"This does not end here!" His rough kiss hurt them both.

She tore her arm from his grasp and stepped out of reach. "It must. If not for my sake, then for the sake of the child growing within me."

He clutched his stomach. Staggered, he braced his hands on his knees. "A child. Are you certain?"

"That you are the sire?" She backed up a few more steps. "I never thought you would be so blatantly cruel."

"I claim the child," he snapped, visibly sweating. Jumping up, he stalked after her. "I am not my father!"

She flinched at his vehemence. It had not been her intention to accuse him of the misdeed he despised Reckester for. "Yelling at each other solves nothing. I—I just wanted you to understand why it ends here. No more games, Keanan. You will have to find your revenge without my help."

"This is your solution? Telling me and then running away?"

"Not running," she shouted at him, matching his volume. "Living!" Seeing his pained expression, she strived to soften her voice. "I am not your mother. My family will not throw me into the streets, leaving me to starve or prostitute myself. My son will not spend his life waiting until he is strong enough to best you for abandoning us."

The tears brimming in his eyes horrified them both. "I never took you for a coward, Wynne. I am not the only one afraid here. You are running so fast, the dust and wind are blinding you."

"I am just simplifying things. You are just upset I am giving up before you."

"I am not the one pulling away."

"Nor have you ever asked me to stay." Taking one last risk, she kissed him on the cheek, tasting his tears. "I will never forget you."

She glanced up at him. He looked furious, purposely keeping his hands at his sides as if he did not trust himself to put his hands on her.

"Nor will I forgive you, Keanan, for not accepting more." She quietly retreated from the room, ignoring the underlying vehement plea she heard when he roared her name.

Keanan blindly walked the streets for hours. The image of Wynne's pale face overwhelmed by quiet misery haunted him. She had asked him politely to leave. No, worse, she was severing all ties to him. Even carrying his child could not bind her to him. Half crazed by desperation, he had run after her.

Bedegrayne had not been as trusting as he had initially

appeared. He and three very determined footmen had tackled him before he reached the stairs. With Keanan outnumbered and not thinking clearly, her father had landed a respectable doubler to his gut and had him thrown out of the house. Disgusted that his efforts to speak to Wynne were proving the old man's argument of his unsuitability, he had stalked away.

Glancing up, he finally noticed that his wandering had led him not to his house but to the Silver Serpent. For a time, this place had been home. When Blanche and her husband had tried taking him in, he had been too wild and angry to accept their caring. A good woman, she had ignored his harsh rebuffs, and time had found a place for her in his unyielding heart. It was now, when he hurt, that he realized she had become family to him.

"Keanan." Blanche greeted him with a kiss. She took him by both hands and guided him to an empty table. Sensing his pain, her eyes filled. Producing a handkerchief, she started dabbing. "I'm so sorry. All your plans ruined. Though, and pardon me for saying so, it was probably for the best."

Hearing his worst fears spoken aloud inflated his suffering. The blow he had taken to his stomach pounded in opposition to each breath. "I handled it all wrong."

Reaching into his fob pocket, he removed the gold fob chain. Instead of seals adorning the end, he had attached a carved cameo. He had given a jeweler the silhouette of Wynne created from that afternoon at the fair. His thumb brushed over her relief carved into stone. Instead of being a symbol of all he possessed, it had become a brutal reminder of all he had lost.

"It is natural you have regrets. Contrary to your beliefs, you wanted acceptance more than death."

Irritated, his fist tightened around the cameo as he tried to pay attention to their conversation. "Death? I will kill any man who tries to harm Wynne."

Confused, she blinked at this through her watery gaze. "Wynne. You have a lady?"

"Blast, woman, I have no inclination for chatter. Is there someone out to harm her?"

"Your lady?" She sniffed, all affronted. "Keanan Milroy, you are closed as wax when it comes to the details of your life. You find yourself a decent woman, and have you brought her around for an introduction? No." She nodded at his confirming wince. "It wounds me deep, knowing you think I am not good enough for her."

He seemed to be offending all the women in his life. Awkwardly patting her hand, he soothed, "Aw, Blanche, she would like you just fine." He did not doubt he spoke the truth. Wynne had her thorny barriers, but she was never snobbish. He should have told her so, he decided, feeling regret. Comforting words had never come easily to him. "It is I who trouble her." He thought of her alone, carrying his child. Perhaps she was still in danger. "Now don't addle me further with this straying. Who is in danger?"

Stunned, Blanche said, "You really don't know, do you? Reckester is dead, Keanan. Murdered he was, just a walking distance from here."

Reeling from the news, his vision went gray around the edges. "When?"

"Last evening. He came to the Silver Serpent looking for you. I was so shocked. Never has he ever asked after you. When I told him I hadn't seen you, he left." She dabbed at her eyes again. "It was the last I'd seen of him." Blanche crumpled her handkerchief and banged her fist on the table. "Of all the rotten luck. One of my best patrons set upon by footpads and struck from behind. Do you know what this will do for my business when word gets around that he was murdered leaving my establishment?"

Her words battered him like dried leaves caught in a whirlwind. "He wanted to speak to me?"

Keanan recalled Reckester's wild confession about his being the legitimate heir, and the talk of hidden proof. It was a tale he had longed to believe, but he had assumed the duke had been drunk, or toying with him. Disgusted, he had thrown him out of his house. "Did he leave me a message?"

Her eyes dulled as she thought back to the encounter. "No. He just said to put the word out that he was searching for you. I told him I'd send a lad after you, but he refused."

"Was he drunk?"

Wrinkling her nose, she shook her head. "Nay. Still, he was acting odd. Anxious. He barely touched his beer and did not even glance at the gaming tables."

Regret over the income she had lost with Reckester's death warred with her concern for Keanan. Watching for the first time his struggle to keep his aloof mask in place, her personal skirmish faded.

"All these years wasted while the pair of you skirted each other's lives. It took his last day on God's earth to find the courage to summon you. Bad fortune is as fickle as good, it seems."

Something had driven Reckester from his pleasures, and it was important enough to send him seeking out the son he had refused to acknowledge. Had he been carrying papers dangerous enough to incite murder, or was he just a victim of fate as Blanche had believed? If his sire spoke the truth, there were several people who would benefit from possessing this information, himself included.

His public dislike of Reckester would probably brand him the likely killer in the eyes of the speculative *ton*. If the old man were not already dead, the unappealing notion would have given him murderous incentive. All he needed was another barrier separating him and Wynne.

"Milroy," Dutch said, lumbering toward their table. His clothes were rumpled and stained; he looked as if he had spent the night brawling. "I heard about Reckester."

His friends stared at him, expecting some kind of grief from him. All he felt was a growing numbness that had started long before he had learned his sire was dead. The lack in him made him uncomfortable, since he should be feeling something. "It's his family who needs your sympathy. He meant nothing to me." And everything. "I have to go," he said abruptly, getting up from the chair.

Blanche clutched his wrist. "Come back if you have the mind."

Ineptly acknowledging her offer with a brief nod, he spun into his friend. The stench of the man's clothes had him shoving the back of his hand up to his nose. "Christ, Dutch, you smell like piss and vomit."

"Well, my apologies for not offering you a perfumed handkerchief for your newly acquired delicate sensibilities."

His friend punched him hard in the arm, making it difficult for Keanan to suppress a wince. "While you lamentably spent the night mastering the folds of your new cravat, my evening included bear baiting, an impromptu fight for the favors of a rather large breasted wench whose name I cannot seem to recall, and several barrels of ale." He sniffed experimentally at the sleeve of his coat. "How I came to smell of fish will remain a mystery."

He could not leave Dutch wandering about in his present inebriated state. The man had a propensity for trouble. "Blanche, could you see to our friend?"

"Of course, Keanan." Pressing her handkerchief to her nose, she was already contemplating the fastest manner for removing him and his offensive garments from her establishment.

Dutch brushed off Blanche's gingerly attempt to help him stand. "Where are you off to?"

"I dislike coincidences," he replied, not having time to explain everything. "Nor do I like having my name tethered to them."

Eighteen

"You of all people should have sense not to come call-ing," Nevin snarled, still flustered from their butler's an-nouncement that a Mr. Milroy wanted to see him. There were purple shadows beneath the raw pain in his eyes, mak-ing him look far worse than Dutch. "My mother has already endured one shock. Seeing you in her drawing room might sweep away what remaining threads of sanity she pos-sesses."

"I did not come to torment her." Once he would have enjoyed curbing her barbed, condescending tongue. "You have a choice. We could stand here in front of everyone bandying back and forth insults, which will provide enter-taining fodder for this evening's assemblies. Or you could invite me in and pretend to tolerate our regrettable paternal ties."

Arms crossed, with his shoulders propped against the closed door, he watched as a carriage slowed in passing, one of its occupants glancing back at them. Nevin whacked his head against the door, his aggravation clearly evident. "Damn." Unwinding from his pose, he opened the door. "Come in. Whatever my choice, I doubt anything we do will silence the talk."

Keanan followed, not surprised by the opulence within the house. The elegant entrance hall bespoke generations of wealth, and a confidence of discernment borne from good breeding. Nevin's direct, quick pace attested that he accepted this house and its beautiful treasures as his due.

Entering the library, he eyed the collection of birds represented in numerous forms about the room. There was a subtle, lingering masculine scent that must have belonged to Reckester. He stroked the feathers of a stuffed kestrel poised on a wooden stand as if it were prepared to take flight.

It had never occurred to him that the man had interests beyond drinking, gambling, and whoring. There he was, standing in a room in which he did not belong, and it took a dumb, dead bird to make him realize that despite all the information he had collected about the duke over the years, he was essentially still a stranger.

Nevin turned, finally noticing Keanan's scowling preoccupation with the stuffed kestrel. "It rarely bites. Not even the uninvited. We might as well sit and be civilized."

Avoiding the massive walnut desk and the cumbersome mantel it represented, Nevin chose one of the solid ivory armchairs, its legs rooted to the floor by four carved tiger paws. Keanan slid down onto the emerald cushion of its twin, his choice keeping an unspoken balance.

"Was he dead when he was found?" he asked, breaking the silence. This was not the first question that had arisen in his scattered thoughts, but one led to another, and he would have them all answered before he walked out of the house.

Nevin's cheek twitched, unable to conceal his tumultuous emotions. "There is some confusion on that. All I can state with certainty is that he was dead when I arrived home." Clearing his throat, he asked, "How did you learn of his death so quickly?"

Keanan removed his hat and dropped it in his lap. Scratching at his head, he laughed at the suspicion in his half-brother's question. "Not by delivering the death blow, if that is what you're implying. I was doing just fine bungling my own life. I saw Wynne this morning."

He had no intention telling Nevin of his failure. Their relationship barely qualified as amicable. Still, they had not been enemies last evening. He might not have spoken the words, but he had appreciated the man's support. It proved they shared more than blood. They also were bonded through Wynne.

"From your expression, I gather she has not forgiven you."

"Can you think of anything more amusing than an honest overture coming from such a dishonorable bastard? Have I given her reason to think different? I confess, my reaction was not to my credit. It confirmed Bedegrayne's worst fears about bad blood. He had me thrown into the street right after doing his damnedest to break my ribs."

The rushed, infuriated delivery of his confession had Nevin gaping. "Her father landed a hit?"

After watching him handle Digaud and his cronies, the man's disbelief was understandable. "His footmen were holding me down," Keanan added, noting the detail did not impress him. "So I let the old man hit me. It was less than I deserved."

"So the incomparable Reckless Milroy is not the invulnerable man he appears," Nevin softly taunted.

"No one is."

"The police suspect robbery," Nevin said, losing interest in provoking him about Wynne.

His gaze sharpened. "Do you agree?"

Flexing his hand over the ivory armrest, he sighed. "A plausible theory, considering his pockets were rifled and empty. No witnesses have been found, so the explanation will do as well as any other."

"Do you hold me responsible for his death?"

The bold question seemed to shock his half-brother from his unfocused bearing. "My father left town without explanation to me or my mother. No one, not even you, could have anticipated his return. Besides, we were together last evening."

Keanan abruptly decided to take another risk. "The proprietress of the Silver Serpent told me he was asking for me there. He was sober and kept away from the gaming tables."

Nevin had made his own inquiries into Keanan's background to learn of his connection with Blanche Chabbert. Discovering that his father's last actions on earth involved finding his unrecognized bastard was visibly disturbing. "You never saw him."

Half expecting some nuance of suspicion, he never took his gaze off Nevin's face. It relieved him that there was no doubt in the statement. "No. I can guess why he wanted to see me." Keanan paused. Once said, their small truce would likely end. "Reckester has been bleeding the family fortune. You have sold off more assets than is common knowledge. Shelve your objection, Nevin, I have made it my business to ferret out your secrets—and have profited nicely from a few of them."

The mild tolerance in Nevin's expression vanished. "Were you blackmailing him?"

"My, my, you do have a nasty opinion of me, brother. To answer your question, no, there was no need for extortion when he was ruining himself without my assistance."

"I was keeping him in line, damn you. He understood what was at stake. Marry an heiress, he said, as if that would have solved everything. He might not have liked it, but he would have curbed his gambling."

Not bloody likely. "Rouse yourself and listen, Nevin. Reckester would never quit. He just switched the game and stakes. Cut him off, did you? He must have been furious. So much so that he was willing to—"

"What? Tell me."

"Reckester claimed he was married to my mother. That I was his true heir. Supposedly had papers to prove it. When he had managed to impregnate both his unsuitable wife and his blue-blooded mistress, the family stepped in to help him correct his mistakes. What was the harm, after all? It only ruined the life of a poor Irish actress. He even had a surplus of heirs to choose from," he said, the bitterness ringing loudly in his voice.

"I—you lie," Nevin hoarsely accused him, his face becoming so white that his lips looked gray. "What purpose does it serve, conspiring such a chimera?"

"Absolutely none!" Keanan thundered. "I have been buying up your precious assets piece by piece as soon as you put them on the auction block. Everything will be mine if I'm patient."

The notion that he was correct had Nevin standing. "Everything but a respectable bloodline and title. You could not buy that, so you thought to steal it."

"Reckester was offering me everything without a whimper," Keanan mocked. "He had two sons: one he had betrayed; the other had betrayed him. When you threatened to cut him off, he made one desperate gamble, thinking I was hungry enough to seize it all and compensate him for his sacrifice. Push down your anger and consider it. He sacrificed one family for greed. Why not the other?"

Nevin staggered backward, reaching out for the chair he had abandoned. Slumping into it, he pressed the heels of his palms into his temples. "What you are saying . . . I cannot believe."

"Neither did I," he admitted. "I distrusted his motives from the beginning and tossed him out of the house." It had been the last time he had seen him.

"You think he had this proof when he was attacked?" The blood was seeping back into Nevin's lips.

"Like you said, for what reason would he seek me out?"

Nevin started at his own words being thrown back at him, and then he began laughing. It was cold and self-derisive. "Well, well, you realize what this means, Milroy?"

Uncertain of his direction, Keanan warily shook his head.

"It means, brother, if true, that I had more cause to murder our father than you."

Pen in hand, Wynne sat at her desk pretending she was writing a letter to her brother, Brock. She had been staring at the same sentence for half an hour. What could she tell him that would not have him sailing for England, intent on challenging Keanan Milroy? Besides, between Tipton and Papa she had more than enough males prepared to defend her honor.

She had done what she had sworn she would never do: gambled on a man who could never appreciate her heart. It hurt to be so wrong about him. She had always prided herself on being sensible, the proper lady her mother would have wanted her to be. If not for the portrait Papa hoarded in his private rooms, her mother's face would have faded from her memories. It was sad, really, she mused, fighting back the tears that surfaced with alarming regularity. All she truly recalled about her dear mama was that she smelled of her favorite strawberry water.

Wynne violently wiped away an errant tear. She had failed everyone. Paragons simply were not supposed to be scandalous. Oh, but what fun she had had, allowing her heart to lead before propriety. Her moments with Keanan had been romantic and magical. Too full of love and hope, she had gone to him, not seeing that it had always been she who had taken the steps bringing them together, while he had backed away. Not that she blamed him. He had not changed. Only her perspective had.

"Miss Bedegrayne," her maid, Milly, said, interrupting her bout of melancholy. "Lady A'Court has come calling."

Discreetly she turned away and wiped all traces of her tears. "Ah, I told you I did not want any visitors." She could speculate on her own about what they were saying.

"I know, miss, but if you pardon my impertinence, the countess looks more miserable than you." Backing out the door, she added, "An' that's a feat in itself. I'll be showing her ladyship to the drawing room." Milly closed the door, fleeing her reprimand.

Wynne opened a drawer and tucked her abandoned letter within. Her artful omissions could be put off another day. She wondered what could be troubling Brook. Nothing important. Her friend had the perfect life. She was happily married to a man who loved her, and now she carried his heir in her womb. It was difficult to be sympathetic to a woman who had everything she coveted. Sulking and already dreading their meeting, Wynne assumed Brook had been ordered by her husband not to associate with her.

Milly had not been exaggerating to lure her mistress out of her chambers. Brook did not seem well. Not bothering to rise at the sound of Wynne's approach, she sat on the sofa, her head lowered, hands clasped in her lap. Normally tidy in appearance, her peach gown was wrinkled, and there was a dark smudge at the hem. She was also overdressed for such a temperate day.

"Brook, dearest, you must be stifling in that gown," she said, her false cheer faltering when she noticed her friend trembling. "Shall I call one of the footmen for something to drink?"

"No, thank you. I am just so cold."

Wynne laid a hand on her friend's cheek. "Hmm, a bit warm. You should have taken to your bed instead of paying calls this afternoon."

Wrapping her arms about her, Brook shivered and rocked in a comforting motion. "I had no choice, you see. Pray, what was I to do?"

The woman's hesitant speech and puzzlement worried

Wynne. "You are not well. I shall send someone for Lord A'Court."

"No!" She rose, her visage twisted in unimaginable terror. "I—I . . ." she panted, gasping for breath. Clutching her abdomen, she collapsed in a dead faint.

"Brook!" Wynne fell to her knees, her frantic fingers unfastening the gold brooch at her friend's neck that secured a diaphanous scarf to her pelisse. Something had upset her friend. Opening up her restrictive clothing would cool her, allowing her to breathe.

Unwinding the scarf, Wynne made a tiny, defenseless sound as she stared down at the mottled bruising marring Brook's throat. "No. Oh, no." Her suspicions were unthinkable. Needing reassurance that her friend was merely unconscious, she seized her limp hand. The spreading bloodstain it had concealed provoked her into action. Screaming for Gar, she ran out the door, her mind already reaching out for the one man who could help Brook.

It was worse than she could have ever imagined.

Tipton and his manservant Speck had arrived hours earlier, under the misconception that Wynne had been hurt. Relieved she was unharmed, her fierce brother-in-law had crushed her ribs with an unusual show of affection and then moved past her to see his patient.

Poor Brook had remained unconscious the entire agonizing wait for Tipton. She barely stirred during his careful examination of her condition, or during the journey upstairs to one of the bedrooms. With Milly's help, they had removed her gown and corset.

Now Wynne understood that Brook's choice of dress had little to do with comfort. From her wrists to her shoulders, she bore numerous bruises, all at various stages of healing. There was an infected bite on her right shoulder, and several more on her breasts. Beneath the bloodstained skirt, a horrifyingly larger stain covered her petticoats. While Wynne was politely offering her something to drink, her friend had been quietly bleeding to death. The smell and sight of all that blood churned her stomach. Rushing to the chamber pot, she disgraced herself by vomiting.

Afterward, Tipton, once he had satisfied himself that he did not have two patients on his hands, had ordered her out of the room. Embarrassed by her weakness, she had dragged a chair near the closed door and waited.

The door finally was thrust open. Tipton started at her presence. Sighing his disapproval, he hunkered down at her side. "I told you to rest."

"What is strenuous about sitting in a chair?" she argued, dismissing his objection. "Tell me the truth. How ill is she?"

He stared at her face for a moment. Assured by what he saw, he reluctantly nodded. "The bruising, although cruel to the eye, is superficial. The bite marks are infected and have brought on a fever."

"The baby?" she whispered, seeing regret in his eyes.

"She lost it. I am sorry, Wynne. I know she is your friend, and someone has treated her inexcusably."

"Not *someone*. Lord A'Court. Her husband. The man who should have been cherishing her. Instead, he . . . he . . ." Her voice hitched at the memory of Brook's battered body. "I will not let him have her. The next time, he might succeed in killing her."

"You are too involved, Wynne, and are not thinking clearly," he murmured, lowering his voice so their conversation did not go beyond the closed door. "No matter what you or I desire, the man holds all the rights."

Tears flooded her gaze. "Rights!" she seethed. "What about Brook's rights? Her unborn babe." It was so awful, she thought. Too envious of what she thought was her friend's perfect marriage to the man she loved, Wynne had not seen the desperation and misery.

Tipton was pushing her back into the chair before she

realized she had arisen to escape. "You are hysterical. I'll send Speck after Devona."

Jerking her arms up and out of his grasp, she sobbed, "No, no."

He maneuvered her into his arms and held her. "Hush. You will hurt the baby, crying so."

Wynne stiffened. Ignoring her damp cheeks, she glared, irritated that he was the one who had uncovered her secret. "How did you guess?"

"Little clues, pet. You are not the first lady I have observed in the delicate condition."

She sniffled, feeling foolish. A year had barely past since Devona had given birth to her son. Logically, he would be more perceptive than most, considering his profession.

"Milroy is the father?"

The bout of tears over, she nodded. Noticing the menacing glint in his knowing expression, she felt pressed to add, "There is no need for that look. The moment you met my sister, you could not keep your hands off her."

"The man has laid more than hands on you, Wynne."

"My choice, Tipton. Nor your concern." Pride made her posture rigid.

Thunderstruck, he sat back on his heels. "Protecting him, too? By this time, I expect your shoulders are wobbling from the strain."

"Stay out of my business. You are worse than Brock ever was," she muttered.

"Milroy has pride too, Wynne. No man wants to hide behind his woman. Nor does he want you to think he needs charity."

Her lips thinned at the sympathy in her brother-in-law's defense, not liking that he was siding with Keanan. Still, she preferred it to the murderous outrage she had glimpsed earlier.

She stood and moved past him. Cracking the door, she

watched Brook sleep, the woman's fear and grief banished by the sedative Tipton had poured into her.

"Some men do hide behind women," she mused softly, wondering how long before Lord A'Court would call upon the Bedegraynes. From her friend's feverish rambling, Wynne had learned that Brook had dismissed her carriage and had walked in an attempt to keep her destination a secret. No matter what Tipton thought was right or legal, she would not return her friend to her husband.

"Damn, uncompromising woman," he swore, understanding that nothing he could threaten would prevent her from protecting those she loved. "Were you listening to me?"

Drawing back, she closed the door. Assuming he was referring to Keanan, she said, "Oh yes, I heard, but you are mistaken. Women, also, despise charity—perhaps even more than men do. I certainly will not marry for it."

Well into the night, Milly roused Wynne from sleep, telling her that Lord A'Court was waiting for her below. Checking the clock on her small mantel, she noted the late hour. It had taken the earl longer than she had expected to locate his wife.

Preferring he should wait, she took her time dressing. With her maid's assistance she donned a modest pale-blue muslin with a short train. Lace edged the rounded neckline, covering more flesh than it revealed. Milly covered her coiled and pinned hair beneath a lace-and-white-beaded handkerchief while she secured the clasp of her mother's pearl-and-gold cross. Pleased with the effect, she made her way downstairs. The realization that Brook's well-being depended on a convincing performance subdued her better than any skill she could muster.

"My lord," she greeted the earl, signaling her footman Gar with a subtle glance to remain close. "My family has been called eccentric, but visits at this hour are highly irregular even for us."

A properly tormented expression firmly in place, Lord A'Court clasped her extended hand. She felt him tremble. "Miss Bedegrayne, I regret the intrusion. Pray, forgive me, but I am too beset for pleasantries. My lady is missing."

Shocked, her hand closed over the cross over her heart. "Poor Brook," she lamented, speaking from the heart. "You must tell me everything."

His gray eyes liquid with emotion, he said, "My business affairs of late have made me a less attentive husband. I was impatient, and we had a row. I locked myself in my study, and she left the house, presumably to shop. She foolishly abandoned the carriage and never returned."

"What a dreadful tale! I assume you have men searching the streets?"

Annoyance flickered in his gaze and then was gone. "Yes, yes. She has vanished like mist in the dawn." He rubbed the wetness from his eyes.

She had to tread carefully now. The man was so expressive in his anguish. If she had not seen Brook's injuries, she might have thought his torment genuine. "It was kind of you to bring this sad news to me in person. I love Brook as one does a sister. Is there anything our family can offer in assistance?"

"Without a doubt, Miss Bedegrayne. You can tell me where my wife is," he insisted. The cold demand had her taking a step backward out of his reach.

She frowned, appearing confused. "My lord, you just told me Brook disappeared whilst shopping. Why would you assume I know of her whereabouts?"

"Why?" He took a menacing step toward her and then halted when he noticed he would have to deal with the footman if he laid a hand on her. Dropping all pretense of distress, he curled his hands into impotent fists at his sides. "Where else would the stupid cow flee, but to London's merciful angel for the downtrodden? Now tell me where she is."

The cross was cutting into her palm, but she did not release it. She was staggered that Lord A'Court knew of her private business. Perhaps Brook had guessed and had innocently confided her suspicions to her husband. Or maybe he had simply beaten it out of her. Wynne tried to conceal a shudder. If there was a manner in which he could use this information against her, this furious man would not hesitate.

"Obviously, I cannot help you, my lord. Gar shall see you to your coach."

He lunged and grabbed her, stunning everyone with his brazenness. Gar ensnared him from behind, but the earl was extraordinarily strong. While the footman struggled to pry him loose from his mistress, Lord A'Court twisted her arm. She could hear Milly sob out her name as she tugged on the back of her frock. The handkerchief tied to her head slipped, falling unnoticed to the floor.

"Let go," Gar roared, striking Lord A'Court in the ear. He yelped, releasing Wynne. They fell away from each other into the arms of the servants.

"Did he hurt you, miss?" the maid asked, helping her stand. Wynne denied it with a shake of her head, concentrating on drawing a steady breath.

"If this is how you treat women, then I am not surprised your wife left you," she said, still shaken by his abrupt attack. "Gar, escort his lordship from this house. Use whatever means necessary. Lord A'Court does not have time for pleasantries."

"Listen, you righteous bitch, I want my wife back. You cannot hide her from me for long. I will find her," he warned, trying to lunge for her again. Gar's impolite grip on the earl's cravat held him in place. "Once I do, I will come back." He sputtered as he was jerked backward toward the door. "You will regret your interference."

At least that is what she thought he said. The strain of

her footman's hold had garbled his final threat. A final savage heave, and he was gone.

Milly fretted, "The fiend meant every word. What'll you do, miss?"

"Nothing. He cannot prove I interfered." The tight hold on the balustrade betrayed her anxiety. Lord A'Court was not the first boorish male she had encountered. She would not bow to his intimidation. Protecting Brook took precedence over her own fears. Besides, she supposed that once Tipton and her father learned of the earl's threats, the man would be more concerned about leaving town than plotting revenge. She clung to that small comfort, fearing the escape of sleep would be denied her this night.

Nineteen

"What were you thinking, allowing that man into our house?"

Drake glanced pointedly at their man of affairs, Mr. Tibal, but the subtle warning for discretion was useless in his mother's agitated state. "Spare me the hysterics, Mother. We have credited too much attention to a singular incident, nor do I have the patience for indulgence."

Still pale from that morning's bloodletting, she sank into the small sofa, appearing fragile and beleaguered. "Something must be done. Without Reckester here to protect us, his bastard will try stealing what is rightfully ours."

The only mercy he had from her rambling screed was when she was sedated in her rooms. Unfortunately, the physician would sedate her for only so many hours. Setting aside the ledger, he said, "We have gone as far as we can with this today. You may leave us, Mr. Tibal, and you have my thanks."

"And you, my sympathy, Your Grace," he replied, his gaze resting briefly on the dowager. It took him minutes to gather the papers into his portfolio and depart.

"Tibal is a good man. He will stop Milroy."

"Stop him from what, Mother?" He spread out his arms, encompassing the study. "Taking this house, or the others in the country? He will have to fight his way through the creditors I have managed to stave off until now. Reckester managed to gamble away most of the family's fortune. Be grateful. Had he lived a day longer, we might not have this house."

The dowager glowered, the look worthy of her former self. "Maligning him is beneath you, Drake. I was not blind to his faults. Still, your father was a selfish creature. He would not have enjoyed being poor."

"I have struggled, replenishing what he has frivolously lost. Instead of seeking a bride who stirs my blood, I have pursued women with the greedy eye of a damnable fortune hunter, all in the name of saving this family."

Chastised, she broke the hold of his persuasive stare. "My intention was not to belittle your sacrifices. You have always protected our name and honor."

"You are correct when you say Father was selfish. He would do anything to protect his interests. Milroy claims Reckester planned to offer him proof of his legitimacy. I believe him."

Visibly curling within herself, his mother hugged a small pillow. "Lies. All lies."

Drake closed his eyes, blocking out her image. His mother was as selfish as his father. He doubted she would willingly admit the deception. "I pray you speak the truth, Mother. If Reckester was truly searching for Milroy the night he died, can you guess what fascinating papers his killer has in his possession?"

"Lord A'Court has vanished," Sir Thomas announced to Wynne, frustrated his quarry had eluded him. "His servants have not seen him for two days."

She followed him upstairs to his private chamber, not pleased to see the blunderbuss pistol in his possession. It made her very nervous seeing a weapon in her volatile father's hand. This had been his third attempt to track down the earl. To her relief, even with Tipton's and his manservant's assistance, they had not discovered the man's whereabouts. As far as she was concerned, Lord A'Court could remain lost. She wanted neither Brook nor her family confronting him.

"Perhaps he left town?"

Tossing the pistol on his bed, Sir Thomas barked out the open door for his valet to bring him his dressing gown. "Not likely, gel. You stood between him and his wife. He will be wanting her back, and a settling with you. Not that he will get a chance." He sighed heavily. "It took courage defying him. Can you give me one reason why I should not put my hand to your backside?"

It was time to tell him the truth. "I carry your grandchild."

His eyes boggled at the news. "A stunning reason, it is." He scowled at the appearance of his valet. "Why are you hovering? Get me a drink," he ordered, sending the servant scurrying off.

Wynne walked to the mantel, where the portrait of her mother beckoned. The resemblance was strong between mother and daughter. "You must be disappointed."

"That you anticipated your marriage bed? You are not the first," he said gruffly. "I saw how that Milroy looked at you. Nothing short of death would have kept him from having you."

"I wanted him too, Papa." Summoning the courage he swore she possessed, she turned to face him. Instead of the anger she expected, he seemed astonishingly resigned. "I want your oath you will not go charging after him, pistol in hand."

"Depends on when the banns will be posted." His silver-winged brows drew together as his blue-green eyes narrowed. "Oath be damned. That rogue will marry you or face the consequences."

"Do I not have a say?"

Sir Thomas frowned at her surly manner. "From my way of thinking, you had your say, my gel, when you chose the man for a lover." His face darkened at the impropriety of their conversation.

"I cannot marry him," she said, bracing for the worst.

Her father did not disappoint her. "You will marry him!" he roared. "Whether you continue on as his wife or his widow depends on his cooperation."

"You cannot bully me into accepting him. Neither of us would be happy with the results."

"Whoever said marriage and happiness shared the same bed?" he snapped, exasperated. "Most men I know barely tolerate their wives. Half have mistresses, and half again do not like even them."

Taken aback that he expected a similar fate for his daughter, she stammered, "W-what of you and Mama? Was it merely tolerance on your part? Did you rejoice in the arms of your mistress when she died?"

"You go too far, gel," he said, insulted. "No woman could have bewitched me from your sweet mama. She was everything to me. Losing her almost destroyed me!" The pain of his loss was still as fresh as if it had taken place yesterday instead of years earlier. He snatched the drink off the tray his valet carried, and dismissed him with a curt nod.

"I know. I take it all back." She bit her lower lip, horrified that her careless words had stirred his endless grief. "Is it wrong for me to want nothing less?"

"No," he conceded somberly. "Are you telling me this Milroy feels little for you?" His expression revealed his skepticism. Both were recalling Keanan's last visit to their household, and the near violence it took removing him.

"He pursued me because Lord Nevin was interested. Somewhere along the way, I became more than a faceless pawn. I doubt he understands his feelings any more than I do."

"My opinion still holds. Keanan Milroy is not worthy of you." He put his hands on her shoulders. "That lad has pursued his demon sire for most of his life, not knowing if he would embrace or kill him when he cornered him. Having another to blame for Reckester's murder might allow him to bury his anger. Give him a chance to hunger for more than vengeance."

She circled in his arms to face him. "The duke is dead?" A wave of dizziness swept over her. She grasped her father's arms to keep from falling. The insidious thought that Keanan might be responsible whispered though her, though all the while, her heart denied it. "Have they caught the killer?"

"No." Understanding softened his grim features. "Ah, Wynne, my gel. As much as I would relish young Milroy out of your life, even I can see he is not the sort to hide in the shadows and murder an unarmed man."

Finding comfort in her father's assurance, she asked, "So you think he is incapable of murder?"

"Not exactly," he hedged. "If a man like Milroy wanted you dead, he wouldn't be skulking in street filth at midnight. He would meet his foe direct, and there would be no mistaking his intentions."

"You speak as if you understand him."

Coaxing her head to his chest, he rocked her gently, as he had done when she was a child and had need of his comfort. "I do. Any man who arrogantly declares my daughter his, warrants investigation."

"His life has been so horrid," she said, recalling what he had told her about his childhood.

"Parts. We all have sadness in our lives. Still, he managed to make something of himself. That should tell you something."

Curious, she looked up.

"Milroy might have been thrown out of this house, but he will be coming back."

* * *

Brook awoke at Tipton's touch. Terror surfaced when she noted her state of undress.

"You are safe, Lady A'Court. Do you know who I am?"

Touching her various bandages, she slowly nodded. "Yes, you are Lord Tipton."

"My apologies for awakening you. The duration of your sleep had me worried that I had overlooked an injury to your head."

The lingering lethargy in her gaze vanished. She would have sat up if he had not pressed her shoulder back into the pillow. "I must leave."

"You have trusted me until now with your care, Lady A'Court." He did not mention that she had been unable to do otherwise. "Do you recall who did this to you?"

Tears drenched her pale-blue eyes. "He hurt me—m-my husband."

His jaw clenched in restrained fury. This poor woman had endured enough violence at the hands of a man. She lacked the disposition for witnessing it unleashed even on her behalf. "How long has he been abusing you?"

"My husband has not been abusing me, my lord. It is his right to correct me," she said without inflection, as if the words had been branded into her memory. "I have always been an impulsive, spirited child. I was honored he chose me to be his countess and showed enough interest to guide me when I erred." The well of tears overflowed, slipping down her cheeks.

She had to be addled if she believed such tripe, he thought in disgust. "Well, madam, you almost did not survive your husband's last instruction."

Wiping her tears with the back of her hand, she said, "It was a mistake. Usually, he is careful not to leave any visible marks. He was just so angry, you see."

"All too clearly, Lady A'Court." He suspected from the scars on her back and abdomen that she had been mistreated from the day she was wedded. Not all the injuries were superficial. Her mental state concerned him, if she truly believed she deserved this vile handling.

"I hurt so. There was the baby to think of. I had to get away. I did not dream Wynne?"

"No. You arrived at the Bedegraynes' and collapsed. Wynne summoned me immediately."

Her hand slid down, resting over her womb. "The babe. He is well?"

Tipton could see no alternative for softening the truth. "I am sorry. Your child did not survive. The injuries you sustained—" He halted, watching her curl away from him. Her wretched sobs slashed at him.

"My fault . . . my fault," she repeated over and over.

Helpless, he held her hand and allowed her to cry out her grief. He could tend her wounds, but not the one shattering her heart. Choosing to focus on the details he could control, his dark thoughts turned to the elusive Lord A'Court. The man deserved the lash. Until he could be found and caged like the animal he was, Tipton would make certain his patient remained out of his reach.

"Mr. Milroy, you are too kind, indulging an old woman's whims," Aunt Moll cheerfully flattered, while they enjoyed an afternoon stroll in Kensington gardens.

Purposefully keeping pace with her limping stride aided by her cane on one side and his strong arm on the other, Keanan smiled down at her. "Ma'am, be fair. Your invitation was a royal summons, one I humbly heeded."

She snorted in disbelief. "I am wise to you, sir. If you are humble, it is a method of gaining what you desire."

"Let us not be coy. We share a mutual goal, one you have supported from the beginning."

"My niece," she agreed, seemingly pleased they could speak so forthrightly. "You have been a most difficult suitor, Mr. Milroy."

An image of Wynne, her stubborn chin set, rose unbidden in his thoughts. She had sent him away, believing she was less important to him than claiming his inheritance. Once, he would have agreed. "Then we are even, for I have never met a more headstrong woman."

Stopping, she admired the view of the palace on the horizon. "So what are your plans?"

He kicked at the stones on the gravel path. Considering her friendly, conspiring demeanor, he suspected Wynne had not told her aunt of the child she carried. "Things have been confusing of late. It is best I keep my distance. Sir Thomas has probably issued orders that I be shot if I dare approach the house again."

Aunt Moll lifted one of her dainty gloved hands and whopped him on the ears. She put enough strength into it to make his ear sting.

"What was that for?" he demanded, rubbing his injured ear.

"For giving up too easily. You should be willing to endure all manner of hardships to secure her hand."

"She will not have me," he admitted, the bitterness still strong.

"Wynne has pride and temper and can wield them like a weapon if someone has hurt her. Woo her, Mr. Milroy. Show her that she has a place in your life."

"And do I have a place in hers, Aunt Moll? I will never be the sort of man Bedegrayne wants for his precious daughter. True, I have money. She would not starve in my care. Even so, I will always be Reckester's bastard. There will be talk. How long do you think she will stomach the stares and cruel gossip before she starts resenting me for it? And what of our children? My shame stains them as well."

Noticing the movement of her hand, Keanan prudently stepped out of range.

"You underestimate Wynne if you think she would abandon you because a few insignificant individuals speak unkindly. And what about you? How can you prove that you covet more than her name and body?"

If a man had asked him that insolent question, he would have struck him down. "I walked into a club and challenged five ruthless men for besmirching her honor. Those belligerent fellows are most likely plotting my demise. I ask you, what more can a man do to prove himself?"

Sensing his fear, she was sympathetic. "By not walking away."

After he had returned Aunt Moll to her house, Keanan resisted the urge to call on Wynne. Instead, he drove the carriage, another recent acquisition, home. Despite her aunt's assurances that Sir Thomas's concerns were more for his daughter's happiness than for his bloodlines, he doubted he would ever be the old man's first choice for Wynne's husband.

Married.

The direction of his thoughts stunned him. One afternoon with her dotty aunt had him foolishly weaving impossible dreams. The lady in question did not trust him, and her father wished he would simply die. It was a dubitable beginning for all, and he had seen too much hardship in his life to trust in happy endings.

"Sir, a word, if you please."

Too lost in his unpleasant thoughts, he had not heard the boy approach. Judging from his ragged clothing, and a sober wariness that only pain could bring in a child his age, Keanan recognized a part of himself in that young grimy face.

"Have you eaten?"

" 'Avent come a' begging, sir. I've been employed to deliver ye a message," the lad said, puffing up with importance.

Climbing down from the phaeton, Keanan let his groom take his place and see to the horses. "Well, let's hear it."

The boy scrunched his face, concentrating on the exact words he had been paid to repeat. "I was to tell ye that a certain gentleman 'as papers of vast importance to ye. They're yours if yer willing to pay their worth."

He had anticipated this offer, understanding the temptation Reckester's missing papers provided. Still, it could be a ruse. "How much?"

"Thirty pounds," he said, confirming it with a nod when Keanan lifted his brows at the amount. "The meeting is set for ten o'clock in Common Garden. Come alone, 'e warns, and no pops, else 'e'll peddle the papers to some other chap."

The man had chosen well. Covent Garden was a perilous area at night, filled with thieves, whores, and gamblers. No one would stir at the sound of a discharged pistol or a desperate plea for help.

"You can tell your employer I will be there."

"No need to, sir. The cove never doubted yer answer."

Twenty

The family had united against her. After a private, heated discussion with Aunt Moll earlier in the afternoon, Sir Thomas had reluctantly agreed that hiding from polite society might lend credence to the circulating rumors about Wynne, Keanan, and a certain group of gentlemen who were nursing varying degrees of injury, but all had been amazingly close-lipped on the subject. Wynne had opposed the family evening out. She was overruled.

Only when her father reminded her that his reasoning went beyond her personal comfort, did she relent. There was also Brook to protect. Lord A'Court could make all the accusations he wanted, but he had no proof that Wynne had anything to do with his wife's disappearance. Strangely, for a man certain she was the key to finding his wife, he had not voiced his suspicions to the police. Perhaps he was worried what she might say if pressed. Regardless, she assumed he was having the house watched. This presumption had kept her from returning to her friend's bedside. It was safer this way, and besides, she trusted Tipton and his people to protect her.

"It appears Reckester's demise has not diminished the turnout, though I can think of few who would truly mourn him," Sir Thomas said, frowning at the room filled with people. He was never comfortable with so many females fluttering in their finery. "There's my gel!" He opened his arms to his youngest child.

"Good evening, Papa." Devona greeted her father with a kiss. Her gaze shifted to her sister. "Wynne, you look splendid. I envy you for that gown," she complimented, her casual words spoken for the curious. Leaning forward, she brushed a kiss on Wynne's cheek. She whispered, "Tipton assures me his patient is well. You are not to worry."

Pleased by the news, Wynne was not feigning her delight. "We will endeavor to keep you amused despite your husband's absence." Together the trio strolled the corridor, ignoring the flurry of interest their arrival heralded. "A pity Irene is not in residence. She could instruct us all on the precise conduct of this essentially awkward situation."

Devona hid her laughter behind her fan at their father's stern expression. "Leave your elder sister be," he dutifully admonished. "She has never stood a chance against the pair of you saucy wits."

A shared amused expression passed between the sisters. Since baiting their paragon sibling was best in her presence, they yielded to their father's request.

"Ah, there is Amara." Devona acknowledged their friend from across the room. "And her horrid mama." Fanning herself, she observed Lady Claeg restraining her daughter before she could cross the room and greet them. Looking miserable, the young woman met Wynne's gaze and offered a silent apology. "Lady Claeg despises me," said Devona. "Do not be hurt by Amara's rejection. Her mother is formidable, and she will never forgive your kinship."

Too aware of what Brook had endured behind locked doors, Wynne wondered what price Amara paid for her defiance. "I regret my association with Amara has only increased her hardship."

"Tosh," Sir Thomas objected. "Miss Claeg values your friendship above any reprimand her stone-hearted mama bestows. Besides, she is a sensible gel. Provoking Lady Claeg into a confrontation with our family would not add polish to either of our houses."

"You are correct, Papa," Wynne murmured, noticing Lord and Lady Lumley moving toward them on the right. If anyone had expected to find her quivering in some dark corner after all the nasty speculation linked to her name, they would be disappointed. Chin high, her eyes green pools of cool reserve, she confidently walked over to the couple, leaving her family to follow.

At the stroke of ten o'clock, Keanan was prowling Covent Gardens. He was not the only predator hunting for prey. The fireworks display in the piazza had drawn an impressive mob of spectators. Vendors, pickpockets, and prostitutes shifted through the restless crowd, each eager to separate the gull from his purse. Resting against a stone column, Keanan watched them all. The smell of gunpowder and greasy food lingered heavily in the air, while the smoke of the discharged fireworks diminished his visibility. Celebratory music and laughter drifted in the distance, casting an eerie mood since he was there to meet Reckester's killer.

"Lovely night."

He would have turned, but the pistol pressed against his spine discouraged any risky movements. "You're late."

The unknown man chuckled. "Keep your hand on the stone, an' the other behind your back where I can see it." His voice was soft, almost effeminate, but it sounded unnatural. "The fists of Reckless Milroy are to be respected. So is my popper."

The hand leaning against the column tensed, curling into a fist. "You were the one who called this meeting."

"Aye. You brought the ready?"

He sneered, "On me? I would be a fool, considering you are the one poking me with a pistol."

The man cursed, grinding the barrel against bone. "You wouldn't be here if you weren't planning on coming to the mark. Where is it?"

"Close."

Staring ahead, Keanan was certain he appeared to be just another spectator enjoying the fireworks. Everyone was too absorbed with the display of light and smoke to wonder about the two gentlemen engaged in a serious conversation.

Shutting out the noise around him, Keanan focused, trying to pick out details about his unknown adversary. The hand clutching his at his back was rough, not the hand of a gentleman. His breath smelled of spirits and sweat, but he did not seem careless or drunk. Judging from their proximity, he sensed the man was tall and probably outweighed him. None of those details bothered him. It was the placement of the barrel, and the man's growing jumpiness, that worried him.

"Stalemates are not to my liking. I prefer being the winner."

"Give me my thirty pounds and we'll both walk away richer," the man said, his voice dipping lower as his anxiety mounted.

Brooding, Keanan's eyelids narrowed. "So speaks the stranger holding the pistol at my back."

"See here, those fists of yours can be punishing when you have the mind. I needed something you'd respect."

Oh, indeed. He had an immeasurable desire not to have the damn weapon exploding his spine into insignificant fragments. "I'm here. You have my interest. Standing about all night will not get you that blunt."

The man was wavering; he could feel it. Keanan smiled, imagining the retribution he would deliver.

This delight illuminating from his handsome profile had not gone unnoticed. A dark-haired woman caught a glimpse of his wicked grin. Mistaking it for an invitation, she was already counting her coin when she sauntered next to him.

"You have the look of a real bone setter, m'lord," she cooed, jutting her bosom forward to offer him a view of the pleasures for purchase. Spotting the man behind him, her greedy eyes widened a fraction. "I'm game for a pair, or do you prefer to watch, luv?"

Flustered, the man took a step back, trying to hide deeper in the shadows. Keanan moved the second the barrel shifted away from his back. Whirling, he threw a wild punch, clipping the other man on the jaw. Stunned, his opponent staggered, discharging the pistol into the ground. The prostitute screamed. Enraged, and not about to allow him to escape, Keanan lunged, tackling the man by his calves. Wiggling free, the attacker kicked, missing Keanan's throat. The blow landed on his collarbone.

He sucked in a harsh breath; the bone felt as though it had been cracked in two. Climbing to his feet, he pursued the fleeing man, zigzagging through the crowd. The activity around them became an infuriating blur of obstacles. Keanan leaped over a small fire, blocking out the angry shouts from the men warming themselves by it. Blood pumping to the point that he felt his heart would burst, he was moving more by instinct than by sight.

The chase took him down King Street. Sweat burned his eyes as he skidded to a halt. His vision sharp even at night, he scanned the street crammed with small empty shops and dwellings. A coach rattled down the street, probably heading for the inn. Two women were arguing; their escalating voices floated from an open window above him. Across the street, three boys were gloating over the rats they had killed. If his quarry was there, his movements were drowned out by the nocturnal sounds of the city.

Panting lightly, his cambric shirt glued to his skin, Keanan wiped the sting from his eyes. There were hundreds of places on this street alone where the man could be hiding. In his arrogance, he had thought he could bring down this man alone. Disgusted by his failure, he spat on the ground. It was a curse—and a promise.

"This isn't finished."

* * *

"I never imagined I would ever feel indebted to a man like Reckester," Devona admitted hours later, when they had escaped to the withdrawing room put aside for the ladies.

Wynne used a comb to sweep up her sister's unruly curls that had come undone at the back, and pinned them in place. She kept her voice low, so the other women in the room could not overhear their conversation. "With Middlefell and the others not discussing the outcome, most have lost interest in whether the wager was real or simply rumor. Besides, how can speculation compete against the shocking murder of a duke?"

She adjusted another pin. Behind her calm facade, she was practically giddy with relief. Keanan had done it. The power those men had held over her—or rather, she silently corrected, the power she had relinquished to them by keeping their harrying a secret—had vanished. Reckester's murder had stimulated the room into conversation. Some reminisced about his old scandals. Others discussed his numerous enemies. Overall, everyone was aghast that someone of quality had been snuffed out in such a grisly manner.

"You should summon him."

"Who?"

"Your Mr. Milroy. Even Papa could not contest his assistance."

Finished with her adjustments, Wynne moved, giving her sister access to the back of her head. "It is more complicated than an untangling of misspoken words and unsolicited feelings, Devona," she argued defensively, wishing she possessed more of her sister's passionate nature. Nothing short of death would have barred her sibling from the man she loved. She admired the sentiment, but her pride was the only thing holding her together most days. Keanan was correct. She was a coward.

Leaving her sister's hair untouched, Devona stood. "One does not tamper with beauty's pattern card."

The flash of disappointment she glimpsed in her sister's eyes left her oddly hurt. Wynne watched her depart, knowing Devona would see to their father while she quietly rebuilt the rigidity of her crumbling composure.

Rising, she glanced over at the other women present. Four women draped in leisurely poses were sharing anecdotes concerning their various admirers. No one was showing more than casual interest in her. Wynne sensed the invisible barrier separating her from these women and wondered whether the isolation was due to fate or choice.

Not expecting an answer, she passed the women, acknowledging them with a polite nod, and left the room. Her thoughts focused inward, she collided with one of the guests. The apology on her tongue dissolved. Lord Middlefell was close enough that she could smell the hock on his breath. Stepping back, she noticed Lord Lothbury next to him. Both men bore the abraded scabs and colorful bruises of Keanan's displeasure.

"Lothbury, the lady looks faint. Perhaps we should whisk her into a private room and open a window. Lord knows I have an itch to cut her corset strings."

"Stay away from me," she frostily warned, remembering other instances when the man had described in detail all the horrible things he would do to her if he ever caught her alone. Realizing they would never allow her to pass, she pivoted, but stopped at the sight of Mr. Therry blocking her way. His soft girth was cheerfully wrapped in a green and yellow striped waistcoat.

"Where are the others? I was under the impression scrubs worked in vicious packs."

The viscount's lip curled in an ugly fashion, his ruined nose exposing the ruthlessness he tried to hide behind his charm. "Digaud, the milksop, left London. He claimed his injuries required Bath's soothing waters." Middlefell's expression showed what he thought of that nonsense. "As for Esthill, well, Nevin did manage to break numerous bones. I expect he will leave his bed eventually. How kind of you to inquire."

If a plague wiped them out, the world would be better for it, but she decided voicing the observation was not prudent. "Gentlemen, I have never considered you fools, and will cling to my first opinion. Permit me to pass."

Lord Middlefell matched her step aside and laid his hand on her arm. He bowed his head, leaning close enough for his breath to tickle her ear. "I always thought you were a haughty bitch. You felt you were too pure for the likes of me, but you were a ripe tumble for that Irish whoreson, were you not? The question remains, will you still want him, Miss Bedegrayne, after I have him castrated?"

She met his rigid gaze, immediately understanding this was no longer a game. The man intended to extract his own justice.

"No dulcet pleas for mercy? I might be willing, considering you and I go off privately for the discussion."

"You do not frighten me, my lord. Mr. Milroy trounced all five of you. I cannot think of a man who needs your mercy less, nor would want me to beg for it." Brave words; still, half of her believed them. In a fair fight, she had faith Keanan would triumph over any foe. It was a sly attack she feared. Regardless of the troubles between them, Wynne could not bear for him to be hurt.

Lord Middlefell's fingers dug into her arm. "You spiteful—"

"There you are, Miss Bedegrayne," Amara Claeg said, her greeting brimming radiance and guilelessness. "Holding court again, while there are numerous young ladies pining for these gentlemen's attentions."

Her smile faltered when she noticed the viscount's hold on Wynne. Rallying, she rapped her closed ivory fan across the man's knuckles. He released his hold, more from shock than pain. "Lord Middlefell, you are a shameful scoundrel, flirting with a lady whose heart is already engaged."

Speechless, Wynne forgot she was free until Amara hooked their arms and gently tugged them out of reach. "Lord Lothbury, I am crushed you have no proper greeting for an old friend."

The marquess flickered an uncomfortable glance at his cronies. Clearing his throat, he said, properly chastised, "Miss Claeg, I pray you will allow me to apologize by accepting my invitation for a dance."

Amara lowered her lashes, appearing flustered by the request. Only Wynne noted the uncharacteristic bitterness she veiled. "I shall enjoy your pretty words, my lord."

The inane dialogue had diffused the confrontation as her friend had intended. Lord Middlefell would never attack her in front of a witness. "Excuse us, my lords, I must see to my father. I will never understand why most gentlemen are ill at ease at these gatherings." The men bowed at their departure, although Wynne felt the viscount's glare on her back until she and Amara strolled from their vision.

"Miss Claeg, you were magnificent." She circled her waist and hugged her. "Never a finer performance have I ever encountered. I hope you severely chastise the ninny who dares call you a coward."

Amara blushed, recalling she was the ninny who had used the word. "I saw them together. Lothbury and Middlefell. I knew the viscount would not be able to resist cornering you, since Mr. Milroy is an unparalleled adversary."

"You offend me. Did you not see I had them quite in hand?"

Her friend did not smile and join her in mocking the situation. Instead, Amara's shoulders slumped. "I observed you were vastly outnumbered, and I was partly to blame," she confessed.

"What is this?" Wynne halted, steering her away from the ballroom so they could speak in private. "You had nothing to do with this business. In fact, I must beg your forgiveness for pushing that scoundrel Lord Lothbury at you."

"You do not understand. I was flattered by the marquess's attentions. He made me feel—" She paused, wrestling with her emotions. "He was so interested. I never questioned his subtle inquiries about you. Later, I realized he used my answers to hurt you and Mr. Milroy."

"Ah, my dear friend. What a pair we make, both of us living with our guilty secrets. You are not responsible for those men. Any blame you consider yours vanished the moment you came to my aid."

It was difficult to banish all her guilt. Amara suffered, her heart bruised by Lord Lothbury's flummery. Her first inclination was to hunt down the man herself. However, after witnessing her friend's bold approach when she was in trouble, Wynne suspected Amara was quite capable of exacting her own womanly revenge. "I wager Lady Claeg will require her vinaigrette after she learns you left her side to defend a Bedegrayne."

The tense line of her mouth eased into a mischievous smile. Her mother was known for her spectacular fits. "Yes, I imagine so."

Keanan had caught up with Dutch some time after midnight. His search had taken him through five taverns before he found him quietly sitting by himself near the door of an establishment that Keanan would not have entered unless armed, even in daylight.

"Reckless Milroy." His friend saluted him with his beer, sloshing it with his clumsy movements. "Join me. I hate getting foxed alone."

"The wrist bothering you?"

"Aye, bloody weather must be turning. Sit . . . sit."

Sitting down, Keanan accepted the beer a plump barmaid had set before him. Friendly and almost as drunk as the patrons, she plopped down onto his lap. Feeling nothing, he glowered at his present predicament. There was only one woman he craved, and she would not have him. The maid giggled and snuggled against his chest, aware of his hands on her waist. He unceremoniously shoved her off his lap. The maid landed on the floor. Dutch and several of the patrons laughed while she sat on her rump, screaming foul curses at him. Unmoved by the disruption he had created, Keanan swallowed his beer, his gaze focused on his amused friend.

"If this is your delicate handling of the gentle sex, is it so surprising your lady will not have you?" Dutch teased.

"Wynne will be mine, never doubt it."

The man raised his brows at the resounding confidence he heard. He shook his head. "It is this sad business with the old duke which divides you."

Speaking of it left a burning wound in his gut. "I did not come here to discuss Wynne. I came for the truth. Do you have the papers on you?"

Dutch gulped the remains of his beer. "Papers? I have no papers."

Keanan was discovering that the truth was more difficult to face than his suspicions. Bracing his elbows on the table, he was already grieving when he asked, "You killed him, didn't you?"

Shocked by the accusation, his mouth worked, trying to form a reasonable reply. "Are you daft? I've killed no one."

"You lie," he snapped, the words delivered like a lash. "You have his papers, Dutch, and do not disgrace our friendship by denying it. Did you honestly believe I would not recognize you this night?"

Dutch glanced away. He watched the spurned barmaid flirt with a sailor. Noticing his regard, she smirked and kissed her new champion. "How did you guess?"

"I didn't. Not at first," Keanan said, his gaze fixed on the swelling bruise on his friend's jaw. He flexed his hand.

His knuckles still ached from the punch. "Your disguised voice could not withstand your nerves. Were you hoping I would think you were that fop Digaud, or one of his sinister sycophants?"

"Maybe," he acknowledged. "Can you deny you would have passed on a chance to go at them again?"

No, damn him, he could not. He was not reasonable about these men. They had hurt Wynne. If it were within his power, they would spend the rest of their lives paying for their sins. "You're no killer."

Sensing his companion's tenuous control, Dutch decided he deserved the truth. "You an' me have been friends too long to count. It makes us family in a way. Brothers."

He had wasted so many years plotting Reckester's ruin that he had not treasured the people who had always been there for him. Depending on them would have meant he trusted them, an ability he thought he had lost the cold morning he found his mother's stiff, broken body.

"I would be a difficult younger brother, Dutch."

"Aye, the golden truth, that's for certain," he agreed, his expression a mix of affection and regret. "Someone had to see to you, with you always in a huff, welcoming every rough-and-tumble."

"I've retired."

"A bruiser you are, Reckless. Take the man out of the ring and he is still a fighter." He fell silent, turning the cup in his large, scarred hands. "The old duke was never going to accept you as his blood."

"So you murdered him? If I wanted him dead, I could have done it myself." Had he not envisioned it for years?

"It was an accident. I followed him to the Silver Serpent, knowing his intentions. The man was desperate. He was prepared to cast off one son for the other. Why, I asked myself? It wasn't love or old regrets that moved him. He planned using you, lad. You were so blinded by rosy dreams that he would have destroyed you."

"Did you read those papers you took off his body? They supposedly prove I'm his heir."

"For how long? The wily snake was pitting you against Nevin, or did you believe the lad would toss the title and high water away without a challenge? Blood or by hire, that hoity-toity mama of his would see to it." The wooden cup splintered from the pressure of his hands. "I couldn't let them hurt you. He had to be stopped. I only meant to tap him on the nob and steal the papers, I swear. It ended there, if he lost his wretched proof." The breath he exhaled was shaky with emotion. "I hit him with a board. The weak-necked bastard was downed with one blow. It was like my arms had a mind of their own. I hit him and kept hitting him. I barely remember what made me stop. Maybe a noise from the street? I took the papers and ran."

Eyes dry, Keanan had no grief for Reckester or the violent way he died. His face was a fierce mask as he reached within his pocket for the thirty pounds. "You have to leave town." He did not recognize the rough, strained quality in his voice. Friendship and loyalty had been twisted into a lethal act of devotion, and he was responsible. Right or wrong, he was determined to save his friend. He threw the leather pouch of coins on the table.

Dutch picked up the pouch and tucked it into his waist. He removed the papers from his coat and held them out. The crushed documents were flecked with dried blood. "These belong to you."

"I don't want them."

"The dukedom is yours for the claiming."

Keanan stared at the offered papers and thought of Reckester's shattered skull. "The price is too high."

Dropping the documents on the table, Dutch rose. "Always the noble bastard," he gently rebuked, placing a hand on Keanan's shoulder. "Use them or burn them. The choice doesn't alter the man." He walked out the door into the night.

Palming the documents, Keanan slipped them into an inner pocket. Dutch's parting gift gave him the power to ruin Reckester's family. Despite his protests, there was a lingering temptation to wield it.

Twenty-one

Lady Claeg amused the guests by collapsing when she noticed her daughter had disobeyed her wishes and was chatting with the Bedegraynes. Fortunately, Amara had brought her vinaigrette. Several footmen assisted by carrying the moaning woman off to a private room before she had completely revived. Exchanging private grins with Wynne and Devona, Amara went off to placate her upset mama.

Satisfied that Amara could handle her mother, Wynne made her excuses to her family. She needed to see Keanan. Lord Middlefell's threats echoed in her head. The man might have ended his game with her, but she feared a more dangerous one had begun for the man she loved.

Once her father had learned of Lord Middlefell's, Lord Lothbury's, and Mr. Therry's presence at the ball, he was quite encouraging about her departure. It was mutually agreed that Devona would remain. Neither trusted their father's reaction if one of those men should be imprudent enough to confront him. Still infuriated that Keanan Milroy had protected his daughter in his stead, he longed to make his own impression on the reprobates.

"You are off to see him," Devona said, following her sister out of the ballroom.

Offended, Wynne demanded, "Am I that transparent?"

"Only to me. Have you forgiven him?"

Impatient to leave, Wynne sighed, "Sister, I have no time

for this discussion." Spotting the family crest, she bussed her sister's cheek and ran toward the waiting coach.

As she opened the door she called out Keanan's address to the coachman. Without glancing in her direction, he grunted, acknowledging her order. Puzzled that the leather hoods of the carriage had been drawn up on such a pleasant evening, she was not paying attention when she entered the dark interior. The blunt prod of cold iron against her breast froze her advance.

"Join me, Miss Bedegrayne. Do not fear the pistol. I have no intention of using it," Lord A'Court promised. "It is merely an inducement, lest you underestimate my skills in handling a woman." Gloved fingers seized her by the shoulder and shoved her sideways into the compartment. He barked out an order and slammed the door. The horses jumped at the sound of the coachman's voice.

"No servant of ours would accept bribery. What happened to my coachman?"

"This useless sentiment for the lower classes bores me. Perhaps I can assist in polishing your polite conversation."

"All I require is for you to halt this carriage," she replied before questioning the wisdom of her hasty words. Seeing only a cloaked shadow within shadows, she could not discern if the pistol was pointed at her.

Explosive pain lit up her vision for a few seconds. Cowering, she tried to think beyond the throbbing ache. He had removed his glove and used his bare hand on her. She touched her cheek. The ring he wore had grazed her. The burning scratch almost hurt worse than the blow.

Defiant, and annoyed with herself for stepping blindly into his hands, she said, "Hurting women must be the only skill you claim, you pathetic maggot. Having been deprived of your wife, I suppose any defenseless woman will do." The next blow had her seeing glittery blooms of fireworks.

Fool, she thought, sucking in her breath. Protecting her injured cheek with her hand, she remained silent. No one had ever lifted a hand at her in anger. Having spent a lifetime defending herself against officious brothers, her verbal attack had been automatic. In his present state, A'Court would beat her senseless before they reached their destination.

Panting with suppressed rage and triumph, Lord A'Court pounded the hood. "I *was* correct. You have been hiding her. I thought maybe she went crying to her mother. However the last time she dared, the dear matron was kind enough to return my lady. A pity you were not as cooperative."

Wynne shut her eyes, feeling a sliver of the despair Brook must have felt. How could a mother send her daughter back to the man responsible for abusing her? Her hand slipped protectively over her womb. She feared for her child. Any man who battered his own wife until she aborted their child would show no mercy for hers.

His continued silence increased her anxiety. Burrowed into the seat, her body tensed, waiting for another blow. She thought him unbalanced, and his actions seemed to confirm it. Why was he not interrogating her about Brook's whereabouts? The question circled around in her frantic brain until his earlier comment triggered a baffling realization.

"You were uncertain I had knowledge of Brook. Yet you attacked my coachman and kidnapped me. It was a considerable risk for mere speculation, though what grievance you may charge me with is perplexing."

"Someone of your admirable intelligence should understand that a proper lady does not speak without permission." He kicked; his boot unerringly connected with her right knee.

She choked on her insuppressible plea for him to cease. Biting her lower lip, she refused to satisfy his perverse pleasure by revealing her pain. The confines of the compartment gave him the advantage. Provoking him further might make an escape attempt impossible. So she curled away from him and employed what even he had praised her for possessing. She would use her intelligence.

Keanan pushed his way through the crowd.

He might have arrived bearing no invitation, however, the hostess, recognizing the ingredients of a good scandal, practically dragged him through the front door.

Exasperated, he wondered if he would spend the rest of his days chasing down the elusive, headstrong Wynne. He had wasted an hour first bullying his way into the Bedegrayne residence, and then once he was convinced she was out, he tried ascertaining her whereabouts.

Only later it occurred to him that her aunt might know—if she had been conveniently at home. A discreet bribe to a departing underbutler and a scullery maid revealed the old woman's destination. His patience waning, he hoped his search had ended.

The ballroom was overheated and stuffed beyond a tolerable capacity. Locating one particular lady held its own challenges.

A hand shot out from the shifting throng. Halting, Keanan pivoted. The identity of the annoyance had him snarling, "Lothbury, you dare much crossing me this eve." The residual feeling of his friend's betrayal surged to life.

Clearly uncomfortable, the marquess said, "Circumstances have prevented me from approaching you sooner. I do not expect you will ever shed your malice toward my deplorable actions. Even so, I sincerely regret the breach I have caused between us."

Stiffly, Keanan shook off the man's touch. "You regret the loss of friendship, but not your actions?"

"Honestly, Milroy, whom do you blame? Me alone? We both understood your interest in Miss Bedegrayne was less than honorable. You seduced her. I just wagered on the outcome."

"Wrong," he corrected softly. "You declared war on an innocent woman. Unfortunately for you, this dumb fighter had more honor than you credited him with. If you are fond of your pretty face, I would keep to the horses."

He did not spare his former friend a parting glance. A minute later, another hand touched him. His hand fisted as he whirled.

"Goodness, Mr. Milroy! What a formidable greeting," Lady Tipton said, enjoying his embarrassment. "My sister must have felt she was teasing a tiger when she dealt with you."

"Is she here?" he asked, unconsciously comparing the similarities and differences of the sisters. The countess was a striking woman with her fiery tresses and blue eyes. Regardless, another overshadowed her beauty. He was completely beguiled by an incomparable blond with dreams in her eyes and who burned at his touch.

"No, she left to see you."

Joy arose in his chest. Wynne had not given up on him. Or them. He took up her hand and gallantly kissed it. Giving her a devastating smile, he broke into a run.

Admiring his imperious exit, Devona exhaled slowly as she fanned herself. "My dear sister," she murmured, "you have not only courage but amazing restraint."

This was a terrible dream, she prayed. Lord A'Court wrenched her arm behind her back, urging her toward the silent house. The last time she had arrived here in the night, it had been raining. The edgy yearning linking her and Keanan had erupted into a night of discovery and love.

Now the earl had brought her back. Her throat strangling on fear, she watched helplessly as a floating light from within moved closer to answer the pounding summons.

The door opened. A man dressed in his nightclothes glared at them through one bloodshot eye. "Be gone! The master is not home." The sour expression diminished with recognition. "Hair like moonbeams, the master tells me. And eyes, the tranquil pond in summer. You be his lady? Miss Bedegrayne?" She lifted her head, illuminating the side of her face. Seeing the mark on her cheek, he lifted his candle higher, intent on inspecting it.

Lord A'Court pushed Wynne into the startled servant. Colliding with him, she held on, preventing both of them from falling. The butler wavered, struggling not to set their clothing afire. The flame flickered precariously, its smoke curling into a hypnotic dance.

"Accommodating as always, my lady," the earl mocked. The pistol was pointed at the servant's heart. "Now it is your turn, old man. When do you expect your master?" The butler hesitated. "Lie, and Miss Bedegrayne will pay the forfeit."

"Don't know. I'm his butler, n-not the warden."

Lord A'Court shook his head. "Pitiful." He looked at Wynne for agreement. "I will wager a house of this size is insufficiently staffed. How many servants?"

"I don't see how—ten in all, sir," he lamely finished when the barrel of the pistol shifted to her.

The earl's eyes beamed approval. "Excellent. Now if you will show me to their quarters, we will begin."

The man turned, leading them to the stairs. He slammed the silver butt cap of the pistol against the back of the servant's skull.

Wynne shrieked. She dropped down beside the ubconscious man, gently examining the bleeding wound that was already beginning to swell. "What kind of a monster are you, attacking women and an old man? The blow could kill him!"

He reached down and hauled her up by her neck. If his fingers had been positioned differently, she would have been throttled under the pressure. "This conversation bores me, Wynne. Do you need reminding how strongly I detest being bored?"

"No!" she hissed. She stood up on her toes, lessening the strain on her neck.

"Good girl." He pressed his lips to her cheek until she felt the scrape of his teeth. "It is Milroy who needs your pity."

Lord A'Court was too efficient for this to be an impulsive plan. The coachman appeared at the front door, carrying rope. He bound the butler and towed his unconscious form into the drawing room at the earl's command. The servant would secure her cooperation, she was told.

Once a fire was built up in the hearth, the coachman had disappeared. She assumed he was checking the servants' quarters. Even though he worked alone, there was no doubt he could easily subdue a handful of sleeping servants.

Curled up into an oversized tub chair, Wynne concentrated on the changes in the drawing room instead of watching the man pacing in front of the hearth. The room had been finished in her absence. The walls and ceiling had been painted a pale green. The rococo plasterwork was finished, and a gold chandelier was suspended from the ceiling. Gazing upward, her eyes traced the ornate circular design surrounding the fixture. Tilting her head, she realized these were not abstract scrolls as she had first believed. Overwhelmed by sentimentality, her eyes welled with tears. Keanan had had their entwined initials worked into the ceiling's plasterwork.

He had decorated this room for her.

She dashed at the wetness under her eyes, relieved that Lord A'Court had not noticed. He prowled the room as if seeking out weaknesses in his foe. The pistol rested against his leg. Despite his assurances to the contrary, he appeared quite capable of firing the weapon if provoked. The poor unconscious butler reclined on the floor. He had not moved or made any noise indicating he had survived the attack.

"Keanan will be no help to you. He does not know where

Brook is hidden," Wynne said, making another attempt at understanding his motives.

His back to her, he removed a small frame from the wall. "When I ask for the location of my wife, I have every confidence you will tell me," he said, his calm assurance scaring Wynne more than his irrational rage.

Facing her, he flipped the frame over so she could see what had caught his attention. It was her silhouette. "This is you. Rushed work rendered at a fair generally produces poor quality. However, Graley on the Strand is a remarkable artisan, do you not agree?"

She straightened in the chair. "How did you know about the fair?" A rush of insight left her cold in spite of the fire. "You were there. Watching." She pressed her hand to her lips, feeling sickened. Innocent actions suddenly seemed sullied under his covert gaze.

"I did much more than observe you play your taunting games, flirting between indifferent innocence and eager Haymarket ware." Smiling, he stepped over the butler's prone body. Caging her with his body, he tapped the barrel of the pistol against her knee. "I, too, touched you that day. Do you still dream about our tête-à-tête?"

Wynne knew the exact moment. Fear had scored the scene forever in her memories. "The lions," she said, the words barely audible. Where her voice lacked strength, her gaze was pure green fire. "You pushed me into the path of those half-starved beasts."

"Did you hope I would forget? The forfeit has not been met."

He was addled, she was certain. "Forget what? I have done nothing!"

The slap hit her like a clap of thunder. Gasping for air, she fought the looming blackness.

"Liar!" he roared. The pistol jerked wildly in his other hand. "Minutes after our introduction, I wanted you for my wife. Surrounded by half a dozen suitors, your eyes begged me to rescue you. Our hands clasped, and I was lost, so lost." He closed his eyes; his body swayed to some forgotten music of the past.

Wynne bit down on her lower lip, stilling the trembling. She had no clear recollection of their first meeting. Over the years, she had accepted his invitations to dance. Oh, he had flirted like most of the gentlemen and had composed a poem or two in honor of her beauty. It had been harmless. "I t-think you are confusing me with Brook. She was the one—"

"No! No!" Lord A'Court stomped out his denial. "So sweet and cool at once, you reminded me of a peach ice from Gunter's. Hundreds of people could be in the room, and I could still pick you out at once."

"My lord, I was not aware of your feelings."

He scrunched his face into a horrible mask. Flinching, she stared at his large unfettered hand, expecting another slap. He shook his head. "You were afraid. I took too long declaring myself. You questioned my regard."

"I introduced you to my dearest friend, Brook," she gently reminded, worried she would provoke another rage. "You both were instantly smitten. It was never me."

"She was the after," he said, pointing a finger at her. "Chaff. I called on your father, declared myself. I was prepared to offer you everything. Do you know what that nasty piece of work called me?"

"No." Her father had never mentioned Lord A'Court's visit. He had probably thought he was protecting her from the ugliness she was witnessing now.

"Conceited and high-strung. A stronger man was needed for his demanding daughter. I wanted you for my countess, and he walked out of the room. Do you recall what you did when I approached you that night at the ball?"

What night? she frantically wondered. What ball? "I—I cannot recall."

"You were vexed Lord Nevin was not crawling on his

knees, humbling himself before you, and instead had an eye on your baby sister. You refused my overtures and spent the evening wiling Nevin into your venomous embrace."

He spoke of a night that had occurred years ago as if it were just days past. Had she been so blind that she had not seen his pain, or were the events a twisted fantasy he had conjured? There had been a brief moment years ago when Lord Nevin had expressed interested in Devona. Tipton had ruthlessly crushed the notion.

"Lord Nevin is a friend. I would never accept his proposal."

"Nor any man's, it seems," he scorned.

"Even if I were unintentionally cruel, the offense hardly deserves murder."

This slap was expected and well deserved. "The forfeit," he reminded her. "First, I married your good friend. I gave her what you tossed away."

Brook had endured daily beatings and a tyranny that would leave permanent scars.

"I could not stay away from you for long. Especially when my spies uncovered your latest ruse."

"The Benevolent Sisterhood? Your spies are slow-witted, my lord. I have been enjoying that particular subterfuge for years."

"You swallowed my tempting bait quick enough," he smirked. "Young Miss Jenny Egger. The poor sacrificial lamb for a very ungentlemanly sport."

Wynne did not conceal her incredulity. "It was all a trap?"

"I cared nothing about the girl's fate. You were the one Egger was after. He had orders to bruise you a bit before he stashed you away in the stews. I intended to be your first customer that night."

Acid rose in her throat. "Keanan rescued me."

"Mr. Milroy will soon learn the full extent of my displeasure, never fear." There was a maniacal cast to his face, which craved Keanan's death.

Memories shuffled through her mind like a deck of cards. "What else? You have been following me around for weeks. What is my forfeit, my lord?" she demanded.

Too drunk on his supremacy, he was beyond hearing her sarcastic inflection. "There were so many choices. At first, I thought to leave you in the hands of Middlefell, for his and the others' malevolent pleasure. You suffered so beautifully. Unfortunately, Mr. Milroy once again deprived me of your ruination. Another forfeit. So here we are, awaiting your filthy lover." Tapping the barrel against his cheek, he mused, "I imagine learning that his beloved whore has chosen his half-brother to wed will put him in the appropriate killing rage."

The possibility jolted her, and she was shamed by it. Keanan might be capable of violence, but he would never hurt her. "He will never believe it!"

The earl gave her a roguish grin. "Dead participants rarely protest, Wynne. Now our enraged Mr. Milroy will use those prized fists of his on you. The betrayal, you see," he explained. "I had planned that, in a crazed fit of grief, he strangles you, but that does not sound quite right. After all, he is a fighter. I would not deny him his nature. Once you are dead, he will, of course, regret his violent actions and"—he called attention to the pistol—"take his own life, thus depriving Sir Thomas of justice. What do you think? I rather like it."

A noise in the entrance hall silenced them.

They both glanced at the door. Keanan had arrived home. Lord A'Court tensed, preparing for an ambush.

She acted before she noticed the movement at their feet. Headfirst and arms extended, she crashed into the earl. The awakened butler brought his knees up. Together, they knocked the earl off his feet.

Wynne rushed for the door. Screaming Keanan's name, she threw the latch. Lord A'Court bellowed his denial, as he fought to untangle himself from the servant. This had not ended. A madman was demanding she pay a forfeit for her imagined crimes. If she ran down to Keanan, there was the risk he could be shot.

Lights flickered below. A single sconce glowed from the landing above. It took only seconds to make her choice. She started her swift ascent up the stairs. Shouting a warning for Keanan, she tripped on a cloth carelessly draped over the steps. Her palms pushed off on the steps above her as she resumed her climb. Distantly she realized this level of the house was still being renovated. She reached the top floor, littered with lumber and chunks of stone.

"Wynne!"

She was so winded she could not identify who yelled her name. The feel of the railing beneath her gliding hand kept her bearings. Suddenly, the railing ended abruptly. There was a jagged gap. Most likely, the workmen had been pushing heavy objects through the opening.

"Damn it, woman, answer me!" Keanan demanded from below.

"Watch out, he has—" She gasped, a noise from the left startling her.

Lord A'Court emerged from the shadowed stairs, blood trickling from one of his nostrils. He broke into a full run when he saw her. Screams in her ears, he tackled her to the floor. They tumbled over pieces of discarded planks, sending plaster dust into the air like resentful ghosts. Fighting for her life, she clawed his face and chest until suddenly she was grasping air. Crying out, they fell through the ragged opening. Someone shouted. Her breath was knocked out of her from the unexpected impact. They had landed on scaffolding positioned three feet below. Too narrow to hold them both, the earl bounced on the edge and toppled, taking her partly with him.

Legs dangling, she gritted her teeth as his weight skidded her to the edge, slamming her chest into the support post.

Her right arm instinctively curled around it for purchase. Lord A'Court had stopped his fall by seizing her around the waist. The strain of his additional weight was unbearable. Desperate, she kicked out and hooked her foot around the opposing post. The one digging into her chest was cutting her in two. She did not know if she could support them both much longer.

"Wynne," Keanan shouted. The terror and determination in his voice rung overhead. "Hold tight. I'm coming."

"Not the plan," the earl panted, slipping an inch. "She was never meant to be yours, Milroy," he called out, the ferocity of the vow ruined when he yelped, his fingers losing their hold on her waist. Clutching fistfuls of fabric, the seam of her gown rent, costing him precious inches. "Poetic, I think. Us dying together."

Wynne wanted to roll away, but his fingers were too firmly imbedded into her gown. She brought her left fist down on his grip. He grunted but maintained his hold.

Reaching behind her, she groped for anything to help her break his hold. Nothing. Refusing to give up, she searched the area above her head. Keanan was shouting—or cursing—but she blocked him out. One finger scraped against a brick. Stretching, she fought the pull of the earl's swinging deadweight. It took several attempts, but she managed to drag the brick closer using her fingertips. Wrapping her hand around it, she clasped it to her breast.

"It's too late!" Lord A'Court said, swinging his body closer while he tried to catch his foot on the wooden scaffold. If he succeeded in gaining a foothold, his efforts would force her over the edge. Wood creaked around them, and Wynne felt the pain bone-deep. It only fueled her determination.

Heaving it back with all her strength, her knuckles connected with something solid. Ignoring the masculine bellow from behind, she smashed it into the earl's elbow.

Later, it would come to her in pieces. First, she saw the

startled look in Lord A'Court's eyes, just before they glided into horror. Fingers one by one freed themselves from the torn fabric. There was a buoyancy of both body and psyche, and finally, the shadowed descent of a dying man. Darkness veiled the gory collision of flesh and bone into the marble flooring, but the sound of the impact would never diminish in her memories.

Keanan grabbed her before her weakened muscles could fail her, and hauled her limp body into his embrace. Rocking her, he murmured incoherent phrases meant to comfort them both. Wynne closed her eyes, relishing the warmth of his body. She felt so cold.

"Christ, Wynne, I thought I'd lost you." He shuddered, pressing her face into his pounding chest. "I spent half the night searching for you, needing to set things right between us. Where do I find you? Here, in my own home, fighting off a madman."

"I had little choice, although I cannot think of another place I would rather be." Wynne nuzzled her face into his neck. Her hands tightened on his arms. "He was not alone. His man—"

"Is no trouble," Keanan harshly cut in with some satisfaction. "He attacked me on the stairs. He was the reason why I didn't get to you sooner." Heedless of the blood on his trembling hand, he cupped her face. "You were screaming my name, and I saw that bastard chase after you. Why didn't you run to me?"

He was too upset to conceal that her actions had hurt him. "It was an ambush. He, Lord A'Court, brought me here, intent on killing you. I was so frightened he might . . . he m-might—"

"Hush," he soothed, understanding. "Bloody nobility," he sneered, swiping at the blood on his face. "Is this one part of Lothbury's crowd, too?"

"No, not exactly." Stirring from his embrace, she winced. "The tale is long in telling. Can we find a softer perch?"

"Of course," he said, embarrassed that he had not thought of her comfort himself. Scooping her into his arms, he stood. Noticing Wigget standing discreetly at a distance, awaiting orders, he nodded. "Here, man, lend me a hand." As Keanan lifted her up, she reached out for the butler.

"Are you hurt, Wigget?" she murmured, grateful for the man's assistance in her escape.

"No, miss. What good would a skull be if it couldn't take a knock or two." Gently setting her down, he offered a strong arm to his master.

Wynne seized the balustrade, finally seeing the extent of Keanan's injuries when he climbed into the candlelight. There was a raw scrape on his right cheek. The area around his eyes and nose was discolored and swollen. His frequent swipes with the back of his hand had not stemmed the flowing blood.

His fight with the coachman had been unfair and brutal. Nor had he spoken one word about his injuries. "You fool, why did you not tell me that man hurt you?"

Affronted, Keanan mopped his face with his sleeve. Gingerly he touched his nose and cringed. "He barely tapped me, woman," he growled, renewed anger kindling in his indigo gaze. "You broke my damn nose with that bloody brick!"

Two hours had passed since dawn had chased the shadows from the house. The police had removed the body of Lord A'Court hours earlier, and Keanan's efficient staff had washed away all traces of his violent demise. Even so, it did not prevent Keanan from brooding that it could have been Wynne's body lying broken on the marble.

Too rattled by the events Wynne had told him about A'Court, he had summoned Bedegrayne and the Tiptons, sensing that she needed her family but was too selfish to permit her straying from his side. Her shocked family had rallied around her, shielding her the best they could from the police and their inquiries.

They had believed her to be fragile. Drowsily curled up

next to her sleeping sister, she did appear delicate. Hair askew, and her gown torn at the waist, he saw the fatigue bruising the skin below her eyes. Then again, Keanan had witnessed her strength as she had fought for her life. He was awed if not terrified by it. The lady took risks. Prowling about the drawing room, he doubted he would ever recover from this night.

"Are you settled enough for me to take a look at your nose?" Tipton asked, standing beside him. His testimony to the police about Brook's condition had hastened the process of eliminating any foul play. The earl's henchman, now in custody, had finished their part.

"Leave it," he muttered, though he remained motionless for the surgeon's not-so-gentle prodding. "It's broken. Nothing can be done except allowing it to mend." He shot a glare in Wynne's direction. His vexation made her smile slightly for some reason. It was the first he had glimpsed in days. In that light, it was difficult holding on to his anger.

"Now, Keanan," Blanche soothed. "Would you feel better if you had broken it in the ring?"

"Aye," was his sullen reply. "I will never live this down."

Wynne had insisted on sending for Blanche and telling her what had happened. Keanan had balked, not wanting to bother her with business that did not concern her. He gave in to Wynne's quiet demand, only because he could not deny her anything. Blanche had rushed into his arms on her arrival, sobbing out her fear and concern. Oddly, he had been comforted by her presence.

"A'Court died too painlessly for my comfort," Sir Thomas seethed, too caught up in the circling loop of private misery. Keanan understood his helpless torment. "Honest, Wynne, if I had sniffed out his depraved nature, you would have been put beyond his reach. I thought him spineless. I recall, the man actually wept at my refusal." The memory still appalled him.

"You are not to blame, Papa," Wynne said, her voice

husky from the hours of questioning. "If he was a madman, he was a cunning one. He cloaked himself well. I doubt anyone suspected—except his victims." She stared off, her thoughts directed at herself and Brook.

Entering the room, Wigget announced, "Sir, a—"

The appearance of Nevin at the threshold ruined any sense of formality. The butler skulked off. "Ah, I see it is just family in attendance. No apologies necessary, brother, for neglecting to summon me." He walked over to Wynne and knelt in front of her. His hand brushed her injured cheek. "He hurt you?"

"More frightened than anything," Wynne said, understating the horrifying events. Compassion begot compassion. "I am sorry about your father."

The mention of Reckester had Keanan growing rigid. Nevin continued speaking, but his voice faded from Keanan's ears. In his concern for Wynne, he had forgotten the impetus that had forced him into the night to find her. Absently Keanan's hand rose, touching the documents hidden within his coat.

Nevin admitted, "We must accept that the identity of the killer may never be known—or his reasons."

Sir Thomas awkwardly patted Blanche's hand while she cried into her handkerchief.

Wynne's gaze met Keanan's. The question in hers told him that she sensed his indecision. There had been no time to tell her about Dutch or the papers. His fingers clamped onto the edge of his coat. As he stared at her, she smiled encouragingly, her love and trust forcing the words out.

"I can give you the reason. It cost me thirty pounds." Having everyone's attention, he withdrew the papers. "Reckester's proof."

"Proof of what?" Sir Thomas interjected.

Nevin took the papers being pushed at him. He did not even glance down at them. Resignation darkened his face. "Justice, do you think?"

"No, just a gamble that didn't pay off." Keanan knocked the papers out of his brother's hand and into the morning fire. The flames heightened, greedily devouring the brittle papers. The blatant destruction of the mysterious documents produced startled sounds from several of the onlookers.

Nevin bent down, intent on pulling them from the fire. Keanan stopped him. Whirling away from him, Nevin's anger was unexpected. "Are you addled? There was your proof. Think man about what you are giving up? Everything!"

Keanan turned his back on the fire. Walking up to Wynne, he held out his hand. She stood, and placed her hand into his. "Not everything, Nevin." He scooped Wynne up. "I enjoy being the bastard. The title is yours." Before anyone could react from his announcement, he rushed her out of the room.

Wynne's laughter tickled his throat while he shifted her so he could lock the door of what might have been a music room had it been furnished properly. "Do you think a mere lock will keep them out?" The uproar he had caused seemed to be escalating outside.

"Nay, just borrowing against time. Nevin can handle them." He slid her down the length of him, groaning at his body's painful reaction to her proximity.

Not desiring the separation, she kept her arms circled around his neck, figuring he deserved the torment. "Is it true? Did you toss your right to the dukedom into the fire?"

Uncomfortable under her scrutiny, he shrugged and moved away. "Reckester's blood spattered those documents, as did my mother's." A harsh brittle laugh rumbled in his throat. "The price was too high. Do you understand?"

Pieces of it, she thought. "I do. Nevin is part of your family."

He laughed, "God, save us both. Is it enough if we refrain from raising our fists at the sighting of the other?"

" 'Tis a beginning," she conceded. Slyly, her lashes fluttered upward. "Our child will need an uncle."

Placing his hand on her abdomen, he asked, worrying, "Our babe, he is well?"

She longed to touch his face. However, considering his injuries, she thought he might appreciate her restraint more. "Tipton says our child is well. He will be the child's uncle, too."

The notion brought an oath to Keanan's lips. Suddenly, he grinned. The action had him wincing. "You will have to marry me, Wynne."

She cocked her head up questioningly. "Why?"

His indigo gaze sparkled with deviltry. "You listed two fine ones. My son's uncles are brutes."

"Not good enough," she replied, taking a step forward and pleased with his wariness.

"Have mercy, woman. I gave up a respectable title. Your father will cast me into the Thames weighted with chains for my idiocy."

"Papa has not murdered anyone in years," she assured him, enjoying the game. "Do better."

"Bearing my child alone would make you a ruined woman," he said. The teasing light had faded from his eyes. "I could not endure causing you more pain."

"Why?" She seized him by his coat, refusing him any retreat.

"Is it not obvious? I love you. Marry me for love."

Wynne shrieked and jumped into his arms. They both ignored the pounding at the door. "All you had to do was ask, my love." She kissed him on the lips, murmuring sincere apologies when her nose collided with his broken one.

About the Author

Barbara Pierce resides near Atlanta, Georgia, with her husband and three children.

Readers may write to her at: P.O. Box 2192, Woodstock, GA 30188-9998, or visit her website at: http://www.barbara-pierce.com for updates on her next book.